INCEPTION
OF A BRIGADE

SAGA OF THE
SINGING SWORD BRIGADE

INCEPTION
OF A BRIGADE

J.M. MACLEOD

AMBASSADOR INTERNATIONAL
GREENVILLE, SOUTH CAROLINA & BELFAST, NORTHERN IRELAND
www.ambassador-international.com

Inception of a Brigade

Saga of the Singing Sword Brigade, Book One

© 2019 by J.M. MacLeod

ISBN: 978-1-62020-834-2
eISBN: 978-1-62020-840-3
Library of Congress Control Number: 2019936663

This is a work of fiction. Names, characters, and incidents are all products of the author's imagination or are used for fictional purposes. Any resemblance to actual events or persons, living or dead, is entirely coincidental. Any mentioned brand names, places, and trademarks remain the property of their respective owners, bear no association with the author or the publisher, and are used for fictional purposes only.

Cover Design & Typesetting by Hannah Nichols
Ebook Conversion by Anna Riebe Raats
Edited by Daphne Self

AMBASSADOR INTERNATIONAL
Emerald House
411 University Ridge, Suite B14
Greenville, SC 29601, USA
www.ambassador-international.com

AMBASSADOR BOOKS
The Mount
2 Woodstock Link
Belfast, BT6 8DD, Northern Ireland, UK
www.ambassadormedia.co.uk

The colophon is a trademark of Ambassador, a Christian publishing company.

The sword gleaming with ancient runes,
Pulsing out heroic tunes,
Hummed a strain one cold, fey night,
Ere the battle joined full might,
To keep safe from hurtful woe,
And to guard from death's sorrow.
Hear a tale that will inspire,
Told by every rune afire.
Of cave and snow, hill and dell,
Of taken oath, deceivers fell,
This tale though new, is old as stars,
And blest are all that bear the scars,
Wise are they that live and learn,
Truth their cause, the false to spurn,
To cry out, "Lives for the King,"
And strive to give him everything.

CHAPTER ONE

ARTKA'S HEAD WAS SLAMMED ON the dirt road. Instantly a knee jammed the small of his back and hostile hands pinned and bound his arms. He was jerked upright; shackles were locked around his ankles and he was shoved into a line beside Bilrood, his best friend.

"Should've known it was a trap," Bilrood whispered through gritted teeth. His lower lip was swollen, and discoloration spread across his cheek and around his eye.

Artka gingerly probed a stinging knot forming on his own forehead. "Oooh!"

"Heshup, boy," a sharif inspecting the row of prisoners growled, brandishing a short sword.

Artka glanced aside and saw bushes whipping back into place. "At least some of the gang got away," he whispered.

"Here now, you were warned, no talking," shouted a sergeant rushing at them. Then he turned and ordered the guards, "Load 'em up."

Artka was thrust like a sack of turnips into the canvas covered wagon. Gruff prisoners crowded the benches on both sides of the wagon.

"Ere, yer crimpin' me feet. Git off'n the floor," said a gravelly voice.

Artka struggled onto a small corner of the rough-hewn bench. Craggy faces with cold eyes leered back at him. Directly across sat a man with a vivid chin-to-ear scar that his grizzled beard didn't hide.

The man's lip curled as he said, "Whut be's yer lookin' at? Yer wanted ter be outlaws, now yer'll see whut comes o' thet."

"Ease off the scamps, Rilf," said someone seated toward the front.

"Please, what's going to happen to us?" Bilrood asked, eyes wide, nostrils flared.

Rilf, the man with the scar, said, "Why laddie, yers jest enlisted."

"Enlisted? In the army?" Artka said.

"Aye," Rilf stared unblinkingly at Artka, " . . . less'n yer prefers hangin'. All law-breakers—includin' youthful rascals—either gits hanged or trained fer battle."

Bilrood leaned forward. "But, I'm not old enough—"

"Old enough ter pillage innocent merchants though, aincha? I reckon yer qualifies."

Artka shot a sideways glance at his friend. Bilrood's bruised face paled. His shoulders were hunched and his eyes downcast as he stared at the groaning floorboards.

No one else spoke as the wagon pitched and yawed for the next two hours over the rutted, dirt road toward the capital city, Cosmopolis, and the dungeon situated beneath the emperor's palace.

The wagons arrived just before sundown. The ancient, iron hinges of the fortress gates creaked open as the prisoner wagon lumbered beneath the gatehouse and raised portcullis and out onto the drill field.

Artka peeked through the opening at the rear of the canvas and read Carnalia's motto emblazoned over the inside of the gate:

"LIVE FOR THE MOMENT, DIE FOR THE EMPIRE."

This was the underlying philosophy the empire ingrained in every man, woman and child. Every individual of the empire's confederated nations actively pursued this mandate. Live for the thrill, seek what-ever is fun and exciting, heed no consequences . . . for in the end all things perish anyway, and pleasure will be but a passing sigh, so have enjoyment while you can. Therefore, to die, if need be, for the glory of the empire that encouraged such ecstasies would give a life honor and meaning.

With the mind intent upon obeying the first part of the decree, little thought is given to the latter portion, for it was unlikely to come to that for a very long time.

"Yet," Artka mused aloud, "here I am, facing that final, raw end of the bargain before I got to enjoy the first part."

"Eh, you say something, Artka?" Bilrood whispered.

Artka jerked his head back from the opening. "Uh, nothing important."

The wagons lurched to a stop at the end of the grassy field. "Git out, yer scummy bums, move yer cankered hides!" shouted a guard.

Men were yanked out through the wagon's rear opening and formed into a haphazard line. Artka jumped down, ducking the blows the guards rained down on slow-moving prisoners.

"This is the military post, not the dungeon," Artka muttered in relief as he observed a squad of soldiers performing close-order drills on the other side of the field.

From behind a guard commanded, "Face off . . . left." He cuffed a man on the top of his head that had turned to the right. "I said left, you bird twit."

Artka turned left and choked back a cry of anguish. Looming be-fore the ragged line of prisoners loomed a dismal archway leading down into Cosmopolis' dungeon.

From a portal across the bailey a stocky sergeant emerged huffing toward the prisoners, drawing their attention away from the yawning maw in front of them.

The sergeant stopped before the prisoners, ceremoniously withdrew a scroll from under his arm, unrolled it and read: "You are hereby adjudged guilty of any number of these high crimes and/or misdemeanors against the empire: murder, thievery, pillage, treason, sedition, brawling, usury, insolence, abuse—verbal and physical, rapine, hate crimes, drunkenness, resisting arrest—and whatever else you may or may not have been charged with, and are hereby sentenced to death by hanging." He looked up from the scroll and smiled. "Because of the emperor's fondness for his subjects, however, he offers to pardon you . . . conditionally. That condition being, you must enlist in the emperor's legions to fight any and all enemies of the empire, both foreign and domestic. Those who refuse his eminence's gracious offer are to be hanged forthwith."

A half-masked, black-garbed executioner stepped out from behind a tall oak on the edge of the drill field and tossed a series of nooses over a stout, lower limb that would serve the purpose quite well.

"All wishing to enlist, step forward."

Leg-irons clanked as the entire line of twenty prisoners shuffled forward.

The sergeant snarled something to the guards and the prisoners' arms were unbound. Sighs filled the air as they massaged and flexed their aching muscles. The leg-shackles, however, remained.

The sergeant smiled again. "Good. Now, raise your hand—either will do." He waited until all prisoners complied. "By your upraised hand you signify that you are able and willing to bind your eternal soul to live and die in service to your emperor; to resist and kill his enemies; to unquestioningly follow every command given or else suffer the wrath of our lord in this life and fiery torment in the ever-after."

The references to "fiery torment" and "ever-after" puzzled Artka, for Carnalia's rulers officially ridiculed anyone who believed such things as suspicious. Nevertheless, as superstitious, Artka, along with every other prisoner in line, raised a hand and took the oath to obey the emperor upon pain of death and eternal torment.

"Alright now lads, off to the tombs with you until enough volunteers are gathered to complement a full brigade." The sergeant nodded at the lead guard, did a smart about face and returned to the portal from whence he'd come.

The guards wasted no time prodding the prisoners with swords and clubs, herding them like cattle, as it were, toward a nearby table of stacked bowls. Beside the table sat a three-wheeled cart bearing a cauldron of foul-smelling, greasy gruel. Serving girls ladled the gruel into bowls and handed one to each prisoner shuffling past.

"Eat up," said a smirking guard, "it's all you're likely to get 'til morning."

"What's in it?" Artka sniffed the bowl. It made his nose tingle and his eyes water.

"You're better off not knowing, lad. They call it B'n'B broth. More than that you don't want to know. It's what they feed prisoners. Once you begin training you'll get better fare."

Artka sniffed again and squinted. "I'll learn to fly before I drink this slop!"

"You'll take it, and be thankful," the guard rested his club menacingly on Artka's shoulder.

The man behind Artka dumped his bowl to the ground. "Hain't fit ter eat."

The club whipped off Artka's shoulder and rammed with the blunt end into the man's nose. He sank like a brick.

The guard returned his glare to Artka. "Now then . . . "

Artka considered the unconscious man at his feet, narrowed his eyes at the guard, hefted the bowl to his lips and gulped. It nearly scalded his mouth and once swallowed, felt like a stone in his belly.

"That's more like it, then," said the guard lowering his club. "It don't taste so good, but it'll ward off starvation. Now get moving. Come on, all of you get along now."

With shackles clanking, the gagging prisoners were herded into the yawning, dark cavern in front of them, the entryway to the dungeon.

"Keep your bowl," advised another guard standing at the top of a stone stairwell. "It's your water and food dish until your training is completed."

Stone slabs, slime-coated and only supported by undergirding iron beams protruding from the granite wall spiraled down into the dungeon's murky depths. The way was dark but not entirely lightless. Torches provided dim, smoky light at each landing.

"Where are the handrails?" asked a tall, thin man at the top step.

"Ain't none," sneered a guard. "You'll just have to watch your step, won't ya?"

"But these leg irons might trip us—"

"Your tough luck. Just don't take no one with you if you fall."

Stench a dozen times worse than the B'n'B broth greeted the descending prisoners. Artka's stomach revolted at the combined smells of urine, feces, and mold added to the foul aftertaste of the B'n'B broth lingering in his mouth. He tried panting, but it didn't help.

At each level guards shunted a couple of prisoners off to a side tunnel and into cells. Tears of irritation brimmed in Artka's eyes as they descended to the deepest, most fetid depth where, on the last and lowest level, the corporal leading them paused, fiddling with the key ring, biting his lip, looking back and forth from the remaining prisoners to the only cell door on this level.

He finally found the right key and unlocked it. "Oh well, it's only for a day or two . . . " then he took the torch from its sconce and led inside. "Come on, move it. Here's where you will lounge away the hours until we're ready to commence your training. Pick a spot along the wall and get comfortable, heh, heh."

Artka backed against the moist, stone wall and slid to the floor. A chain was threaded through his ankle irons and linked to the remaining prisoners.

"Nighty-night," a guard mocked as he stood ready to close the cell door. "Don't let the bed bugs bite—nor anything else!" He laughed as the door clunked shut.

The cell was in absolute darkness. A sob escaped from Artka. Bravado wasn't needed in this anonymous darkness. Others also gave in to pent up emotions for a few minutes. If only he and Bilrood had escaped like most of their gang. He shook his head to clear his thoughts.

He mustn't give in to regrets now or he'd never survive. Nevertheless, regrets surfaced as he thought of his parents—and what they would think. And his sisters, especially his own fraternal twin, Jeda? Would he ever see her again? Or any of them?

Bagged like a goose for the Winter Solstice! Fun and pleasure seeking had consequences after all. But didn't everyone in Carnalia "Live for the Moment"?

Wasn't he just living for the moment when he and Bilrood formed their band of brigands? Why had he and Bilrood lost their right to fun and pleasure to have to go fight—perhaps die—for the empire? Artka swiped at a tear trickling down his cheek. The second portion of the motto—"Die for the Empire"—he now realized, was a consequence, not a patriotic, second option. But, what choices had he had, really? As oppressive as the empire was at times, didn't that decree only encourage what came naturally?

Bilrood's voice spoke out of the nearby darkness, "Does anybody know how long we have to wait here?"

"Till yers rots," said Rilf's gravelly voice right next to Artka.

Artka had been so full of self-pity that he'd failed to take note of his nearest chain-mate.

"That's just like you Rilf," said someone several feet away, " . . . keep tormenting the lads. Ain't there enough Pitland in this stink hole without you adding to it? Don't pay no nevermind to Rilf there, leastways, long as he can't reach out and throttle you."

That comfort was a pail without a bottom.

"We'll be here a day or two, I s'pect," said another. "That ought to give 'em long enough to collect more ruffians and cutthroats to fulfill the brigade's numbers."

Artka stretched out his cramping legs, paying little attention to the continuing banter around him until someone loudly hissed, " . . . but the emperor is up against a hard enemy that can topple him. He should recruit brave, stalwart men—"

"Wrong, wrong, wrong," said another, "the emperor especially wants criminal types. He needs all the felonious help he can get, even the likes of drunks, cut-throats, robbers and thieves. They're easier to train for the killing and harder to be tricked into changing sides. Even so, the emperor hain't never beat the king, and likely never will."

Several seconds of silence passed before anyone dared respond. Even acknowledging such a statement was punishable by a messy, painful, prolonged death. "Bah," Rilf spat out, rattling his—and Artka's—section of chain. "No enemy kin stand agin' the emperor. I kens. He gots powers. An' besides, he gots all kinds o' phantom beasties whut does his biddin'. Yer'll never persuade me ter believe the emperor be's hard put. Summat day soon he be's gonna launch a campaign agin the 'Clessites and drive 'em into the river. Mark me words. Thet, me hearties, be's why he picked scum the likes o' usn's ter fight fer him."

"Well, Rilf seems to have a point," said someone from a distance, "the emperor never bothered garnering baby-highwaymen, drunken cutthroats and total losers so thoroughly from his highways and by-ways before."

"How you talk. He's never been face to face with the king," said another.

"You're mistaken," said yet another unseen shackle-mate from the darkness. "There was a time, long ago, as the legends tell it, when our emperor ran in terror from Ecclessa's prince. Tell me, does anyone know if Logon's Bridge still stands?"

"What in the name of Pitland is Logon's Bridge?" a youthful voice asked.

"Bah! And double bah, says I." Rilf hacked up and spat a wad of phlegm at the unseen shackle-mate seated across the walkway. "That business 'bout Logon's Bridge—hain't nobbut nonsense."

"Then . . . King's Gate guarding the bridge has been taken?"

"What's so important about Logon's Bridge and King's Gate?" repeated the youthful voice.

"What are they teaching youth nowadays? Is the younger generation so ignorant as to not know the legend of Logon's Bridge?"

"Lookee here," Rilf said, " . . . yer be's ignorant scum just like us'ns, an yer gots no bizness fillin' our ears wi' Ecclessite lies. Logon, if'n he ever existed, got kilt by assassins. No tales 'bout him still bein' alive is gonna change thet. So quicher moanin' 'bout Logon's Bridge. Thet fable don't mean nothin'." Rilf rattled his chain again for effect.

"When Logon's Bridge, and the King's Gate Fortress guarding it," continued the mysterious speaker, "falls into empire hands, disasters heralding the destruction of the world are supposed to be unleashed."

"Shut . . . up!" Rilf's coughing spasm preventing him saying more.

"The myths say that a great conflagration will overwhelm the empire—"

From deep in the recess of the cell, farther back than any prisoner had been chained, erupted a raging howl that increased in volume until the prisoners couldn't hear each other. The unnatural wail resounded for several minutes, forcing the prisoners to cover their ears. Then the roar gradually died away, leaving a stunned silence in the cell.

"Whazzat?" whispered a cellmate, daring to break the stillness. "It sounded like one o' them half-men howling an' a'beatin' on his chest."

No one replied. They scarce breathed.

Then someone whispered, "Great dreads of the gate, they put us in here with ravenous beasts!"

More silence.

At last one of the prisoners whispered, "Whatever it is, it must be caged, or it would've attacked by now."

"Yeah, you're right," said another, sighing.

"Ecclessites believe horrible beasts will be loosed upon humanity toward the end," said the man who knew about Logon's Bridge. "That creature might be one of those monsters, chained up in this hole to be released at the end of the world."

"Nah! I agree with Rilf," Bilrood said no longer whispering. "That end of the world stuff sounds like the enemy's lies to make us fearful."

"Oh? And are you so wise? You're but a youth, by the sound of your voice, barely draftable, I'd guess. But you can discern fact from fable?"

"Well, just who are you, that you know so much?" retorted Bilrood.

"I marched with the kingsmen, once. They have runes . . . magical, hidden, engraved runes on their swords that suddenly light up and tell them what's going to happen. The prophecy of Logon's Bridge is one of those mystical runes."

"And you believe that claptrap? You're a fool," said another.

"Very well, laugh. You wanted to know about Logon's Bridge. There it is."

A taunting wave of laughter coursed among the prisoners.

"Treason, traitor," someone shouted. "You should be sent to the White Priestess in Pitland and be tortured."

The cell door lock clicked. All conversation immediately ceased.

The door creaked open and several soldiers scurried in. A blaze of fiery torchlight temporarily blinded Artka. Low-ranking soldiers methodically went man to man, stooping over unlocking the chain.

"All right, on your feet," barked the sergeant.

While the prisoners got to their feet, the sergeant took two corporals and went deep into the cell's recess, followed by the eyes of the curious prisoners. There in the torch's glow squatted an immense man hunkered down, shackled both feet and one hand to the wall. There was something vaguely familiar about his features. His beard and hair were long and unkempt, his face grimy. It slowly dawned on Artka. This was none other than the most notorious face on wanted posters scattered throughout Carnalia. Here, locked in the same dungeon cell with him was the most infamous outlaw in all the empire, Turit!

Already in chains but still classified as a wanted outlaw? What was going on? Was he the source of that ear-splitting roar? What was this all about?

For a chilling moment Turit's hate-filled eyes locked with Artka's. A chill went down Artka's spine, his hands and feet turned numb as he tried to set his eyes elsewhere, but in vain. The monstrous man held Artka's eyes against his will, as if trying to control . . . no . . . more than that, as if he were trying to somehow invade him. But the spell broke when a guard smacked Artka and shoved him into line. But Turit's feral glare remained in Artka's mind's eye.

"I didn't know where else to put them, Sarge," a corporal whined as the prisoners shuffled out of the chamber. "All the cells above were already full or else contained captives from the warfront. I'm under strict orders to not let that kind mingle with common prisoners and weave their mesmerizing spells. Those orders are from the top."

"But, not in here with him, you spore-brain," said the sergeant. "He's not fully conditioned yet. Any outside contact or information might undo the invested effort. You'd better hope there's no harm done, or you'll answer to Hod-ya herself, and that'll mean the rack. I'd wager a month's rum on that. Might as well pull them out of the other cells too, Fitcher says we'll start this brigade's training short-handed. Head 'em all the way up."

CHAPTER TWO

ARTKA WOKE WITH A SHUDDER. Harsh reality burst in on him in the clamorous form of a brutish sergeant striding between bunks smacking procrastinators' feet with his quirt and shouting, "Get outta them racks."

"Ah," said the sergeant pausing and observing Artka and Bilrood trembling in the early morning chill at the foot of their bunks, "now they've sent me nursing whelps to babysit." The man's muscular shoulders seemed as wide as a door. His jet-black eyes matched his close-cropped hair and chin-line beard. "Well, if you lads survive my boot camp, I reckon you'll survive anything."

He turned and strode down the barracks' center line. "I'm your new owner, your mentor, your mommy and daddy, your teacher, disciplinarian, lover and . . . your worst enemy. At first, you'll hate me That's good. But be assured, before you finish training you'll loathe me. I care for none of that—I care only that you pay strict attention and obey me." He paused in front of Rilf, with his hand, reached and turned Rilf's head to the side. "I see you still haven't learned to keep out of trouble, Rilf. That gash I put on your face made you prettier. Let's hope I don't have to open up the other side. I'd hate to mar a work of perfection."

Rilf lowered his eyes.

"I have power to make you happy . . . " said the sergeant, resuming his swagger, "or sad, very sad, at my whim." He suddenly whirled, cold-cocking a man whose eyes had been wandering about the barracks. The

20

trainee collapsed in a heap. A dark scowl from the sergeant discouraged anyone who even thought of rushing to the man's aid.

"My name is Sergeant Love, understand?"

Every man in the barracks stared in horror at the unconscious fellow on the floor.

"Answer me, or I blast your louse-riddled hides! DO YOU UNDERSTAND?"

"Yessir!" The men snapped out of their trance.

"What's my name?"

"Sergeant Love, sir!"

"And don't forget it." Sergeant Love proceeded to spew staccato instructions about daily routines, policing the barracks, respecting officers and getting outfitted with weaponry, clothing, food and various supplies. When finished, the sergeant strolled to the door at the end of the barracks, pausing only briefly beside the unconscious victim on the floor, scanned each man on both sides of the aisle, and said, "At my whim."

Then he exited.

Corporals shouted instructions, trainees fumble-fingered their bedding or set about straightening items while two orderlies carried the stricken man outside. Artka's eyes met Bilrood's as they attempted to make the bedding on their cots wrinkle-free. Sergeant Love had singled them out, making a special point of their youth. Would he try to make examples of them as unfit?

"Where did you take him?" Artka asked one of the orderlies returning from carrying out the unconscious man.

"The infirmary," said the aide. "But—if you're wise, you'll not investigate how he fares; in fact, you'd best forget you ever saw him."

Artka and Bilrood again exchanged knowing glances.

"Let's get our stuff," Bilrood said, "like the sergeant told us."

They joined the rear of a line at the outfitter's where they were is-sued coarse-woven tunics of a dun hue, stiff leather breeches, a leather breastplate, thick-soled, hob-nailed boots that laced securely around the calves, a helmet sans plumage, a rucksack for personal items, and a bedroll and fly that doubled as a rain slicker.

Their primary weapon was a three-foot broadsword made of fire-hardened hickory wood. One side had been sharpened to a hair's-breadth. The other was half an inch thick.

"This," the supply sergeant said, "must never be out of your reach until you earn an iron sword."

Artka was hustled on so quickly that he had no time to ask what merited bestowal of an iron sword.

So, began Artka's and Bilrood's rigorous martial training that honed them from untrained, roguish youths into dangerous, skill-ful manslayers.

~

"Wake up," Sergeant Love shouted, silhouetted against the rising sun in the barracks' open doorway. "Today you graduate. I've rarely had the pleasure of training so proficient a company of troopers. I'm proud to be your trainer. Three months ago, I wouldn't have traded a cockroach turd for the lot of you. But now, though short-handed, I'd pit you against any fighting unit that ever marched off to war—Ecclessite, Eroton or Carnalian. I'm proud to be chosen to lead you into the high-est calling a soldier of the empire can attain, the blood-fest of battle.

"The fortress gates will remain open to you for three days. Just show your pass and you'll not be hindered. For those three days you have earned the right to free reign of the city to go anywhere and do whatever you want—within reason. Your only law is to be back here at daybreak four days from now, ready to put in a full day of marching."

"Sergeant, when are we issued iron swords?" Artka asked.

Sergeant Love smiled and pointed to a man behind Artka.

"Why laddie-boy," said a familiar, snarling voice from behind, "yer'll earn yer iron when yer've kilt a enemy wi' yer hick'ry."

"I don't believe that." Artka turned and curled his lip at Rilf. "The emperor wouldn't send us out to fight his battles with nothing but toys."

Rilf mockingly shook his head side to side as he smirked.

"Nay, he's right, boy." Sergeant Love laid his hand on Artka's shoulder. "Your first kill will have to be with that hickory. But it don't necessarily have to be in the heat of battle, nor does it need to be a man for that matter," he winked at Rilf. "If you catch my drift. Why lad, first enemy dwelling or outpost we come to, go find a man, woman, or a child. We care only to see blood on the blade—just make sure it's Ecclessite blood."

Raised amid Carnalia's greed and cruelty, Artka, though disgusted at the suggestion, wasn't all that shocked. He watched Sergeant Love walk down the center of the barracks shaking hands with trainees, congratulating them one by one, saying something personal to each.

Bilrood sauntered over and said, "Artka, come along with me. We'll get gloriously drunk," he urged, "and find some like-minded companions and spend three days in revel."

"I don't think so," Artka said, bundling up his rucksack. "I need to let my family know what's become of me. They haven't heard a word the entire three months we've been training."

"Are you sure you wouldn't rather celebrate our graduation and get drunk?"

Artka nodded.

"Well, I guess I understand. My mam and pap don't care. They're probably glad I disappeared. Well, if you change your mind, I'll be at the Boar's Tusk Inn. In fact, you'd better come get me or I might not make muster."

The two gripped each other's right wrists, grinned and parted: Bilrood eager to splurge his wages; Artka back to the haunts of his youth, back to his father's house.

CHAPTER THREE

THE DOOR OPENED. "MASTER ARTKA!" said the plump maid, Gwinnid. Her eyes widened for an instant upon seeing him. "Oh, come in, come in. I never expec—We thought you'd been kidnapped or something dreadful. But, look at you. Why, you've filled out and are a full-grown man now. Well, don't just stand there, come in."

Gwinnid led him down the hallway and into a main room where a crackling fire warded off the early autumn chill. In the northlands of Eroton snow would soon cover the ground and every fireplace in those dwellings would be aflame. But here, in Carnalia's milder clime, one good fire a night was all that was needed to ward off the chill.

Artka, feeling more a guest than family, obediently followed Gwinnid through to the reception hall and made himself comfortable in a stuffed chair while she went to announce his presence. How long had it been since he'd enjoyed the softness of such a seat? Everything in his training had been hard, hard and difficult. No ease, no comfort to be found . . . and if by chance he found a moment's ease, Sergeant Love soon descended and made life twice as unbearable. Artka smiled at the memory. But it was enduring all that hardness that made him one of the champion swordsmen in his company.

"Artka," said his mother upon entering, " . . . oh, my dear, dear son, where have you been?" Her tone changed from dripping sweetness to mock scolding in mid-sentence.

"I . . . I joined the army, Mother." She still treated him as if he were her little boy. He hoped to avoid explaining the circumstances under which he'd joined.

"The army? Oh, Artka, how common." She sashayed in front of him and purred, "You haven't said anything about my gown. I'm told it's the latest style. Do you think the color too muted? I thought the train a little long, but Gwinnid assures me it's no lengthier than other dignitaries' wives are sporting. Do you like it?"

"Uh, very fetching, Mother." She hadn't changed, unless it was to be even more self and status-obsessed. He tried once more. "Mother, I've been away training these last three months with a regiment that will soon—"

"I know very well you've been off playing at army. Haven't I lost sleep worrying? You know how much I need my sleep," she patted the underside of her chin with the back of her fingers, "to keep wrinkles away. Artka, I'm afraid you should have been more considerate of our family status."

Artka shrugged. Well, he tried. "Where's Father?"

"Your father? Ah, I believe this is his day to attend to the Lord High Secretary's Council on Crimes and Misdemeanors. He's become a very important man now, very important indeed. The name and title 'Lord Kekinor Kway' is known in every household throughout Cosmopolis. When you settle down, our family name will open many doors for you, son. Come along now."

Artka rose from his chair and followed his mother into another room, eyeing the multi-colored tapestries and exquisite furniture as they passed. "I see you've added some décor and replaced furniture since I was last here."

They entered a great room where logs crackled in the fireplace, sending out warmth. He longed to explain that he wasn't "off playing at army" but decided she wouldn't comprehend; it was outside her realm of pomp and parties. And she'd said nothing about his staying overnight, either. Well, that was to be expected; he'd made it clear a year or so ago when challenged for staying away from home for days at a time, that his loyalties were to the gang in the hills. This unenthusiastic homecoming was all he had a right to expect. And yet . . . he'd hoped for some display of maternal affection.

A rustling of petticoats from a double doorway interrupted the uncomfortable silence. Jeda, his fraternal twin sister, swept into the room, followed by the younger twins, Velnu and Cornil.

"Ooh, you really are here," squealed Jeda as she flitted lightly across the room and embraced him. "You shameless scoundrel, how dare you stay away months on end?"

Velnu and Cornil crowded close, voicing agreement. They were still little girls in Artka's eyes, but his own twin surprised him. She'd blossomed into a beauty. Her long blonde hair fell delicately about her shoulders, framing her finely featured face.

Her large, blue eyes glinted with merriment as she said, "They were all sure you'd gotten arrested and thrown into the emperor's dungeon. But I knew better . . . "

Artka coughed, then said, "Ah, actually, I've, er, joined the army."

Color drained from all three girls' faces. Even his mother seemed to have finally understood the implications.

"Oh no, Artka, but you can't," Jeda said. "I mean, it's not final, or anything, is it?"

"Afraid it is."

"Mother, tell him no," Jeda said.

"Listen to me," Artka threw back his shoulders, " . . . it's done. I'm a soldier now. Childhood is behind me. I'm my own man, able and free to choose my own path." He hadn't realized until he said it aloud how untrue it was. It wasn't his choice . . . he wasn't free . . .

"But the army . . . " his mother sighed. "Just a common soldier, without officer status? Oh dear. What will the other wives think of me? Really, Artka, how could you?"

"Actually, I didn't have much choice at the time."

"Why not?"

"I'd rather not go into all that. Look, I have only three days till I march to the front. I'd like to spend them at home, if that's alright?"

"Well, er . . . Artka," his mother whined, " . . . you were gone so long this time, I assumed you wouldn't be back. We made your room into a servant's quarters. I'm afraid there's simply no place here for you anymore."

"Mother please," chorused the younger twins. Jeda looked on pleadingly but held her peace.

"Well, alright, my darlings. Artka, you may stay in the great room if you like. I'll have Smid put bedding out there. I must warn you however, I don't know how your father will react. He's very important now, has a lot on his mind, and he doesn't like surprises."

"I won't cause any trouble, I promise."

"What's army life like?" Velnu asked as she and Cornil took Artka's hands and led him to the divan and sat on either side of him.

"Oh yes, leave nothing out," Jeda had tagged along and was forced to sit without any pillows for backing. The younger twins quickly absconded with them, leaving Jeda to deal with the deprivation.

Artka leaned back on the couch and said, "Well . . . I don't know what you want to hear."

Jeda, uncomfortable, left the end of the pillow-less divan and settled on an ottoman directly in front of Artka, hugging her knees, watching Artka with wide eyes. "Is life very harsh?"

"Harsh . . . ?" Artka thought back to Sergeant Love clobbering a man senseless the first day of training. " . . . there were times—"

"Let's see your muscles," Cornil wheedled. "I bet they worked you real hard."

Artka laughed, rolled up his sleeves and flexed his biceps. "Push-ups, chinnings, running fifteen miles a day, weapons drill, tactical and strategic studies morning, noon and night . . . and wrestling competitions. Yeah, I'd say they worked us real hard."

"Us?" Jeda asked.

"Bilrood was caug—er, joined when I did."

"Bilrood? Wasn't he part of your gang?" Jeda looked up into his eyes.

"Tell us about the fighting," Velnu interrupted, giving Artka yet another chance to evade Jeda's pointed questions.

"Yes, how many kingsmen have you killed?" Cornil said.

"I haven't been in battle yet. I'm 'raw meat', as they say." Artka chuckled and pointed to his helmet. "See, no plume. They only award a plume after you prove yourself in battle. But I've won the broadsword competition three weeks in a row now. No one in the brigade can match me—except our sergeant, of course. And I'm almost the best wrestler . . . "

"Well," said their mother from the archway, "Since I'm known as Dame Kway, I have a trousseau to choose, which is what I was doing when you showed up, son. The Cosmopolis Ball is coming up soon, and alterations must be made. Come along girls."

Cornil and Velnu happily excused themselves to help their mother try on various garments.

After their mother and the twins left, Jeda whispered, "I've been so lonely here without you to confide in. I wish I could run off and join a gang. Then I wouldn't have to put up with being ordered about by everybody, especially our younger sisters. Mother always favors them so . . . "

Artka stared into the fire.

"Why do mother and father cater to their every whim, but treat us little better than servants?" Jeda asked. "They always treated us like we were inferior. Since you've been gone they treat me even worse." She searched Artka's face. "Maybe one day I will just slip away and disappear, like you did."

"No!" Artka roused from his reverie. "You mustn't. A boy gets into enough trouble on his own in Carnalia, but a girl . . . a girl would be better off dead than on her own in Carnalia."

"Artka, did you get in trouble?"

He hung his head. He couldn't deceive Jeda. "I was . . . "

Outside, the sky faded from late afternoon to twilight blue, dusky cobalt, and finally pitch black as Artka related his capture by the merchant's surprise cargo and being forced to choose between hanging as a criminal or joining the military. On and on he talked, reliving episodes, both good and bad times. He said nothing, however, of the mysterious Turit, not wanting Jeda to face repercussions of knowing that the empire's most wanted criminal was already secretly in prison and being 'conditioned' for some enigmatic purpose.

Jeda shuddered when Artka told her that Sergeant Love smashed the jaw of a recruit the very first day. "What cruel irony for him to be named Love."

Artka prattled more than he'd intended, unable to stop, as if talking to someone who cared somehow cleansed him.

Jeda turned her gaze to the fire when Artka mentioned how he was advised to earn his iron sword. She dabbed at a tear.

"Jeda, are you weeping?"

She turned away.

"I'm sorry. I've said too much. You're the only person in the world who really cares about what happens to me. I never meant to upset you."

"Artka, what's the purpose of it all?" Jeda turned to him. Tears had left glistening trails on her cheeks. "Is life nothing but hardship, cruelty, hurting others or being hurt, all for selfish gain? Isn't there somewhere people are kind and care for each other?"

"Be thankful we live in Carnalia, short lived as our liberties are. During training we learned about the king of Ecclessa. He's far worse than the emperor, allowing his people no pleasures at all, not even natural pleasures. He hates his people, making them obey strict, ritualistic, bitter laws, and working them to exhaustion until they're all used up."

"How awful."

"And besides that, he's enlisted a powerful Magician to mesmerize and drive even his own troops to their destruction." He paused, remembering the empire's slogan. How different were the two kingdoms, really?

"What?" Jeda asked.

"Something reminded me . . . oh well, there isn't much use in questioning the order of things."

Cornil stamped her foot on the landing and called, "Didn't you two hear the dinner bell? Mother is getting impatient." With a sassy toss of her curls, the young twin turned back to the dining room. Artka and Jeda followed.

Father's place at the table was empty, his chair backed away to a corner.

"We're sorry mother," Jeda said, " . . . we had so much to catch up . . . "

"See to it that you're on time from now on, or you'll go hungry."

"Father's not coming?" Artka slid into his seat.

"He's still working at the palace." His mother stuck a fork in the roast.

The meat on the platter was garnished with peeled, boiled potatoes drenched in butter and topped with a sprinkling of herbs. Additionally, there were the side dishes of varied vegetables—some raw, some cooked, some swimming in sour cream. Blood oozed as the knife sliced into the beef. "I received word that your father won't be home till late. Just think, children, the chief men directly under the emperor know your father personally. How important we're all becoming."

A procession of laden servants paraded in carrying three more courses, followed by trays of puddings, cakes, and other confections. Artka stuffed himself till uncomfortable, making up for all the mess hall slop he'd had to swallow in the last three months.

After dinner, in an unusual move, his mother invited, "Artka, since you've entered a man's world, coarse and common as the military is, you're entitled to share a man's simple pleasures. Come, have some brandy with me."

Though it meant leaving Jeda to fend for herself, Artka was pleased that his mother wanted him to accompany her into the sanctum of the visitor's parlor where his parents entertained empire dignitaries. His parents—Adana, his mother, in particular—had spent a small fortune making it lavish. A cask of brandy sporting a highly polished brass spigot in the bunghole sat on a filigreed silver stand against the far wall. Expensive crystalline glasses were displayed in a crafted cabinet above and on either side of the cask. Adorning one entire wall were empire banners and plaques. The opposing wall bore family portraits, crests and heraldic emblems. One could not help but associate Kway family ancestry merging with Carnalia's dominion and destiny. His mother's contrivance, no doubt and quite effective, too. As important personages were ushered into this room for political discussions or even just casual visits, his father's rising prestige would correspond to the lowering level of liqueur.

"Very shrewd, Mother."

"Thank you," she said, handing Artka a snifter half-filled with golden liquid. She stood before an oil portrait of herself and her husband. "I only wish I'd hectored your father more. Who knows what heights he'd have attained by now? Sometimes I wonder if your father has enough ambition to sustain his success." She took a sip and lowered her glass to the table. "So, you joined the military. It's obvious that, though you have the potential, you don't have much ambition either, just like your father."

Artka settled into a comfortable, overstuffed chair, only partially listening as she rambled on about her being the one responsible for the family's ascending status. Artka gradually realized that his presence wasn't even needed for this performance; indeed, he had the feeling that she often came alone to sip brandy and harangue the pictures on the wall. Tonight, at least, she had a live audience. A comfortable drowsiness overtook Artka. His eyelids grew heavy and his breathing slow and deep. His mother's droning voice faded into the background as memories of sword duels and wrestling matches swam lazily across his mind.

When he awoke it was dark. Cramped, cold, stiff, and alone he felt his way through the dark hallways to the great room where bedding waited beside a cozy fire. A dull ache throbbed behind his temples. Ah, he forgot . . . he was going to spend more time with Jeda before bed. He was sorry, he'd make it up to her in the morning. Thus, salving his conscience, he stretched out and was instantly asleep.

Awareness returned. The room was gray with the approaching dawn. Glad to be away from the barracks, he rolled over to his side to resume the luxury of sleep when the sound of someone's breath close by alarmed him.

Artka spun over to his back. A shadowy form loomed over him. "Who's—who's there?" Artka tried to make his voice menacing as at the same time he groped for his wooden sword that should have been alongside. It wasn't there. He'd been too inebriated to perform his nightly routine.

"So, the highwayman wakes." His father's tone was cold and hard.

Artka sat up, re-kindling the pounding in his head. "It's early. What do you want, Father?"

"What do I want? You come here to associate yourself with my name after being nabbed as a common criminal, and dare demand answers from me?"

"You know about that?" Artka held his head in both hands.

"Not much goes on in Cosmopolis that I don't know about. I know you're to march in three days' time. Is that why you're here, to see if I can get you a deferral? Well, I could, but I won't."

"You never did understand me. How did you find out?"

"What does that matter? Enough people have access to the rolls of prisoners enlisting in the legions. If anyone makes the connection between us . . . you must leave the house, now."

"Right this minute?"

"Immediately, while fog enshrouds the streets, so no one will recognize you. As far as we—me, your mother and sisters—are concerned, you're dead. No one in this house is to ever hear from you again, understand?" Kekinor Kway spun on his heel to leave.

"Can I at least bid farewell to Jeda?"

"I said leave now! She'll be gone soon, too. The two of you never did fit in. You've found what you're best suited for. The emperor will find a suitable use for your twin, too. Don't bother coming to visit her, she won't be here." He vanished into the gloom of the hallway.

Artka rubbed his brow and stared at the dying coals in the fireplace, collecting his thoughts.

Two men swaggered into the room.

"Yer be's trespassin'. The master wants usn's ter escort yer off'n his property," sneered one.

Artka nodded and stood. The pounding in his head increased. "Just give me a minute to get my things."

"Usn's already gots 'em. Let's go."

They prodded Artka through the darkened room, past curtained windows, down long, dark corridors, passing silent, luxuriously furnished rooms. At the outer exit to the street Artka turned to his escorts, "May I have my things now?"

"Sure, why not?" The bodyguard handed over Artka's rucksack containing all his personal items and leather armor, bedroll, clothing, a short knife and a notebook of tactics. The other guard still fiddled with Artka's hickory blade.

"My sword?" Artka said, waiting in the doorway, extending his hand.

"Yer means this here toy? Not till yer down the walkway, acrost the lawn an' off'n the property an' out on the road, laddie. C'mon, move it," said the shorter one, giving Artka's spine one last savage poke.

Artka spun around and faced his tormentors, his face flushed and muscles tense, but a season of Sergeant Love's tutelage had taught him to master impulsive reactions.

The bodyguards noticed him stiffen. "G'wan an' do it yer little snake. Come fer usn's," said one fingering the knife in his belt. "I sees the anger in yer eyes, boy. Like ter kill usn's, wouldn't yer, huh?"

Artka studied the gnarled hands, sinewy arms and flinty faces of the two thugs. They could kill just for fun, and probably had. He turned and started down the stairs.

"Hah! See whut fer kind o' recruits the emperor gots now, Blatch. Afeared o' every shadow. We'll hafta defend the empire ourselves if'n all they gots is blokes the likes o' him."

"Right yer be, Orvy. Pretty poor pickin's, I'd say," said the other. He jabbed Artka between the shoulder blades with the hickory sword.

Artka's rucksack hit the stone walkway as he spun around in a blur, grabbed the hickory blade and tugged the unsuspecting goon off balance. Blatch's arms flailed and his hand released Artka's sword. Quick as a spark Artka flipped his weapon to his sword hand and in one motion whacked the thick side against Blatch's neck. Blatch grunted and sprawled headlong.

Orvy yelled, "Hey! Watch thet yer—"

Artka leapt at the other tough, brandishing his "toy."

Orvy backed away, fumbling for the knife in his belt.

The sharp side of Artka's sword sliced down through homespun fabric, skin and into Orvy's elbow. A muffled snap resounded as bone and tendon spliced free of each other. Orvy cried out and fell face down on the stairway, unconscious, his arm bent unnaturally beneath.

Artka's head was clear; the headache gone. He lifted his sword and prepared to roar the brigade's battle cry in triumph, but then paused as he said, "Blood on my blade—but not Ecclessite blood. Only trouble will come of this." He knelt and wiped his sword clean in the dewy grass.

Blatch moaned. Artka went over and, with a foot, prodded the man.

Blatch rolled over and blinked, staring up at Artka. Artka touched the sword point to the bodyguard's throat. "Listen good you maggot, tell my father that I'll be back, and I'd better find Jeda here, and safe, or he'll pay more dearly than your pig-faced friend. Got that?"

Blatch made no response. Artka pressed his sword's sharp point a tad deeper. A spot of crimson appeared. "Got that?"

"Awright, I'll tell him."

"And if I ever see you or your comrade again, I swear by the dreads of the gate I'll finish what I started and lay your skulls open." Then, turning toward his father's house, he shouted, "I'll return. Count on it."

A curtain moved ever so slightly at an upstairs window.

CHAPTER FOUR

ARTKA LONGED TO WIPE AWAY the beads of perspiration trickling down his forehead into his eyes and hanging off the end of his nose, but mindful to maintain discipline, he forced himself to focus on swinging his arms and marching in step to the cadence of the pace-drum. Coughing and sneezing from those on his left reminded him that, he at least, had the fortune of being placed on an outside column, unlike most recruits who marched inside the columns where swirling dust clogged nostrils, made eyes water and teeth grit.

Artka faced rigidly forward but his eyes strained right, drinking in the lush scenery. Fields nearby stretched into distant, grassy knolls, which then emerged as forested hills and mountains ablaze with autumn's yellows, oranges, reds and russets. At the foot of the mountains, but still near the road, were peasant cottages interspersed between patch-work gardens and paddocks. "Peasant" was a derisive term Artka had used freely like his comrades, but now, seeing the hard scrabble-life these serfs endured, Artka regretted his disdain. Indeed, the empire owed its life to these over-worked, over-taxed, unappreciated soil-turners who supplied the hands and backbone of the Carnalian economy.

As Artka passed by an ancient farmer busily hacking and stacking stalks into sheaves to provide bedding and fodder so his livestock would survive the approaching winter, he became fascinated. Deep, weathered lines etched the old man's leathery face and white hair poked out oddly here and there from beneath his knit cap; his gnarled knuckles evidenced the ravages of flexing thousands of times a day for years upon years. The serf briefly looked up and, in that glance, Artka sensed the man's drudgery. He had a sudden, inexplicable urge to step out of line and ask the old farmer why he worked so hard if he took no joy in his labor or had no hope that life would improve. But that was impossible. Artka passed by the aged cotter who remained unimpressed by the robust, parading martial column.

Hours and hours of dusty leagues the martial column trod under a brutal sun. Grime caked on faces, necks and any exposed skin. Artka fared somewhat better than the inner columns, but eventually even he felt the grit of dust between teeth, itchy eyes, and an annoying tickle in his nostrils.

Sergeant Love's training was serving him well. His pack, like the pack of every soldier around him, jounced in perfect syncopation with each drum throb. Up until he'd passed the hoary peasant, Artka, like everyone else in the regiment, eagerly anticipated fighting at the front. But now what was it all for?

"Prepare . . . to fall out," non-commissioned officers echoed down the line. The drum stuttered to a different rhythm, then a rapid drum-roll, and a sudden stop. Every boot halted in unison.

"Fall . . . out!"

Men dropped out of line and reclined on either side of the road, partaking freely of water bags and strips of dried meat.

Artka sauntered over to Bilrood who sprawled on a tussock. "You look awful."

Bilrood rinsed his mouth with water. "Sure, and I'd look like a daisy too, if I were in the outer column. How'd you manage that appointment?"

Artka shrugged. "I don't know."

Bilrood's lips turned down at the corners and his eyebrows rose.

"Honestly, I don't know. Sergeant Love pulled me aside and showed me my place in the outer column."

"Humph! All I know is that only revered veterans or wealthy recruits are allowed in the outer columns."

Artka frowned. "What are you insinuating?"

"Your family is well off, isn't it? Lord Kekinor Kway . . . "

"My father disowned me. You know that."

"You explain it then." Bilrood poured water onto his cupped hand and splashed his face.

"I can't."

"Hmph!"

"All right, be that way." Artka turned to leave.

"Wait, Artka, I'm sorry. I'm just fed up with dust gritting between my teeth and burning my eyes. Don't leave."

Artka smiled. "That's more like it." He opened his leather pouch and withdrew a strip of jerky, tearing off a bite with his teeth. "Did you ever see a peasant, close up, I mean?"

Bilrood, also chewing jerky, looked at him. "Are you serious? Who wants to look at peasants? Unless, of course, you mean peasant girls. That's a different matter."

"Be serious. I saw an old man working close by the road today. Our eyes met for an instant."

"Yeah, so?"

"He had this expression—"

Bilrood's eyes widened. "Do you think the peasants are planning a revolt? Maybe we should report this."

"No, no, no. Listen to me. I somehow knew that he felt like his life was just one long, useless misery."

"Ah." Bilrood settled back on his haunches. "Probably wishing he was young enough to quit slaving in the fields and march off to glory with us."

"I don't think so. He was barely aware of us. It was more like . . . like he was just going through the motions of life but forgot the reason why."

"The reason why? Nobody knows why. We just do, that's all. What's the matter with you, are you feeling all right You got sunstroke or something?"

"I can't explain it. It was like he gave up caring."

"Caring? About what?"

"About the purpose of life."

"Oh, no! Not you, Artka," Bilrood said with a guffaw and turned to others nearby in the grass. "Our Artka here is a philosopher, searching out the mysteries of life. Artka, listen to me, the purpose of life is survival, and as you do, get all the fun you can. 'Live for the moment' remember?"

"Yeah, and 'Die for the Empire,'" Artka muttered under his breath. He tied his pouch shut and determined to never express personal thoughts or feelings again—at least not to fellow soldiers. "Yeah, I guess you're right."

Their conversation drifted to lighter things as they gnawed jerky and sipped lukewarm water from their canteens.

The call came down the ranks, "Form up." Gear rattled, and feet scuffed as soldiers rousted themselves back into their positions. Artka slung his pouch over his shoulder and re-cinched his pack.

"I guess we'll march now 'til we make camp," said Bilrood. "It's only a couple more hours 'til sunset. Probably cover another couple of leagues . . . "

"We'll bed down side by side, okay?"

"Good. See you then."

Artka arrived at his position in the column just as the preparatory drum roll *rat-a-tat-tatted*. Then Artka, along with every soldier in the regiment stepped in time to the deep, booming pulse of the pace drum.

A sense of pride flowed through Artka as he beheld all the colorful banners painting the breeze as uninterrupted ranks and files of black-garbed men with crimson-trimmed capes and polished black helmets sporting red plumes surged forward *en masse*. Most warriors in outer columns sported bright-red, feathery plumes, denoting their battle experience, while the innermost files contained mostly non-plumed soldiers. Artka's and Bilrood's nemesis, Rilf was one of the few in the inner columns sporting a plume; he'd been in the wars before but seemed to be perpetually in disgrace. Artka's helmet, like all recruits, sported no such plume.

Almost every plumed soldier also possessed a coveted, black iron sword. Artka's eyes fixated on the warrior's sword immediately in front of him. The three-foot blade hung suspended from belt to ankle, swinging hypnotically with each stride. On each back swing the glossy black metal reflected the sun's rays into Artka's eyes. One edge was honed to razor-sharp keenness, the other edge was thick, dull, and blunt. The black Carnalian iron sword was deadly in the hands a skilled fighter. Warriors with twenty confirmed kills were awarded a ruby to adorn their sword's pommel.

Sergeant Love was a sword-master; his rigid training imparted his skills to his trainees. "One side keen," Sergeant Love drilled into them over and over, " . . . to slice through armor, clothing, skin and muscle. The other side blunt for splintering bones and smashing skulls . . . "

Each brigade's sword handle differed from other brigades, depending from which brigade a soldier haled. Brigade emblems ranged from fearful animal mascots such as wolves, tigers, bears, water-dragons and wild boars to mythical entities such as flying dragons, fire-drakes, and dreads. The blades of different nationalities also varied in design: long and straight, or else broad and short for most Carnalian brigades, curving scimitars for Craniantiumite and Pitlander forces, and even curiously-wrought wavy blades for the despised Erotons. The sword handle dazzling Artka's eyes had intertwined serpents forged in such a way that as they curved upward they spread to form the hilt guard where pommel merged into blade. This pommel was a lion's head with jaws agape; clenched in its teeth was blood-red ruby. Its owner had dispatched at least twenty enemies in his service to Lurcan. It was an enormous satisfaction marching amongst such dangerous men.

During boot camp, recruits constantly bragged about winning their own iron. The first recruit of the brigade to earn his own real sword would be the envy of all the others. They boastfully strutted as they envisioned how they'd be among the first to claim the honor of sporting a ruby in their sword handle, sure of their prowess. Artka marched bedazzled by the ruby's gleam as he desired his own "iron" as much as he'd ever craved anything.

CHAPTER FIVE

SWAMP TOPHET WAS THE SOURCE of unspeakable horrors told to children to make them behave. Despite the efforts of the empire's Hall of Re-Education to disparage such beliefs, rumors persisted among the general population of tophets—fanged brutes with bulbous eyes and bloody claws that crept out of the swamp to snatch and devour unwary children, the sick and those injured in battle. The credibility of these rumors of monsters being invisible or enshrouded in thick fogbanks was not diminished. Artka's nanny knew enough Swamp Tophet legends to enthrall, and terrorize, the Kway children for hours.

Artka thought he'd outgrown those childhood fears until word passed down the line that the regiment would bivouac a mere half mile from Swamp Tophet itself.

Mists drifted freely across their campground, as if sent by heavier mists and fogs to spy on the intruders. Recruits freshly arriving in camp were jumpy, disobediently turning heads to investigate the slightest noise. Their sergeants wisely relaxed the protocols. Even plumed veterans, who should have known better about such things, acted nervous.

Bilrood was so tense that he made critical mistakes as he tried rigging a rain fly over his bedroll. Attempting to break his own jitters as well as Bilrood's, Artka crept up behind his friend and whispered, "How can you tell when a tophet is stalking you? Give up? When you're looking from the inside out! Get it? You're no longer outside the invisible monster, but insi—"

"It's no laughing matter, even if the old fables aren't true." Bilrood scowled as he tore down the rain-shield and started over.

Artka turned back and focused on rigging his own gear. Snapping twigs from the forest drew his attention. Were faces glaring at him from the wall of fog? He gripped his hickory sword tight and watched, as did Bilrood.

Rumor and myth aside, Swamp Tophet was a foul location, placed as if by sinister design between the nearly impenetrable Wind Break Forest and the Forbidden Mountains. The swampland had formed countless ages past when the Flaming Sword River overflowed its banks and back-eddied over Carnalia's flood plain, leaving a glut of stranded waters in low-lying hollows. The waters never evaporated but collected more and more runoff every passing year from the Forbidden Mountains, evolving into the miry, noisome system of muskeg, marshes, quicksand, and treacherous waterways that defied anyone entry, let alone habitation. In the early years intrepid hunters tried, but were frustrated by lack of game, or edible fish. Then rumors of loathsome, unnatural creatures growing in the swamp's interior grew into legend. Then hunting parties venturing in failed to return, spawning tales of invincible monsters. Ever since, the entire area, regardless the time of day or prevailing weather conditions, was perpetually shrouded in fog.

Not far from the swamp huddled several ill-disposed, wood-frame structures known as Tophet City. Lurcan established a fortress this side of the Wind Break Forest to deter Ecclessite invasions across Logon's Bridge that kidnapped empire residents and make them kingsmen slaves. A fortress needed a supply source; thus, Tophet City was founded to provision the nearby empire outpost. The emperor purposely chose to establish this fortress because King's Gate Fortress sprang up merely a league away, situated on the Carnalian side of the Flaming Sword River to guard Logon's Bridge. Thus, the broad plains between the swamp, the outpost and Tophet City were a prime staging area for the empire's assaults on Ecclessa. However, as things turned out, Swamp Tophet also was a significant target for kingsmen to invade Carnalia, thus preventing the empire's invasion into Ecclessa.

"Prepare to halt," cried a muffled voice through the mist as another company arrived. Artka and Bilrood sat on their bedrolls watching as new arrivals made camp nearby.

"Halt!" Feet and drums stopped simultaneously. "Fall out." Veterans and recruits scattered to pick places for their bedrolls around fire rings.

Sergeant Love loomed out of the fog, inspecting his squads and appointing various ones to gather firewood. Usually recruits were chosen, but tonight, Artka noticed, veterans were designated this menial chore. Any complainers were silenced by a no-nonsense glance. The sergeant also disrupted the practice of segregation by ordering veterans to bed down among recruits.

"Sterk," Bilrood turned to the grim veteran squatting at their fire, "why is Sergeant Love making vets camp with recruits?"

Sterk rolled his eyes and said, "So's yer wet-nosed runts doesn't git no idees 'bout runnin' off cryin' fer yer mammy." He kicked a bedroll away from the fireside and replaced it with his own. "Yer'll soon be scairt o' yer own shadow," he said, sliding beneath his blanket.

"Tell 'em the real reason, Sterk," said an all too familiar voice. Rilf strolled into their circle and dropped his gear.

Sterk sat up curling his lip. "Yer tell 'em if'n yer so keen." He lay down and turned his back to the fire.

"Because we're so close to Swamp Tophet so the officers are afraid we might get skittish, right?" Artka ventured.

"Partly, laddie-boy, partly," Rilf said, picking bits of meat from between his teeth with a small knife.

"Well, what's the other part?" Bilrood asked.

"Ah, now fer t'other part," Rilf said, " . . . t'ther part gots ter do wi' a certain mysterious Ecclessite." He unrolled and began sorting his gear. Other recruits rimming the fire ring sat up, all ears.

"Is-is it the Ma-Magician? The m-man that can c-control a body just with the s-s-sound of his voice?" said a skinny, pale recruit. It was a wonder Sergeant Love had qualified him for duty; he wasn't skilled at anything, nor was he quick or strong; most expected him to be among the first casualties. For that reason, no one befriended him.

"Out with it Rilf," Bilrood said. "If you know something, spill it." Sometime during the last weeks of training, and more so on the march, Bilrood had lost his fear of Rilf.

"Doncha git sassy wi' me, boy. I could rip yer heart out if'n I was minded." Rilf made no move to back up his threat. "If'n yers wants ter ken more, it'll cost. I overheered the officers, so it be's bonafide information."

"How much?" asked another.

"Oh, I knows yers hain't got nuthin' now. But, bye'n'bye yer might. All's I wants is ter be able ter claim summat whenever I sees fit."

"That's pretty vague," Artka said. "How do we know you're not making the whole thing up?"

"Naw," Sterk said, rising on an elbow. "He gots summat ter say all right." He pointed at the stuttering recruit and ordered, "Promise him yer next rum ration so's he kin git his tale off'n his tongue an' I kin git some sleep."

All eyes fixed on the nervous youngster, who reluctantly nodded.

"Done, then laddie," said Rilf. "Whut be's yer name?"

"Poppitt."

Guffaws and laughter greeted this disclosure. Even in the flickering firelight an embarrassed flush covered the lad's usually pale complexion.

"Poppitt, yer rum it be's then. And here's me tale. When yer marches inter battle tomorrow, if'n yer sees a tall man wearin' a hooded robe o' gray, stop yer ears an' flee. Thet'll be the Magician. He been spotted lurkin' 'bout the swamp."

"And there's another good reason we shouldn't have camped near this cursed swamp," Bilrood said. "I didn't think any king's men dared go near that vile place."

"More dangerous to you is King's Gate Fortress," said Sergeant Love appearing out of the mists again. "You just worry about dispatching kingsmen."

"King's Gate Fortress?" asked Rilf and Sterk in unison.

"That's right. Now, one more thing, keep your campfire high. And no matter what you hear, don't leave the circle of firelight." Sergeant Love studied those gathered around the fire ring, chuckled, then disappeared as phantom-like as he'd appeared.

Artka, brimming with questions, looked to Bilrood, who merely shrugged. Sterk was of no use, either, for his back was to the flames and them as well. "Rilf?" Artka hated to ask but had no other choice.

"It'll cost."

"Boar's bowels, Rilf! Do you have to put a price on everything?" Bilrood demanded.

"Live fer the moment . . . eh?" Rilf turned to Artka. "Well?"

"A pint of rum," Artka grudgingly said, then added, "it better be worth it."

"Oh, it is, it is. And lots more. But I'll tell yer fer a pint. Them doesn't much like the light o' campfires. Makes 'em keep their distance."

"What?"

"Why, I be's truly surprised. A lad as old as yer hain't never heered tell o' the Swamp Tophet creatures?" Rilf licked his lips.

"Now look here, Rilf." Icy fingers tickled Artka's spine. "Do you think you can scare us with ghost stories? There are no invisible monsters in the swamp, or anywhere else."

"Jest the same, yer'd best mind the fire, like the sergeant said."

"W-w-will creatures c-c-c-come out of th-th-the swamp?" Poppitt said, his eyes bulging.

"By the dreads," Sterk rose on his elbow again. "How yer drags things out, Rilf. W-w-w-will they come out of the sw-sw-swamp? Yes, yer little bug-eyed mouse, where else does yer think Swamp Tophets comes from? They'll come creepin' an' crawlin' outta their haunts durin' the darkest hours o' night when the mists rises off'n the marshes. Now, I be's supposin' summat gots ter ken why?" He coughed and spat phlegm into the fire. "Because the emperor has summoned 'em ter join the attack. That oughtta satisfy yers. Kin I finally git some sleep now?" Sterk lay back down.

Bilrood frowned. "Do you expect us to believe—?"

"Grrrr! Yers'll believe afore the nights over," Sterk said, sitting up. "Yer'll hear 'em when they comes, most likely smell 'em first, if'n the wind's right."

Poppitt dodged under his bedroll.

The others stared into the flames wrestling with their own fears. Sterk grunted, stood to his feet and threw a fair-sized log on the fire, then re-settled into his bedroll.

Rilf stretched his arms, prolonged a yawn, then lay down, covering himself. "Yer'd best see ter it thet someone keeps the fire goin' bright," he said and rolled over.

Poppitt uncovered his head and said, "I'll w-w-watch . . . can't sleep now, anyway."

Artka caught Bilrood's glance and nodded back. They'd wake periodically and check the fire. Pulling their blankets up, they soon drifted off to sleep.

Artka dreamt he was in the dungeon with the notorious Turit. The massive, hulk of a man rose in rage at Artka. With a mighty tug, Turit yanked the chain's ring out of the granite wall and whipped it around into Artka's ribcage. Stunned, Artka fell back. Turit leapt on Artka, eyes gleaming like coals as he commanded, "Look at the fire in my eyes, boy. Look at the fire. Look at the fire." Again, the chain slammed into Artka's ribcage.

"Artka, look at the fire . . . " urged Bilrood, poking Artka. "Look at the fire. Rain is putting it out."

Artka shook his head trying to differentiate between dream and reality. Bilrood crossed over to the woodpile, saying, "Quick, help me rebuild the fire before the coals die."

Artka threw off his bedroll. Cold rain penetrating his clothing restored his senses. He got up and tossed smaller sticks onto the hissing coals. Smoke mixed with steam, then tiny, orange flames hungrily licked at the new fuel. Larger branches were piled on; the fire revived.

A vice-like grip seized Artka's arm as he was about to toss another log. Sterk hissed in his ear, "Lissen." Artka and Bilrood froze, rain dripping off their noses and ears. Through the patter of rain and the crackling fire, faintly at first, then louder they heard the unmistakable sounds of something immense crawling—or being dragged—just outside the light of their fire-ring. "More wood, afore them be's on us," said the veteran.

Artka and Bilrood furiously flung wood from the pile to the fire causing sparks to soar upward. Soon others at nearby campfires roused; muffled curses mixed with the hiss of heavy rain and the snapping of igniting twigs filled the night.

"Phaaah!" Bilrood spat. "What stinks?"

Artka's nostrils caught the rotting smell of decay. His heart thumped against his chest. He dumped another log atop the pile. Bright flaming spurts shot through the bramble of wet sticks, casting a reddish glow on soldiers scurrying here and there with armfuls of firewood or else standing with swords at the ready.

"Them won't come closer," Sterk said. "Where's thet little bug-eyed kid? He was supposed ter be watchin' the fire."

"Here he is, in his bedroll, fast asleep."

"Passed out from nervous exhaustion, I'd guess," Artka said, "the way he was shaking and all. He missed all the excitement."

"Hain't no sense tryin' ter git any more sleep ternight," Sterk said, draping his bedroll over his head and shoulders as he squatted down. "Soon enuf be daylight, anyhows."

Seeing the veterans relax their guard, Artka breathed a sigh of relief. He and Bilrood sat by the fire, covering against the rain, each keeping a wary eye on the darkness toward the swamp. Rilf started for the sleeping recruit intending to skin Poppitt alive, but Sterk intervened, staring Rilf down and shaking his head. So Poppitt slept on, blissfully unaware how close he'd come to encountering his worst nightmare.

"Sterk," Bilrood said in the hush of the wet, smoky camp, "why does the emperor use those—those—?"

"Tophets?" Sterk said. "Sarge said they's gonna be a big push for the King's Gate Fortress. They's several kingsmen brigades at King's Gate, and whut with the Magician bein' sighted . . . it figgers ter be a hard battle. Tophets be's needed ter oppose the kingsmen's brights—"

"Brights?" Artka asked.

"Yeah, yer kens, brights be's summat like tophet creatures whut's fights on the enemy's side. Only difference is, tophets be's jest as likely ter turn agin usn's. If'n yer smells ary rotten or swampy stink durin' the fightin', yer best be a skedaddlin.'"

CHAPTER SIX

"RATHER THAN KILL, THE KING'S armies will attempt to capture you." Captain Fitcher paced on foot, encouraging his troops.

Artka exchanged a knowing glance with Bilrood.

"Your sergeants informed you of living conditions in Ecclessa by now," Fitcher continued. "The king of Ecclessa's strict rules and severe punishments are intolerable for freeborn Carnalians. Ask yourself, does the emperor ban pleasures and strictly control empire citizenry with spells to keep them in line until they die?"

And yet, Artka mused, here he knelt, in ankle deep mud on the edge of Swamp Tophet in a soaking rain, ordered to risk life and limb for the emperor's glory.

"The enemy is so naive as to think that once they lie to you about their lifestyle, you'll want to join them. If by some circumstance you get captured, pretend to join them. Later you can make your escape and find your way back to our lines."

The attack had been postponed due to the dismal weather. As a result of the down time, discontent had arisen in the rank and file. Even experienced veterans were complaining, and recruits were squabbling with each other, sometimes erupting into fisticuffs. To quell the moodiness, the captain decided to personally address the men.

"Take care, though," Captain Fitcher said, "kingsmen are clever spellbinders and have actually caused some of our best warriors to turn traitor. And never, I repeat, never, let them touch you with their swords. There's an unexplained force at work in those weapons. You've been well-trained. Use your weapons first to cut, slice and batter your opponent before he gets a chance to use his weapon. If you do so with maximum efficiency as you've been taught and summon your courage, you will give a good account of yourself."

Artka glanced down at his trustworthy hickory. He'd mastered the skills Sergeant Love had taught, using it to disarm most of those he'd trained with, and winning every duel except against Sergeant Love.

"Then, there's the possibility you might meet the Magician," Captain Fitcher wheeled about and retraced his steps as he reached the end of the line of kneeling soldiers, "in which case flee, or if unable to flee, slit your own throat while you retain possession of your mind. The Magician has some kind of mental prowess he uses to strip away a man's sanity and leave him a mindless, whimpering wretch. There's no shame in avoiding such a fate. Get away from him at all costs.

"You recruits should stay close to, or even behind seasoned warriors who know what they're doing. Any recruits that do manage to slay an enemy, bring your bloodied hickory to the quartermaster after the battle. You'll be able, upon presentation of kingsmen blood, to trade it for an iron blade." Captain Fitcher took the reins of his horse from an aide and prepared to mount. A lieutenant approached and whispered in the captain's ear. The captain nodded, climbed aboard his stallion and added, "Oh yes, one last thing, do not, under any circumstances, wander into foul-smelling fogs. Don't ask too many questions either, there are some things you're better off not knowing for the time being."

"Sergeants, see to your men," a lieutenant barked.

From the saddle of his steed Captain Fitcher reviewed the kneeling rows of troopers as non-commissioned officers scurried about with last minute instructions, appointing men to squads.

"You two shadow me," Sergeant Love said, laying hands on and commandeering Artka and Bilrood to his squad. "Artka you on my left, Bilrood on my right. And . . . " he said looking around, "oh yes, you too Pupsy, or whatever your name is, you tag along behind."

"Be's yer sure o' whut yer doin', Sarge," said Rilf with a smirk. "A couple o' whelps the likes o' them could git yer kilt."

"Telling me how to run my outfit could *git yer kilt*, so stay out of my way, or I might forget which side you're on," Sergeant Love said.

Captain Fitcher, slowly reviewing the troops, paused in front of Artka. "You there, soldier, do I know you?"

Artka's cheeks reddened. "I-I don't think so, sir."

"Have you family in Cosmopolis?"

Having been unofficially disowned, Artka was unsure how to answer. "No, sir, that is, only a twin sister."

"Ah-ha! And would her name be Jeda?"

Artka's mouth fell open.

"I thought so. Good luck on the morrow, son. You're led by a worthy sergeant." Fitcher directed his horse toward the next company, his bodyguard following right behind, sending muddy chunks flying in the air.

"Thet," Rilf rubbed his stubbly chin, "explains why Artka gits ter march in the outer file, an' gits chosen fer the sergeant's squad. Twin sister, eh? She must be a looker ter catch a captain's eye."

Without thinking Artka lunged and seized the Eroton by the throat, sending both of them sprawling into the mud. "Shut your mouth, you slimy slug. I'll not allow trashy comments from the likes of you about my sister."

The two rolled in the mud. Artka attained a position atop Rilf and his thumbs found Rilf's windpipe and squeezed.

Eyes bulging, gasping for breath, Rilf vainly battered Artka's arms.

The flat edge of Sergeant Love's sword tapped Artka's forearms. "Let him loose. Save your anger for the real men you'll meet tomorrow."

Artka reluctantly released his grip and got off Rilf.

Rilf rolled over to his stomach, squeaking with each breath, glaring hatefully up at Artka.

"If he ever insults my sister again, I'll finish it." Artka slogged away through the mud toward his gear.

Bilrood fell in beside him grinning ear to ear. They knelt in the mud, pretending to examine their kits. Bilrood spoke lowly, keeping his eyes downcast, "You showed him. But how do you think the captain knows Jeda?"

"No idea," Artka said curtly. As hard and cold as their father had become, might he have followed through on his threat to send Jeda to the emperor's palace to be . . . ? Is that how Captain Fitcher knew her?

Sergeant Love splashed over to Artka and Bilrood. "I told Rilf I wouldn't intervene again. Just so you know, Artka, I'm responsible for putting you in the outside file, and choosing you for my squad, not the captain."

"Why?" Artka said, squinting against the rain.

"'Cause of how you handled your father's bodyguards. That shows real ability. I know those two rascals. They're dangerous men."

"How do you know about that?"

"It's my business to know such things," the sergeant said with a shrug. "I also know about the three blokes that got you drunk, Bilrood, robbing you blind the first night of your liberty."

"You do?" Bilrood said, a flush rising to his cheeks. "Who are they? When I get my hands on them—"

"Now, now sonny, not so fast. Even I wouldn't tangle with that bunch, at least not alone. Save your rage for the enemy tomorrow."

"Bilrood, you should've told me," Artka said.

Bilrood tugged and retied the rigging on his breastplate. "Nevermind."

Sergeant Love stood and looked toward the sky. "Blasted rain. Mucks up everything. Rest well tonight men. Tomorrow, if the weather breaks, you'll both earn iron." He trudged off into the swirling drizzle.

Artka picked up his hickory sword. It had served him well during training and in the fight with his father's thugs, yet he couldn't wait to trade it for a lion-head sword, proud emblem of the Roaring Lion Brigade. He envisioned himself surrounded by kingsmen and defeating them all, earning a ruby in one battle. "Hah! Here I'm daydreaming about rubies and haven't even been in a fight."

"What'd you say," Bilrood said, pulling his hood up against the rain.

"Oh, nothing." Artka's thoughts returned to Jeda. Was she a slave, or safe at home? For sanity's sake he must choose to believe she was safe; the fact that Captain Fitcher knew her was purely coincidental. Yes, of course, as a military leader, Captain Fitcher would've been on the Cosmopolisian social registry, and as such, been among his mother's invited guests. The captain had probably met Jeda on a social visit to the Kway estate. There was a strong resemblance between brother and sister and with the captain's eye for detail and sharp memory, he must have made the association. That was it, it was all very innocent. He sighed, and the corners of his mouth turned up slightly.

A veteran trudged by, splashing the pair. Bilrood called out, "Hey, watch it, Sterk."

Sterk growled back, "Watch it yerself," affecting annoyance.

"While you're here, maybe you can give me an answer, earlier today I had a thought—"

"Congratulations. I hopes yer gits another someday." Sterk took another step.

"No wait, seriously, I have a question . . . after the battle gets under way, why has no one suggested picking up an Ecclessite sword? There ought to be plenty scattered around. Wouldn't that be better than fighting with a wooden sword?"

"Dreads o' the gate, boy, doncher ken nuthin'?"

Bilrood looked blankly back, as did Artka.

"No, I kin see yers don't. Well, it be's a longish story, an' I hain't gots time fer it now. Ask me ternight around the campfire." Sterk continued on his way muttering, "Cain't hardly believe whut they ain't teachin' recruits nowadays."

"Seemed a reasonable question to me," Artka said, tightening his backpack straps.

That afternoon the misty drizzle turned into a hard rain and the temperature dropped. Struggling fires again sprouted up as night settled in, but the smoky fires did little to elevate the dark mood of chilled men huddling together for warmth.

Artka and Bilrood returned from guard duty to find Poppitt tossing wood on their campfire. Rilf's bedroll and gear were gone from the makeshift lean-to. In Rilf's place was a grizzled, one-eyed veteran who lacked the last two fingers of his sword hand.

"Will they come around again tonight?" Poppitt said, jerking suddenly to check out every sound from the surrounding darkness.

"Who?" Sterk sent a puff of steam from his lips into the night air.

"The—oh, you know," Poppitt said.

"Oh them," Sterk winked to the new man beside the fire. "Nah, they's picketed on the eastern edge o' the Wind Break Forest ter thwart kingsmen surprise attacks."

"How far away is that?" Poppitt asked.

"Yer'll find out tomorrow. Trust me, they won't come 'round hereabouts . . . unless—shhh, whut's thet I hears?" He sniffed the air. "Does yer smell it? Oh! It be's headin' right fer usn's! I'm a gittin' outta here!"

Poppitt, ashen-faced, eyes wide, nostrils flaring, jumped to his feet, grabbed his sleeping gear in a bunch and scrambled to get his hickory sword.

Coarse laughter checked his panic.

"That's not funny," a crimson-faced Poppitt returned to his bedroll by the fire.

"Yer be's askin' fer it laddie," Sterk said. "Now, doncher be worryin' none 'bout them tophets no more. They avoids open spaces, only venturin' out when forced, or drawn by a cravin' fer vengeance or fresh blood, like as be's found after a battle, if'n yer ken whut I means."

Poppitt grimaced.

Although no one asked, Sterk continued, "Them likes the Wind Break Forest . . . it sorta be's like their swampy haunts. It stops the wind from blowin' the sweet smells and pleasant sounds of Ecclessa acrost the river. I guess that's why they likes it, though it lacks the smell an' feel o' their swamp."

Artka spread his bedroll beside Bilrood's.

"Smag," Sterk said, " . . . these be's the other two I tole yer about. The taller one's Bilrood, an' that there be's Artka. This here's Smag. He be's replacin' Rilf. I think the sergeant was afeered yers would put Rilf outta his misery durin' the night."

"So," said Smag, eyeing them as they settled near the fire. "Sergeant Love chose yers fer his left an' right bowers, eh? Yers don't look so special. Well, tomorrow we'll see whut yers be's made o'."

With dismay Artka noted that Smag's dialect was Eroton, as was Sterk's. The fact that Rilf also was Eroton didn't help matters. Artka, like most Carnalians, despised Erotons' slovenly ways, cruelty, and excessive pleasure seeking. Even so, over the years Eroton-ish practices, as well as shades of the dialect crept into Carnalian culture.

"At least Rilf won't be slitting our throats as we sleep," Bilrood said laying back on his bedroll, fingers interlocked behind his head.

Artka gnawed some jerky while Sterk and Smag traded stories of gore and glory. Artka's eyes caught a brief glint of firelight from Smag's sword handle and saw it sported a ruby.

Bilrood draped the fly of his bedroll around his neck and shoulders. "Sterk," he said during a pause in the story swapping, "you were going to tell us why we shouldn't pick up dropped Ecclessite swords."

"Be's they serious?" asked Smag, lifting his head.

"Feered so."

"Pitland's Priestess! I thought everybody kenned 'bout them blades."

"Musta skipped summat o' trainin' ter git 'em out ter the front quicker. All right yer recruits, listen up, cause I only wants ter say this oncet."

All attention riveted on him.

Sterk said, "A long time ago, afore the Magician appeared, the king's soldiers changed battle tactics, becoming bolder, more aggressive. Our spies thot it due ter Prince Xychirion's presence. Whatever the reason, empire troops began losin' battle after battle. Even cusps and tophets gave way ter the king's armies.

"In them days Xychirion hisself marched at the head of their columns. They come acrost the Flamin' Sword River in droves an' built a fortress this side o' the river callin' it King's Gate West. The foundation o' the bridge, which be's the only crossin' inter Ecclessa, was established by none other than Xychirion hisself."

"What's all this got to do with their swords?" Bilrood asked.

"Patience, laddie," said Smag, "let him say whut he gots ter say. They's more ter be learnt than whut yer asked."

Sterk continued, "As I be's sayin', the king's son, Xychirion, built the bridge acrost thet river. No one kens how he done it. Right after it got built, the king's armies invaded Carnalia, buildin' outposts wherever they went. Empire city after city fell under kingsman domination. Things begun lookin' mighty rough fer the empire.

"Only Cosmopolis an' Mammon remained free o' Ecclessa's influence. O' course, the entire country o' Eroton was free, but if Cosmopolis fell, it would o' been jest a matter o' time afore Eroton fell, too." Sterk threw a couple of branches on the fire.

"In desperation the emperor rallied his crack blackguard troops," Sterk continued, "boldly attacking Logon Xychirion. The attack succeeded 'cause Lurcan cleverly infiltrated a betrayer into Xychirion's inner circle. Xychirion got captured, tried fer hate crimes, condemned, and impaled on a post alongside the Flamin' Sword River so's all the king's forces on t'other side could look acrost an' see whut become o' their prince.

"Ecclessite outposts got razed an' kingsmen went inter hidin' or back acrost the river. The emperor reclaimed all his rightful territory this side o' the river . . . 'cept King's Gate West. A couple o' days after thet the Magician appeared an' made Xychirion's body disappear from the impaling post.

"Emboldened by their new leader, kingsmen made sorties acrost the bridge again. No matter how hard the empire fought, they couldn't take King's Gate West 'cause the Magician was castin' spells whut protected Ecclessa."

"Jest luck, says I, t'warn't no spells," said Smag hugging his knees.

Sterk tilted his head and gave a slight shrug. "Anyways, kingsmen surged inter Carnalia again and re-built their outposts. But their plans got confused, Ecclessite captains didn't cooperate wi' each other. Their goals seemed ter be the enslavement of Carnalians rather than takin' control o' territory."

Bilrood, hands widespread, interrupted, "But what about the—?"

Sterk ignored the interruption. "The same time thet the Magician appeared, the king's soldiers wielded a new type o' sword which, instead o' killin', only wounded. Wounded Carnalians was carted off ter Ecclessa and enslaved."

"Wh-wh-what happened to them?" Poppitt asked, the whites of his eyes fully visible.

"They done lost their minds and spent the rest o' their lives in forced hard labor, an' git this . . . they was deceived into thinkin' they liked whut they was a doin'."

Firelight flickered on somber faces.

"At first," Sterk resumed, "the quality o' iron in their swords seemed superior ter Carnalian swords. Now mind yers, them swords only seemed superior, as if made o' better metal, yer kens? Empire alchemists examined Ecclessite swords and declared 'em inferior ter black swords. Even so, ours often break when we crosses blades wi' an Ecclessite what gots a glow on his weapon—which don't happen too often no more, eh, Smag? The Priestess o' Pitland declared Ecclessa's swords be's under a charm. This got confirmed when several Carnalians went inter battle usin' kingsman swords they picked up off'n the field o' battle. Them 'Clessite swords kept turnin' an' aimin' fer the hearts o' the empire men whut wielded 'em. Some stabbed themselves in the chest and run over to surrender ter the enemy right off. Others had ter fling 'em away lest they got cut ter ribbons by the sword in their own hand." Sterk laid back, finished.

Smag added, "It be's no coincidence thet the Magician an' them glowin' swords appeared about the same time. So be wise, earn yer black iron. Fergit about even touchin' one o' them accursed things."

The squad of recruits stared at sparks rising into the night sky.

"How can we fight the Magician and . . . and spell-bound weapons?" Poppitt wrapped his sleeping bag tighter around him. "I mean, th-th-those tophet creatures are bad enough, and they're on our side. We have to guard against them, and face an unconquerable foe, too?" The recruit shook so violently that the pine tree he was leaning against showered him afresh.

Smag reached over and smacked Poppitt upside the head, sending him sprawling. "You whimpering little pup. I oughtta slay yer now an' be done wi' yer."

Poppitt picked himself out of the mud, no longer quivering, a three-fingered hand emblazoned on his cheek.

"Yers needn't be worried 'bout them swords glowin'," Sterk said. "Most kingsmen jest carries 'em fer ornament anymore. They don't hardly kens how ter use 'em like kingsmen o' old. If'n by chance yer sees a kingsman whut kens whut he be's doin', let a veteran handle him—or a tophet."

"Naw, it hain't like the old days, eh Sterk?" said Smag revealing emptiness above two knuckles of his right hand. "Not like when I lost me digibles. Why, I remembers . . ."

As the two vets traded war stories on into the night, Artka drifted off to sleep determined to never touch an Ecclessite sword.

CHAPTER SEVEN

THE HAIRS ON ARTKA'S NECK stood on end as he moved tree to tree, then stopped to investigate any movement or analyze every sound. It was raining again. The predicted break in the weather never came. Chilly rivulets trickled down his open neck and inside his leather breastplate, yet he didn't mind.

Sergeant Love, a panther on the prowl, stalked a dozen paces to his right. Bilrood was a few steps on the other side of him; and strung out past them, barely visible in the swirling fog, were the other soldiers of their brigade gliding through the mist-enshrouded Wind Break Forest like phantoms.

The Carnalian battle line was set in three waves, each wave a double file. Veterans and worthy recruits led, followed by those of more doubtful ability. Sergeant Love had been granted the northern-most edge of the assault wave where fierce resistance was expected. Artka, his mind alert and nerves taut, basked in being appointed flank man in a wave five thousand strong, a position of responsibility and honor.

All account of time lapsed as the battle group stealthily crept through the forest searching their quarry. Artka slipped noiselessly, cautiously to another tree trunk and peered around it at the mists ahead.

Muffled shouts and clanging iron suddenly broke out somewhere on the right. Blood pounded in Artka's temples. His muscles twitched as he gripped his sword tighter.

"Come on then, lads," Sergeant Love hoarsely whispered, " . . . let's see what disturbs yonder glen, eh?"

Artka ached to rush ahead, but faithful to his training, stayed in position alongside his sergeant. The squad wheeled to the right, toward the shouting and clanging sounds of scrimmage. Other soldiers, anxious to be in the fray, peeled off from their squad leaders, joining themselves to Sergeant Love's advance. His silence was taken as permission. Artka vaulted a downed tree and found himself in the midst of a thorny thicket. He hacked and pushed through the prickly bushes, emerging alongside Bilrood and Sergeant Love. The squad crept over a ridge. Sounds of a mêlée echoed from the bottom of a fog-obscured draw. Sergeant Love raised his hand. The swollen patrol paused.

Bilrood, his hickory straight out before him, leapt several yards downhill, challenging, "What are we waiting for?" Several non-plumed soldiers started to go with him.

"Hold up!" Sergeant Love hissed. "Where do you think you're going?"

"To the fight," Bilrood said back in frustration. "It's just down there, Sergeant. Can't you hear it?"

"Do you see a battle? How do you know it's not the Magician luring you with battle noises?"

Bilrood fell silent.

"Never. NEVER," Sergeant Love said, "charge into anything you can't see, especially when the Magician is rumored to be about."

Bilrood and the others with him shamefacedly clambered back up the ridge.

The sergeant sniffed, listened and stuck out his tongue tasting the air. "All right," he said, "fan out, advance slowly, until we know what we're dealing with."

Only a few wooden swords bristled among the many black iron swords leveled downhill as the troopers navigated over large rocks, wet leaves and slick, fallen branches.

Whoosh, *thunk*.

A Carnalian arrow vibrated right beside Artka's head in an oak tree. Artka stared open mouthed at the "friendly" arrow.

At that moment Sergeant Love reared back his head and raised their regimental battle cry, a Craniantium lion's roar—the signal to attack—adding to the growing clamor in the foggy draw. Artka joined his voice to the swelling roar that was calculated to make the blood of the most stalwart enemy warrior run cold. Artka cut to the left and froze as he heard a twig snap.

A sandy-haired, Ecclessite youth loomed into view from behind a tree. He wore only a light tunic with no battle armor and wielded a sword that glowed a few inches from the tip. Artka lunged toward the shadowy figure. The kingsman's eyes widened. His breaths were shallow, but his jaw was set in a determined grimace. Artka halted five feet away. They stood for a few minutes taking each other's measure.

The kingsman's trembling voice said, "Your sword is merely wood. It's no match for my metal. Come, lay your weapon down, join us, seek the king's amnesty." The kingsman stepped forward, his sword aimed at Artka's chest.

Artka furrowed his brow as his eyes narrowed. His opponent didn't seem hostile, nor under a spell, but almost . . . friendly. Artka felt drawn to accept the invitation even as the kingsman's sword drew within inches of his leather breastplate. At the last minute Artka shook his head to clear his thoughts and slapped away the kingsman's weapon with his hickory, then threw his head back and roared their regimental battle cry.

The Ecclessite flinched and took a step back, his weapon dipped down.

Artka smiled. The lad was dead where he stood. Artka launched, swinging his hickory in deadly, overhead arcs. There was no possible defense.

Quick as lightning the Ecclessite sword swung upward, fending off Artka's strikes.

Rebuffed, Artka staggered backward, nearly losing his footing. He regained balance and wheeled about to defend against counterattack.

But the kingsman merely crouched, panting through his mouth.

Artka examined his hickory. The blows hadn't hurt it.

"I wish you no harm," said the kingsman. "I could have struck when you stumbled, had that been my intent. Don't you see how I withheld?"

"I see only that you're faint-hearted, and that will prove your undoing." Artka lunged again with a fusillade of blows intended to penetrate his opponent's blocking defense, but each and every time the glimmering-tipped sword turned from an indefensible position to deflect Artka's thrusts.

Artka whirled around behind the kingsman and again spun about to defend but needn't have bothered. The young warrior held his ground but didn't press his advantage. Artka circled warily. How was this stripling repelling his best attacks? No one in his company had been able to withstand these attacks on the practice field. So how was this inferior kingsman able to do so?

Artka shouted to disorient his foe and feinted to the right, then reversed, springing left with a vicious stab at the youth's ribs. The kingsman teetered on one foot off balance. Artka knew he had him. He again savagely thrust his hickory, this time at his opponent's exposed spine. Instead of piercing flesh and bone however, his sword merely swished harmlessly through a corner of the warrior's white tunic. Then a sudden jolt numbed Artka's arm.

Artka backed away incredulous, rubbing his wrist, analyzing his attack. The Ecclessite had somehow knocked away the lethal stroke. In a flash of insight Artka muttered, "The sword is fighting me. There *is* a spell on it . . . " Artka's confidence wavered until he noticed his opponent's brow drenched in sweat and his eyes darting about with the furtive look of a cornered animal.

"How long do you think the spell will last?" Artka said. Not all battles are won by skill and strength. Demoralization drills were about to pay off. "Spells weaken with use, you know."

"There are no magical spells in the king's service," the Ecclessite said. "But this sword does have power, for Xychirion brought its molten metal from beyond the stars, and during forging, engraved the king's decrees upon it giving it strength and agility."

"Then I'll defeat your Xychirion and his decrees when I defeat you." Artka leapt at his foe slicing, chopping, and stabbing to wear down his enemy, but somehow, despite his opponent's obvious exhaustion, the glowing sword repelled every assault. Artka pressed the attack several more minutes, but then, with a two-fisted upswing, the kingsman's sword knocked away Artka's jab. A reverberating crack echoed through the glen.

Artka jumped back and examined his weapon. A split ran the entire length of the blade, even into the handle. His stomach tightened. His hickory had only one or two blows left, then it would be kindling. No longer so confident, anger at not being sent into battle with a real sword flooded through him.

Artka's rival leaned back against a tree sucking in great draughts of air. The glowing sword point rested in the decaying leaves of the forest floor. The kingsman had stood his ground, but barely. He couldn't withstand Artka's attacks much longer. But now that Artka's weapon was compromised . . .

The Ecclessite took a deep breath and leveled his sword, uttering, "A life for the king!" he charged.

Artka twisted aside and easily slipped his damaged sword beneath the oncoming blade, diverting it. A shiver went through his wooden weapon and the split ran the rest of the way down the haft. Stringy fibers were all that held the wooden sword together. A bitter taste of fear and outrage filled Artka's mouth.

The kingsman's weapon, however, fell from his hand and skittered across the ground. The youth stumbled after it, reaching, sprawling headlong to retrieve it.

Without thinking Artka lunged and drove his riven hickory into the Ecclessite's exposed ribcage.

Crimson spurted up. The young warrior shuddered, arched his back, then went limp as a prolonged sigh escaped his lips. Artka fancied he saw a slight smile cross the kingsman's lips at the last instant.

Dazed and nauseous, Artka fell to his knees. It had been hours since he'd eaten, so there was nothing to void. Nonetheless, he retched until he had no more strength. When the purge passed he sat back against a tree. His strength would return in a few minutes. He'd rejoin the battle then.

He stared at the lifeless form lying a few feet away. "I'm sorry," he said. "I had to do it. Another time, another place, we might have been friends. But, here today, it was you or me, understand?" Tears, rain, blood, sweat and mud mingled on Artka's face. He leaned back against the trunk of a tree and sobbed.

The sound of battle had already receded from the foggy draw.

CHAPTER EIGHT

"Artka, lad, be's yer alive?"

Artka grunted and opened his eyes. He was propped against a tree. He stared up into Smag's grimy face. "I must have passed out."

He struggled to his feet. His hand automatically checked his belt for his sword and found empty space. Then he remembered. Turning, he saw the kingsman lying where he'd been killed. Sticking straight up out of his ribcage was the barely connected shards of his riven hickory sword.

"Musta been summat o' a fight, lad. An' wi' a Sharpointer, too!" said the veteran. "Yer finished him off in the nick o' time by the look o' things."

Artka made no reply as he extracted his all but useless sword. He studied it with downcast eyes. His trusted hickory that had taught him the art of war and served him through training was now just two long, blood-coated sticks tentatively held together by slivers.

Artka looked at Smag. The veteran's breastplate was blood splattered. "The battle?"

"Over fer now. Jest how long yer been sleepin' here?"

"I . . . I don't know. It's hard to tell exactly how long since I fought—killed him. Must've been mid to late morning."

"C'mon. We'd best git outta this wood. Nightfall is almost on usn's. Them tophets is already eatin'. They hain't bein' particular atween the quick and the dead, neither. We hain't got a minute ter spare."

"What about Bilrood, Sergeant Love, and the others?" Artka said.

"No time fer questions, laddie, heshup an' follow." With that, the Eroton vaulted a fallen tree and was off at a rapid jog. Artka, hadn't realized how stiff and sore he was, and therefore hard-pressed to keep up. One mile, two, and yet another passed as they sprinted across wet leaves and leapt over rocks and logs, yet Smag never slackened his pace. Darkness closed in. Artka labored for breath. Smag merely breathed hard.

At one point, Smag paused to sniff the wind. Artka gratefully stopped, but then was instantly alarmed at the scent of tophet.

"Not thet way," Smag said as he turned downwind. Artka gritted his teeth and bounded after his guide.

Smag nimbly scudded down a slope dodging barely-visible rocks and trees in the dark. Artka did his best to keep up with Smag's shadowy form. His best hope of eluding tophet creatures was to stay close to the grizzled, old vet who was experienced in such things.

Smag uncharacteristically paused halfway up a ridge. Artka stopped a step behind him, hands on knees, rasping for breath. "I can barely see you," Artka whispered to the motionless form in front of him.

No response.

"I can barely see you," Artka repeated. Still no response. Artka reached out to touch the older man's shoulder and gasped. It was a rotting tree stump! Smag hadn't paused after all but had run on past the stump—which Artka mistook for the veteran.

"Alright now, don't panic," Artka told himself. "What did I learn in training? Take stock of the situation. I'm lost and all but blind in this darkness and fog. I'm also famished, exhausted, alone, cold, wet, weaponless—and perhaps behind enemy lines. It couldn't possibly be any worse." Artka looked around and called softly, "Smag . . . Smag," desperate for a response.

He cupped his hands around his mouth to call yet again when a crunching, rumbling, sucking sound in a hollow stopped him. Artka froze. The breeze shifted, Artka's nostrils repelled the overpowering stench. There was no doubt—childhood nightmares had sprung to life—he was being stalked by a tophet.

Artka bolted heedless of direction or obstacles, smashing through saplings, stumbling over downed trees and tearing through brambles that snagged flesh and clothing. He burst free of the forest and sped down a grassy slope. His only thought was to flee! Heart and legs pumped his lungs past exhaustion. His bloodied, riven hickory sword was clenched in his right hand. Objects hurtled by in a blur as he alternately crossed wooded fringes and grassy meadows, through bushes and vines, over rocky terrain, across creek beds, crashing through or around whatever lay in his path. His legs, arms, hands and face were bruised and scratched from downswept branches and briars.

He stumbled, as a black veil lowered over his eyes in mid step and he collapsed. His cramped fingers tightly clinging to his sword.

~

A dim, gray light woke Artka. That, and the growling of his stomach. Where was he? He had a vague recollection of endlessly running through darkness. He stared at his hand . . . a bloody, split sword! Then he remembered chasing after Smag, the endless chase through foggy woods, the stench of a tophet . . .

Recalling that, however, did nothing to ascertain his whereabouts. So, where was he? On a grassy muskeg where mists swirled freely. It was still too dim to see much beyond his outstretched hand. And it was drizzling. He scrunched deeper into the grass. He was hungry . . . no . . . ravenous, chilled to the bone and ached from head to foot. He was, however, despite his discomfort, rather pleased at having survived. And . . . when he found his way back to the Roaring Lion Brigade, he had a right to claim a black, iron sword. Ah, the tales he'd tell around the campfire.

Rustling sounds stirred in nearby grasses. Artka's mouth went dry. He sniffed the air, but the noise was coming from downwind. He couldn't smell it . . . but might it be smelling him? Don't panic. Last night he'd fled blindly, too exhausted to think straight. By sheer luck, he'd survived. Now reason must prevail. He dare not trust his luck again so soon. He eased into a comfortable position and slowly raised his head to have a look around.

Several blue dots of light were heading toward him—a kingsmen patrol with their shiny swords meandering through the bog. Artka saw only glowing sword tips, and they were but small, hazy pinpoints in the dense fog.

"Patrol, hold up," said a quiet voice to Artka's left.

Artka ducked down.

"Is it safe to talk, sir?"

"I think so, but quietly. Those foul creatures were closing in on something down here. I doubt we've driven them away for long."

"Disgusting, smelly, evil brutes."

"Probably after some carcasses. After all, there was a lot of carnage yesterday. They were more than likely sniffing out some of the dead."

"Or wounded."

"Should we call out to see if there's anybody that needs help?"

"Not much point. Kingsmen would see our swords and call out to us. Carnalians aren't likely to answer unless desperate."

"How about a fire? The men are hungry, sir."

"No. We haven't finished our search grid yet. Just take a breather, but no sleeping, this is no place to bivouac."

"Aye sir. Fall out and rest, men."

The order was greeted with several good-natured grunts as soldiers sank down to sit among the grassy tussocks, hemming Artka in on all sides. There were at least twenty glowing sword tips surrounding him. A clump of grass before him quivered and a dark form thudded to the sod. A large man in a kingsman tunic and assorted battle gear sat with his back to Artka. Artka's eyes were drawn to the man's sword. Except for the very tip, it had hardly any glow, and even the tip was dim. Artka hadn't even seen the man approach. Why was his sword different from the sword of the Ecclessite he'd slain? Was the spell wearing off this one?

Another kingsman settled in beside the large man. This soldier's sword glowed brightly for three inches from the point. "Rarn," the newcomer said, "how are your wounds?"

"Better, thanks, Gase," the larger man said.

"You were told to hang back until called for. You could've been killed, running out into the fray like that. Lucky for you I managed to get between you and that nasty bloke with the scar. He was hard-core, a vet of many campaigns," Gase said.

"I know. I'm sorry. I'm so used to charging in I thought strength and zeal would make up for what my sword lacked. I still don't know how that little bug-eyed kid knocked me down and cut me. He caught me by surprise."

Artka grinned. Were they talking about Rilf and Poppitt? Now that would have been a sight to see—little, stuttering Poppitt, knocking down a hulk of a man like this.

"Haven't you learned anything, Rarn?" Gase said. "Your physical prowess has little to do with fighting for the king. Everything depends on the brightness of your sword."

"I know. It's just that it's hard to believe merely sharpening my sword will make me a better warrior."

"The sword is the warrior, Rarn, not you. Your part is to keep tolling it. Just look at your sword. Only the tip glows."

Rarn lifted his sword, sighed and placed it back on the ground. "It's so hard to sharpen, Gase. It's the hardest thing I've ever tried."

"It takes time, but it gets easier with effort. Come on, what say we toll our blades now?"

"Well, alright."

The kingsmen withdrew files from their belts and started honing their swords. The sound of grating metal shattered the quiet of the marshland.

"Here, what's this, what's this?" Someone charged through the grasses straight at Artka.

Artka gritted his teeth and gripped his broken hickory to defend himself. But the man ran right past Artka.

"It's just us sergeant, sharpening our swords," Gase said.

"Put your tollers up, lads. This isn't the time to prepare for battle. Those swords should've been sharpened last night, before the battle. Now look what you've done. Any Carnalian within a hundred paces has heard you two filing away."

"Sorry, Sergeant, I was just encouraging Rarn to toll his weapon regularly and thought this might be a good time."

"Alright but put your tollers away. When we get back to camp you can sharpen your weapons all you want." The sergeant receded back into the mists passing within an arm's reach of Artka.

"Hey look, Gase, the bleeding stopped."

"Good. Here, let me repack that cut. Hold this while I tie it tight. There, how's that feel?"

"Smarts a bit, but okay."

"Rarn, that kid probably earned his iron because you bled all over everything."

"I said I was sorry. Quit rubbing it in."

Gase apparently hadn't heard. "And I almost had him persuaded to let me pierce his heart, too."

They sat in silence for a minute, then Rarn said, "I won't do it again, Gase, I promise."

"Well, okay. I just hope someone else brought that kid in. That was some fight, wasn't it? Can't wait to see Pelton. I wonder how he made out. He always does well. Good thing for us there were several brights keeping tophets at bay."

"Hmph!"

"What do you mean, 'hmph'?"

"I only saw that we were swarmed by more Erotons and Carnalians than I ever saw in one place before. As for your so-called brights, tophets and such, well, I have a hard time believing things I can't see. I'll grant the captains fret about them, but all I saw, besides empire warriors, were fog banks and sunbeams."

"Oh, Rarn, it takes light from your sword to see them. With your sword dull as it is, it's a wonder you can see your own two feet."

A hushed call to form up was passed down line through the mists.

The two Ecclessites stood, picked up their gear and returned to the sweep formation.

None too soon. The vapors were beginning to lift, revealing more of the meadow. All around Artka, kingsmen were becoming visible. In a few more moments he'd have been discovered.

A command echoed down the rank and file, and as suddenly as they'd come, the patrol disappeared into the gray mists.

Artka breathed out a sigh of relief and congratulated himself on escaping yet again. His luck seemed to be holding.

Daylight increased. Although the grass was tall, it wasn't very dense, providing less concealment than he'd have liked. Rising and stretching, then crouching low, he moved in starts and stops, a deer on the sneak advancing through the bog. Such stealth however, depleted his already sparse physical reserves. His need for food was becoming acute. He'd been trained to ignore hunger, pain, and fatigue, but there were limits. He hadn't eaten since . . . when? When had the battle been, a day ago, two days? It felt like a week. Gradually the pain subsided, and he was able to straighten up.

The mists had dissipated, but the sky was still overcast, preventing a fix on the sun, so Artka had to guess which direction to take. He angled across the field with his eyes on a distant hillock to keep from circling. A rabbit dashed from beneath his feet. He considered giving chase for a brief moment, but the effort was bound to end in futility, further draining him. Besides, the commotion could draw unwanted attention.

Another half-hour of slow creeping brought him to a wooded, hillside tract. The mists had evaporated affording him a commanding view from the top of a knoll. He squatted, studying each bush, rock, and tree in front of him. Only after careful scrutiny did he venture from the high grass into the woods.

He leaned against a tree and took a deep breath. There was no noise other than leaves rustling in the breeze or an occasional rumble from his stomach.

Artka checked the grassy plain behind in the hopes of identifying where he'd been. Color drained from his face as he realized he'd slept the night on the fringe of Swamp Tophet. He shook his head, incredulous at his luck, then edged around the side of the tree, discovering this wasn't a forest after all, but merely a copse of trees in a sea of grass. He had no option but to keep trusting his luck. He moved tree to tree, heading toward the other side of the copse, picking seeds, berries and nuts as he went. They were bitter, dry fare but he managed to chew and swallow them. Halfway through the wood he slaked his thirst at a trickling brook. Rising from the water's edge he painstakingly resumed his course, pausing to scrutinize each new vista before advancing.

An hour later his nostrils caught the acrid smell of smoke. A wildfire set by the enemy to flush out hiding Carnalians? But no, if that were true, there'd be more smoke not just a whiff. He flattened to his stomach and crawled into the breeze. He crested a ridge and peered over. In a clearing below him was a cobblestone fire-ring. A small animal roasted on a spit as low flames danced playfully above the coals. Nobody was in sight. Artka was hungry enough to eat the varmint raw, yet, caution had been drilled into him by Sergeant Love. A wayward breeze carried the tantalizing aroma of roast rabbit. His nostrils twitched, and his mouth watered. Need pressed the argument against prudence.

Easing behind some bushes he studied every nook, rock, tree and shrub in the hollow. Confident he was alone, he plotted a course down to the fire ring. He wasn't about to jeopardize his freedom for a morsel of food. Kingsmen, he'd been warned, set clever traps. But, was it a trap? For this trap to be effective, the meat must be kept warm enough for its aroma to ride the breeze. If the fire burned out and no one appeared to re-stoke it, he could safely assume this was no trap. Since the fire was down to just coals, it would soon need tending. He'd wait a little longer and see. After all, it wasn't out of the range of possibility that someone started to cook their game and got frightened away by something.

Hunger gnawed inside Artka's belly as the coals blinked out one by one, yet he remained motionless, watching, waiting. The last coal finally expired with a final wisp of smoke curling up to the sky, yet Artka continued his vigil.

Three quarters of an hour later, persuaded there was nothing more dangerous than a chipmunk in the hollow, Artka decided to risk it. But should he rush down, seize the prize and scamper away, or creep down, prolonging his exposure but creating no stir? He decided on the latter method. The rushing down would make him vulnerable to snares and pitfalls. He preferred fighting to being snared. Besides, he was certain he was alone. He rose from behind the bush and descended, probing with his split sword beneath dried leaves for traps.

He arrived at the fire-ring without incident. He stretched his hand out and lifted the skewered rabbit to his lips. He hesitated, but all remained still. He bit into the flesh. The meat was tender and sweet. His eyes closed in delight. He swallowed and tore off another leg.

He was just about to bite down when a voice said, "It would have tasted better when it was hot."

CHAPTER NINE

ARTKA SPUN AROUND IN A circle. There was no one there! "Wh-where are you?"

"You need not fear," said a voice. "I'm not your enemy."

"Show yourself then and declare your intentions."

The top half of a boulder shifted, and a slate-colored cloak was tossed back revealing a gray-robed man. "Behold," the man stood and spread his arms, "my intention is for you to enjoy your meal." Sparkling eyes shone from beneath a cowl while the rest of his face was in shadow. "You won't get much more use out of that weapon."

"Who are you?"

The stranger laughed, and as he did, the surrounding trees and shrubs rustled as if in a breeze. "You trespass my campsite, grab my food, and then dare to challenge me. Hah, but you have gravel."

Artka defiantly tore off another piece of rabbit. He lowered his split sword but kept a wary eye on his mysterious host. The man placed some sticks atop the cold ashes then touched them with his staff. Fire immediately sprang from the dead coals, igniting the newly placed sticks. "Would you like to warm your meal?"

Artka stepped back, his eyes wide.

"Ahh, you fear I am some sort of magician? I'm not. You don't believe me? Very well, believe what you wish. I'll neither harm nor control you in any way, I promise. Please, sit and keep me company."

"Who are you?" Artka repeated. He took another bite and squatted to his haunches keeping a safe distance.

"I have many names. Most call me Logon."

The name was vaguely familiar. Where had he heard it before?

"It means 'demonstrated power'."

Artka jumped up. "Power? You *are* the Magician!"

"Don't be ridiculous. There is no Magician. What have I done to make you think I was?"

"Fire from dead coals, and your name . . . "

"You merely thought the fire was dead, you didn't see the hot coals beneath the cold ash on the surface. Don't take things for what they may appear. As for my name, I truly am the demonstration of the one who sent me. Now, does that make me some sort of magician? Have I captured your mind?"

"I . . . uh . . . I'm not sure. How would I know if you were controlling me?"

"A fair question. Switch places. How do I know you're not the Magician?"

"Well, if I was the Magician, and you were within the sound of my voice, I suppose you wouldn't even think to ask that question . . . I suppose."

"So, are you able to think for yourself?"

"You're trying to trick me with riddles." Artka's cheeks warmed at the man's condescension.

"You have your answer, if you care to accept it."

"Well . . . " Artka hunkered back down on his haunches and took another bite of rabbit. "Anyway, Logon, which side are you on? The king's, or the emperor's?" Artka gnawed the leg bone clean and tossed it to the mossy turf. "I mean, not that it matters at the moment," he said, eyeing his riven hickory blade.

"That question applies only to you, lad."

"Artka, my name is Artka. I'm no longer a 'lad'."

"Yes, so I see, Artka," Logon said, glancing at the hickory. "It was a difficult fight, was it not?"

Artka squinted. "Yes, it was."

A breeze lifted a corner of the cowl off Logon's face. For a terrifying instant Artka thought he saw the features of the Ecclessite he'd killed. Was this his enemy's ghost come to haunt him?

"Fear not, Artka." Logon stood and threw back his cowl revealing himself, tall and regal. "You caught a glimpse of Pelton in my face just now. That's because I share in the life and death of all my subjects."

"His name was Pelton?" Artka asked.

"He proved most faithful. I love him greatly."

"He was your subject?" Color drained from Artka's face.

"Steady, Artka. All your life you've been lied to about me. I'm not the one who hates you. Your emperor, who coerced you into pledging your life to die for the Empire, is the one who hates you. And die in his service you will, unless you pledge troth to me. I can break that oath, but I must have your permission."

"You . . . you're the prince!" Artka backed away.

"I am Xychirion, the one who died, but lives. I am the bane of that 'Cringing Dog'—Lurcan, as he is known throughout all my father's house for the hateful liar he is."

Artka turned to run.

"Before you flee, consider have any of the things you heard about me proven true? Were you stricken mindless? Do I seem dangerous?"

Artka looked back, his lips pursed, his brow furrowed.

"You were told I was dead. Lurcan knows I live. He invented a myth about an evil magician to keep people from seeking me and the amnesty only I can bestow."

Artka backed away, unheeding of tree roots poking out of the ground. His heel snagged, and he fell. His sword skittered across the leaves and landed at Logon's feet.

Logon extended a hand.

"You tripped me!" Artka squirmed away and struggled to his feet. His heart pounded. Something about this man aroused more fear than tophets.

"Don't forget this." Logon pointed to Artka's split hickory. "You'll need this if you want to claim your iron. But you may renounce the empire's black iron and use this." From beneath his cloak Logon produced a sword like Pelton's, offering it to Artka handle first.

Artka stared at the blade, torn between running away and his desire for a real sword. An incomprehensible urge to fall prostrate and beg mercy for killing Pelton stole over Artka. Logon's demeanor promised forgiveness. Yet, it was too simple—just renounce the empire and swear allegiance to the king? How could he reject everything he had ever believed? This must be a trap.

"Artka, you must come to me of your own will."

Artka eyed the sword. The haft simulated two birds in flight back to back. Their wings outspread to form the hilt-guard, tail feathers splayed out at the bottom. One side of the handle was a gentle dove with an olive branch in her beak, the other a fierce eagle with penetrating eyes and grasping talons. The double-edged blade was silvery gray from haft to point. Both sides of the blade bore runes in an obscure language. There was, however, no blue glow anywhere on the blade.

"That sword has no charm upon it. You lure me with a useless weapon?" said Artka.

"Not so, Artka. You accuse me of what your emperor did. The wooden sword he provided seemed adequate until you met a warrior with a real weapon. Neither your hickory nor black iron swords have any effect against your true enemies. This sword, however, when my virtue is upon it—after you pledge allegiance to me—will overcome your enemies."

"Hah! Now I know you to be a weak spellbinder. My sword might only have been wood, but it bear's my enemy's blood."

"Pelton wasn't your enemy. That hickory bears the blood of one that only meant you good. Look at me. What do you see in my eyes, Artka?"

Artka dropped his gaze to the ground, afraid to look.

"Artka," Logon said, "do you see hate, guile, revenge, malice. Or do you see forgiveness and love?"

Artka cast his eyes about the campsite, everywhere but at Logon. "I . . . I can't look."

"Then at least behold the price of your amnesty." Logon opened his robe. "Who is more powerful, the one who kills, or he who lives again after being killed?"

Artka couldn't help himself; his eyes were drawn to Logon's chest. The wound where Logon had been impaled was closed, but not entirely healed. Blood seeped around the edges of the chest wound.

"I allowed myself to be impaled in order to break Lurcan's claim on humanity. My blood breaks Lurcan's oath, but you must ask for it. There is nothing more Lurcan can do to me or those who appeal to me for amnesty. Your emperor hates you. He plans to consume you until there is nothing left. In the depths of your heart you know this is true. Come to me, Artka. I offer an opportunity for you to share in my own life."

"I can't. I just . . . can't." Artka leapt forward, seized the hickory remnant from the leaves at Logon's feet and fled.

CHAPTER TEN

RUNNING WAS HIS ONLY EXISTENCE: despite the chilly air, sweat drenched his clothing. Artka's heart pounded. His lungs ached. Benumbed feet relentlessly hammered the ground. One thought possessed his mind—run from the menace; run, push the limit; run, don't think; run, embrace pain—pain helped him forget. Run and forget; flee the unthinkable.

~

Corporal Lewt of the Eroton Boar's Head Brigade savored supper's final bites. His squad sprawled beside him on a grassy knoll not far from the mess tent. "One thing about Eroton brigades," he said to no one in particular, "usn's eats high." Lewt patted his distended belly with both hands, emitting a loud, satisfied belch. "Now if'n we only had summat wine." He stretched and gazed across the grassy plain rolling down to the Flaming Sword River and Ecclessa on the other side. "Someday I'm gonna git me summat o' them lovelies o' thet land."

"Whut're yer sayin', Corp? They gots purty women in Ecclessa? Whut a waste," said a cocky recruit sporting a new plume in his helm.

"Does they gots purty women? Boy, hain't yer never heered o' the fair maidens o' the Truthful Valleys?"

The recruit looked around bashfully. Was he the only one who didn't know?

"Ahh, now there be's women," Lewt said, gazing across the distant river. Suddenly Lewt sat upright, shading his eyes. "Whut be's thet now, does yer think?"

The others roused. "Whut, where?" said one.

"Cain't see it now—wait—there it be's, over there, see it?" The others followed his point.

"Thet little black speck?"

"Summat be's a runnin', hain't it?" Lewt said.

"Uh-huh," several agreed.

"Looks ter be a man fleein' summat. I see nobbut chasin' him, though. Let's go see whut his hurry be's."

The squad jogged down over the rolling hills in pursuit of their leader. Lewt calculated an intersecting point along the runner's path and deployed his men so at least one or two of them would encounter the runner. He belched again, ruing such strenuous activity so soon after a hearty meal. The squad scattered, crouching low in the high grass.

Moments later their quarry approached, laboring for breath.

Two of Lewt's men sprang.

"Harrrgh!"

"Oomph!"

A lion's roar broke the quiet of the peaceful meadow. Lewt recognized the battle cry of the Roaring Lion Brigade.

A wailing cry rang out, "I be's stabbed ter me death!"

The rest of Lewt's squad churned through the thigh-high grass, convening where one of their mates thrashed in agony with a piece of wood sticking clean through his leg; another Eroton soldier slumped unconsciously in a heap. Standing over them was a young Carnalian warrior, panting heavily, clutching a sword from one of the downed men.

"Surround him, but don't get too close," Lewt said. They obediently, cautiously circled the stranger, cutting off any escape. "Easy lad, we be's yer friends. Whut be's a chasin' yer?" Lewt said in a calm, comforting tone.

Spittle drooled from the young man's mouth; his sunken eyes darted fiercely back and forth at the men encircling him.

"Who . . . be's . . . yer?" Lewt said.

"He plumb loco, Corp," said one of Lewt's soldiers.

"Aye, mad as a fever. Lookit him, poor beast. Summat scairt him witless."

"Whut could do thet ter a man?" asked another.

"A hunnert different things. Judgin' how worn out he be's, he come a good piece. Mighta been a tophet, or mebbe a bright. Poor divil."

"Brights kin do thet?"

"Aye, 'specially if'n he seen one fully manifested. If'n yer seen a tophet wi'out his fog, yer'd drench yer drawers wi'out so much as a 'by yer leave', so yer kin imagine how seein' a bright could make a man go daft."

The Carnalian sank to his knees, growling. His breathing slowed.

"Will he stay mad?" said a recruit.

"Cain't rightly say. Mebbe he will. Mebbe a good night's rest and a warm meal will set him ter rights." Lewt turned and ordered, "Bawker, git yerself up ter supply an' bring back a net. An' hurry."

"Aye, Corp."

"Hey, Lewt, lookit here! There's dried blood on this here piece o' hickory in Rumpit's leg," said the soldier tending the wounded man. "Hain't this one o' them swords Carnalians uses afore they gits their iron?"

"So, it is. I'd wager this lad gots a tale ter tell."

Several minutes later Bawker arrived with four curious Erotons tagging along. Lewt, glad for the extra hands, said, "Awright, now, easy lads . . . hey yer oaf! Keep thet net outta sight. We'll never catch him if'n he sees it. Bawker, yer an' a couple o' men sneak around behind. When I distracts him, fling the net. And don't miss. We'll have only one chance. If'n yer misses, we'll hafta wrestle him, and summat's gona git hurt."

The Carnalian turned as the netmen circled, keeping them in sight.

Suddenly Lewt, squealing like an enraged wild boar, jumped forward to distract the Carnalian.

Taking their cue, the netmen pitched the net.

The runner let out a lion's roar as he leapt high in the air and to the side, startling the entire squad.

The net arced off course.

The Carnalian, wielding a captured Eroton sword, tackled Lewt who hadn't had time to recover from his feint.

The net-men, having missed their target, tumbled backwards to the turf, their net empty.

Lewt and the Carnalian rolled over and over in the waist-high grass, each seeking a grip on each other.

Suddenly the attacker sprang free, spun around and began a two-handed assault with the wavy-bladed sword. Lewt struggled to his feet and tried to intercept with his own sword. The Carnalian's blade descended and sliced into Lewt's shoulder.

Searing pain exploded in Lewt's collarbone as the Carnalian extracted the sword. Lewt staggered a couple of paces, then fell. The last thing Lewt saw was carmine spurting onto green grass and the high grasses swishing behind the departing Carnalian.

~

Artka sat up. His head throbbed, a petulant hunger gnawed at his stomach and every muscle ached. And if that wasn't enough, abrasions covered him from head to heel. He groaned as he stiffly rose from the mossy embankment. There was an unfamiliar weight in his hand. A curvy, iron sword? With an effort he straightened his cramped fingers, letting the weapon fall to the ground. "What's this? What in the name of Pitland have I done since . . . since?"

His last recollection was of creeping through foggy damps in the Wind Break Forest as Sergeant Love's left bower. Artka bent over and scooped up the fallen weapon. Well, at least it was an empire sword, not Ecclessite, but it wasn't Carnalian. Instead of a roaring lion's head, its handle was fashioned like a wild boar's head with mouth agape. Its tusks extended outward from the bottom of the shaft to prevent slippage. The blade itself was wavy, not straight like a decent Carnalian sword nor arced like a Craniantium scimitar. It was shorter, too. And there was blood, fresh blood. Had he dispatched an enemy, or . . . ? He must remember.

A sudden, intense headache burst like lava in his head and only abated when he ceased trying to remember. But then that deep, unknown sorrow like a thousand years of regret flooded the pit of his being. He sank to his knees and passed out.

Artka awoke some time later, hungry and sore. He stood and arched his back. Groaning and grunting he worked out the kinks in his legs and back.

"Why do I feel like I've lost something valuable?" He shook his head and spoke to the sky. "Because," he answered his own question, " . . . whatever I've been doing has drained all my strength. In fact, I'm probably lucky to be alive." He flexed his limbs. When sufficiently limber, he tucked the boar's head sword inside his belt, then climbed a knoll and surveyed the countryside. His vantagepoint overlooked the white-water rapids of a river.

Artka had heard about, but never seen the Flaming Sword River, the barrier between Ecclessa and the nations of the empire. It was said that the river ran deep and savage from source to mouth. No Carnalian could cross it. No bridge had ever been built from the empire side. No narrows had ever been forded or swum; boats and rafts that attempted were dashed to pieces and sank beneath the turbulent waters. The only crossing into Ecclessa was the extremely narrow bridge located at the King's Gate Fortress which guarded the bridge night and day. No one crossed that bridge unless pledged to serve the King of Ecclessa.

Artka didn't know where that bridge was, nor did he care. His intention was to go the opposite direction and find his battalion. He gazed one last time across the treacherous waters to the pleasant, rolling grasslands of Ecclessa.

A stiff breeze ripped across the river carrying a zesty scent and promise of good things. Carnalia's Wind Break Forest impeded that breeze elsewhere, but not here, where the forest's tangled undergrowth and thick-boled trees had not yet grown. It looked so peaceful on the other side, so calm.

An inexplicable longing stirred in his breast, tempting him to abandon recognition and rank, urging him to desert the empire and flee to Ecclessa. He had to summon all his willpower to resist running to the shore and flinging himself into the swirling waters.

"Control. I am master of my destiny," he quoted one of Sergeant Love's maxims. He slapped his face so hard tears came to his eyes. "What am I thinking? One glimpse across that river and I'm ready to abandon everything I've striven for? I'm acting as if I was spellbou—!"

Flitting before his mind's eye came a vision of a hooded figure arising from a rock.

Blinding pain knocked him to the ground, disrupting further recall. But that slice of memory was enough. He'd encountered the Magician! He'd been under an enchantment but was he not himself now? Except for his memory blackout, this recurring headache and the strange longing to go to Ecclessa, he was quite himself again. But the headache would eventually pass, as would the perverse desire to desert the empire. The spell was weakening.

"Well, Magician," he arose and taunted the wind blowing into his face, "it seems I've escaped your spell." He thrust the boar's head sword aloft in his hand and yelled, "Death to Ecclessa!"

Acute hunger pangs doubled him over. He retched but nothing was voided. He struck out across the fields, heading away from the river. Sooner or later he'd encounter empire troops.

CHAPTER ELEVEN

ARTKA LAY ON A LEDGE atop a flat rock scanning the glen below. Empire irregulars were camped below him. Men lollygagged around campfires talking, gambling, arguing, sleeping, and eating. A rumble from his stomach reminded him he hadn't eaten for how long? Two . . . three days? He forced his attention back to the lounging soldiers below who weren't clothed properly in Carnalian black uniforms. Their helmets were regulation black with red plumes, but their uniforms—if such could be called uniforms—were mixtures of greens, tans, and browns. Many didn't even have polished, leather chest plates, sporting buckskins and furs instead. A glint from a sunbeam briefly sparked off a wavy sword like the one in his belt.

Erotons! He'd stumbled upon a regiment of Erotons. They were just as vulgar in appearance, speech, and manner as he'd heard—the dregs of empire population. It was natural for men to fight in their country's defense, but to enjoy brutality and plunder . . . not to mention slovenliness . . .

Artka tried to remember where and how he'd obtained his Eroton sword since a Carnalian recruit bearing a wavy Eroton sword was bound to attract curious, if not hostile, attention. Difficult questions would be asked.

His headache increased, threatening another black out. He quit trying to remember and resumed studying the picket line around the encampment. It was a sloppy set up, even a raw recruit could infiltrate it. The Erotons were either over-confident or just plain lazy . . . or stupid.

Though reluctant to do so, Artka needed to reveal his presence. His hunger was severe and his strength at low ebb. If he crept away he might blunder into a kingsman patrol and be unable to fight. As much as he detested Erotons, revealing himself to them and seeking their aid was his only choice.

Should he sneak into their midst? It could easily be done. But they might take offense. Should he just stand and reveal his position? No, the pickets might attack first and ask questions later. He'd already penetrated too far into their defenses, and though he was a soldier of the empire, being Carnalian wasn't in his favor.

He slid backwards down off the rocky escarpment. As soon as his feet touched the ground a stern voice said, "Easy now laddie, usn's been lookin' fer yer."

Another said, "Raise yer hands away from yer belt an' lace yer fingers behind yer neck."

The Eroton set-up wasn't as porous as Artka thought.

"I'm a Carnalian warrior, Roaring Lion Brigade, in service to the emperor," Artka said. "I've been separated from my outfit for . . . for . . . well, I'm not sure how long. I think it's been a few days."

They studied him, saying nothing.

"I'm near to starved."

"Does yer think he be's the one, Orf?" asked the taller of the two.

"Hain't nobbut other Carnalians wanderin' about. It's gotta be. Now then lad, gi' us yer blade, real keerful like. Yer be's wantin' no trouble from the likes o' usn's."

Both men were unshaven, disheveled, dirty and tough. It was impossible to tell their ages; hard times had etched deep lines on their faces; their features were craggy, indiscernible. They could have been twenty-five—or sixty. But they weren't to be taken lightly. Both evidenced skill in the craft of war; their faces and limbs bore scars of past frays, their battle gear likewise, was pockmarked with holes and slices.

"Best ter take him in," the taller of the two said. Then to Artka, "Walk. We're takin' yer down ter our captain. He'll ken whut to do wi' yer."

Artka sauntered into the encampment in front of his captors as if these roughnecks meant nothing to him. Men stirred from various campsites along the camp's center pathway to come hoot and stare at Artka, but his captors were given hearty congratulations.

"Hey, Orf, yers found him."

"Good fer yers."

"How 'bout that, hey Kint."

"Whut're yers gonna do wi' all thet rum?"

Kint retorted with a laugh, "We's gonna drink it all, jest usn's. So, don't git no notions 'bout bummin' some."

"Thet's right," Orf said, "we caught the Carnalian, we deserves the reward."

"Reward?" Artka asked, alarmed.

"Shut yer mouth, grub. Lewt was a good corp. Yer'll pay fer whut yer done," replied Kint.

Artka was guided to a tent situated in a grove of linden trees. Orf went inside without announcing himself, contrary to Carnalian military etiquette—but then, this was an Eroton brigade. Muffled voices came from inside, then four officers stepped out, followed by Orf.

"Well, well. So, you have, m'lads, so you have," said a captain in regulation Carnalian garb. Accompanying him was a lieutenant, also dressed Carnalian. The other two were Eroton sergeants clad in animal skins. The captain walked around examining Artka front and back, then came to the fore again. "You don't look crazy to me, soldier. Are you mad?"

Artka replied smartly, "No sir."

"No, I'm quite sure you're not. Sergeant," he said to the nearest man, "see that these men get a half-keg and three days excused duty."

The sergeant saluted, "Aye sir," then led Orf and Kint, grinning widely, away. The other sergeant followed.

The captain turned his attention to Artka. "Who are you? What brigade are you with? How do you explain your exploits of yesterday?"

"I'm Artka of Kway, assigned to the Roaring Lion Brigade, commanded by Captain Fitcher. As to my doings of yesterday . . . sir, I'm afraid I have no recollection or memory of anything since I went to battle in the Wind Break Forest."

The Captain looked up in surprise. "Indeed? You remember nothing since three days ago?"

"It's been that long, sir? All I can remember is waking up this morning by a swift-flowing river."

"You were by the river?"

"Yes sir."

"And you were able to walk here unhindered?"

"Yes, sir."

"Hmmm. And how did you happen to come by this sword?" The captain held the incriminating cutlery up in front of Artka.

"I-I found it in my hand when I woke this morning, sir."

"And you have no idea how you came to be in possession of it?"

"No, sir." What was he suspected of? "Uh, sir, I'm very hungry," he tried to direct the conversation to his needs.

The captain regarded him momentarily, then said to an orderly, "Bring this man some stew, a double portion. And a tankard of rum." The orderly scurried away as the captain returned his attention to Artka. "Artka of Kway, I believe you. If I didn't, you'd be disemboweled where you stand. I'm Captain Sarcas. So, how do you explain your memory loss?"

"Sir, the only thing I can remember is a hooded figure rising up from a rock. Everything else is blank. I get a tremendous headache—"

"The Magician!" Captain Sarcas said and emitted a low whistle. "It's as I suspected. Lieutenant, didn't I tell you the high command was lying? I knew he was nearby." He paced back and forth rubbing his hands, his cloak billowing behind. Then he stared directly at Artka, demanding, "Where were you when you saw the Magician?"

"I'm not sure, sir. There were trees and a field, I think. That's about all I remember. I get a terrible headache if I try to remember more."

"Still under the spell, some, I would guess. You'll soon be set to rights. Ah, here comes your meal. Eat hearty, lad. You'll stay with my command until we meet up with your Captain Fitcher. He'll know whether you're a coward or a warrior, and how to deal with you. Until then, so I can keep a close eye on you, you're assigned to my bodyguard."

Before attending to other details Captain Sarcas told Lieutenant Diak to instruct Artka as to his duties. The lieutenant introduced himself, explaining that he was from the town of Lustre, near the Eroton border. "I tell you Artka, Erotons are swine. I never knew humans could live so low. In truth, I'm half-afraid of them. But Captain Sarcas keeps them in line."

"Where's he from? Near the Eroton border, like you?" asked Artka between mouthfuls, savoring the venison stew.

"He's from Sofista, in Craniantium. A very forceful and cruel man, that one. Sometimes I don't know who I fear most, Erotons or him."

Artka consumed his meal, only half-listening to Lieutenant Diak as he explained the duties of the captain's bodyguard.

"We're a small contingent of Carnalians—the bodyguard and a few officers. I'm afraid you're the only recruit in camp, but the other Carnalians will be glad you're here. See, that's the Carnalian tent over there." A large, brown tent was pitched amongst the trees. "I'll get you some bedding. I have to sleep alongside the command tent with another lieutenant by Captain Sarcas' tent, or I'd keep you company. But, as I see you're about done eating and will want some sleep I should think."

Artka was stuffed. The food was immensely pleasurable. Under any other circumstances, the food would have been considered superior. He burped unintentionally.

"Go ahead, belch away," Diak laughed heartily. Then his tone changed. "Say, you really don't know what happened yesterday, do you?"

"Not a hint."

"I'd better tell you then, so you'll know to keep an eye out. The man you killed was a good warrior who knew how to make life, uh, shall we say entertaining for his men."

"That I . . . killed? I don't remember killing—" A scene flashed across his mind; a fair-haired youth with a glowing sword charging him, shouting, "A life for the king." The entire scenario unfolded until he saw his own hickory sword sticking up from the inert kingsman's ribcage.

"Artka. Artka!" Diak grabbed Artka's shoulders. "Are you all right?"

"Uh! Headache. But . . . it's passing. I just remembered a duel I had with a kingsman."

"Did you win, or—?"

"I slew him," Artka said flatly. "His name was Pelton, and he nearly pierced my chest. I got him, instead."

"You knew his name . . . you talked with him?"

"We talked. I guess he told me his name, but, I don't remember that. Funny, I remember everything else."

"You'd best forget whatever the kingsman said. It'll poison your mind. I've seen hard-crusted warriors forsake the pleasures of the empire and run off to join Ecclessites after merely talking to some prisoners of war. By the dreads, Ecclessites are dangerous."

"Not half as dangerous as their swords."

Lieutenant Diak's eyebrows rose. "Do you mean to tell me you fought a kingsman that had a glowing blade—and won?"

"I'd have made quicker work of it if I'd had an iron blade instead of hickory."

"What? With only a hickory training sword? Oh, this is too much! Are you sure you remember it right? How much of the kingsman's blade was glowing?"

"A hand's span, maybe more. I remember it all right, although it gives me a headache trying to remember beyond that."

Diak muttered to himself and rubbed his chin, momentarily oblivious of Artka.

"What'd you say?" asked Artka.

"Huh? Oh, just thinking out loud. That would explain how you got the drop on Lewt."

"Just who is this Lewt?"

"Artka, listen to me," said Lieutenant Diak. "Just once in a lifetime a warrior appears—a champion—so agile, so powerful, so determined and naturally skilled—one who is destined for greatness."

"What are you getting at?"

"Artka, you're just a recruit, yet you've killed one of our most experienced fighting men, not to mention maiming two others. And not only that, but you bested a blue-blader. Didn't your sergeant warn you to leave kingsmen with glowing blades alone? It's best to let experienced veterans handle them."

"I thought he meant that we should only challenge younger men like ourselves, you know, recruits."

"Artka, there are recruits, and there are recruits. Most of the king's recruits aren't prepared to fight—though they think they are. Their blades hardly glimmer, and sometimes not at all. They may be physically strong and able, but their swords are sluggish in their hands. Those recruits are easy marks. But when you see a sword with light on it, even a small amount, you're in for a real fight. Let experienced soldiers deal with them. There are enough foolish kingsmen surging up to the battlefront with no shine on their swords. Until you've had more experience, stick to dull-sword recruits. You've got rare potential, Artka. I'd hate to see you fall prey to a blue-blader before you reach your prime."

"You make it sound like defeating an experienced Ecclessite is impossible."

"Artka, you have a gift. If I'm right, you'll be of great service to the emperor—for which he'll reward you handsomely. And me too, if you'll let me be your special trainer and adviser."

"I don't know, lieutenant. I've had only one fight which I barely won."

"Don't forget Lewt."

"But, I don't remember any Lewt."

"Well then, let me tell you," Diak said. "Just after suppertime yesterday, Lewt and his squad saw a man—you—running across a field. They placed themselves in your path. Two of them jumped you. You kicked one so hard he still can't walk straight. The other was crippled for life when you stuck your split hickory sword through his leg. He'll never walk normal again. And Lewt, poor, old, lecherous Lewt. You broke his collarbone and severed a major artery. He bled out in seconds. That, my dear Artka, is what you did yesterday."

Artka was dazed. As Diak recounted the battle, visions flooded Artka's mind: the net-men circling behind, the piercing squeal of a wild boar, the warm gush of crimson on his hands and the surprised expression on a man's whiskered face. "I remember," Artka said in a subdued voice. "By Pitland, I remember. What have I done?"

"Hey, hey, it's no big loss. I mean, after all, they're only Erotons. You ought to be proud. Like to made the rest of the maggots soil their breeches, too. Aw, come on Artka, don't feel so bad. I wish I'd done it. Then they'd have some respect for me, by the dreads."

Artka regained his composure. "It's not only that."

"Oh? Then what?"

"I wish I knew. Sometimes I feel so empty inside. And it hurts, like an ache without real pain. Do you know what I mean?"

"That's what comes from talking to kingsmen. Their words keep fighting even after they're dead. Drink your rum. I'll get you another tankard. Sleep is what you need now. Don't worry about a thing. I'll see you're protected." Diak started to leave then paused. "You've got a destiny Artka. Wait and see. You'll be as renowned as Claygall, the betrayer. Too bad Logon Xychirion isn't alive for you to battle, eh?"

The rum and rich food were taking effect, a pleasant dizziness settled over Artka. Something about Lieutenant Diak's last comment needed correction, but Artka couldn't decide what just now. He'd rest awhile, then decide what was wrong with Diak's last statement.

Artka, with his head pillowed on his arm and sleep stealing upon him, barely heard Lieutenant Diak returning or the tankard of rum set before him.

CHAPTER TWELVE

A CRISP, AUTUMN BREEZE BLEW away the few lingering, morning mists. The sun ascended toward zenith promising a beautiful day. Artka's leather shin guards rustled in the knee-high, dewy grass as the Eroton band trotted over knolls, down ravines and across meadows, passing copses of trees and swampy bogs on a seek and destroy mission.

Captain Sarcas, with his bodyguard, preceded the main column. Artka was in the rearmost echelon of the double-timing bodyguard running behind Captain Sarcas and his spirited mount. Artka jogged alongside a grizzled old veteran who looked and smelled more Eroton than Carnalian yet wore full Carnalian appurtenances. Behind them jounced three hundred slovenly Eroton soldiers: out of step, nonconformingly clad, some half-sober, all hardened killers.

Though no one had dared say anything aloud, Artka was the recipient of sullen, even hostile stares from many in the Eroton contingent.

Captain Sarcas showed unusual deference to Artka, as did Lieutenant Diak who kept fawning over him. Artka's tattered clothing and torn battle armor had been replaced with fresh Carnalian gear. His helmet hadn't been issued a crimson plume though. Confirmation was lacking that he'd ever engaged the enemy but everything else had been re-supplied.

The wavy-bladed boar's head sword hadn't been returned to him, instead he was issued a Carnalian-iron straight-sword with a bear's head handle, the insignia of Sarcas' bodyguard. The grip and heft were to Artka's liking. There had been some discussion as to whether Artka deserved iron, but since the brigade carried no hickory training swords, and the riven slats of Artka's own sword bore dried blood, the captain dismissed all contrary arguments and issued Artka the iron, albeit without any pomp or ceremony.

Artka mentally took stock of himself as he ran despite still having a slight headache. Three days of Eroton cuisine and grog had had a restorative effect; he was ready for anything. Memory gaps between fighting the kingsman and killing Corporal Lewt nagged at him, as did the thought of any potential revenge Erotons might be plotting. Lieutenant Diak had assured him that no one would dare try anything. Captain Sarcas had put the word out that the "crazy Carnalian" was under his personal protection. This was some comfort, even so, Artka had heard too much about the Eroton code of vengeance and so, kept a wary eye.

As he ran, Artka's thoughts drifted to his twin sister Jeda, bringing a stab of doubt. Where was she? Was she safe? And what of Bilrood? How had he fared in the Battle of the Wind Break Forest? And Poppitt? And . . .

"Company, halt!" Lieutenant Diak shouted back over the column. "Lunch break. Disperse, take nourishment, and rest."

Artka gladly sank to the ground. Others fell out all around him grumbling about having only jerky to eat. Artka smiled, knowing how much of a sacrifice this jerky ration was for them.

Lieutenant Diak settled beside Artka. "How goes it, Artka? Can you keep pace?"

"I've never felt better. Why do you keep checking on me?"

"Let's just say I feel much like you do about marching with Erotons. Besides . . . " his voice trailed off.

"Come on, out with it," Artka said.

"Well, if you must know, I believe you have a destiny."

"Not that again."

"No, I mean it. You could become one of the great ones, like Hittel, or even Claygall, betrayer of the prince."

At mention of the prince, Artka's stomach tightened. In his mind's eye he saw a tall man throwing his cloak open to reveal a chest wound. A phrase, " . . . my blood breaks Lurcan's oath . . . " echoed in his mind.

"By the dreads, Artka, what's the matter? Are you all right?" Diak grasped Artka's arm to keep him from toppling over.

Artka dry-retched; his head throbbed, but the vision passed. "I'm okay. I just remembered something."

"Quick, tell me, another fight, another victim?" Diak thirsted for every gory detail.

"I don't really know. I saw a bloody wound in a man's chest, yet he spoke as if he wanted such a wound."

"A kingsman?"

"Yes, I think so. He said something about power in his blood breaking Lurcan's oath."

"Hush your mouth," Diak said, putting his fingers on Artka's lips. "Merely saying such things is treason."

"Why? I only said what I remembered, and only a fragment at that."

"Never mind. What you said borders on the enemy's lies. Immediate death is decreed to anyone propagating such lies. I'll forget you said anything. You should, too."

"But, it happened."

"How do you know? Do you remember anything else?"

Artka shook his head.

"Then can you be sure it isn't just part of the Magician's spell, making you think you saw and heard things you didn't?"

"No, but—"

"Right. Now then, say no more about it."

Artka gnawed off a piece of jerky.

"And, if you happen to remember anything else along those lines, I don't want to hear about it, understand?"

Artka nodded, his mouth busily chewing. As he swallowed, he thought he detected a faint scent. "Lieutenant?"

Diak turned around. "Yes?"

"Did you smell . . . something?"

"No, why?"

The odor was gone, and Artka hadn't had enough of a whiff to be certain. "Oh, nothing. I just thought I smelled . . . something."

"Look Artka, if you're fatigued, just tell me. I've mentioned your potential to the captain, and he agrees that you might have a destiny. So, if you have trouble keeping up, tell me."

"Lieutenant, I'm fine. It's these memory flashes. They catch me off balance. I never know when one is coming. I'm fine now, see? Please, don't give me any special treatment."

Diak smiled like a proud father, then strode away to attend the troops.

Artka leaned back, propping on his elbows, enjoying the fresh air, sunshine, and clouds drifting lazily overhead. An Eroton scouting party trotted over a remote hillock and reported to Captain Sarcas, drawing Artka's attention. The scouts kept looking and gesturing toward the way they'd just come. Artka sat up. Their indistinct words didn't carry to him, but their actions bespoke something alarming to them.

Artka gathered his gear and stood to his feet even before Lieutenant Diak, who had been summoned hastily by Sarcas, called the column to fall in. Ill-natured grunts and expletives greeted the premature command. Within minutes the column formed and stood ready. It was then that Artka caught the wind-borne odor again and recognized it.

"Ugh! Tophets be's upwind," said the man beside him. Tension rippled down the rank and file.

"On the double, march," Lieutenant Diak ordered, acting as the captain's mouthpiece. The captain's steed veered left instead of following the previous course. The column dutifully followed like a giant, mottled snake slithering through the high grass.

Captain Sarcas constantly kept looking over his shoulder.

After some rapid-paced miles the less fit soldiers began lagging behind, sergeants clubbed the worst stragglers, forcing them to keep up. Artka fared well enough, as did most of Sarcas' bodyguard, but no one could keep pace with the captain's mount indefinitely.

As if in conjunction with Artka's thoughts, the captain reined his steed aside, turned in his saddle, and with a hand shielding his brow squinted at the elongated column. The bodyguard deployed around him as the column trotted on by. Sarcas waved Lieutenant Diak over to him.

Diak nodded, turned, and with hands cupped around his mouth called out, "Column . . ." Diak sucked in another deep breath," . . . slow."

The Erotons slackened the pace as the command echoed down the line. They'd covered two leagues since their last halt; the fetid odor of tophet no longer hung in the air.

Sarcas fitfully tugged his mount's reins as he scanned the horizon in front.

"Column . . . draw up . . . and . . . halt," Lieutenant Diak ordered.

The men obliged, many bending over with hands on their knees for support as they sucked in great draughts of air.

"Close up those ranks, stand in place." The Erotons who'd stayed to the pace huddled around their commander, looking up expectantly.

From atop his horse Captain Sarcas surveyed his bedraggled command. "Here's the situation," he addressed the huffing, perspiring soldiers and officers clustered close enough to hear. "Some of you might have smelled tophets back yonder. We're not fleeing them. They were sent to be our rearguard. Our scouts spotted a legion of brights that landed on our side of the river. It seems they were heading straight for us. The tophets held them at bay so we could get away. From here on we go full tilt. Keep up as best you can. If you fall behind, you know what awaits you. There'll be no more breaks 'til we reach battalion. Lieutenant, order triple-time."

"Yessir. Column . . . stand ready . . . triple-time!" Diak called back over the weary brigade.

Captain Sarcas spurred his mount to an even faster pace than before; the foremost section of the column managed to stay intact for another twenty minutes; but gradually even the fittest lagged; the column stretched out over a mile. Artka noted that fear of the mysterious brights pursuing them inspired these hardened Erotons to even greater effort than their sergeants' clubs or fear of tophets. How much worse could brights be than tophets?

The prolonged exertion made Artka's legs weary. He needed to draw on some inner source of strength to keep pace. He found it in bitter hatred—toward his father, the source and focus of all that had ever gone wrong in Artka's life. That smoldering, angry coal in Artka's breast was fanned to flame as he ran, providing his limbs with renewed energy. He was so inwardly focused on his hatred that he failed to notice that the captain reined his horse to an abrupt stop. He collided into the soldiers in front of him, incurring curses and rebukes.

"I knew it! It's a trap," Captain Sarcas said, scanning the field ahead. He turned and stared at his command strung out behind and swore. "Lieutenant," he said lowly, "summon the drummer to beat, 'Imminent Attack—Prepare to Defend'."

"Sir," Diak said with a smart salute, and scanned the extended, disorganized column. "Sir," said Diak wincing, pointing at the fields behind, "I believe the drummer is back there. His drum must have hindered him."

Sarcas' teeth gritted. When he finally spoke, his voice was malignant. "Lieutenant, go find that worm of a drummer and tell him to beat out the command. If he's dropped or thrown his drum away, cut off his hands and feet and leave him for the tophets."

Diak paled. "Sir." He pointed at two Carnalians, "You, and you, come with me. Oh, you too, Artka."

"No," Captain Sarcas spat vehemently. "Artka stays with me. Quickly man, kingsmen are advancing!" He shielded his eyes and peered at the rolling hills ahead. "How did so many blue-blades get this deep into Carnalia?"

Lieutenant Diak reluctantly left Artka and headed back through the contingent searching for the drummer.

Captain Sarcas dismounted and looked toward a distant forested hillside. "They'll be here in minutes, get ready. Artka, you stand here, in front of my horse, so I know your whereabouts."

"Yes, sir." Artka drew his sword and stepped directly in front of the steed. Artka's neck tingled under the war horse's hot, moist breath.

A hail of arrows pelted down around them—Eroton arrows. Archers in the distended column had panicked, shooting at the Ecclessite lines from too great a distance. Their anxious sergeant had ordered the volley on his own initiative. An arrow grazed Sarcas' steed's flank. It whinnied and tried to rear but the captain tenaciously held him. The spate of missiles stopped as suddenly as it had started.

The rumbling sound of a waterfall came rolling over the brow of the hill. Artka's heart thumped against his ribs. Every muscle in his body reverberated with the thunder of approaching kingsmen beating swords against their breastplates. A multitude of blue tipped swords loomed over the crest of the hill, held aloft by grim warriors advancing through the high grass, chanting, "Lives for the king!" With a unified shout and blare of bugles they charged, swarming the strung-out, pathetically ill-defended Eroton column.

Artka crouched, re-gripped his sword and prepared to engage as many enemy soldiers as he could. Two kingsmen with blue only on their sword tips made straight for him. Artka sprang ahead, slashing his sword, sounding forth a fierce lion's roar.

Both Ecclessite swords collided with his. Artka's hand stung from the jolt. He dropped to the turf, rolled away and crawled into the waist-high grass, massaging his wrist. Shouts and the din of clashing weapons filled the air all around.

"Ow! I thought you said he'd be easy," said one of Artka's assailants.

"He had no plume," said the other. "I thought he had no battle experience. Be careful, he's hiding in the grass."

"Let's wait for help. He knows what he's doing better than we do, plume or no plume."

That was all Artka needed to hear. He sprang from cover, his sword thrust out before him, sounding forth his war cry again, expecting to unnerve and quickly dispatch the kingsmen. His attack stopped short, however, for instead of the first two assailants, he met a veteran Ecclessite warrior blocking his path. The kingsman had close-cropped, fair hair, eyes of deep blue and a confident smile. But Artka's attention was drawn to the kingsman's sword. It glowed brightly along both edges and had engraved runes shining from the fuller and flat from point to hilt. The other two kingsmen took refuge behind their champion.

All around the crescendo of metal on metal reverberated over the once peaceful meadow. Shouts of triumph and agony intermingled amid the clash of weapons.

"So, a roaring lion gambols amidst these swine, eh?"

"You're the swine," Artka spat back, "and this lion is your sworn enemy." He quickly sized up his foe by the criteria Sergeant love had ingrained into him. He'd need all the strength and skill his strength, hatred, and anger could spawn. Loathing against his father, Sergeant Love, Rilf and tophet creatures surged as one through his veins. But . . . he also must keep his head. Mistakes against this adversary would prove fatal. At least there was a real weapon in his hand this time and not a wooden sword.

A voice choked with venomous hatred disrupted Artka's preparation to fling himself against the kingsman.

"Traitor! Maggot! How dare you show your face, kingsman? After all I did for you."

Artka turned to make certain it was Captain Sarcas. The captain, having remounted, spurred his steed past Artka, spewing epithets as he charged. His vitriol was drowned out by the clash of black iron on blue steel as Captain Sarcas, his war horse, and the Ecclessite merged in combat. The captain rained a storm of savage blows, but each strike was met and turned aside easily by the Ecclessite's sword. Sarcas flipped his blade to the hammering edge.

Artka ached to join the fight, but the circling, stamping war horse prevented closing in to lend a hand.

After several moments of fierce chopping and parrying, Sarcas steered his mount a few paces away, giving it, as well as his arm, a rest.

The kingsman hadn't yielded an inch of ground. "Sarcas, I'm not the traitor, but rather, your emperor is."

"Stop! I've heard all those lies before, and I'm no more moved to believe them now than when I first heard."

"Well, since your troops are hopelessly outnumbered, if not for yourself, for the sake of your men, order a surrender before they injure themselves. See for yourself if I speak truth or not."

"Never! After teaching you everything I know, embracing you as my own son, sharing my home and possessions, you repay me by deserting and joining the enemy? That's all I need to know about that kingdom—stab your friends in the back. You were my friend once, but never again. You're just another enemy. I'll drink your blood in celebration of my victory."

Sarcas spurred his horse forward, sword angled low, ready to strike whichever way the kingsman jumped. The kingsman stepped left, avoiding a trampling. His glittering sword sliced the air so keenly that Artka fancied it hummed.

A piercing collision of weapons and the horse's painful shriek mixed with an agonizing human scream, temporarily deafening Artka. As Captain Sarcas' sword descended it was deflected by the kingsman's weapon into the great, war horse's neck, paralyzing it, sending it crashing to the ground. Sarcas rolled away from his fallen mount and lay among the weeds, a gurgling sound emitted from his throat: loathing and fear glared from his bulging eyes.

Artka stared dumbfounded. A shard of the captain's own sword had split off and burrowed into Sarcas' own throat.

Artka raised his eyes from his fallen leader; it now fell to him to avenge his captain. But this kingsman had just downed a champion warrior and his horse in one fell blow; he was invincible.

When Artka fought Pelton, Pelton's sword had done most of, if not all, the fighting. This Ecclessite, however, manifested unity of sword and soldier. Fit as he was, Artka's youth and inexperience was no match for this seasoned warrior, and yet honor left him no alternative.

Surrounding sounds of battle had all but ceased. Empire warriors had either fled or died. Artka alone still bore arms for the emperor. Defiantly he raised his sword, sounded the lion's roar and gathered himself to avenge his captain.

"Hold on, friend," the kingsman said. "I've been sent to rescue the lion from the swine."

Artka dug his heels into the ground, skidding to a halt. "Rescue? You're my enemy, not my rescuer."

"I'm Tren," the kingsman said, stepping toward Artka with his glowing sword leveled at Artka's chest. "The 'Roaster of rabbits' sent me to fetch you."

Artka's face paled and his sword drooped. His memory—from killing Pelton in the Windbreak Forest to waking on the banks of the Flaming Sword River was fully restored. The headache, though dreadful, quickly passed, but the restored memory of his encounter with Logon Xychirion ignited a deep, desperate ache in his heart.

A circle of Ecclessites closed in around him. "A life for the king," Tren said as he thrust his sword into Artka's chest.

Like a withered leaf, Artka's leather breastplate peeled away from the kingsman blade. Artka had no strength to even try to raise his sword, let alone fight. The Ecclessite's blade pierced skin, muscle, bone . . . and heart. Something warm flowed from the sword into his heart. Artka sank to his knees.

Then all became dark.

CHAPTER THIRTEEN

SOUNDS OF A BUBBLING BROOK woke Artka. He opened his eyes and to his horror, found he was by kingsmen enjoying a hearty meal of eggs, venison, and some greens.

"Ah, the rabbit-eater awakes. Join us."

Artka twisted around. Tren, the kingsman warrior who had stabbed him, sat just behind. Alongside him were several good-natured Ecclessite soldiers at another campsite munching a breakfast of black-bread, berries, wildfowl, and a couple of fish.

"I thought you stabbed me." Artka touched his chest and discovered a painless, but open wound.

"I did," Tren said. "Clear to the heart. Tell me, what's your name?"

"Why should I tell you?" Artka said, gingerly examining his wound.

"Why shouldn't you? You're one of us now . . . well, almost."

Artka looked up, his jaw set forward and his brows scrunched together. "What do you mean, one of you?"

"Well, do you still feel loyalty to your emperor?"

"He's not my—"

"Uh-huh. No one who's been pierced to the heart by a Child of the Stars can still owe allegiance to his former master."

"But, I'm no kingsman."

"You soon enough will be. Logon has summoned you. My sword's wound awakened a desire for truth in your heart, and now you need Logon's healing touch. So, what's your name?"

"I—I do feel kinda different."

"Of course, you do. You don't want to belong to Carnalia anymore do you?"

"No."

"Why not?"

"It's a selfish land, ruled by an evil leader, full of nasty, vile people. Strange, even though I knew all that before, I was never bothered that much . . . "

"Could that be because you were just as evil, *friend?*"

Artka lowered his eyes. "I'm as vile as any." He'd never before understood, nor cared about his own selfishness. He now understood why he'd fled from Logon. Even Tren, a minor reflection of Logon, caused Artka to cringe and want to hide. "You've made a mistake, Tren. I don't belong here. I'm corrupt. I loathe Carnalia now, but fear I'll spoil Ecclessa, though . . . I wish I could belong." Artka fought back tears.

"Take courage." Tren laid a hand on Artka's shoulder. "That's the result of my sword, Star Splinter, one of the Children of the Stars, wounding you. Look," Tren opened his tunic revealing a scar on his chest, " . . . see, I received just such a wound myself. For weeks I suffered until I found healing. Then I was given this sword," he said, tapping the sword in his belt. "And assigned to an Ecclessite brigade to begin training to rescue others, such as yourself. Now I fight, no longer to kill and injure like the empire trained me, but to rescue."

"But you killed Captain Sarcas."

"His own resistance to the truth killed him. No one regrets my former friend's death more than I. I'd hoped to pierce his heart, but alas, it was too hard, too full of bitterness for even this sure blade. His own weapon, in which he placed his trust, failed him and ultimately destroyed him. Now, about your name?"

Artka asked, "What did you call your sword, a 'Child of the Stars'? What does that mean?"

"All the king's swords are Children of the Stars. But, that tale isn't for now, nor for me to tell. First we must get your wound tended."

Artka looked around the Ecclessite camp. "I see no medical tent. What does getting my wound tended involve?" A curious reluctance stole over Artka.

"You must seek out Logon."

Artka cringed. "Logon! He mustn't see me in this wretched condition."

"Did you think he doesn't know?" Tren asked. "It's your opinion of yourself that's changed; he knew what you were before he sent for you. He waits for you by the river."

"I'm so ashamed."

"He'll not reject you. Your heart won't heal without his touch . . . *friend*."

"Artka."

Tren smiled and stood to full height. "Artka. Well Artka, come have breakfast, then we must be off. Oh, don't fret about your wound, it won't fester. It will only make you aware of what you were, but that's a pain of the heart, and though severe at times, isn't fatal. If, however, you resist Logon's will, it'll cause discomfort, though your body will wax stronger. As long as you obey the awakened conscience of your heart, the wound won't bother you, but I warn you, your body of flesh will find ways to resist."

Artka followed Tren to a fire-pit where several game fowl roasted in a spit over coals. Tren handed him a glistening, slightly browned grouse still. Artka sank his teeth into the delightful, yielding flesh.

Tren thoughtfully chewed a morsel, looking east as if checking the weather. Artka concentrated his full attention on breakfast. He hadn't eaten since early the day before.

"Tren," intruded an authoritative voice, "we would have a word with you."

A kingsman captain strode toward them, flanked by four lieutenants. Nearby other soldiers looked up and quickly excused themselves.

Tren rolled his eyes. "Captain Basso. Yes, of course, come, sit down. Shall I get you—?"

"We've eaten," the captain said curtly. "We'd like to discuss a private matter."

A resigned smile played at the corners of Tren's mouth. "I think I know what you want, captain. You may talk freely in front of Artka, he'll soon to meet with Logon."

The officers regarded Artka kindly, then turned stern again as they paid attention to Tren. Captain Basso resumed, "Very well, I'll come right to the point. It's obvious, Tren, that you're a skilled warrior. Your record bears that out. But, why do you insist on bringing up controversial notions? Don't misunderstand, we're grateful for your participation yesterday. Having you along expedited matters, but, fuddle it all, why don't you stay with your own type of brigade? Your presence confuses our recruits, especially about sharpening their swords."

"And veterans, as well," added a lieutenant.

"Yes, and some veterans as well," Basso said. "Every time you're with us, arguments arise about your methods, and, and . . . "

"Fairy tales?" Tren wryly suggested.

"Precisely! Fairy tales. You see, even you know how preposterous your ideas sound."

Tren scrutinized Captain Basso. "It's no fairy tale. My sword does sing, just as yours would, if you'd let it."

Captain Basso withdrew his sword. Like Pelton's, it glowed several inches from the tip with a bluish light. Artka blinked in amazement. Were Tren and Basso going to fight each other?

But Captain Basso merely lay the sword on its side and pointed at a mark along the blade. "Look here, Tren, this rune makes clear how mistaken you are. It says:

> This point of life,
> With edge defends,
> This mark of strife,
> Must make the ends.

"See? No one's permitted to sharpen past this rune. That's where the sharpening ends."

"You're the one misinterpreting it, captain," Tren said. "Look here," he extracted his fully shining blade and subjected it to the captain's inspection. "This rune, though not yet visible on your less tolled sword, is in conjunction with that one, expanding the meaning:

> This point of life,
> With edge defends,
> This mark of strife,
> Must make the ends,
> The darkened life,
> To start anew,

With glories rife,
And learn the true."

Tren lowered his sword. "Since the rune ends—not where you thought—but up here, you've limited the fuller—and truer—understanding of the rune."

"No, no, no! Tren, your application is wrong. You're making those obscure lines—beyond the allowable area, I might add—fit your beliefs. That's dangerous. I want you to stay away from my brigades if you insist on teaching men to sharpen more of their blade than they should."

"Captain, I regret the contention, although in truth, it's *your* refusal to acknowledge all of Logon's blade that's the real controversy. Furthermore, I must go where Logon bids me. Look, doesn't my success in battle indicate the validity of what I say?"

"Wherever Logon bids you, eh? That brings up another issue. You claim to hear directly from Logon? We're Sharpointer officers, don't you suppose he'd communicate as clearly with us as you claim he does with you? As for your victories, they only indicate that your foolishness hasn't yet overtaken you."

Tren sighed. "Aren't you in contact with Logon when you toll your swords?"

"Yes, of course, but, only by the runes, not 'some voice emanating from the sword.' If you ask me, that sort of thing borders on empire sorcery. You're dabbling in practices that sound more like the doings of the White Priestess of Pitland."

"It's not a voice from the sword, captain, it vibrates, and if I listen carefully—"

"Oh, what's the use?" Basso threw up his hands. "We've been over it a hundred times, Tren."

"We can't both be right, Captain. I was trained as a Sharpointer, like yourself. I learned the arguments against sharpening the entire blade, but all that training of what not to believe didn't help on the battlefield. I now know that the fully sharpened blade efficiently rescues more lives."

"You're incorrigible. Don't come back to my command until you've abandoned your fairy tales."

"I'll honor your wishes, unless . . . Logon orders otherwise. Artka, I think I've worn out my welcome." Then Tren added, "One more thing, captain."

"Well, what is it?"

"Logon puts the glow on his swords in response to our tolling, does he not?"

"So?"

"So, if it isn't Logon's will to sharpen the entire sword, why does all of mine glow?"

"Your trouble, Tren, is that you're too independent. You have no respect for what the ancients taught. You always go one step beyond. Well, mark my words, someday it'll catch you up."

Tren stepped so close to Captain Basso that their noses almost touched. "The ancients sharpened the entire sword, so who's defying the tradition of the ancients, you or me?"

"Gentlemen," interrupted a muscular lieutenant with hair and beard glistening as if recently anointed, "may I respond to that?"

"Please do, Crand," Captain Basso said. "Tren, Artka, this is Lieutenant Crand. He's distinguished himself in training and service as well as on the battlefield and is well known for being a scholar of ancient ways and runes. Do yourself a favor, Tren, listen to him."

Crand cleared his throat as if preparing to address an audience. "The original generals had unusual abilities available to them for a variety of reasons: first, the swords were newly forged and as yet, un-runed; second, the king had no set limitations on the powers his generals were to use because the enemy was more powerful in those days; thirdly, tophet creatures and cusps were more dangerous and more numerous back then. Therefore, hardly any kingsmen fought alongside the generals at first, so the swords the generals wielded needed to have greater capabilities than we now need."

Tren shifted his weight to the other foot. "I've already considered—"

"Then," Crand continued, ignoring Tren, "as recruits were added, some misused their swords, hiring out as mercenaries instead of fighting for the glory of the king. That's when Logon inscribed runes on the blades—to keep error from the king's armies. Surely you see the wisdom of not expecting these swords to be like they were in the days of the generals. Only harm can come from pretending things should be now as they were then. The unstable will try to imitate ancient acts of valor if they follow your beliefs. When they fail—which is inevitable—they'll be discouraged, demoralizing the entire outfit. Do you really want to be responsible for that?"

"As it is now," Captain Basso said. "My command is divided because of you. I must keep unity at all costs."

Lieutenant Crand smirked.

"Unity at what price? Truth?" Tren said. "Unity is to be built on truth, not truth on unity."

"How you twist my words! Tren, finish your breakfast, and be off. I can no longer abide you. As for you, young man," Captain Basso turned to Artka, "the wound to your heart is true because it comes from a

Child of the Stars. But don't trust everything Tren says. He's deluded about some things. After you meet with Logon, it would be best if you came back to us for training, lest Tren fill your mind with silly notions."

Artka looked from the captain to Tren.

"He should go where Logon directs," Tren said.

"Aye, but make sure Tren doesn't trick you into thinking something Logon hasn't said. We'll bivouac here for another week. That should be time enough for you to meet Logon and return. See you then, m'lad, I'm sure." The officers turned and left.

"What was all that about?" Artka asked, watching them go.

"I'm sorry you were exposed to that, Artka, but, I suppose it was important at the outset of your new life that you learn how the emperor has had influence even among the king's armies. Oh, that kingsmen would trust each other long enough to search out the truth without feeling threatened when there are differences of opinion. We're a divided, fractured army, Artka. It's only by the king's great power that we haven't already been defeated. Come, we need to be on our way."

Tren glanced again at the eastern sky as he readied his knapsack. "I'm uneasy," he said. "My sword's runes advised me to move swiftly, we'd best hurry."

Artka looked up and frowned doubtfully but said nothing. Might the captain be right about Tren's delusions? "Wouldn't it be just as good for me to stay here and begin my training?"

"Artka, you've entered into a higher plane of existence. You're in the process of being, as it were, born a second time. Everything in Elyon's kingdom is the reverse of what you learned in Carnalia. So many sudden adjustments will be difficult. I promise to not force my opinions on you, but you must allow me to guide you to Logon. Your wound won't be healed unless he touches you. Your new life won't start until Logon heals your wound. Even Basso agreed that since I rescued you, I had the right to present you to Logon."

Artka nodded and stuffed some items into his sack, then rose and said, "Ready." He suddenly realized he was weaponless. "Wait . . . Tren, where's my sword?"

"Empire weaponry has no place in the king's army. I destroyed it." Tren led off through the encampment.

"But . . . I feel defenseless," Artka said, keeping pace.

"And how should a prisoner of war feel?" A smile played on Tren's lips.

Artka silently walked alongside Tren. Several kingsmen called greetings as the pair passed while others turned their backs or stared sullenly. If Tren was bothered, it didn't show.

"Tren, where are the others?"

"What others?"

"Others, like me, captured in yesterday's battle. Shouldn't they also be on their way to Logon?"

"You're the only one, Artka."

"But, I mean, the Erotons who surrendered, why aren't they going with us? I saw some lay down their arms. What's happened to them? Where are they?"

Tren's pace quickened. "Most of them feigned surrender, then ran for the cover of the woods. Tophets waited there. Tophets are merciless, torturing as they eat. Our pickets heard screams all night long. If only they hadn't resisted . . . "

Artka made no reply. Did Tren have any idea that he hadn't just let his heart be pierced, that he'd wanted to resist, he'd tried with all his might but had been stricken paralyzed? Nevertheless, now that he was among kingsmen, he desperately wanted to belong.

"Leid," Tren addressed a perimeter guard, "I see you've been tolling your sword's edge. Keep it up. By the way, I sense trouble brewing. Keep a sharp watch."

"I shall, Tren. I sense it, too, something stirring in the east. I hoped I'd see you before you left. I wanted to tell you . . . it hummed a little the other morning."

Tren smiled. "This is Artka. He's on his way to Logon, a prize from yesterday's fray.

"King's road to you both," Leid said.

"Were you on duty last night?" Tren asked as an afterthought.

"No, but I heard about it." He shook his head. "King's road to you."

CHAPTER FOURTEEN

Tren led the way southeasterly through marshes, fields, and wooded tracts. With each passing mile Artka's heartache lessened, but strangely, despite his physical conditioning, his limbs grew wearier, as if lead weights had been sewn into the seams of his Carnalian clothing. By early afternoon he asked Tren to slow the pace.

"We'll rest soon enough, Artka," Tren said. "I know you're tired, but we mustn't slacken our pace. You're in great peril."

"From what?" Artka said, leaning on his knees, breathing heavily.

"I'm not sure. I've seldom felt such an oppressive atmosphere," said the kingsman. "We have far to go and must be well away from here by nightfall."

"A storm?"

"Yes, and something more. Are you able to quicken your step?"

"I'll try. If only my gear wasn't so heavy."

Tren smiled. "It's not your gear, my friend. It's not the wound to your heart either. Your decision to seek Logon weighs heavily on your flesh. Your body is still under the oath you swore to Lurcan. Your awakened heart continues to strive against the weight of the curse your body is under."

"But, I had no choice," Artka said. "It was either take the oath or hang. I never thought there might be an alternative. Back then I thought the king was evil."

"Would it have made any difference?"

Artka struggled to come up with a believable defense, but every excuse sounded hollow even to him.

Tren broke the silence. "Artka, you were born under the emperor's shadow, born with a craving to serve yourself. You could have done nothing else, no more than fire can help but consume dry kindling. The emperor's corruptive influence shapes each Carnalian into a self-serving being. Some people are worse than others, but everyone is far less than what King Elyon requires."

"Live for the moment, die for the empire," Artka mused. "The last half is a result of the first."

"Ah! So, you do see?"

"But, I no longer want to obey either part of that decree."

"A change has begun in you but isn't complete. Logon must further what Star Splinter started. This sword pierced through the lies exposing the excuses that shielded your heart from truth, now that light has entered, your heart hungers for more. Only knowing Logon can provide that."

"I did meet Logon, once."

"I know, but your heart hadn't been pierced nevertheless, didn't you sense some quality about him that made you cringe, but at the same time, desperately wanted?"

Artka recalled his conflicting emotions, especially when Logon revealed his chest wound.

"He would have pierced your heart and healed you then and there," Tren said, "if you'd have let him. But your heart and mind were still under Lurcan's influence. You still had selfish ambitions and didn't want your true desires exposed, so you ran and forced yourself to forget."

Artka hoisted his rucksack and nodded. Tren smiled, patted Artka's shoulder and headed up the trail, setting a demanding pace for Artka who could only trudge behind. Tren had an even lighter step. As they hiked, the struggle between Artka's will and body intensified; every joint and muscle ached. Did Tren's pace have to be so rapid? Artka lagged several paces behind.

Tren marched on, oblivious.

Artka wrestled against the desire to just fall out and sit along the roadside reconsidering his decision to go to Logon. His footsteps slowed and in response, his bodily aches subsided. But his heart felt like a stone. He watched Tren recede into the distance and a thought crossed his mind that if he lost track of his guide he'd lose the something of the greatest valuable. He summoned all his willpower and forced himself onward. The weight on his heart instantly decreased, but at the same time his limbs felt heavier.

Up ahead, Tren turned and watched, sensing Artka's small victory. He paused on the top of a rise and called, "Choosing to keep to the course seems like such a small decision, Artka, but no choice you ever make will be more important than the one you just made." He waited and encouraged, "We've another day and a half to Logon's Rock, no doubt you'll face that decision again between here and there. When we approach Logon's Rock you'll feel even greater temptation to turn back. So, brace yourself, ask for my support when you need it. But don't ask me to slow the pace. It's imperative we waste no time getting you to Logon's Rock."

"Why? What possible difference could a few hours, or even a day or two make?" Artka said, catching up to his guide.

"I don't know, exactly. Runes on my sword warned me to not delay."

"But I'm so weary. Maybe, like Captain Basso said, you're just imagining your runes said something. Maybe there's really no danger. The sky is clear, I see no sign of storm."

"I've learned through hard experience to not put aside the warnings from my sword, no matter what the environment indicates," Tren said.

"But, how do you know for sure? Couldn't it just be your feelings?"

"Feelings? Whoever said anything about feelings? I knew it in my inner self—where the Advisor dwells—it has nothing to do with feelings. Look Artka, I've learned a lot about feelings, mostly that they're influenced by my surroundings. My inner sense tells me different. I can't explain how, but I know that danger pursues, and it's not after me, but you."

Artka looked up. "Me? Who could possibly know where I am, or even care?"

"I don't know. But someone knows and cares a great deal. Come, we must hurry. We have leagues to travel before it's safe to sleep. Danger could be lurking anywhere in Carnalia and will find us if we make camp too soon. Besides, even if I'm imagining the danger, what's the harm of getting you to Logon sooner rather than later?"

Artka smiled. "You have me there. Lead on."

They traversed the pathway over grassy hills, past marshy lowlands, through glades and wooded dales, constantly heading south by southeast. Daylight faded to twilight, then dusk; but Tren kept to his pace.

Artka lagged several paces behind in the growing gloom. Had it not been for Tren's glimmering sword swinging back and forth on Tren's belt, Artka would have lost sight of his pathfinder. When it was quite dark Artka was so far behind that he even lost sight of Tren's sword.

He was about to call out when the shining blade reappeared on a rise and came to a standstill.

Forcing his legs to keep churning, sucking in deep breaths, Artka drew alongside Tren. Tren had both hands scooping something out of a tree crotch.

"What are you doing?" Artka huffed.

Tren turned and smiled. "Well done, Artka. We'll make camp here, though it's not as far along as I'd hoped. To make up for that, we must be on our way well before sunrise."

Artka sank gratefully to his knees, then slumped over on his side without removing his pack.

"Don't sleep. First, we must eat, and then you must observe while I toll my blade."

"You're joking! I'm bone weary. Can't hardly keep my eyes open."

"Hold out your hand. Here, eat this."

Artka extended a hand. Tren placed a sticky, gossamer-like substance on his open palm. He sniffed. A delicious aroma reminding him of roasted meats, vegetables, sweet breads, and confections tantalized his nostrils.

"What is this?" he asked rubbing the substance into a doughy lump and tasting it.

"Exactly," Tren said with a hint of mirth.

"No, I mean this food. It's delicious, but," he took a mouthful and swallowed, "I've never had anything like it. What is it?"

Tren chuckled. "That's right."

"What's right? And what are you smiling at? And what is this I'm eating?" Tren's attitude was becoming irritating.

Tren laughed aloud. "I'm sorry. I couldn't help but tease you with a Wholeblader joke. The food you're eating is called manu, which is from a rune that means 'what is it?'"

"I don't get the humor," said Artka, taking another bite. "But whatever you call it, it's toothsome."

"I guess it takes a Wholeblader to appreciate a good rune joke. The ancients discovered manu when Somem, the lawgiver, led them out of what was then Psychanan into a country of their own. They needed to eat while they established fortresses and villages. They discovered that manu formed on certain trees at night and was easy to gather in the morning. Once their crops matured and were ready for harvest, the manu all but disappeared, but by then, they no longer needed it."

"How is it you have some, if it disappeared?"

"I said it 'all but' disappeared. Manu still forms sparsely here and there. Not many know it exists anymore, or how to find it. I found out by—"

"Let me guess," Artka said, "your sword's runes told you."

"The evidence is in your mouth. Did you see any manu in Captain Basso's Sharpointer Brigade?"

"No," Artka said, taking another bite, too hungry to care.

"That ought to help keep you awake while I sharpen my sword." Tren licked the last bit of manu off his fingers then withdrew his sword. Its glow lit up their campsite brighter than their fire. He slowly, deliberately applied his file to the razor-keen edge, first one side, then the other. As he honed, certain runes on the flat of the blade flared reddish-orange, which Tren briefly studied before tolling by other runes. Artka watched fascinated as the edges glowed a little brighter wherever the file touched. He was especially fascinated when runes appeared from what seemed to be a blank part of the sword.

As Tren concentrated his tolling on one such rune, a faint hum resounded. Artka craned his neck looking around for the source of the sound, then, realized that the musical tone was vibrating from Tren's sword.

The hum swelled into a robust, joyful tune. Its music whirled exultantly around them as the sword waxed brighter, shining like the noonday sun; and the melody intensified, rolling like ocean waves. Surrounding trees, rocks, and plants became starkly visible in the brilliance of the singing sword.

Artka felt he would burst with amazement.

Tren leapt to his feet, thrust his sword high overhead and chanted along with the vibrant melody:

"*Great gusts of wrath are blown astray,*
Fierce howls of hate are held at bay,
When comes Defense of Gavan-Laye,
To render justice with coming day,
Crushing the crusher; undoing the stay,
Protecting pilgrims from all harm's way,
To battle the night, words of light say,
Slack not nor stumble 'till path has sun's ray,
A comfort sends king to lead safe away,
And hold the son's course, lest lies cause dismay,
For mettle with metal is proved in the fray."

The sword's intense light faded to normal. Tren lowered it, but still stared at the sky drinking in the last of the exhilarating experience. Night flooded again into the dell leaving the campfire and the blue of Tren's sword for light.

Artka's eyes were fixed on Tren. He too, had felt the vibrations of Tren's bold runesong coursing through his being, a restorative balm.

Tren resumed his seat beside Artka. Several moments passed; neither spoke.

At last Tren said in a choked voice, "It . . . it isn't like that very often. Usually, when the sword sings it's a gentle melody, comforting and refreshing. Powerful warrunes, like that one, are usually a preparation for battle."

Artka, overcome by the power and beauty of the runesong, merely nodded his head, saying nothing.

"Time to sleep," Tren said. "I now know for certain that peril lies in our path."

Artka tugged his cloak around him and lay back, staring at the stars shining through the tree canopy. Ruby-studded empire swords no longer held any fascination for him compared to Ecclessa's glowing, singing swords. Just before slumber overtook him, Artka fancied seeing a column of twinkling lights hovering between himself and Tren. He drifted off with visions of Tren's brightly shining sword resonating sweet, musical strains.

~

A hand clamped tightly over Artka's mouth, waking him.

"Make no sound," Tren whispered. "We must leave. Enemies draw near." Tren removed his hand.

The putrid odor of tophet permeated the air. Artka shivered. The fire had gone out; no hint of life was left in the coals. His leg muscles were sore, but his heart felt lighter than ever. But for the threatening presence of tophets, he would even have enjoyed rising so early.

Tren wrapped his cloak around his sword, allowing only a pinpoint of light to guide them over the exposed roots and rock-strewn forest floor. Instead of a rapid, punishing pace, Tren circumspectly picked their way through the trees. A breeze sprang up carrying the scent of storm, thunder, lightning, and a hard, driving rain.

Stumbling along behind, Artka focused on the sword's pinprick of light, trying to be as quiet as possible. Tren silently trail-blazed through the dark grove.

Large raindrops splattered around them and the temperature dropped several degrees as wind whistled through bending tree limbs; leaves skittered across their path as flashes of lightning outlined the horizon. Artka paused to secure the straps of his cloak; when he looked up Tren was several yards away. He was about to cry out when Tren's blade was suddenly uncovered, a blue flame flaring in the stormy wood. Artka watched as a crawling fog bank advanced on Tren, obliterating Artka's view of the sword. Artka gasped—the fog bank was unaffected by the howling wind! It was a tophet!

A shiver ran down Artka's spine that was unrelated to the storm. A blazing lightning flash revealed Tren standing like a statue, his rain-drenched face grim, sword raised in combat with the fog bank!

In all the childhood legends Artka had ever heard, mortals never came off victorious when battling tophets. What was Artka to do when Tren got killed? He wrapped his arms around a tree trunk for balance and watched in despair as Tren's blade flashed, darting back and forth. He wanted to help, but unarmed and exhausted, joining the fight would be utter folly.

Tren's voice carried to him on a gust of wind, "In the name of Xychirion, I deny you your quarry." Tren's sword slashed again and was promptly obscured behind the tophet's foggy shroud. Tren's voice came again, but the howling wind distorted the words.

A crunching sound from behind drew Artka's attention. He turned and stared into the darkness. A lightning bolt split a tree into flames fifty feet away. In the flash and fury of the moment Artka identified two more fog banks dogging their trail.

"Ohh-hh!" he uttered and tore himself loose from the tree and fled toward Tren.

An inhuman, ear-shattering shriek sounded above the tumult of the storm. Tren stood silhouetted for a brief moment as a fireball screeched up and away above the treetops, speeding away south.

"Glory to Logon!" Tren shouted, waving his sword overhead, doing a sort of shuffle in the leaves as a victory dance. Then remembering himself, he turned and called, "Artka?"

"Here," Artka gasped, stumbling to his knees beside Tren. He pointed behind, panting, "More tophets."

Tren lifted Artka to his feet. By just that touch Artka felt a renewed strength flow into his arms and legs.

Soaked to the bone they jogged onwards through the woods and found a clearing. Artka, clung to the shirttail of Tren's tunic. They crossed the uphill, clear terrain and paused on a hilltop. Thunder and lightning crashed on all sides. Tren wiped the rain from his brow to get a sense of direction.

"East now, Artka. If anything happens to me, keep heading east until you reach the river. You must get to Logon before this day passes."

"Where are you going?"

"Nowhere . . . but, just in case . . . "

"Shouldn't you cover your sword again?"

"Not much point in that now. They've picked up our trail. Seeing they have a Wholeblader to contend with might make them think twice. How are you doing?"

"I'm fine as long as I hold on to you. But, before we set off again, what happened back there? Did you actually kill a tophet?"

"Kill it, no. It's impossible to kill them. I merely struck its mortal form a fatal blow, which, as you no doubt witnessed, transformed it to its original form as a fiery specter. When they lose their assumed form, they're catapulted back to their swamp to take on a new shape all over again. It takes them months to form a body and gather a cloaking mist. By that time, they're ravenous."

"How did you know where to strike? I mean, with all that darkness and fog . . . "

"Ah, that's what Star Splin—"

Voices like a rockslide swelled in a blood-chilling chant:
>*"Give us the lad, the master wants him back.*
>*Give us the lad, the master wants him back."*

The gravelly incantation continued its odd cadence. Another flash of lightning exposed a tightening circle of fiends surrounding the hillock where Tren and Artka stood.

Tren defiantly raised Star Splinter. "I declare victory over you in the name of Xychirion." Several runes on Tren's sword flared reddish-orange, even where no runes had previously been visible. Tren whispered, "Hold my belt, and don't let go."

Artka slipped his fingers inside the back of Tren's belt. "Why, what're you going to do?"

Tren ignored Artka's question and shouted, "Centipede, I overcome you in the name of Xychirion."

Looking over Tren's shoulder through Star Splinter's glow Artka saw a giant centipede three times the size of a man. It reared its head and snapped mandibles at them with a loud "clack."

Tren rushed forward, yanking an incredulous Artka along. The creature, caught off guard, tried to swerve aside as it thrust a rending claw at Tren. Star Splinter flicked to the side; the claw was split open.

A smoky, green effluent spurted from the rent member; eye-watering stench filled the air, as did a horrible screech. Before the maimed creature could retaliate, Tren's sword swung back in an uppercut, dividing mandibles, mouth, and head. A sulfurous explosion engulfed the two men as a howling wail ruptured the stormy night. The fireball fled south through the stormy night.

The other fog banks stepped back from Tren.

Tren waved his sword. "Such will be the fate of all who stand in our way."

Artka, still peering over Tren's shoulder, saw the faintest outlines of a spider, scorpion, beetle, and shrivel-winged wasp backing off. Other loathsome creatures behind weren't as discernible.

Artka tugged Tren's belt, "Do your victory celebration later, okay? Let's get out of here."

Tren laughed. "Right you are, Artka. We mustn't keep Logon waiting." Then at the tophets he shouted, "Go tell your master that the lad chooses to meet Logon."

Tren's sword swished back and forth, opening a swath through the growling band of tophets. The two men passed unhindered down the rain-slick, muddy hillside and into the wooded vale beyond.

CHAPTER FIFTEEN

ARTKA AND TREN TRAVELED THROUGH the mid-morning hours with few stops. The thunder, lightning, and gale-force winds ceased at sunrise, but torrential rain continued. Even leaning upon Tren's supporting arm, Artka's pace faltered. His legs felt like tree trunks. Making matters worse, his dull headache now throbbed. His physical discomfort subsided whenever they stopped to rest, but then his heartache increased. Resuming the journey lessened his heartache, but the physical aches returned.

By midday Tren had decided to take a brief rest and shelter from the intensity of the rain in a hemlock grove.

"I'm hungry, Tren. Do you think there might be any manu around?" Artka sank to the ground.

"I doubt it, Artka, spike trees don't grow in this area, but I'll look. Stay in this refuge. Enemies are likely prowling about. No doubt those tophets we fought our way through have sent for reinforcements. And they know our destination. The closer we come to Logon's Rock, the greater our danger, so stay in hiding. I'll be back in a few minutes."

Artka leaned against the trunk of a great hemlock and closed his eyes. He closed his eyes for a moment and beheld a vision of Logon waiting atop a wooden bridge, smiling, beckoning. As Artka approached Logon's smile changed to a leering grin. He withdrew a sword and told Artka, "You don't belong amongst true kingsmen—I must slay you."

Artka jerked awake. He fancied seeing a shadow dart behind him around the hemlock bole. He blinked and looked again but saw nothing.

"Such dreary weather." He leaned back again, and his eyelids grew heavy. Artka forced his eyes open. He dared not doze lest he have another bizarre dream. He studied his surroundings, peering beneath the down swept branches of the surrounding trees, anxious for Tren's return.

Shouldn't he be back by now? Had Tren abandoned him? Or . . . was Tren part of some sinister plot? Was that dream a warning? And what about the king's brights, feared by hard-hearted Erotons more than tophets? Maybe Tren was really leading him to be tortured by a gathering of brights? Had that been his plan all along?

"I must escape," he told himself. "I, I mustn't follow Tren any more . . . he's leading me into a trap. I should've seen it before. I can find my way back to Captain Basso's brigade . . . Tophets can be avoided, I've done it before, but brights? I don't even know what they look or smell like."

He stood, his limbs reinvigorated, but the ache in his heart deepened. Artka crawled out of the shelter. Several minutes later he ducked beneath some tightly interwoven, hemlock branches and discovered a large, open space that had been formed by succeeding generations of trees spreading outward in widening circles from the parent tree. Looking from the inside, the outer perimeter of interlocking branches gave the appearance of walls, complete with a ceiling of overhead, entwined boughs above a floor of silent needles. The downpour did little more than drip through to where Artka knelt examining this sanctuary. He could see out well enough, but nothing could see in. And nothing could enter without a commotion. Feeling secure, Artka stretched out on the soft needles.

Out of the corner of his eye there was a slight movement in the outer branches, but upon closer investigation, it was just a shadow of a tree limb swaying in the breeze. But, shadows in such dim light? He shrugged, dismissing the mystery and was about to close his eyes when another motion drew his attention.

Rainwater cascaded off branches. Someone was pushing their way into his hiding place. Had Tren located him so easily? Artka sat up, his heart pounding and his stomach tight.

But it was a vulture pushing beneath the trembling branches. Artka's steamy breath rose overhead. The large bird shook its wings, spraying water everywhere. It eyed Artka, cocked its head, took a step closer, then turned and walked back out underneath the branches. Artka heard its wings flap as it disappeared to parts unknown.

"Where are you going, stupid bird? Don't you know it's pouring out there?" Artka shrugged, dismissed the matter and resumed lying on the soft needles.

He dozed again. He didn't know how long, but a vague memory of foul dreams lingered in his mind. He rolled to his side and started to close his eyes when he heard, faintly at first, then more clearly, though nearly drowned out by the drumming rain, a human voice. He lifted his head.

Tren? How did Tren know he was here? Was his sword guiding him? What would Tren do to him for running away? How could he persuade Tren he didn't want to go to Logon's Rock anymore? Tren was a deceiver, not to be trusted . . .

"Artka, where are you?" Tren waded into view through ankle-deep waters and swirling mists, headed directly toward Artka. Did he possess powers that enabled him to see through branches?

Some forty paces away Tren paused. Was he looking for a way to get through the branch wall? Artka's pulse pounded in his ears.

Then Tren turned away, cupped his hand to mouth and called, "Artka . . . Artka, can you hear me?"

Before fading from view, Tren stopped again.

Was he playing cat and mouse? How wicked, how sly.

"Artka," Tren plaintively called. "If you can hear me, please, come out. This wood isn't safe."

Safer than being with that monster, Logon.

The vehemence of that thought surprised Artka.

"We're closer to Logon's Rock than I thought, Artka. Can you hear me? This is the Valley of Shadows, a dangerous place. There are cruel agents here who are as dangerous, if not more so, than tophets. Artka. Artka." Tren sank to his knees and looked up at the sky, sobbing, "Oh, King Elyon, I've failed. Help me find him, or, or send a roamer to guide him. I don't know where else to look. He could be anywhere by now. Forgive me. I should have recognized this area. Help me find him before they do."

Tren stood and continued down the trail, calling, "Artka, where are you? Don't believe the lies, Artka. Floodwaters are rising. It's not safe to hide." Tren disappeared into the mist and rain. The echo of his voice vanished soon after.

Artka's shoulders slumped. Tren appeared to be genuinely grieved. For a brief moment Artka considered bursting from cover and chasing after Tren, but then the atmosphere in the hemlock grove—like a dark wave rolling along the forest floor—turned a shade darker, and Artka's urge to go after Tren dissipated. Without any breeze rustling the branches, shadows glided across the needled floor from every direction. At the same time voices crowded out his own thoughts.

"Tren will torture you."

"He'll betray you to the brights . . . and who knows what they'll do to you."

"Afraid! You are deathly afraid! You're afraid!"

"You can't move, you're paralyzed with fear."

"Wait here until the dread comes to rescue you."

"We have him. He nearly slipped away, but now we've got him."

The confusing vortex of voices talked about him as much as to him. And there was an undertone of evil laughter that mocked Tren and Logon, reciting all manner of foulness, especially against Logon.

"You can't resist, surrender. There's no escape. You belong to the empire."

Suddenly the voices shrieked, "Ayyyh! How did it get here?"

Another voice—calm and authoritative—drowned out the tormenting cacophony, "Your heart, Artka, what does your heart seek?"

The hideous voices receded to the background. He was again aware of his own thoughts.

Artka's eyes opened. Between him and a legion of jostling shadows hovered a twinkling column of lights. "Follow your heart's new desire, Artka."

"No, no, Artka, fear him. He'll take you to Logon, the Tormenter."

"Logon will not torment you, Artka. Logon will torment these cusps—at the proper time. Remember the desire awakened in your heart by the Child of the Stars."

"My . . . heart?" Artka uttered. "In my . . . heart?" What did his heart want? Artka recalled waking up with a pierced heart, desiring to be good, clean and honest, and . . . forgiven.

"No! He'll kill you, he'll torment you," clamored the shadows. Their number increased; they surged against the column of light.

"Lo—gon . . . help . . . me—ee," Artka sobbed as he struggled to his feet and stumbled through the hemlock branches. His foot snagged on a root and he fell.

The shadows rushed forward, their voices yammering, "Give up, lay still."

The calm voice overrode the nagging voices, "Rise. Flee to Logon. Greater danger approaches, a prince above my ability."

Artka's limbs were suddenly heavier. He pushed through the agony and gained his knees—blood thumped in his temples. He tottered a few steps and clung to a sapling for support.

The twinkling column repositioned itself between Artka and the shadows. "Hurry, Artka, there's not much time." Artka staggered to another tree, but with each faltering step his heart was rekindled with desire for Logon.

Where was Tren? He remembered. Tren admonished him to head east if they got separated. Artka guessed which way east was. His body begrudged every step, yet his yearning for Logon overcame the resistance. He must get to Logon.

He staggered several hundred yards with the mob of shadows dogging his heels but kept at bay by the column of lights.

Flapping wings and a shrill, "Yeeeark," startled him. A vulture—was it the same as in the grove?—circled overhead. It swooped down, then up, screeching, "Yeeeark," then sped away.

The waters were calf-deep, and there was an undercurrent causing his feet to feel as if they would be swept from under him. More shadows had arrived and were surging past the column of light.

A second column of twinkling lights glided past Artka. He watched the strange apparition join side by side with the first, both barely visible through the downpour. The two columns arrested the advance of the twitching mass of shadows. A sudden rumble of thunder sent the shadows scrambling back several feet, but the horde came back immediately.

"Artka!" Tren, with drawn sword, splashed around a tree trunk. "Thank the king, I've found you!"

"T-T—Tren, I'm s-sorry! I—"

"Save your breath, Artka, all is forgiven. We must hurry. Powerful evil draws near."

"Yes . . . the shadows," Artka pointed.

"No, stronger than those cusps. I've never encountered anything like what I now sense." Tren gripped Artka's arm and Artka was infused with strength. "Come, time is short."

They emerged from the woods and saw a distant cliff looming through the fog. Tren waded onto the flood plain dragging Artka along.

"Yeeeark," sounded from above, accompanied by a low-pitched chuckle.

A cold chill enveloped Artka; he lost his grip on Tren's belt and stood shivering in the thigh-high waters.

"Artka, why did you release—?" Tren said, turning. "We're almost there. See that rocky crag? Logon waits there."

A powerful depression held him transfixed.

"Artka," Tren implored, anxiously glancing at the deepening waters.

In a daze Artka said, "It's no use Tren, I can't move. Save yourself. I'd never have the strength to climb Logon's Rock, anyway."

"Then I'll carry you." Tren hunkered under Artka, hoisting his waist onto his shoulder. "Don't worry about climbing the rock. As soon as—"

"Stop fools!" rasped a deep, malevolent voice. "You cannot escape Neask."

"Neask?" Tren craned his neck around.

Artka lifted his eyes and beheld the dread.

Neask, half the height of a tree, garbed in black pelts from shoulder to knee, stood on the edge of the river bank watching. Angry red coals gleamed from recessed eye sockets beneath overgrown eyebrows that met at the root of his flat nose. Huge ears rose above the sides of his head like horns. Out of his sneering lips flicked a split, serpentine tongue. In each of his six-fingered hands were weapons. Rain turned into steam as it hit a glistening black sword in his left hand, his right fist coddled a mace, also steaming in the downpour.

"Artka, just who are you that Lurcan sent a dread to retrieve you?" Tren said, staring at the monstrosity.

"Dread?" Artka echoed vacantly.

"Haw, haw, haw," sneered the giant. "Little maggot, you took an oath; you received special training. I'm sent to fetch you. There's no escape from Neask. No mortal can resist me."

Tren shuddered involuntarily as he backed away.

"Stop fool, or I'll take you back with him, and you know what Brida will do to you. Release him, and I'll make your death quick."

"You have no authority over me," Tren retorted. "Your words don't root my feet. Furthermore, you recognize Xychirion's authority in my Star Splinter and know that I'm not reluctant to invoke it. Return to your master and tell him, 'Artka chooses Logon.'"

"Har, har, har! Such boasts from one about to die. As for your shiny needle—" and with a flick of the wrist Neask's mace hurtled unerringly at them.

Tren's sword met the spiked ball and chain. The resulting shower of sparks was accompanied by a dull snap. The dread's weapon splashed hissing into the floodwaters behind the pair.

Tren groaned, his knees buckled, and he and Artka dipped beneath the surface.

Artka rose choking and spitting out a mouthful of water. He regained his feet and beheld Tren, Star Splinter in his other hand, facing the oncoming giant. Tren's right arm hung at his side.

"Tren, save yourself. Leave me to my fate."

"Stop that nonsense," Tren said through gritted teeth. "Grab my belt, and don't let go."

"But Tren, I—"

"Do it." Tren grimaced, keeping his eyes on Neask.

"How touching," mocked the dread. "How noble. Fools! One blow of my 'World Heart' and your other arm will shatter as well. How then will you hold your shiny needle in my face? Your sword's metal is strong, but you lack the strength to wield it against me."

"Yeeark!" cried the vulture circling overhead.

"Har haw haw. My spy wants your eyes as his reward. What say you to that? I'll pluck them out while you're still alive, so you can hear my pet gulping them down." He chortled and flicked stiletto-sharp fingernails one at a time.

"You dare defy the king's son, in whose name I take authority over you?" Tren grunted and lifted his sword as high as he could.

Star Splinter blazed from blue to bright reddish-orange, and the air suddenly hummed with a sweet, musical strain.

Tren broke out in a chant:

> *"Oh, great and mighty king,*
> *The arrogant have risen,*
> *Violent hands have sought my life,*
> *They have not honored your commands,*
> *Grant us strength to fight,*

Save your servants, oh king,
And show me a sign of good,
Let those who hate me see it,
And silence them,
Because you, oh king, will rescue,
And comfort me at the last."

The giant's sword arm froze in mid-swing, his eyes widened, and his mouth gaped as his forked tongue flopped down over his chin and dangled in the breeze.

A sudden, swelling wave buoyed Tren up—with Artka clinging to his belt—up, into the very face of the astonished dread. Tren's sword slashed. Neask's head dodged, but the long, serpentine tongue trailed behind.

The swell swept the two men around and past the howling dread. Cusps scattered back into the forest, screeching in confusion.

Artka's eyes fixed on the falling forked tongue. Just before it hit the water a dark form swooped from the sky and snatched it.

The vulture squawked before gulping the slimy muscle down its gullet as it sped away.

CHAPTER SIXTEEN

TREN'S SWORD FADED TO BLUE. Some mysterious force propelled
Artka and Tren against the current, heading toward Logon's Rock.
Artka's cramped fingers clung to Tren's belt while Tren struggled to
keep his sword pointed at the shoreline. His right arm trailed behind
in the floodwaters.

The dread's outraged shrieks rang out anew over the flood plain as a
sudden, torrent swept him with his entourage of cusps into the marshes.

With dismay Artka noted as they drew near the stony shore that
two shallow caves above the cliff base gave the appearance of a skull.

Tren and Artka washed ashore more than crawled out of the surf.
Atop the cliff stood a cloaked figure watching silently.

Groaning, Tren pulled himself out of the lapping waves, hugging
his injured arm to his chest. Artka, on hands and knees, followed.

Upon seeing no sign of their enemy Tren sighed and reclined.
Through gritted teeth he said, "Artka, go to Logon, he waits."

Artka stared up at the sheer cliff, drenched and fatigued beyond
exhaustion. "I . . . can't move."

"Tap the hunger for Logon that brought you out of hiding to me."

Yearning for Logon stirred afresh. Artka's limbs were no less resis-
tant, but his heart's desire overruled his body once again. He crawled
over jagged stones to the base of the cliff. Artka saw no visible handholds.

"Reach out believing, Artka. You'll find the way," Tren said, his face
to the ground.

Artka stretched out his hand.

Logon's voice came from above, "Would you come to me if you knew I would slay you?"

Artka looked up, his fingertip a hair's breadth from the rock-face as he said, "My liege couldn't prove so false, not after all I've been through."

"All who touch this rock must forfeit their life."

Logon's eyes removed any doubt. If Artka touched the cliff he would die. Echoing memories clamored. "The shadows warned you—Logon would slay you! The tophets warned you—Logon was the enemy!"

Artka could no longer abide the empire's darkness. The sword piercing his heart brought a glimpse—nay, a promise of light.

"If I perish, I perish." Artka touched the rock. His limbs went numb, his heart fluttered, bile welled up in his throat, his eyes closed . . .

~

A gust of wind into his lungs revived him. Artka's eyes opened. He stood atop the cliff face to face with Logon. Logon's hand was just withdrawing from Artka's chest. All physical weariness had vanished.

"What . . . ?"

Logon smiled. "Exactly what I promised. You died."

"No, I'm not, I'm still alive."

"You don't understand. The Advisor will teach you, as will the sword I give you. What do you see on my fingers?"

"Blood?"

"My life's blood, applied to your wound, healing your heart. My blood now courses through your veins." Logon stepped back and swept his arm in a circle around the stone mound they stood upon. "I was impaled here. All who touch this rock acknowledge guilt in murdering me and are under a death sentence."

"But I'm very much alive."

"I've experienced and overcome death. Therefore, I share my victorious blood with all who voluntarily touch this rock and join in my death. At the end of Lurcan's reign, this rock will grow into a mighty mountain filling all the earth. Those upon whom this rock rolls will be crushed without hope. You were dead, Artka, though you thought you were alive. My blood now gives you true life. This rock can no longer harm you, for now you are in me, and I am in you, therefore, you also died, and were brought back to life here."

"Am I still me?"

Logon laughed, and as he did, all things surrounding vibrated with merriment. "Yes, Artka, you are still you, your likes and dislikes, your thoughts, your body, your feelings. You are still you. But, you are no longer your own. I bought you. Your life is now mine. To help you, I've placed my guide—the Advisor—within you. Your oath to Lurcan is broken. He can never control you again—unless you allow."

"No fear of that. I'll never go back to Carnalia."

"How will others know to seek my amnesty unless those who've received my life return to Carnalia and rescue them?"

"Like Tren did?"

"Like Tren. And Pelton."

"Oh, I see."

"No, you don't, not yet. Come, sit. We have much to discuss."

Artka sat on a boulder beside his new master. Then he remembered Tren. "Oh Master, Tren received an awful wound. I fear his arm may be shattered. Can you help him?"

"Tren is in little discomfort at the moment. He'll be alright, though time is needed for his bones to heal. He's in good hands, tended by roamers, or as Erotons call them—brights."

Artka shuddered. "If you say so Erotons are more terrified of brights than tophets."

Logon smiled. "Artka, you've seen them. The night the rains began I sent one to guard you and Tren as you slept. And the two roamers that kept the cusps away from you as you searched for Tren."

"Th-those twinkling columns of light were . . . ?"

Logon nodded. "They assure that whoever seeks me isn't hindered. Nevertheless, they must seek with all their heart, else roamers won't be able to render much assistance."

"I'm not sure I would've come had I known I was coming to die."

"You made your choice by touching the cliff. Your heart longed for me and the freedom from evil that only I can give. That was enough."

"Why did I flee when we first met in the wood?"

"Your heart wasn't pierced, it was too encrusted in self-love. A Child of the Stars needed to pierce that callous flesh and expose you to your heart's corruption. You abhorred learning that about yourself, so you fled. I sent Tren to find you and pierce through your heart's destructive self-love."

"I remember. Tren did say he was sent."

"Tell me Artka, when Tren pierced your chest, did you feel anything unexpected?"

Artka recalled vainly trying to parry Tren's thrust, and the moment the sword pierced him. "Yes, something flowed into me from the sword."

"I spoke my words upon the Children of the Stars while they were being tempered. Those words entered your heart and would give you no rest unless and until you sought me. My word always accomplishes my will."

"Is that why you didn't help in the fight against Neask, because we—I—had to exert my own will despite overwhelming opposition?"

"I gave the help you need: the roamers, the floodwaters, the wave. I'll always send the help you need, though it may not be the help you want or expect. My life is within you Artka, so I'll always be there in your need."

It was then Artka noticed he no longer wore Carnalian clothing. From neck to knee was a white, spotless, woven tunic. On his feet were dun-colored sandals secured by crisscrossed straps around his calf. "When did I get dressed like this?"

"All your Carnalian clothing fell off when you touched my rock. I clothed your lifeless form as I carried you up here. I myself wove this tunic when, as a weaver in Carnalia, I taught my father's ways. This is the garb of a servant. In my kingdom we serve each other, not ourselves. Though it is but servant's attire, it is highly honored in my father's realm. This garment isn't soiled by what touches it, but by what touches your heart. When you honor me, your garment will be as white and bright as it is now. But, should you desire Carnalian things, or revert to Carnalian ways, this tunic will turn dingy. If you persist, it will get stained."

"Can I get a new tunic if this one gets stained?"

"No. This is your tunic. I wove this one specifically for you. It will never wear out. If it gets stained, there is only one way to cleanse it, by coming to me and confessing that you have put your Carnalian self higher than loyalty to me. Some find it difficult to admit, thus deepening their stains, resulting in hardened hearts. I warn you, watch your motives. You'll be summoned by my father someday. That summons will be without notice, so keep your tunic spotless."

"Don't worry, I'll never want anything Carnalian again."

Logon beheld Artka for a long moment, then said, "Don't boast of things you know little about. You know nothing of Lurcan's subtleties. Many an Ecclessite stains his tunic because he fails to take Lurcan's shrewdness into account. Stained tunics inevitably lead to defeat. Have you not seen captive kingsmen in Cosmopolis?"

Artka remembered the emperor's dungeon where Ecclessite prisoners were chained to the walls, their clothing dingy, their faces hopeless. "Yes, I've seen them."

"They didn't fall away from their love of me all at once. It began when they allowed Carnalian luxuries to replace me in their affections. They soon became enmeshed in Carnalian ways, neglecting to call upon me to cleanse their garments. They convinced themselves that sooner or later everyone stains their tunic, thus their stains go deeper, and their swords become dull, forgotten. Such soldiers lose their vigilance, and thus are captured and taken to the dungeons of Cosmopolis, Pitland, or Hadel Prison where they remain in bondage to what they once had escaped."

"Can they be rescued?"

"That depends, but first we must speak of other things before I send you into Ecclessa, to the Prophecy Mountains."

"What?"

"Your parents."

Artka turned away, unable to hold Logon's gaze.

"Artka, you must differentiate people serving the empire from Lurcan and his agents. Lurcan, and lesser entities of his order like dreads, firedrakes, tophets, and cusps, freely chose to hate my father and me, knowing full well the consequences of their choice. Mankind, however, was deceived into hating us.

"I came to earth to show that my father and I love them and are willing to forgive. I send those who are rescued to bring truth to those who are duped by Lurcan that they all might have opportunity to escape.

"My armies face overwhelming odds with nothing more than love in their hearts and the Children of the Stars in their hands. Lurcan's armies are well armed, supplied, trained in savagery, and given to all manner of violence. My armies do not harm, instead rescuing their enemies by acts of sacrifice and love. My warriors must love their enemies as much as I do. There must be no hatred, no thoughts of vengeance, regardless of how deep the offense."

Artka hung his head. "You don't know what my father did to us."

"Yes, I do."

Artka looked curiously at Logon.

Logon continued, "What's more, I know why."

"Why? I . . . I just thought we were a burden."

"That's what he thought, too. But it's unnatural to love oneself more than one's offspring. He was deeply under Lurcan's power. Both your parents said and did things even they didn't understand, for it brought agonizing guilt. But, as slaves to Lurcan, they had no power to resist."

"That doesn't excuse them," Artka said.

"It shows how helpless they are. The closer to Lurcan—and your father has become quite close—the more influence Lurcan exerts. Lurcan made them think you irritated them, building resentment and bitterness in you. You nursed hatred because it justified your rebellion. You only lacked exposure to cruelty, so Lurcan arranged for you to be conscripted to the Roaring Lion Brigade—as complete a collection of cutthroats as ever cast a shadow. Even the Erotons you marched with paled by comparison to Captain Fitcher and Sergeant Love."

"That wasn't just chance?"

"Lurcan planned to shape you into one of the most savage warriors Carnalia has ever known. I intervened by sending Pelton."

"But—"

Logon raised his hand. "Pelton knew the risks. He chose the assignment. Now he serves in my father's palace as an honored servant. He started the process that eventually brought you to me."

"I regret his death. And all for the cheap glory of winning a sword."

"His brother will be glad to know you rue the deed."

"His brother?"

"Tren."

Artka's mouth fell open. "Did . . . does he know?"

"Upon hearing of his brother's death, Tren volunteered to complete his mission."

Artka looked over the ledge. "I'm so sorry, Tren."

"He loves you. There's no bitterness in his heart, Artka. Likewise, there must be no bitterness in your heart against those who have wronged you. You are useless to me if you don't forgive."

"How can I deny my feelings?"

"First, you must want to. Do you?"

"I—I don't know. It's all so confusing."

"Because you cling to your hurt. My life within you will evict that hate, but you must allow it to work."

Artka grabbed Logon's hands. "Take it. Take it, my liege. If it's not of you, I don't want it."

"You must tell me you want me to forgive them. You must see them as I do—as what they could become if they forsook the empire and sought my amnesty."

Tears brimmed in Artka's eyes. "Yes, forgive them. I forgive them. I really want to love them." Artka slid to his knees, sobbing, "Can they be rescued?"

"Would you like to try?"

"Yes."

"I guarantee no results. Your obedience is required for such a mission. First, you must be trained. What you learned of Carnalian warfare will not do in my army. You need re-training. Now, let me give you your sword."

"My own Child of the Stars?"

"Your own. You shall call it Sky Saber, for it came from the heavens to cleave the foundations of Lurcan's throne." From beneath his robe Logon produced a double-edged sword, dull gray from point to hilt. The handle was polished ivory: one side carved as a dove, the other as an eagle. Outspread wings formed the hand guard while the tail feathers fanned out to form the pommel at the bottom.

"It doesn't glow," Artka tried to not sound disappointed. "Why, it has no blue anywhere, no runes, or no—"

"Patience," Logon said.

Artka fell silent.

Logon held the blade aloft by the handle, and softly chanted:
> *"Words of the word,*
> *Power of the source,*
> *Light over dark,*

Breaker of the curse,
Opener of the eyes,
Heart, mind, and soul,
Grow ever brighter,
With each stroke of toll."

Logon lowered the handle to the rock and grasped the tip, continuing his canticle:

"Fire of the heart,
Teacher of the song,
Mending broken part,
So, the lost belong.
Future, past, and now,
Humble those who wield,
Strengthen to the vow,
Truth as thy shield."

Several runes lit up at each phrase Logon spoke until the entire sword was afire with blue flame.

Logon's head stayed bowed until the runes faded and the sword returned to drab gray, leaving only the tip brightly aglow. "Take Sky Saber . . . " Logon withdrew a file from his vestments, "and use only this toller to sharpen your blade. Nothing else can sharpen it. And use this toller on nothing else but your blade. You've seen Tren demonstrate some of the capabilities of the Children of the Stars. You will learn those and more if you faithfully toll your sword's edges. The more you sharpen it, the less of a chore and more of a joy it will be. Use it well, Artka. Rescue lives with it."

He placed Sky Saber and its toller in Artka's hands.

CHAPTER SEVENTEEN

"Let me tell you the history of these swords and tollers," Logon said.

Artka inspected the sword in his hands as he listened, his finger tracing the few visible, embossed runes.

"My father and I laid Psychanan's foundations as a most prized possession. Lurcan, or Brida, as he was called then—our Prime Minister—expected the governorship of the planet, and especially Psychanan. My father explained to him that our imprint was manifest in the beings there and that it would be inappropriate for our image to be governed by our other servants, even our Prime Minister.

"Psychanan—as Carnalia was then known—was a free land, each man and woman received instructions directly from my father and me. We walked among them as a father among children. Psychanan was a place of refreshment where we enjoyed the company of its beings. The men and women were inventive, clever, fun-loving, industrious, gentle and kind, creative, artistic, tender, beautiful, gifted in song and drama. All mankind's industry and arts were blessed. We delightedly watched as people discovered the same qualities my father and I possess within themselves and in the surrounding environment.

"When we returned from Psychanan, Brida often asked if there were anything he should attend to or correct. We always told him the same thing, Psychanites did not need his services. We would tend their needs ourselves. It wasn't fitting for those created in our image to be governed by our other servants.

"Brida's attitude soured. Eventually his thinking became warped. He discretely disparaged us to his peers, insinuating we were mistreating them. Brida's lies and accusations swayed some. To quell the murmuring, we held a court. We three addressed Brida's charges."

Artka looked up. "Three?"

"We are three, yet one." It was simply stated. "Do you feel my life within you?"

Artka nodded.

"Yet I'm outside you, talking to you. What you feel within is the Advisor. He's as real as my father and I, though you cannot see him. We three are one. More than this, you're unable to comprehend. If the Advisor doesn't dwell within a person, that person is not mine."

"This is hard to understand."

"The Advisor will teach you, and Sky Saber's runes will give you understanding. Together they'll open the secrets of my kingdom, but, all in good time.

"As I was saying, we held court to address Brida's threat, for an increasing number of our servants came under his influence. Brida actually believed he was strong enough to oppose us. When he had the needed support, he rallied his followers and challenged us to test Psychananites worthiness to bear our image.

"For the sake of those servants who remained faithful we endured Brida's insults. Brida planned to corrupt Psychanan so he could demand stewardship over the inhabitants. Painful as that would prove, we allowed his plot to unfold so the consequences of his rebellion would ultimately be displayed through all realms.

"The terms and time of Psychanan's test were set. But even before that day arrived, Brida's dementia overtook him. War came to Splendora. Our loyal palace guards were hard pressed to repel Brida's deceived minions. I went out alone and faced the rebels, unveiling my wrath for the chaos they'd inflicted on Splendora. The cowards shrank away. I crossed the expanse of Splendora seeking him, and when I found him I seized his throat."

Logon's eyes blazed with ferocity.

"I denounced him: 'Brida, you have befouled your own existence. You've scorned your betters, defiled your peers and have brought contempt into my father's realm, all who heed you are contaminated. You have even corrupted your office. You are disease. No longer are you Brida—Prime Servant, but Lurcan—Cringing Dog—for your jealous howls have echoed across Splendora. You are banished. Your office will remain forever vacant, a warning to all.'

"Lurcan fled on all fours, yelping in disgrace. Even so, many followed him. Lurcan secured a hideout in Psychanan where he and his horde made crude attempts to corrupt the people, but the people were naive and couldn't comprehend the accusations he leveled against my father and me, they considered Lurcan and his minions a bizarre form of amusement.

"Then Lurcan sent a message to Splendora that despite his banishment he expected us to keep our word and test Psychanan, to wit: that if any meteors fell from the sky, they were to be immediately reported to a roamer. Knowledge of a fallen meteor past three sunsets without being reported would warrant the destruction of Psychanan and all dwelling there."

Logon strode to the edge of the rock and stared across the flood plain. "We agreed. Shortly after the decree was given a comet lit up the night sky, crashing to earth in what is now called Cosmopolis."

"Cosmopolis is many weeks march to the border of Ecclessa," Artka said. "They couldn't possibly move a meteor out of Psychanan in three days' time."

Logon sighed. "Roamers fly faster than starshine, Artka, the inhabitants only needed to inform one of the roamer patrols that toured Psychanan on a daily basis.

"Mada was the leader of the people. Lurcan ingratiated himself to Mada with flattery, urging him to notify—not a roamer—but himself, should a meteor or comet ever fall inside Psychanan. At first Mada hesitated, but through, Ivi, Mada's wife, Lurcan persuaded them to disregard the king's edict and instead, obey him.

"Mada turned the meteorite over to Lurcan, who melted it down into black metal and used it to forge weapons. Mada broke communication with us, and using Lurcan's weapons, took ruler-ship over mankind as Lurcan's puppet regent, forcing others into slavery. Thus, selfishness and cruelty introduced death into Psychanan. Roamers reported to us what had happened, seeking permission to destroy Lurcan and his followers, avowing further proof of Brida's pollution wasn't needed."

"Why didn't you let them?"

"Psychanites were also Lurcan's followers, though unwittingly. We loved the people of Psychanan. To visit punishment on Lurcan, we'd have had to do justice and include all Lurcan's followers—human as well as phantom. Long before Brida conceived his rebellion we knew rebellion was forming in him and let Lurcan run his course, to become as wretched and insane as his willful perversion was destined to prove. Thus, Psychanan degenerated into the Carnalian Empire. And it will continue to decline, like a rotting harvest. Then I'll intervene, gathering my own to safety and punishing all rebellion.

"The Flaming Sword River was a barrier between Ecclessa and Carnalia, providing a refuge for those seeking amnesty from Lurcan's madness. Mind you, Ecclessa isn't free from strife, but it has the protection of the Advisor and my swords. All who enter must come by way of this rock and then pass over my bridge. No mortal may cross the Flaming Sword River."

"But I'm mortal, aren't you sending me across that river?"

"Haven't you died?"

Artka grinned. "Oh, so I have!"

Logon continued, "At the crux of time, after the river divided the land, I took on human flesh, entering Carnalia by way of a miraculous birth. In manhood I went throughout the empire exposing Lurcan's lies. Many responded to the truth and expressed desire to follow me. From them I selected a small band of stouthearted warriors who believed me—all that is, except one. Together we roamed throughout the lands as I taught the truth about my father and his kingdom.

"But Lurcan controls human rulers like marionettes. He vaunted himself as a dark emperor. Mankind obeyed out of fear. Several times Lurcan tried to ambush me, but I eluded him. Finally, he exploited a weakness in one of my men—greed. That man was Claygall. Lurcan promised him power and wealth if he'd lead me into a trap. I knew what Claygall was doing when he led me to this rock where a concealed band of cutthroats waited to seize, bind, and impale me.

"My followers fled. I was abandoned to face the agony alone. Lurcan gave orders to not gag me. He wanted Ecclessa to hear my anguished cries. I, however, remained silent in suffering.

"Lurcan expected I would free myself and immediately seize and torture him for attempting to kill me. He comforted himself with the thought that my father would be forced to destroy his prized possession—mankind—when he destroyed the rebellion. If we had punished only Lurcan and his fallen roamers, but spared the rebellious Psychanites, Lurcan would have accused us of injustice. It was a consolation he would nurse through the eons of his much-deserved judgment.

"But, I gave him no such satisfaction. Lurcan didn't realize that I took mankind's treason upon myself, fully paying for their guilt in my silent agony. Had the ethereal rulers known, they wouldn't have impaled the Prince of Splendora.

"This rock is where I hung suspended between Carnalia and Ecclessa, between earth and sky, between life and death, my innocent life's blood flowing down over it. Our loyal roamers were appalled and had to be restrained from wreaking vengeance as I hung on the spike. This rock, then, became a bane and a rock of judgment for it was here that humanity murdered its Crown Prince. I died, whispering my father's name, begging him to have mercy and to commit Carnalia's judgment to me."

Artka's lips were parted, his eyes intently watching Logon. He sat, his sword across his lap.

"My spirit left my body and soared into the darkened sky, past the confines of air, until, deep among the stars—so far away that Lurcan's name and influence had not come—I found the two meteors my father had prepared beforehand. I drew them into my train as I soared through the core of a distant star. That furnace had no power over me, for there were no impurities in me to consume. The meteors in my train became molten, purged of any contaminants. With them in tow I sped across the expanse of the firmament and re-entered this world.

"I'd been gone three days. My lifeless body still hung on the impaling post. I over-flew Carnalia with the meteors close behind, showing Lurcan and his revelers that I'd returned even greater in power and authority. Lurcan shuddered, realizing he'd fallen prey to his own ambition. Death could never hold me, nor would it hinder my father's cause. Rather, Lurcan's attack on me completed our evidence against him and provided an escape for Psychanites who sought forgiveness.

"I rejuvenated my lifeless body as the meteors crashed into that hillside on the other bank," Logon pointed toward a mountain on the Ecclessite shore. "I lifted myself off the post, searched out my followers, forgave them for abandoning me and commissioned them as generals. I then built a bridge across the river and took those men over the bridge. While the meteors were still molten I taught the generals to forge swords from one and tollers from the other."

Artka gazed at Sky Saber. "This sword is . . . ?"

"Yes, forged from material beyond the skies. Hence they are 'Children of the Stars'. All weapons and tools of this world were polluted with death when Mada joined Lurcan's rebellion, and so, only bring death. My weapons are not of this world but are mighty and free from the taint of death but rather, they dispel death.

"My generals decamped, armed with a new kind of weapon, and thus won recruits by the thousands, such was their zeal.

"Over time, Lurcan's cusps tricked my armies into not using, or else, misusing their swords. So, I had runes engraved on the weapons to alert my warriors to Lurcan's wiles. My warriors were urged to toll their blades daily and encourage one another to keep their tunics clean.

"This is an ancient weapon you hold. Its runes reveal powers that few have fully discovered. Use it well. Apply yourself to sharpening it and be careful to not let others sharpen it for you. If you do, when it comes back into your hand, the shine they put on it will immediately go dull. Others may instruct you how to sharpen it, but the tolling you must do yourself."

Logon turned and faced the ledge. "Tren approaches."

Borne by two roamers, Tren was lifted over the edge of the rock and gently placed beside Artka. The two Ecclessites stood side by side, grinning, but suddenly a shadow crossed Artka's face.

"Tren, about Pelton, I—"

"I told you on the flood plain that all is forgiven. It still stands. You're my brother in his place." The two embraced. Tren groaned.

Artka stepped back. "I'm sorry Tren. I forgot about your arm."

"It's more than his arm, Artka," said Logon. "His clavicle was fractured and both collar bones were severely stressed."

"Logon," Tren said, "the runes say that you heal all manner of hurts, sickness, and pains. Will you heal me?"

Logon looked tenderly at Tren. "You've served me faithfully, jeopardized your own life so Artka could arrive here. For that, I commend you. My runes do declare my power to heal, but, is that what the Advisor speaks to you?"

"No, m'lord. He speaks of patience. I hoped that meant while I waited to be lifted up here."

"You must trust me that it would not be best for you, or Artka, if I healed you now. As your bones knit you will gain appreciation for the limitations of others. You have an arduous journey ahead, and it is not without danger. But, you won't be taxed beyond your ability."

Tren nodded. "As you deem best."

"Excuse me, Logon," Artka said, "but did you say there was danger ahead, even in Ecclessa?"

"Ecclessa is not Splendora. There are no mortals in all of Ecclessa, save those born there, but even they must come and be pierced with a sword and seek me for healing, else they cannot remain in Ecclessa.

"Lurcan's spies lurk even in Ecclessa, discouraging and deceiving my warriors. Many have been deluded, and as such, are dangerous. Sky Saber will guide you. Tophets are there, too. Many cusps have stolen across on air currents infiltrating entire brigades, so heed no voices from the shadows, even if they claim to be sent by me. Reliable messengers will come in my name and will never contradict my runes, but trust not those who use my name but ignore my commands."

"What am I to do now?" Tren asked.

"I'm not sending you back to your brigade, Tren, although you could be of use there. Many leaders have been beguiled by cuspian lies, leading brigades into fruitless activity, though they're sure their busy-ness is accomplishing much. But it's all of themselves, for themselves, and not of me. They've chosen favorite runes and spend all their time tolling just that portion of their sword. Many are proud. And worse, many argue. More cusps and tophets invade Ecclessa every day—drawn by the quarrelsome attitudes and fruitless activities of my soldiers. Yes, you could be of great service there, nevertheless, I have other plans for you. Escort Artka until I indicate otherwise.

"Artka, a new brigade is forming deep in the Prophecy Mountains. Seek out Saygus the Sage. Through him you'll find that brigade. It would be best not to mention that I'm forming a new brigade."

Tren said, "I'll not be able to travel quickly, with my injuries."

Logon smiled. "Yes, Tren, you'll not be able to travel far, but, there is little need for hurry now, yet, don't tarry, either. Get Artka safely to the bridge.

"Artka, now that you own a sword, defense is also your responsibility, so be sure to toll your blade often. Tren, you guide, since you know the way to the fortress and Artka must do any fighting along the way."

Artka looked up. "Fighting?"

With that, Logon faded from view.

CHAPTER EIGHTEEN

TREN AND ARTKA ARRIVED AT the King's Gate portcullis just after dusk. They found the portcullis raised and drawbridge down, but the doors to the keep were barred. Tren leaned wearily against the granite wall. "We shouldn't have taken so many rests, Artka. This door is always open 'til dark, except during siege. We should've been here an hour ago."

"I couldn't stand seeing you in such discomfort. You needed those rests." Artka stood back and examined the parapets. "Don't seem to be any sentries on duty. How do I get them to open?"

"Odd. Watchmen are usually on duty. Nobody up there? Well, I doubt they'll open these doors 'til morning. Ease me down, will you? We'll make do out here."

Artka lowered Tren to the ground by holding his belt.

Tren released a prolonged sigh. "I'm chilly, Artka, would you make a fire?"

Artka dipped his hand into his pouch. "All my tinder is still damp."

"Mine too. Oh well, we'll just have to endure, I guess."

"I wish I had a blanket for you. Isn't it funny how dependent I was on you 'til we got to Logon's Rock and now you're dependent on me."

"Logon's law of reciprocity." Tren smiled weakly.

"Huh?"

Tren shook his head at Artka's confusion. "Later. I'm so weary, Artka. I'll probably sleep until morning despite the chill. I've been trained to ignore hunger and cold, though not in such pain." He leaned his head back and his eyes closed.

"Should I keep watch then?" Artka asked.

"Umm."

Artka hunkered down beside his friend. This was as good a time as any to try his hand at tolling Sky Saber. "Should I start at the point and work my way to the handle?"

No answer.

"Well, that seems logical," Artka said, admiring his blade, "since that's where the glow is." His scraping the metal blade disrupted the quiet. He filed again, and yet again. Sky Saber's dull edge didn't yield easily. Artka's tongue stuck out between his lips as he tolled to get some shine on his sword. Several minutes of determined effort produced only perspiration on his brow. But he kept on, until little by little, a faint glimmer beyond the point began to glow.

An hour later Artka looked up to check on Tren and enviously eyed Tren's fully glowing blade. All his efforts had produced only a mere quarter-inch-glow. Tren had invested hours making both sides of the entire blade glow. Even Captain Basso of the Sharpointer Brigade had evidently spent much time honing his Child of the Stars.

"Well, what else am I doing till dawn?" Artka bent back to his task.

Another hour passed. Tren's deep breathing and the rhythmic scrape of Artka's toller reverberating into the night were the only sounds. A sense of gratitude and love for Logon stole over Artka as Ecclessa's ideals took shape in his mind: selflessness . . . love . . . justice . . . truth. Sky Saber brightened quarter inch by quarter inch, and to Artka's delight, the top of a previously hidden rune began to glow. Though his forearms ached, and his fingers cramped, he was reluctant to stop. Carnalian pleasures were hollow compared to the simple joy of an Ecclessite tolling his sword, discovering secrets about Logon.

Another hour passed. Artka flexed his neck and shoulders and examined his work. The glow spanned three-quarters of an inch on each edge with a half-glimmering rune in the fuller. He was about to re-apply the toller when a twig snapping out of the darkness drew his attention. He peered down the nighttime road whence they'd come, but no one came. Minutes passed with only Tren's deep breathing in his ears.

Artka shrugged, leaned back against the wall and poised his toller over the blade again. As soon as the toller touched the metal another crackle came again. His scalp tingled. Was something sneaking up, covering its noise under his tolling? He slowly stood to his feet and pointed Sky Saber at the surrounding darkness, demanding with false bravado, "Who's there?"

No answer.

"Who's there," he repeated. Still no reply. He advanced a couple of steps, waving his sword back and forth menacingly.

A heavy dragging sound resonated several feet off the trail.

Artka caught his breath, remembering the first time he'd heard that sound.

He looked back at Tren slumbering. Artka steeled himself to face the approaching entity that was no longer making any attempt at concealment.

"I—I've got a Child of the Stars here," Artka said, imitating Tren, "and I'm not afraid to use it."

The breeze shifted. Artka's eyes watered and his stomach lurched at the stench. He held his sword higher.

A swirling, misty fog appeared inches from Artka's sword tip. Artka panicked and glanced backward to the greater light of Tren's sword. With Tren's brighter sword Artka felt he could stand a better defense. He leapt back and seized Star Splinter off Tren's lap.

The glow on Tren's sword suddenly receded, leaving only three-quarters of an inch aglow. Artka broke out in a cold sweat. Could tophets drain Ecclessite swords of their power?

"Artka? What are you doing?" Tren struggled to his feet. "Quick, hand me Star Splinter." Artka gave the weapon to its rightful owner. As soon as it touched Tren's hand a blast of glory sprang from tip to haft, penetrating the swirling fog revealing drooling mandibles, claws and eyestalks of a huge scorpion. "Charge when I do, Artka. My sword knows what to do, though my arm has little strength."

Artka's knuckles went white as gripped the sword and swallowed the lump in his throat. Was Tren really taking him into battle with a being from a higher plane?

Drawing a deep breath, Tren shouted, "Scorpion, I resist you in the name of Xychirion!"

Tren surged ahead as Artka leapt, slashing furiously to make up for his sword's lack of shine.

A spray burst upon them making their eyes water and their skin tingle.

"Venom?" Tren coughed, involuntarily sucking in another breath. "Press the attack."

Dizzy, nauseous, and swinging his sword blindly, Artka slashed at the fogbank until something slimy made him lose his footing. As he went down Sky Saber's point connected with something solid. A shriek filled the night air. But instead of backing off, the tophet redoubled its attack, snapping mandibles, bobbing its tail-stinger overhead. Artka rolled in a feeble attempt to strike with his sword as pincers gripped his waist. Another venomous blast of spray settled on him. Artka couldn't breathe. His vision darkened.

Tren, gasping and weak, but still on his feet, rallied his strength and stormed at the beast's head. The massive scorpion dodged just a moment too late and lost an antenna. Another fierce shriek rent the night as the monster reared up and dropped Artka.

But Tren was spent. He sagged to his knees hugging his injured arm, his face gray.

Artka sucked in a draught of fresh air and crawled to Tren's side, retching as he went.

Scorpion spray showered them again. The surrounding ground, wall and shrubbery dripped with the venom.

Both collapsed, gasping for air.

Artka watched helplessly as drooling mandibles descended toward him again. He whispered, "Xychirion," and waited for excruciating pain in his vitals.

That agony never came. In a haze, Artka fancied blue and yellow lights swirling around him accompanied by angry shouting. The shadowy pincers withdrew. Artka was floating, then everything became orange and warm.

~

Artka allowed himself the luxury of leisurely ascending from sleep. He was warm but very hungry, and his ribs ached. Opening his eyes, he found himself in a richly-paneled barracks with beamed ceiling and trestles for supports. Artka sat up.

Rows of smartly made beds lined both sides of the barracks. Crossed spears, bucklers, battle axes, and shields of battles past decorated the walls. Artka swung his feet over the bed's edge, touching his toes to the worn floorboards. He still wore his Logon tunic, but his outer clothing lay at the foot of the bed, along with Sky Saber and toller. He shivered in the chilly room as he donned his garments.

A prolonged sigh from the next cot drew his attention. Tren lay there asleep.

Artka fastened his weaponry to his belt as quietly as possible. He tiptoed between the empty bunks and exited the doorway at the far end.

A mixed aroma of eggs, venison, and sweetmeats cooking greeted Artka as he found himself on a balcony overlooking a dining hall. Neatly tucked under the balcony was a spiral stairway to the ground floor. Soldiers clustered at various tables sipping from tankards and talking in hushed tones. Good-natured laughter erupted from one group or another, making it an altogether jovial atmosphere.

"What ho! Behold, the nighttime crusader," said a portly corporal spying Artka descending the stairway. "Welcome, lad. Ye look the worse for wear, though not as poorly as when we drug ye in. Will ye no have some of our humble fare until ye can return to your own regiment's more glorious nourishment?"

"Surely the food here must be very good, from the looks of you, sir," Artka replied before thinking.

The dining hall erupted in laughter and someone shouted, "He's pegged you right, hasn't he, Clepy?"

More laughter followed, and the red-faced corporal put a beefy arm around Artka's shoulders. "Well said, laddie, well said. Will ye no come and break your fast?"

No sooner had Artka sat at the table, saying, "I'd like that," than a plate of eggs, fried venison strips, browned potatoes, and dark, buttered bread was plopped down before him along with a tankard of spiced tea.

Several men gathered around, waiting for Artka to finish his meal so they could ask him about the fight with the tophet. Artka finished and pushed his plate away, uncomfortable from eating too much, too fast.

"Now then laddie, are ye minded to share so urgent a mission as brought ye to our gate at such an hour?" Corporal Clepy said.

"Well," Artka began, "I guess it'd be all right. We—that is, I, had just met Logon, and—"

"What? For the first time?"

"Ahh now, is it so?"

"How grand."

Corporal Clepy clapped his hands loudly. "Let the lad speak without fussing and carrying on. Ye act like mother hens. Go ahead, lad, tell us your tale."

"Well, yes, it was my first time—well, sort of—to meet Logon. Anyway, this time he healed my heart—"

Several gladder responses greeted this revelation, but a raised eyebrow from Clepy silenced them.

Artka recounted his story, beginning with losing his way in the Wind Break Forest. He judiciously omitted the duel with Pelton, however, not sure how that information would be received.

" . . . and so, we camped outside the gate, since it was shut for the night. That's when the tophet attacked. I really don't know how we got away."

The men nodded approvingly at each other.

Corporal Clepy said, "A fitting tale deserves a fitting end, as I like to say. Let me apprise ye of what ye don't ken. The tophet's shrieks alerted a sentry. We sent out a patrol to investigate—quite a dangerous thing in the dark of night like that, I might add. Anyway, in the light of our lanterns and torches we saw ye both a-lying on the ground about to get et by the foggy beastie. We charged and drove him off into the forest. That's aboot all there is to tell, except we brought ye both inside, washed the venom off ye, and put ye abed to sleep away the effects. That was two days ago, laddie."

"Two days?"

"Aye, and ye slept like babes all the while. Now, tell me, if ye were at the gate, why did ye no clamor to be let in? Surely ye must ha' known someone would be aboot."

"We, tried, but no one heard us."

"To be sure, things weren't usual that night, it being the captain's twenty-first anniversary with his missus. Most of the watch was called off the wall to join the celebration. Oh, and what a bash it was, too. The more's the pity ye could no ha' been there. Ye'd have had a great time of it, laddie."

The other soldiers, having their curiosity satisfied, drifted away, leaving Artka and Clepy alone.

"How is Tren," Artka asked.

"Ach now, ye know he's received grave injuries to his arm and shoulders, and no wonder, facing a dread of the gate, as ye tell it. The venom ye got sprayed with worsens bodily injuries. But, with rest, he'll soon be set to rights. No need to worry yourself aboot him. He'll likely be the cause of some discussion hereabouts when he wakes, though." Clepy's eyes twinkled.

"What do you mean?" Artka asked.

"His sword, laddie. We seldom see a sword as lit up as his. There be some feel it's improper to sharpen the sword that much."

Artka remembered Captain Basso's hostility. "Will that be a problem?"

"Well now," Clepy said thoughtfully, "for some, it's a pile of rocks for their flinger. Suffice it to say it'll keep things from getting dull."

"If that was an answer, I missed it," Artka said.

"Now, don't trouble yourself, laddie. Ye'll not be the source of contention. Ye're accepted by all good men here, for all can see that ye're but a recruit, as is borne out by your story."

"You can tell?"

"Your sword shows little, but zealous work. Much of what ye had on it has dimmed a mite since we brought ye in," Clepy said with a wink.

Artka examined his weapon. Most of what had been aglow was now gray. Even the top half of the rune was no longer visible.

"It takes persistence, laddie. Dinna forget ye've neglected your sword for two days. But, ye'll find that what was once sharpened will quickly recapture its glow with less effort. Well, I must be aboot me duties. Feel free to wander the fortress. This will always be a place for ye to find asylum on your journeys to and from Carnalia."

Artka took a sip from his tankard as he watched the corporal leave, then surveyed the room. Spying some young men jovially engaged in sharpening their swords at a firepit, he approached, asking, "May I join you?"

"Please do," said one.

Artka sat on a bench and withdrew Sky Saber. His comrades introduced themselves, but Artka was too distracted to remember their names. They returned to their tolling, filling the hearth with the noise of files scraping steel.

"So, Artka," asked one, "to which brigade are you assigned?"

"Logon asked me not to disclose that information, but I think it's all right to tell you that we, my friend and I, are to seek out a sage named Saygus for directions."

"Saygus?" another said. "Are you sure Logon wants you to seek him?"

"Yes, Saygus, that's his name. Something wrong with that?"

"No, not if you like crackpots and lunatics."

His companions chuckled.

"I didn't know Saygus had been re-commissioned," said another. "Not after the court-martial."

"Oh, Saygus isn't the captain," Artka said. "Logon told me Saygus would guide me through the Prophecy Mountains to the brigade."

"Oh well, that's a different matter then."

"I didn't know there were any brigades left in the Prophecy Mountains," said a third man. "How about it Harnet, do you know of any?"

"Mmm, not off hand, but maybe Logon directed one back in again. It's a good place to learn mountain tactics."

"What need is there for defense on that side of the river? We're the frontier, here on this side," said a young man with handsome features and fiery red hair.

"Maybe Logon's plan for Artka doesn't involve a brigade in the Prophecy Mountains," said another with a sly grin.

"What foolishness is that?" demanded the red-haired youth. "Of course, Logon wants him in a brigade. He wants everyone in a brigade."

"Now Reddy, don't get upset. I agree, he should be in a brigade. But, since we don't know of any brigades in those mountains maybe Logon has something else in mind."

"Such as?" Reddy asked.

"Well . . . other than military things, what are the Prophecy Mountains noted for?"

Everyone's toller paused.

Harnet broke the silence with a conspiratorial, "Oh!"

One by one the others caught on, saying, "Oh," winking and poking each other with their elbows.

Artka, feeling the brunt of their joke, said, "What are you all laughing at?"

"Oh, Artka, don't you know what the Prophecy Mountains are known for?"

"Famous for," said another.

Artka shook his head. "Enlighten me."

"Why, the fairest maidens in all of Ecclessa dwell in the foothills of those mountains." Giggles broke into guffaws.

"Maidens?" Artka blushed. "You've got it all wrong. There's a new brigade that Logon is for—"

They all stopped laughing and looked at Artka in surprise.

"Go on," Reddy said. "That Logon is for . . . forming? Is that it? Is Logon forming a new brigade? And he's sending you to be part of it?"

"I wasn't supposed to tell," Artka said sitting back, his toller resting on his knees.

"Well now, isn't that something?" Harnet murmured.

Gradually the tolling resumed, but instead of light banter, each young soldier silently considered the possibilities.

CHAPTER NINETEEN

ARTKA PASSED THE REST OF the afternoon investigating the fortress and meeting new friends. After the evening meal he ascended back to the dorm where Tren still slept off the effects of the tophet venom. Artka sat on his cot, took out Sky Saber, and inspected its partially restored glow.

"Artka," Tren whispered.

"I didn't mean to wake you."

"S'all right, Artka," Tren said. "Ooh! Whassa matter wi' me? I feel drunk. My head . . . Say . . . where are we?"

"Inside King's Gate Fortress. We were rescued from the scorpion tophet, washed, tended, and put to bed. That was two days ago."

Tren grunted, lay back and closed his eyes. Artka stood, intending to go and let his friend finish sleeping when Tren asked, "Tell me they unmade the beast."

"No. Clepy, uh, Corporal Clepy, told me they chased it into the forest."

Tren grimaced as he sat up, bracing his forehead in his good hand. "That's the trouble with Sharpointers. If only they'd light up more of their swords they'd be able to see through the mist to the creature's vitals instead of blindly slashing away hoping to hit something."

"I should think you'd be glad we were rescued."

Tren smiled. "Quite right, Artka. I am thankful. You're learning, that's good." Tren's right arm was splinted and wrapped up to and around his shoulder. His other shoulder was also wrapped but not splinted.

"How do you feel, Tren, not counting the effects of the venom?"

"Not well enough for travel, if that's what you're asking. Otherwise, I'm alright. Venomous spray. Now that's a new one. Never fought a venom-spewing tophet before."

"The garrison here seems to know a lot about spitters, as they call them," Artka said. "They knew we'd sleep off the worst of it once we were washed, and it seems they were right."

Tren dressed slowly. Picking up Star Splinter, he said, "My, my, you certainly look neglected."

"What happened to your sword?" Artka noted with alarm that several inches of Tren's sword had faded. While Artka's had lost only a miniscule amount, Tren's had lost much. "Did the tophet do that to it?"

"The tophet? No, they have no power against Children of the Stars. Don't worry, Artka. It'll come back with a little effort. Didn't Logon tell you if you didn't toll daily the shine would fade?"

"But so much?"

"Only because I have so much to keep sharp. It'll brighten easily again. Now, how about assisting me to the dining hall?"

Artka's arm circled Tren's waist as he helped his friend through the dorm and down the stairway.

Tren was greeted with the same enthusiasm that had met Artka earlier. A platter of venison, eggs, bread, and vegetables was set before him with a steaming mug which Tren accepted without hesitation. Off duty soldiers gathered around as Tren ate, waiting for him to finish.

Since Tren told the same story as Artka, but from his point of view, everyone's curiosity was satisfied. After excusing themselves, most of them wandered off. Artka hopefully kept an eye out for some of the friends he'd met earlier. Not seeing them, he assumed they were on duty.

A group of lieutenants approached and plied Tren with questions about runes, tactics, and long-ago battles. At a loss to understand the complexities of the discussion, Artka wandered away, looking for something else to do. He spied a young man sitting alone on a bench by the hearth and decided to make his acquaintance.

"Hello, I'm Artka."

"Brendle," said the youth, extending a hand. "Yes, I figured you were Artka, and the other fellow must be Tren. You've both gained some notoriety hereabouts."

"Why is that?"

"Oh, it's mostly due to the fact that nothing much ever happens, that's all. You two have provided everybody with something to chat about."

"Surely your warriors have exploits to talk about."

"Oh, there are some show-offs who go out and stir up the enemy, but they always high-tail it back here when it gets too hot," he said with a chuckle.

Artka sat down to work on his blade.

"Why are you doing that, trying to make non-com, or something?"

"Why am I doing what?" Artka asked.

"Sharpening your sword."

"Well," Artka said, "isn't that what we're supposed to do? Especially new recruits like us?"

Brendle stood, his brow furrowed. "What makes you think I'm a recruit?"

"Well, you don't have much shine on your sword."

"That's not the way it is," Brendle huffed. "I've been in Logon's army four years now, assigned to this post three of those four."

"Oh. Sorry I offended you."

"Well, okay," Brendle resettled in his seat.

"But you must've seen some fighting in your three years of duty here. Were you in the battle of the Wind Break Forest?"

Brendle stared unblinking at Artka. "Look, did you come over here to start an argument?"

Artka looked up. "I—I thought maybe we could be friends. Look, if I'm bothering you, I can find somewhere else—"

"No, no. Sit down, Artka. I'm sorry for snapping. It's just that I get harped on a lot about sharpening my sword and preparing for battle."

"Well, shouldn't you?"

"Look, you're a new recruit. You don't know anything yet. Have they told you about when your sword won't glow no matter how hard you try, or when Logon seems to have forgotten you, or when everything goes wrong? Well, have they?"

Artka made no reply.

"No, of course they haven't. I'll bet they haven't even told you that the more your blade glows, the more of a target you are to cusps and tophets, not to mention highly-skilled Carnalians who intentionally seek out 'brightbladers'. You have to fight harder just to stay alive. Well, I've had enough of that. I used to have several inches aglow but let them go dull again. My tip is sharp, that's all I need to be admitted to Splendora when I die. If some Carnalian wants to be rescued, he can come and ask, and I'll be obliged to pierce his heart. But don't expect me to stick my neck out."

Artka sat, mouth open, toller hovering in mid-stroke.

"A rune in the middle of my blade tells an interesting story," Tren said from behind their bench, breaking in on their conversation. He winced as he extended Star Splinter between Artka and Brendle and tapped the rune in question. "Would you lads care to hear it?"

"I don't suppose we can stop you, can we?" Brendle said.

"No, but neither can I make you listen. Will you listen?"

Artka nodded.

Brendle stared moodily into the fire. "Maybe."

"That's close enough for me." Tren settled on the bench between Artka and Brendle. "Long ago, before Logon took on human form, two powerful kings had a disagreement. War, which would have ruined both their countries, seemed unavoidable. But a wise man counseled them to select fifty of their best warriors to fight it out on neutral ground. Seeing wisdom in the man's counsel, both kings pledged to abide by the results of the contest, thus sparing each nation the devastation of war. Champions from each side were chosen and ordered to fight until only soldiers of one side or the other remained, thus settling the kings' argument.

"On the appointed day the hundred combatants were barricaded into a box canyon. A great bonfire was lit at the only exit, so no one could leave until men of one king or the other stood victorious. The battle commenced. Flames were kept high at the canyon's entry. Smoke billowed so thick that neither king could tell how his fighters fared. The ringing of swords, halberds, and axes on shields, along with the cries of the dying, were heard all that afternoon.

"Just before sundown sounds of battle ceased. The fires were doused to let the victors emerge. Through the smoke and steam two men were seen standing side by side at the canyon's far end, weapons lowered. Their uniforms were so besmeared with grime and gore that, in the failing light, neither king could tell which side had won. The kings repeatedly summoned the warriors to come forward and be identified, but neither man moved.

"In frustration, the two kings crossed the smoldering ashes and approached the surviving battlers. When close enough, they were angered to see that one soldier from each side still stood.

"'Kill him!' demanded each king of his champion, pointing at the other's warrior. With grim countenances, each warrior spun about and advanced upon his own king. Unarmed and away from their body-guards, the kings tried to flee. The youthful warriors easily overtook their lordships and threw them to the ground, each putting his sword at his own king's throat. The defenseless kings pled for mercy, promising half their kingdoms if their lives would be spared.

"One of the warriors asked, 'Why should I settle for half, when for the thrust of my sword, I can have all?'"

Tren fell silent.

"Come on, Tren, what happened next?" Artka implored.

"That's all the rune says," said Tren. "But one night as I tolled and meditated, the Advisor had Star Splinter sing the rune's lesson to me."

"And?"

"What about you?" Tren asked Brendle. "Aren't you curious?"

"I think it's a dumb story. No king worth his salt would let himself be caught without bodyguards, or at least his own weapon."

Tren laughed. "Precisely what the runesong taught. Only a fool sits back unprepared for life's battles, letting others do his fighting for him."

Brendle jumped up. "I don't have to sit here and be abused by you glory-seekers." He stalked across the dining hall, frowning at anyone who as much as looked in his direction.

"Artka, have you learned anything?"

"The rune's lesson? I think it means that we're vulnerable if we don't make the necessary preparations to be ready for the fight. Am I close?"

"And they say 'marching with Erotons makes one lose his wits,'" Tren said.

"Why did Brendle react like that?"

Easing against the backrest Tren said, "What specifically discouraged him, I don't know, but I'm certain he's violated one or another of Logon's commands and refuses to admit it, even to himself. I've seen many similar reactions. A man joins Logon's forces, eager for glory, but when he's challenged to a deeper commitment, there's an unwillingness to follow orders. He becomes insensitive to the Advisor. Instead of becoming more familiar with his sword, he doubts that the sword will defend him. Gradually, if he persists in that condition, he'll begin to harbor bitterness, even to the point of baring his teeth at the counselors Logon sends to warn or encourage him.

"You yourself might be tempted to disregard your sword's precepts at some point. But if you rise above the temptation and obey Logon, you'll grow wiser and stronger and more adept at recognizing the Advisor's voice. Never forget: Logon's words are on that blade, and will master all opponents, human or otherwise. But the wielder of the sword must faithfully cling to it."

"Are there many like Brendle?"

"Hmm, I think Brendle is a bit extreme. And I sense something of Lurcan's influence—and that, my friend, is becoming all too common in Logon's brigades."

"Who could ignore such a splendid weapon?" Artka pondered aloud, rubbing his fingers over some visible runes etched on the side of his blade.

"I'm glad that you feel that way but be on guard. Certain influences may entice you with inferior weapons. Back when I was a recruit, four of my friends and I were surrounded by several of our old Carnalian cronies. They tried to persuade us to come back to the emperor's service. When we refused, they tried various tactics to get us to change our minds. Our faces flushed as they ridiculed our glowing swords. They teased us, saying we had stayed out all night catching fireflies to make our blades glow because we were afraid of the dark.

"Finally, when all else failed, they drew swords and challenged us to a fight, offering to let us use black iron Carnalian swords that we'd previously earned the right to bear. Two of my friends had spent little time tolling their Child of the Stars, and so, accepted the proffered empire swords. They fought valiantly but, whilst the three of us stood our ground, even managing to rescue one of our persecutors, the two who resorted to Lurcan's weaponry were captured."

"Well," Artka said, "I've seen your Child of the Stars in action. Nothing can entice me to lay mine aside."

"Don't take it wrong if I say that I hope you keep that conviction. Many begin with sincere hearts, but after a while, lose their love for Logon and his runes."

Artka nodded and gave Sky Saber another stroke.

"This castle doesn't house a regular brigade," Tren said, along another vein. "Many brigades pause here on their way to other places: Sharpointers, Wholebladers, Runers, Onedgers, Tipsters . . ."

"I know, I've seen the different brigades' insignias overtop Logon's tunic. I saw ones that had 'I'm a slave of Logon' tooled into his scabbard. I was thinking maybe . . . of . . . ."

Tren pursed his lips. "How bright were the swords inside those flashy scabbards?"

"I didn't see their swords, exactly, but their love for Logon is certainly evident on their leathers."

"Ah yes, their leathers sure have a lot to say. In fact, I happen to know that that brigade lets their leathers do most of their fighting. When you were a Carnalian, just what would you have thought if you had encountered a kingsman thusly decorated?"

"I guess I would've thought he loved his master."

"Have you so quickly forgotten how Carnalians think? Not that you should live and fight according to Carnalian standards, but keep in mind how Carnalians perceive things. Elyon's warfare requires a fine balance of obedience to Logon while at the same time, not appearing ridiculous."

"I hadn't thought of that."

"Admit it, wouldn't those 'Logon slogans' have convinced you that Ecclessites were bewitched? Is it any wonder Carnalians believe the lie about a Magician mesmerizing kingsmen?"

"Yeah, I guess so. Why don't those brigades understand that?"

"They would if they'd spend more time tolling their blades and less time tooling their leathers. Look at it this way, Artka: Lurcan fears the glow on your blade, the light in your eyes and fire in your heart, not what's emblazoned on your battle gear. Decorated battle gear mainly impresses other Ecclessites. Better their sword should speak rather than their leathers. Your love for Logon will be obvious by how often you toll and follow the instructions of your sword. In fact, during a battle, I once saw leathers boasting fidelity to Logon—on an Eroton who wore it in mockery."

A white-haired sergeant came up and leaned over the back of the bench saying, "Excuse me, Tren, the captain wants a word with you."

Tren looked up. "Barah, my old friend. How are you?"

"I'm fine, as you can see," he said, holding up his sword for inspection. It was halfway aglow with several shimmering runes enhancing the shine. "Sometimes," Barah bent over and whispered, "when cusps close in on me, I get Spark Fire out, and soon it sings, gently, melodically. When I'm finished, the cusps are gone."

Tren smiled. "May I introduce Artka? Artka, this is Barah, an old friend."

Artka clasped hands with the elderly man and was surprised at the strength in his sinewy grip. "You've just been to Logon. I see his glow all about you."

"Barah senses unseen things," Tren said. "It's a gift the Advisor has given him."

"Tren guided me to Logon five, or was it six years ago? Oh, what a time we had of it, eh? What a time."

"Yes, we had a struggle, didn't we? Uh, hadn't you better lead me to the captain, old friend? It's been so long since I've been here, I'm not sure where his HQ is now. But don't go too fast, for I've been slowed down, as you see."

"Eh? The captain? Oh, the captain! He wants to see you, but I already said that, didn't I? He did say to hurry—but he always tells me to hurry. I sometimes get distracted. Say, did I tell you that—?"

"I think you'd best tell me later. You were going to lead me . . . ?"

The old sergeant chuckled, tugging playfully at his white beard. He led Tren across the dining hall to a torch-lit passageway with a massive, inset oaken door.

Artka bent to tolling his sword and was soon caught up in the joy of belonging to Logon.

"Say, you're coming along very nicely," Artka looked up at a dark-haired, young man who motioned to an empty bench. "Mind if I join you?"

"Not at all, after all, this is more your fortress than mine," Artka said.

"Well, we're all wanderers, especially on this side of the river. This fortress is a gathering place for those coming and going—or not sure what to do. Allow me to introduce myself. They call me Debator, though my actual name is Reasno. I hail from Sophista, in Craniantium, but was trained in Ecclessa near the village of Conformity."

"Artka, from Cosmopolis. Seems strange to say that. I keep thinking of myself as an Ecclessite now, though I've never even been there."

"Ah, yes. Well, as I said, you're doing a nice job on your blade."

"Thanks. Like Logon said, the more I apply myself, the less of a chore and more a joy it becomes. I hope to get more of this blade shining before I see combat."

"Oh, so you're headed to the front?"

"I didn't mean it like that. Sorry, Reasno—"

"Debator. Everyone calls me that, and I prefer it."

"Okay, Debator. I'm going to Ecclessa for training as soon as Tren gets well enough to travel."

"Oh, so you and your friend are, shall we say, rescued at the gate the other night."

"That's right. We were nearly killed. Fortunately, the night watch came when they did and drove the tophet away."

Reasno smiled dubiously. "Come now, Artka, you don't have to pretend with me. I'm enlightened. I know there wasn't a real tophet. What really happened out there? Over-imbibe some Carnalian brew, or something?"

Artka's eyes narrowed. "I misunderstand you, sir. Could you speak plainer?"

"If you like. We both know tophets don't exist, I mean, really. They're a legend made up by the emperor to keep his populace in fear of the king. Even Logon, when he lived as a man, merely used the terminology of the culture so that people could relate to his concepts. I have to laugh whenever I hear someone telling me how he struggled with a cusp or a tophet. I know they're just covering up for some indiscretion."

"You—you don't believe tophets exist?"

"Of course, they don't. That's how I know you two are covering up something embarrassing. Oh sure, you fooled most of the soldiers here, they eat up that kind of talk. But we both know you didn't really encounter a being from a higher plane the other night, don't we? So, what really happened?"

"Sir, I—"

"Debator, please call me Debator."

"Sir, if you're calling me a liar—and I think you are—then I must—"

"Now, now Artka, nobody's calling you a liar. Besides, what is a lie, really? Even truth can be told in such a way as to deceive, and

falsehoods often convey truths, you know. If Logon used the terminology, why shouldn't you? I'm merely inquiring as to the real nature
of your, er, discomfiture, that's all. Liar? Splendora, no! I'd never call
anyone a liar. A manipulator of facts maybe—all quite permissible,
mind you. But if you're not inclined to reveal what really went on,
that's fine with me. Why you don't is obvious, but I don't mind. Your
business is yours. By the by, do you mind if I sharpen my weapon?"

"Like I said before—"

"I know, it's my fortress more than yours. A position you seem to have
arrived at merely because you think I've been posted here longer than you."

"Haven't you?"

"In one sense, yes. In another sense, you have a right to claim exclu-
sive right to this area before the hearth on the same grounds—previous habitation. On the other hand, I could challenge that argument
by questioning whether anyone has the right, indeed—if even Logon
has the right to est—"

"You speak a lot of words that say nothing. I see why they call
you Debator."

"I hope you're not offended. I really can't help myself. I mean
no malice."

"I'm not sure what to think of you, yet. But, you're welcome to
share the fireside."

"You know, you really are quite a personable fellow, albeit laden
down with out-dated notions and who knows what shameful practices,
but you have a nice personality."

Artka longed to convince Reasno that the tophet attack had been
real, not a fantasy. He wanted to prove that Reasno was mistaken about
tophets and cusps, but an inner caution prevented him.

Debator rummaged beneath his cloak and extracted a dagger.

Artka could scarce take his eyes off the dazzling, beauteous knife. It was fashioned like a Child of the Stars, and although it sparkled brightly, had no glow of its own. The eagle/dove handle was made of polished mother-of-pearl; the silvery, double-edged blade reflected red, blue, and orange gleams from the fireplace made it appear to be high-quality steel.

Debator, nonchalantly filed away with a common, iron file, pretended not to notice Artka's admiration of his dagger.

"What have you got there?" Artka finally asked, still eyeing the elegant cutlery.

"What, you mean this?" Debator held up his knife. "Why, this is what I use most of the time in combat. It's much easier to handle than those unwieldy swords. Look closely," he urged, holding the dagger up for Artka's scrutiny. "See? All the hidden runes of either side are revealed. It's much easier to file, too. Just a few minutes honing makes it sharp. And it stays sharp until used. Here, have a look."

Artka took the dagger in his hands, careful not to smudge the blade. "It's beautiful. Did Logon make these, too?"

"Logon? Well, in a way he did. Yes, in a sense you could say that Logon made them, as he made all things. This weapon taught me the art of debating. I can win almost any argument against Ecclessites or Carnalians. Sometimes even Craniantiumites. I've nicked a good number of them in open combat, I don't mind telling you."

"I wish Logon had given me one of these, too," Artka said wistfully. "I appreciate Sky Saber, but—"

"Sky Saber? You believe that legend about twin meteors following Logon through some distant star and all?"

"Yes. Logon told me—"

"There you go again. Everything Logon said wasn't meant to be taken at face value. He often reverted to the terminology and concepts people of that era understood. Don't you get it? The runes aren't the real truth, but only the relative truth. The real truth is hidden inside the relative truths." Debator smiled as he eyed Artka. "I can get you one of these, if you'd like, but I doubt it'll do you much good, seeing you still cling to superstition. I was trained how to use this dagger at the Daggerman Brigade. A couple of years there would do you a world of good. For one thing, you'd be spared needless hours of tolling but still only have relative truths whereas daggers divulge the real truths straight off."

"But I really did see tophets."

"You know, I believe you think you did. You must want the relative truth so badly that you've deluded yourself. You'd better get hold of your senses before you become a fanatic like those fools in Wholeblader Brigades. Wait here. I'll bring you a dagger. The daggers show what Logon really wants you to know. But don't use your toller on it. For some reason tollers just tear daggers apart. Uh, if you're finished, can I have mine back?" Receiving his dagger back, Debator winked and headed for the stairs. "I'll be back in a jiffy."

Artka watched Debator walk away, then stared into the fire and scratched his head. He absent-mindedly placed Sky Saber and its toller on the bench. Reasno's dagger still danced in Artka's mind's eye. Its cool touch lingered on his fingertips.

"Why shouldn't I have one, if Logon made them? Why shouldn't I receive advanced training to sort out the relative truth from the real?"

CHAPTER TWENTY

"ARTKA?"

Artka started.

Tren was walking across the great hall. "Artka," he called again when he drew near, "Captain Metid wants me to stay a few weeks to instruct his troops about sharpening the entire blade. Are you alright with that?"

"Uh, sure, sure."

"After all, Logon said we need not hurry, and it's going to be weeks until I'm ready for sustained travel. We might as well make ourselves useful while we're here, right? Say, are you okay? You look kind of distracted."

"Huh, oh, I was just thinking. I'm fine. Maybe a little tired. It's been a long day."

"For me too, though I've only been up a couple of hours. I'm still weak from that venom. How about you?"

"Venom? Oh that! Uh, yeah, I'm still tired, too."

Tren bent over and looked closely at his charge. "Something's wrong. Tell me."

Artka snapped, "What makes you so sure something's wrong?"

Tren's eyebrows rose. "That does." Tren grasped Artka's chin with his good hand, forcing eye contact. "What went on here in the last half hour? Do I sense a cusp's influence?"

Artka tried to pull away.

Tren winced but held Artka firmly.

"Let me alone, Tren." Anger flashed in Artka's eyes. "You wouldn't want me to have one, but it's all right because Logon made them."

"I want whatever Logon wants for you." Tren released Artka's chin. "What thing? I won't deny it to you. You alone must make those decisions. I'll offer advice, but what you do is up to you. Whether you're right or wrong, I'll not interfere other than give counsel."

"Really?" Artka squinted at Tren out of the corner of his eye.

"Really."

Artka dropped his gaze to the stone floor. "Do you know Reasno?"

"I don't think so. Why?"

"He's also called Debator."

"Debator? The Daggermen recruiter? Oh, Artka, say no more. He's tempted you with a dagger."

Artka blushed.

"Yes, didn't I sense a cusp?"

"Logon made them, Debator said so," Artka said, an edge in his voice.

"Are you so ready to entertain lies and doubt truth? Think man, do you love Logon more for having been exposed to a dagger? Don't answer. Let me tell you what I know about those daggers."

Artka folded his arms and stared sullenly into the fire.

"Many runes were inscribed on our Children of the Stars by Atel," Tren began, "although those nearer the tip were made by Logon's original generals. In the intervening years following Logon's resurrection to await his triumphant reclamation of this world, Lurcan deluded certain kingsmen creating confusion among Ecclessa's rank and file. Emboldened, Lurcan spawned counterfeits of the Children of the Stars.

"One of the dreads, Broack, master of cusps, was skilled in metallurgy. He labored long years, finally producing imitations of Ecclessite swords. But, they were flawed, falling to pieces when clashing with real Children of the Stars. Only a few kingsmen were fooled by them.

"Then Broack tried shrinking the fake swords which strengthened their structural integrity; thus, daggers were invented. Thousands and thousands were forged in those days. Rumor had it that Broack's own sweat tempered the steel so that anyone possessing a dagger would fall under his influence.

"Some half-committed Ecclessites were deceived with promises of wealth and power, and so, wittingly or unwittingly, smuggled daggers into Ecclessa, passing them off as a complementary weapon. Anyone who received a dagger soon grew cold of heart toward Logon while those who relied only on their swords remained faithful to Logon. It was then that Logon instructed Atel to inscribe runes on the Children of the Stars, providing a safeguard for differentiating truth from lies.

"This rune," Tren tapped the middle of his blade, " . . . reads:

'The Children of the Stars,
Sent with Logon's breath,
When wielded by one faithful,
Will conquer even death.
This only weapon given,
Will all sufficient prove,
When warrior is devoted,
His hope will not remove.
A life alive it rescues,
For Logon is its word,
And justice surely given,
For those who keenly heard.'

"Logon has sanctioned no other weapon to teach kingsmen how to live and rescue lives. In the empire you were issued all manner of body armor; but among Ecclessites the sword provides the basics of our protection. The world's weaponry can bring only death. Keep in mind Artka, we don't slay or harm our human enemies, but instead, seek to rescue them. Daggers wound and kill. And when fighting tophets or cusps—would a dagger be a good weapon choice?"

"But, it looks so innocent, so regal . . . so . . . "

"Seductive?"

"That's not exactly the word I'd use."

"It's more accurate than enticing, though, isn't it?"

Artka hung his head.

"Artka, I'm going to show you a rune that isn't ordinarily revealed to recruits. But, I think you need to learn it now."

Artka glanced around the room for an excuse to leave, but he and Tren were alone in the keep's great hall. He sighed and leaned back.

Tren touched a glowing rune half-way down his blade and said, "Every moral failure comes through one of three avenues. The first, things that bedazzle your eyes. All Carnalia lies paralyzed by the baubles Lurcan openly dangles before them. Carnalians see only what they want to see, and nothing else. But, your eyes, Artka, have been opened to the true nature of things, thus you should be able to see through the glitter of trinkets—such as daggers. When an Ecclessite yearns for sparkly things the way Carnalians do, he loses the ability to discern the fraud in them and is drawn back to serving Lurcan."

Artka squirmed.

"The second is bodily appetites. Once you allow your eyes to wander, it isn't long before your body craves what your eyes behold.

The Carnalian pleasures you once indulged replay in your memory. Kingsmen returning to Carnalian pleasures soon fall under the power of revived appetites. They no longer heed Logon and are useless for rescuing lives from the empire."

Artka stared at his feet.

"Love for Logon is forgotten. Guilt for disobeying is aroused, further weakening one's good intentions. There's a rune that says, 'You are owned by your pursuits'.

"Unchecked, those two avenues lead to the third failure, which is exalting one's own plans without a care as to whether Logon approves. Such individuals no longer receive correction. They're convinced they already know all that's worthwhile. Logon and the Advisor are soon forgotten, oh, their lips give him polite recognition, but their heart is full of Carnalian pride. Sadly," Tren shook his head, "such ones sometimes enjoy prominence in certain brigades. They add nothing and detract much. Their swords are forgotten, losing all keenness."

"Don't they die in battle?"

"Battle? Such men seldom, if ever, see battle, or if they do, the enemy recognizes them as double agents and leaves them unmolested. Logon will eventually deal with them, though. Now, has this poisonous process begun in you?"

Artka raised his eyes to Tren's. "I suppose maybe."

"Um-hmm, are you willing to forsake it?"

Artka sighed and nodded.

"Say it out loud, Artka. I want to hear you promise that you won't seek a dagger."

Artka shuddered briefly. "All right. I promise. I won't seek a dagger." Two simultaneous things occurred as he spoke: a sense of loss, but deeper, in his heart, the joy of Logon returned.

"I see Logon's light springing to your eyes again, Artka. That's good. I must warn you of one more thing, then we're off to bed."

Artka scanned the dining hall. Debator hadn't returned, but, Artka would stand by his decision: when he saw Debator, he'd say firmly, "No, thanks!"

Tren resumed, "Whether because of Broack's sweat or just that they're Lurcanish in nature, cusps lurk near daggers—even in Ecclessite fortresses. Cusps will whisper things like, 'They're so desirable,' making you think it's your own thought, so be warned. Toll your Sky Saber since only light drives away shadows."

"Thanks, Tren," Artka said with a smile. "I'm glad you made me listen."

"I'm glad you listened. New recruits are targeted by cusps who hope to reclaim them before they get established in Ecclessite ways. Come, it's time for bed."

The two ascended the spiral stair to the dormitory, put their garments on the foot of their beds, and slipped beneath the covers. Soon sleep claimed Artka.

~

Early morning light crept through the small portal windows into the dorm. As Artka rolled over his foot felt something weighty. He sat up; no one else in the barracks stirred. There was something sparkly by his feet. He squinted in the dim lighting and caught his breath as a stab of the sun's first light streamed through the window.

Glinting in the dawn's early rays atop his coverlet lay an exquisite, sparkling dagger.

CHAPTER TWENTY-ONE

TREN SPENT A GOOD PORTION of the morning getting re-wrapped by the post's surgeons. Their diagnosis: three weeks at least before he could travel. Fighting was out of the question, though less strenuous exercise, if not too uncomfortable, might prove beneficial.

While Tren was thus occupied, Artka took the liberty to explore the fortress. There were ten barrack rooms arranged like the one he and Tren occupied, five on the ground floor and five on the upper level, all opening into the keep's great hall. The banqueting hall could accommodate several hundred people at a time. Ground-floor exits led outside to training fields. The outer wall of the castle was foursquare with bastions on each corner. The crenellated ramparts rose thirty feet above the ground and had five-foot wide runways behind an outcropping that discouraged scaling. Towers perched on each of the corners maintained constant vigil of the approaches. Unlike empire towers, however, these parapets lacked catapults and pitch pots. Apparently, these towers were for observation or hand to hand combat only.

Two gates admitted entry to the fortress, one in the middle of the westerly wall that opened to the very road Artka and Tren had recently traveled and the other, an exit, was in the center of the easterly wall, opening directly onto Logon's Bridge which crossed the Flaming Sword River, ending at the King's Gate Fortress East in Ecclessa.

"King's Gate Fortresses have never been breached," boasted Reddy, Artka's guide, "though there've been several near calls." Artka stood upon an eastern parapet and watched banners across the river unfurling in the breeze. "But each time sack and pillage threaten, a champion arises to rally the troops and turn the tide. However, this fortress is eventually destined to fall, as foretold on the Children of the Stars. That downfall—all in King Elyon's plan, you understand—will mark the beginning of final judgment on Carnalia. A devastating chain of events will follow, ending with Logon Xychirion riding forth in fury to destroy Lurcan, the empire, its warlords, soldiers, and citizens."

Artka couldn't help but think of Jeda and his friends who'd be forever lost.

"Hungry for lunch?" Reddy invited. "The dinner bell's about to sound, marking the end of my duty. I'm right glad, too. The wind has turned raw. Atop this pile of rocks is no place to be in harsh weather."

Even as Reddy spoke a clanging gong resounded in the bailey below. Reddy and Artka, along with a dozen other watchmen, filed out of the tower into a biting wind. They scurried for the corner blockhouse where a dining area was maintained for soldiers on watch.

They encountered their replacements heading the other way. One of them encouraged, "We've got a real trainer now. Had him this morning. He sure knows what he's about with a sword. You'll likely be assigned to him this afternoon."

"I hope your ignorance hasn't drained him of everything he knows, Harnet," Reddy teased.

Harnet's only reply was to cross his eyes as he trotted to his post.

"He probably means your friend, Tren," Reddy said as they hustled into the dining room. Four long tables with benches filled the room;

a cheery fire blazed away in a corner fireplace. Men from the south tower already occupied one of the tables.

As soon as Artka and his companions were seated, the door blew open again admitting a blast of frigid air and a dozen more watchmen.

"Them poor blokes a-havin' ter come all the way round from the nor' tower in this wind" laughed a gigantic newcomer dressed in animal furs and leggings instead of normal military attire. He towered above everyone in the room. His beard, long and thick, had no whiskers where he'd obviously been scarred from previous battles.

Artka stared at the hulking man. "Eroton!" he muttered loud enough to be heard. "I'd know that dialect anywhere."

"Shh," Reddy tugged Artka's sleeve. "He *was* an Eroton. Now he's Ecclessite, like you and me . . . well, almost."

"I didn't know they could come to Logon," Artka whispered. "I was with Erotons when Tren captured me, but no one else was rescued."

The huge Eroton stopped in mid-step across from Artka, turned and glowered at Artka.

Artka, a lump in his throat, smiled weakly.

The Eroton slammed both fists on the table, making silverware and mugs jump. "Steward, I'll take me meal wi' the east tower lads." He grabbed the man sitting opposite Artka by the nape of his tunic and lifted him clear out of his seat. "Find anuther seat!"

The startled man picked himself off the floor and scrambled for a different place.

Artka stared at the man. His arms were scarred; his beard splotchy from scars; his metallic, gray eyes unblinking; his furrowed, shaggy brows met over a broad, oft-broken nose as he filled the vacated seat.

"Boy," rumbled the giant, "yer gots summat agin Erotons?"

Artka gulped.

"I used ter eat the likes o' yer fer breakfast, so if'n yer gots summat ter say, spit it out now, fer I'm gittin' hungry, and yer lookin' mighty tasty."

Artka glanced sideways at Reddy who sat frozen, staring straight ahead. In fact, everyone in the room was petrified.

"I-I meant no offense, sir," Artka said.

"No offense says yer," the Eroton thundered. "Steward, fergit me food, I'll eat this 'un, raw! What says yers, lads?"

"Aye, Scang!" everyone, including Reddy, shouted.

The Eroton's hands lunged across the table at Artka.

Artka jerked backward, eyes wide, jaw slack, face white as he nearly fell to the floor before hands caught him from behind.

Everyone dissolved in laughter.

The Eroton grabbed Artka's hand, pulling him upright and saying, "Welcome, laddie."

"Did you see the look on his face?" said someone, doubled over in mirth.

"He actually thought Scang meant it."

"Did you see how wide his eyes were?"

"I did, I did."

The laughter continued.

Artka, sure that his face was a bright crimson, smiled sheepishly.

The door opened and a group of chilled guards from the farthest blockhouse entered. A chorus of, "Oh, you lads missed it," and "Scang did it again," greeted the newcomers.

As the newest arrivals seated themselves, stewards stepped lively from their kitchen with steaming bowls of stew, which soon quieted the hubbub.

Scang grinned and said, "I hopes yer doesn't take offense at me little joke."

Artka swallowed. "I'm glad you weren't serious, I'd have had some difficulty discouraging you." They both laughed again. "I was with a band of Erotons when Tren rescued me. Ever hear of the Boar's Head Brigade under command of Captain Sarcas?"

"Boar's Head Brigade, eh? Yeah, thet be's a nasty bunch, awright."

Artka judiciously omitted his previous feelings about Erotons. Nor did he feel it necessary to mention Corporal Lewt and his untimely end.

"I didn't ken any o' 'em myself, nor Captain Sarcas," Scang said, "but I heered enuf. Some said he was as full o' hate as Lurcan hisself. Even so, it be's too bad he ended thet way. Yer friend, Tren, must be a mighty warrior."

"He is." Artka related how Tren led through the Wind Break Forest, fought off tophets, rescued him from a horde of cusps, and did battle with Neask.

Scang was spellbound, as were the others who hadn't heard.

"And this be's the man leadin' the trainin' this arternoon? Thet settles it fer me, I'll gladly sit under anyone whut faced off wi' a dread."

Several others chimed in agreement.

When they finished eating, a lieutenant, duty roster in hand, stood in the doorway reading off the names of those assigned to various details, then added, "The rest of you report to Captain Tren for sword drill. Oh yes, I believe there's a recruit, Artka, among you. Ah, I see you. I'd like a word with you after the others leave."

Everyone sat still, squeezing the last moments of leisure out of their lunch break.

"Which is NOW!"

Benches toppled as men scurried for the portal. Artka approached the sergeant after the last of them had gone. "You wanted to see me, sir?"

"Son, I'd like to examine your sword."

Artka withdrew it from his belt.

"Good, very good. I usually have to stand over recruits making sure they work on their swords, but I see you need no such supervision. You've even got a rune beginning to glow. I'm impressed. Some recruits take as long as a year to accomplish that. Keep it up, lad."

"Thank you, sir."

"There's one more thing."

"Sir?"

"Captain Metid wants you assigned to regular duties as long as you're here, so I'm listing you to the east-tower squad. Corporal Clepy will fill you in. You might as well join them out on the practice field if you have no other questions."

"I do have one, sir."

"Well?"

"You referred to Tren as 'captain'?"

"You didn't know?"

"No, sir."

"Does that not reveal something of his character?"

"Yes, sir. But I wish he'd have mentioned it."

"To what purpose, lad? He doesn't want your honor, he wants you to be more like Logon, which is his own goal as well. Not everyone is aware of Tren's commission, and that's how Logon seems to want it. Now, you'd better get along to the drill field. Dress warm, it seems winter is setting in early."

Artka descended the solid stone staircase three steps at a time, bounded through the banqueting hall, and out the courtyard postern, grabbing a cloak off a hook and wrapping it about himself as he went. A few men standing idly beside the well caused him a moment's hesitation, but they were only chatting. He lowered his head into the wind and trotted toward his squad, slipping into formation beside Reddy.

Tren, just emerging from a portal of the keep walked slowly onto the drill field, accompanied by two sergeants. He winked at Artka as he passed him.

"My name is Tren. Captain Metid wishes me to inform you that I have a commission, though not through regular channels. As you see, I've been injured, but Captain Metid has encouraged me to stay active while I recuperate. So, I won't be able to personally demonstrate many of these lessons myself. Nevertheless, I trust you shall apply yourselves to my instructions and draw what benefit you may from the exercises. If there are no questions . . . let's begin. Company, present arms."

The assemblage snapped to, feet slightly apart, sword hilts grasped by both hands and points resting on the ground. Tren stalked up and down each row examining each soldier and sword, occasionally stopping and asking how long a man had known Logon or when was the last time he'd seen combat or how many had he guided or sent to Logon's Rock.

As he stood in line Artka's mind drifted back to what seemed a lifetime ago since drilling under Sergeant Love. He hadn't really exercised other than trekking since before the battle of the Wind Break

Forest—Erotons tended to be lazy about such things—and he was now eager to indulge in some physical activity.

His inspection finished, Tren strolled back around front. "I have three weeks, maybe a little longer, to train you men, so pay attention, do your best, and we'll lose no time in repetition. Marching files. Fall in."

Men scurried to their positions. Reddy showed Artka his place.

"Double time." The company leapt into motion. Sergeant Barah, ran alongside, vocally setting the cadence and calling turns at each corner of the field. Tren, snugging his cape tighter, turned as they ran and analyzed each member of the circling troop. Twice, thrice, four times the company jogged the perimeter of the paddock. Many were wheezing as they turned the corner on the fifth tour around.

Artka, however, was just getting his second wind and reveled in the exertion.

"Twice more, Sergeant," Tren called, his shrewd eyes studying each man. On the final lap the order was given to return to formation. Not all had kept pace. Dozens straggled back to their place in line huffing and coughing.

Tren paced between the files again, separating the fatigued from the fit with a tap on the shoulder signifying they were to join a group off to the side. Artka noted that those in the worst physical condition usually also had the least glow on their blades.

"Men," Tren said, "some of you seem to think that your disciplines ended at Logon's Rock. Well mister, you're of little use to Logon if you neglect your Child of the Stars and your own physical condition. Those of you who have been lazy will go with Sergeant Barah who will re-introduce you to some basic calisthenics. At a time when some of you have known Logon for years and should have progressed to more advanced tactics and strategies, you need to repeat basic training again," he said, shaking his head. "Sergeant, see to your charges."

Artka had never seen Tren so stern; wielding authority with confidence, yet he wasn't proud as men in power often were. After Sergeant Barah's squad left the parade grounds, Tren addressed the remainder, "I'd like to evaluate your abilities in hand to hand combat. Pair off, men."

Reddy and Artka nodded at each other, forming a dueling pair. Soon everyone was matched with a partner except Scang, the oversized Eroton.

Sizing up the situation, Tren said, "Scang, go join those two," indicating Artka and Reddy. "I believe you all know each other."

"Oh no," Reddy muttered. "Scang doesn't know his own strength. I'm afraid we're in for a drubbing."

"Well, well, me wee tidbits, let's play," Scang said with a chuckle. "I'll take it easy on yers."

"Then we won't learn much, will we Reddy?" said Artka.

"Hush, Artka. You've no idea what 'playing' with him is like. This is no lunch-time prank. He really gets into it."

"Listen, I've battled a tophet, so I'm not afraid of him. It's all safe. I mean, nobody gets hurt. Logon's swords don't cause harm, especially to Ecclessites, right? We won't benefit if we aren't tested."

Scang smiled. "Awright laddie, if'n thet's how yer wants it ter be, thet's whut yer'll git. I'll try not ter knock yers around over much." Scang spread his feet and raised his sword, facing off against Reddy and Artka.

"In this drill," Tren continued, "your swords will act as normal swords for the most part. Mortal or wounding blows will be deflected, however, so don't worry if you're overmatched. Children of the Stars won't inflict severe injury on flesh and blood, they can however, give you a deserved welt or bruise if you're not careful. As long as you cling to your sword you'll come to no harm. Remember, in this simulated battle, your swords won't fight as much as they would in real combat, for Logon's words will not oppose themselves. Now, you're to duel until one of you in each match yields. Any questions?"

"Sir," Reddy raised his hand and said jokingly, "What should I do?"

Without hesitation Tren replied, "Assist Scang."

Guffaws and chuckles erupted up and down the lines.

"Commence."

Metallic clangs and hearty shouts filled the air. Men grunted as they pivoted, lunged, withdrew, parried, feinted, and circled.

Artka fended off Scang's downswing with an upward blow, stinging Scang's hand and surprising the giant. Scang stepped back, rubbing his wrist, re-assessing his opponent. He circled his opponent, eyes locked on Artka's.

Artka erupted in a lion's roar and charged, swinging his sword in small figure-eight arcs.

Scang yielded ground, frantically warding off each blow. But the former Eroton showed evidence of being war-hardened from many campaigns. He lunged at Artka, then faded to the side, twirling to throw his opponent off balance. Artka feinted right, then spun around left in a risky maneuver, temporarily losing sight of his opponent to gain the advantage of surprise. He finished his maneuver directly behind Scang where Reddy, mouth agape and still facing Scang, locked eyes with Artka.

A resounding smack from Artka's sword to Scang's buttocks released a yowl from the Eroton.

Scang's bellows drew the attention of other combatants. But the Eroton was far from intimidated. He turned and slashed with his sword, brushing the loose folds of Artka's tunic. Instead of parrying Scang's lunge, Artka dodged safely out of reach.

Not meeting expected resistance and drawn off balance, Scang teetered forward. As the Eroton stumbled past his opponent, the other side of his backside received a stinging thwack.

Scang yelped again and tears rimmed his eyes, to the immense enjoyment of the spectators.

"Careful Artka," someone called out, "Scang hasn't been an Ecclessite all that long and he might temporarily revert if pressed too hard."

Laughter erupted from the onlookers but Artka ignored it, focusing on his nemesis.

They lunged again at each other, grunting with each thrust and parry. Beads of sweat broke out on their skin despite the biting wind. After several frenzied minutes, Scang stepped away to catch his breath.

"Well, c'mon Reddy. Do like the cap'n says an' gi' me a hand."

Reddy nervously stepped to Scang's side. "Remember Artka, this is just a drill."

"I'll pay yer back in kind, boy," threatened Scang, gasping and gingerly probing the welts on his backside. "Go gittim, Reddy."

"Me! Why should I go first? After all you're the one he—"

Artka's lion's roar drowned out Reddy's protest. Sky Saber swiped low at Reddy's legs, forcing him to jump and tuck up his legs. Artka's shoulders rammed into Reddy's midsection, driving him backward into Scang. The three tumbled to the ground.

The watching circle of soldiers cheered.

Out of the jumble of flailing arms and legs two swords skittered free. Sky Saber rested firmly in Artka's hand.

Artka rolled free, gained his feet, put a foot on Scang's chest, and touched his sword to Reddy's chest. Scang and Reddy offered no further resistance. Artka threw back his head to roar out his victory.

"Stop, Artka!" Tren commanded, stepping in. "Well done, but never again use that lion's roar. That and other regimental battle cries of the empire mustn't be used by kingsman.

"You men have witnessed an important lesson—determination. You must be determined to win, especially when up against superior odds. Do you remember the fervor you had as a recruit, like Artka here? Summon that zeal to again ignite creativity. Anticipate your enemy's moves, and never let loose of your sword."

Tren continued their training the rest of the afternoon, emphasizing gentle persuasion as the best offense, and keenness of sword as the best defense. "When, and only when, your opponent no longer resists should you pierce his heart."

"How will we know?" asked Reddy.

"The Advisor will show you. It's different for each one. Some will trust you, and yield. Others try desperately to not believe you, but when they realize your weapon is superior, they'll surrender. Then there are those who keep resisting against all reason, like they'll never surrender. But in a brief instant they let down their guard. That's when you strike. Then there are some," Tren winked at Artka, "who want to resist but have no more strength to fight. Be determined to fight as long as you can, and then go a little further. It's always too soon to quit."

"Now," Tren pulled his cape snug around his neck, "unless you're enjoying this frosty wind, let's go inside where it's warm by the fireside and discuss tolling techniques."

The company gladly followed Tren, chatting among themselves.

Upon arrival at the castle entry marked as an officer's portal, the men paused, uncertain. Sensing their awkwardness, Tren asked, "What's the problem?"

Scang answered, "Usn's hain't allowed thru officers' areas."

"Taradiddle! Does Logon's commission mean lordship, or servant-hood?" Tren asked. No one answered. "Then come." Tren led under the archway and opened the portal with a grunt.

Several lounging junior officers jumped up and barred the way at the sudden intrusion of trainees traipsing into their domain. "Now see here," said one, "you can't just march through these quarters. We have regulations you know." Several lieutenants backed him up, murmuring in agreement.

"I see," Tren said, his lips a narrow line and his eyebrows bunched. "Did Logon issue these regulations, or did they originate elsewhere?"

"I fail to see how that has any bearing, rules are rules," the lieuten-ant said. "The point is that as long as anyone can remember, officers' quarters have been off limits to recruits and regulars. The rule is a good one. It keeps respect for officers, and that is one of Logon's laws."

Scang whispered to Tren, "It be's no problem, sir. Usn's kin go around like always. You go thru, usn's will meet yer on t'other side." The company behind Tren fidgeted, glancing nervously about.

Tren ignored Scang's suggestion. "It never fails to amaze me when someone commissioned by Logon clings to Carnalian ways. Logon, though being the king's son, never demanded to be revered. Rather, he lived as a humble servant, as his officers ought to do. Now, lieutenant, step aside and let your brothers pass."

The lieutenant clenched his fists. His jaw muscles twitched. Finally, he broke off staring at Tren and stepped aside. Disapproval rumbled from the other junior officers, but no one stepped forward to challenge Tren.

"Thank you," Tren said evenly. "All right then, let's go, men." He stepped in and off to one side as the trainees passed.

Someone called from the back of the clustered junior officers, "You men have been noted."

Tren's face reddened as he said, "How dare you call yourselves king's officers? How dare you put unnecessary hardship upon those that Logon died to rescue? You may have been commissioned by some brigade HQ, but no true officer of Logon would lord it over his charges. Have you forgotten how Carnalian rulers made you grovel? Is that how you want these men to think of you?"

"And just where did you get your commission?" said the cheeky lieutenant in the rear. "I understand there's some question as to whether you even have papers. We'd like to see your commission as an officer, if you don't mind."

"Lieutenant," Captain Metid barked coming up behind Tren. "I'd like to see your orders to challenge a superior." The captain's bulk filled the doorway, eyes flashing beneath bushy brows. The lieutenant backed away. "Now, all of you, hear me well," the captain continued,

"I'm satisfied with Tren's credentials. He's recognized in this post as an officer. I'll tolerate no debate on this issue. Is that understood?"

A few junior officers mumbled a weak affirmative.

"You're to give him the respect and obedience the rank of captain deserves." Then turning away from the officers, he said, "Tren, dismiss your trainees. You and Artka come with me." Captain Metid stalked through the midst of the lieutenants and headed for his office.

Tren nodded at his trainees, dismissing them, then, with Artka, followed Captain Metid.

They entered a large, richly paneled room replete with table, benches, a trio of overstuffed chairs before the hearth, and a massive desk and chair by the wide window. Metid motioned for Tren and Artka to have a seat beside the fireplace. Creases lined Tren's face as he eased down. Artka glanced out the captain's window that overlooked the courtyard; large, wet snowflakes swirled driven by a gusty wind. Remembering Tren's unwelcome status in Captain Basso's brigade, Artka wondered if Captain Metid was about to rebuke Tren and send him away.

For several moments the captain leaned against the mantel staring into the crackling fire. At long last he asked, "Tren, you aren't a captain, are you?"

CHAPTER TWENTY-TWO

"No, Captain, I'm not," Tren said.

For several long moments the only sounds in the room were crackling sparks escaping up the flue.

Artka's knuckles gripping the arms of the chair went white.

Captain Metid leaned forward, his unblinking gaze fixed on Tren; then leaned back again, deep in thought. Finally, he raised his head and said, "General?"

Tren shifted his weight, settling deeper into the cushion. He glanced at Artka. "Does it make any difference, Captain?"

"Have you come to replace me?" Captain Metid's lips trembled.

Tren leaned forward. "No, not at all. Why would you ask that?"

Metid's shoulders sagged. "Well, I uh, thought that Logon, well, he . . . ."

"Be at ease, Captain," Tren said. "Artka and I are on our way to the Prophecy Mountains, as I've told you. Nothing more. Why do you suspect Logon wants to replace you?"

"Oh, it's a long story, and one I'm not eager to tell, especially with Artka present. It might discourage him."

Tren groaned as he extracted Star Splinter and laid it across his knees. With toller poised he said, "Share your burden. It may help Artka understand what he faces in Ecclessa."

Captain Metid sighed, rose from his chair and paced to the window. "Snow came early." Then facing his companions, said, "Very well, I must tell someone, or my heart will burst. The troubles began about a year ago. They seemed insignificant at first. I thought I was being overly critical. You know how Logon dislikes criticism. Well anyway, there was enemy activity in the forest, and I suspected Carnalia was planning a roadblock. They do that periodically, trying to re-capture recruits between Logon's Rock and here. Most of our trustworthy forces were out on foray, so I sent across the river for reinforcements.

"Two days later a Sharpointer Brigade arrived, and just in time too, for an enemy brigade—Wisests, the ones that act, talk, and even sometimes dress like Ecclessites—were actively subverting recruits."

"Recruits often get led astray after meeting Logon because no one guides them immediately to a brigade," Tren explained to Artka. Then he turned to Metid, "I wonder how the enemy is so successful in re-capturing so many."

"Beguiled with miniature imitations of the Children of the Stars, among other ruses," said Metid.

Artka shuffled his feet and resisted an urge to chew on a fingernail.

Metid continued, " . . . though nowadays the enemy usually uses those foul, black Craniantium swords. Well, as I was saying, many recruits were ambushed and waylaid. Finally, across the river comes Captain Basso and his men."

"Excuse me, you did say Basso?" Tren said.

"You know him?"

"I was accompanying his brigade when Artka was rescued, that's all. Did you by any chance meet his second-in-command, Lieutenant Crand?"

"Lieutenant? He was only a sergeant when they were here. In fact, he's the source of my troubles."

"I see. Go on."

"At first our counterattack went beautifully. The Wisests were driven back, and many that had been re-captured were brought back to Logon. We sent them post-haste into Ecclessa without further ado. Because of the stormy weather—remember how the storms came a few months ago?—Captain Basso requested that his men be sequestered here. Naturally I agreed. But after some days in the course of performing my daily duties I observed things that caused me to suspect Sergeant Crand was intentionally manipulating Captain Basso."

"Such as . . . ?"

"Well, Crand would interrupt Basso as he set patrols or watches, you know, suggesting a better way of doing things."

"Officers ought to be open-minded," Tren said. "Some men are more gifted in administration than others."

"Oh, I completely agree. But, with Crand it was more the way he offered suggestions—never in private, always with an audience. It wasn't long until, seeing Basso continually second-guessed by a non-com, the men lost respect for their commanding officer. Some looked to Sergeant Crand for his concurrence even while Basso was giving orders. Crand would nod discreetly, and the orders would be carried out."

"And Basso let this continue?"

"He was unaware. I took him aside and tried to tell him, but he wouldn't listen. He praised Crand as wise, brave, insightful. He had no idea that his troops were shifting their allegiance to Sergeant Crand." Metid paced to the fireplace and leaned with both hands on the mantel as he stared into the flames.

"One day I heard voices outside my chamber. I opened the door just in time to hear Crand say to one of my junior officers: 'The old man must not appreciate your abilities since he assigns you to stable detail so often.' Upon seeing me he clammed up. My junior officer scurried away. Crand, however, stood there, brazenly staring at me. When I reprimanded him, he acted outraged that I dared discipline another officer's non-com. Before I knew it, I heard myself apologizing."

The flickering flames cast shadows across Metid's face. "Shortly after that incident I noticed the attitude of my own men changing. Oh, they still obeyed, yet something was amiss. Officers shouldn't demand respect, nevertheless, it behooves the rank and file to give it. It's one of Logon's paradoxes.

"Crand always seemed to be slinking about the fortress, spreading discontent; leastwise that's my suspicion. Tren, you're aware that this fortress isn't a typical brigade. It's a mixture of many brigades. With Logon's counsel, I've managed to smooth frictions between various brigades. But it took Crand mere weeks to engender strife. He'd climb on a chair and hold his sword aloft pointing out runes, arguing that Sharpointers were the only true brigade. Onedgers, Tipsters, Runers, Wholebladers, etcetera, according to him, had become seduced by Lurcanish agents. Fights broke out. Some men left for other posts. Some just disappeared—my guess is that they went back to Carnalia. Quite a few transferred from their brigades to join Basso's Sharpointers, which is all right, I suppose, except I suspect they did so because they were persuaded by Crand instead of at Logon's direction.

"Finally, I'd had enough, I told Basso to keep Crand out of the fort, to assign him to duties in the field. Basso acted cusp-touched. He wouldn't even hear me out. He declared he and his men would leave and swore that none of his troops would return to Ecclessa as long as I was commandant of the gate-side fortress. His brigade has been in the field ever since. That's why I thought that maybe you had come . . . "

"Have you talked to Logon about this?" Tren asked.

"I have."

"And?"

"Through the Advisor he tells me to be patient. Nothing else."

"As I see it Captain, your main duty is to defend the road and Logon's Bridge. Logon doesn't expect us to alter what he hasn't charged, nor would he, without a direct order, have you lay down a responsibility he appointed."

"But I'm no longer worthy of my post," Metid moaned.

Tren looked deep into Metid's eyes. "Go on."

"I'm the reason you were mauled by that tophet. I was touring the wall that night. I recognized the glow of your sword as you came up the road at dusk and thought Logon had sent someone more qualified to replace me. I watched you make camp at the gate. I withdrew the guards from that section of wall under the pretense of my anniversary party, hoping that tophets, cusps, or possibly a Carnalian war party would find you."

Metid crossed to his desk and sat, occasionally dabbing at his eyes. "But the guilt for what I'd done eventually overcame my sense of self-preservation, and though it was hours later, I sent men to check, not knowing whether you were alive or not." He sobbed, "Can you find it in your heart . . . to forgive . . . me?" His cheeks glistened with moisture in the soft firelight.

Tren struggled to his feet and looked somberly at Artka. "Can we?"

Anger stirred in Artka; his bruised ribs still ached from the scorpion's pincers, then just as suddenly, he remembered the wound in Logon's chest, and how great his own offenses were—and Logon's forgiveness.

Artka stood with Tren and lay a hand on the captain's shoulder.

"Brother . . . we forgive you," Tren said for both.

Captain Metid wept.

~

Later, seated before the fire in the otherwise dark room, the discussion turned to Crand. "Since your arrival, Tren, many of my men have again taken up their Children of the Stars. Disputes have died down—except among a few junior officers. Crand developed a special rapport with them, and as you experienced a short while ago, they have a haughty attitude. If Crand could do all that in the short time he was here . . . poor Basso must be totally under his spell."

Tren stretched his legs. "Artka, I've been thinking, due to my injuries, it's necessary I remain here. I can best serve Logon by training troops here in the fort, and hopefully re-align the junior officers."

"That's fine. I'm assigned to a patrol, so I'll have plenty to keep me busy until you heal."

"No, I think it best that you not delay. Logon wants you, er, to be, in, uh—you know, the other brigade."

"You may speak freely Tren," Captain Metid said. "It's widely known that Logon is forming a new brigade."

"How did you—Artka?"

Artka was suddenly fascinated with the slate stones beneath his feet. He replied without looking up, "It was an accident. They tricked me."

"Who tricked you? The junior officers?" Tren's voice had an edge.

"No, no, my friends. We were sharpening swords. They teased me about the maidens of the Prophecy Mountains. In self defense, I just blurted it out."

"'They' would be Reddy and Harnet, among others, would it not, son?" asked Metid.

"Yes, sir."

"They, along with several others, have put in for transfers to this new brigade."

Tren thoughtfully rose from his seat and ambled to the fireplace, massaging his shoulder. "Artka, this was to be kept secret. Now the whole fortress knows. Mistakes like this can put the king's work back for months."

"I'm sorry, Tren. It just slipped out."

Tren's features softened. "Well, whatever harm comes of it, you'll have to bear the consequences. For my part, when my arm heals I must confront Crand and put a stop to his divisiveness. I'm afraid, my friend, we've reached a parting of the ways."

"But . . . but, Tren, I know nothing of Ecclessa. I'll get lost. I don't want to go without you."

"I must obey Logon, Artka. It's abundantly clear that I'm the only ranking authority nearby that's capable of dealing with Crand, even if they don't recognize my authority."

"Then I'll come with you and vouch—"

"Artka, we must follow the paths Logon has set for us. I love you as my own brother and want to make sure you get safely to your assignment, but, duty demands I try to undo Crand's mischief. You must find Saygus and get his directions to the new brigade."

"Tren is right, Artka. Never resist Logon's will. Anything else, no matter how noble or urgent it seems, will only cause more grief in the end."

Artka folded his arms and stared at the fire. Tren had done so much for him. "I never thought obedience to Logon would be painful. We will see each other again, won't we?"

"Only Logon knows, Artka. I hope so. But until we enter the king's palace in Splendora, we must accept the possibility of not having each other's company again."

Artka jumped from his chair and embraced Tren, mindful of his injuries. "I love you, Tren. I've never said that to anyone outside my own family, except Logon. I love you almost as much as I love Logon. I'm going to miss you."

The dinner gong sounded, muffled though it was through the thick, oaken door.

Artka, his eyes moist, stepped back and beheld Tren full in the face.

"Artka," said Captain Metid, "why don't you join your friends for dinner while Tren and I discuss other things."

Artka nodded and went to the door. As he pulled the latch he asked, "Can I at least stay for a little more training?"

Tren and Metid glanced at each other. "We'll let you know," said the captain. "Inform a steward to send Tren's meal here with mine. Oh, by the way, would you inform Harnet and Reddy that I'd like to see them? After they finish eating would be fine."

"Yes, sir. I hope my mistake hasn't gotten them in trouble."

"Each bears his own responsibility. Don't you worry about them, you've got quite enough to be concerned about, I should think."

"Yes, sir." Artka left the chamber, closing the door softly behind.

Harnet and Reddy had saved a seat at their table, and espying Artka exit the captain's chambers, waved him over. Scang was with them. He'd left his usual cronies to be at Artka's table—unnerving the recruits who usually dined with Harnet and Reddy.

Artka took his seat. A hot plate of mashed potatoes with roasted venison and assorted vegetables was set before him. Before he lifted a bite of food questions flew at him from all sides. He gave vague answers. Throughout the conversation Scang sat directly across from Artka, silently watching Artka's every move.

Upon being informed that the captain wanted to see them, Reddy and Harnet lost their appetites. They looked at each other, slumped against the backrest and half-heartedly pushed food around their plates.

With those two subdued, the conversation lulled, prompting Scang to say, "Ere, now Artka, yer like ter beat me black'n'blue this arternoon, dinch-yer?"

Everyone at the table tensed.

Gravy-drenched mashed potatoes dropped back to Artka's plate. He met the giant's steely gaze. "It was practice, Scang, a game, sort of. I meant no harm."

"Yer like ter made a fool o' me out there."

"Scang, I meant no—"

"Save it laddie." Scang stood. All chatter and clatter in the dining hall stopped. Scang's demeanor was not the fake belligerence of his practical joke in the watchtower dining hall, his facial muscles were rigid as stone.

"I gots nobbut respect fer anyone whut handles hisself like yer done. I'd be honored if'n yer'd call me yer friend." A beefy hand extended across the table.

Artka clasped the overlarge hand, "My pleasure, Scang." The entire dining room breathed a sigh of relief. All except Reddy and Harnet, that is, who, their appetites quite vanished, decided to face the unpleasant business and trudged to Captain Metid's chambers.

CHAPTER TWENTY-THREE

REDDY AND HARNET EMERGED FROM Captain Metid's chamber grinning ear-to-ear. Stewards scurrying about the mess hall paid them no mind, but Artka and Scang, having been shooed from their table to the great fireplace, paused tolling their swords as their friends drew near.

"Well?" Artka asked.

"We're going with you," Reddy beamed. "Can you believe it? The captain wants us to accompany you to the new brigade."

Laying his sword on the bench, Artka embraced his friends. "And you weren't scolded?"

Their smiles dimmed. Harnet said, "Well, we were admonished about teasing and all, but we never suspected you harbored a secret. So, he believed us. Do you forgive us, Artka?"

"A thousand times, yes! It's not as if I was offended. Besides, I'm relieved that I don't have to go to Ecclessa alone. Isn't that great, Scang? Scang?"

Reddy pointed toward the captain's chamber where Scang stood knocking and was admitted even as they watched. They grinned at each other. Moments later Scang re-emerged and shyly said, "I hopes yers don't mind puttin' up wi' the likes o' me, 'cause I'm goin', too."

"Of course not," said Artka, warmly clasping the giant's hand. "I'm glad you're coming. Your company gives me even greater peace of mind."

"Me, too," Reddy said. Harnet nodded.

"Then, it's the four of us off to Ecclessa," Artka said. "Have any of you ever been to the Prophecy Mountains?"

After a pause Reddy said, "We've all been to Ecclessa for basic training, but since there's no known brigade near the Prophecy Mountains, not many kingsmen have reason to go there."

"No one knows the way?" Artka asked.

"Well, not exactly, but we know it's southeast out of the other fortress," offered Reddy.

"I'm sure somebody will point out the right road," Artka said.

"Ecclessa has few roads," said Harnet. "Logon wants us to discover our own way as he leads, not always travel the same worn trails that others have trod. Ecclessa should be new and exciting to each traveler, no matter how many times he returns."

"And Ecclessa is full of surprises," added Reddy.

Artka considered a moment then said, "Logon warned that I'd face dangers in Ecclessa. I'd hoped Ecclessa would be safe. I guess only the king's palace is safe. I wish Tren was coming, he has so much wisdom and experience, not to mention light on his sword."

"No more light than could be on ours," Scang said. "We'll jest hafta learn how ter light our'n up more."

"Artka," Harnet said, "Captain Metid also said we have a week to sit under Tren's tutelage. Officially, we're to say we're accompanying you to your assignment, even though everyone in the fortress knows about the new brigade."

Over the next few days Artka and his companions diligently applied themselves to Tren's lessons. Fellow soldiers wished them well, some with a wink, others with longing in their eyes.

Tren taught the lessons he deemed would be most useful to the four travelers: silencing cusps, defense against tophets, and most important—instruction on sharpening their swords. Tren spent off-duty hours with Artka as his friend, but also wisely encouraged Artka to cultivate relationships with his new companions.

The week passed quickly. On the evening before their departure, Artka, during his last tour of guard duty, glimpsed movement on the lower end of the moon-washed mead. The watch commander agreed; something was astir, but being half-a-league or more distant, it was difficult to identify in the bleak light of the moon. Even as they watched, clouds scudded in from the west preventing further observation. The officer of the watch thought it prudent to summon Captain Metid to the ramparts, but by the time he arrived it was too dark to see anything; nevertheless, he put the fort on alert.

A cold front was moving in. Those on watch endured the icy sting of wind-driven snow pellets. The very atmosphere was charged with electricity, as if more than a storm was brewing. An hour later Artka's shift gratefully greeted their relief and hustled down to the warmth of the dining hall and a hearty meal.

After eating, Artka went straight to bed. He was asleep before the sheets covering him warmed.

Hours later, in the quiet darkness, Artka awoke to a slight pressure on the foot of his bed. "Who's there?"

"Captain Metid sent for you," Tren whispered.

"Is it time?"

"Yes. Your companions are also being roused. There's a blinding snowstorm outside, and the fortress is under siege."

"Siege?" Artka swung his feet to the floor and pulled on his cold weather garb. "Who?"

"Can't tell for sure. The storm makes it difficult to identify whether it's tophets, or cusps, or just men, or all three. There's also another stronger presence of evil, can you feel it?"

"Now that you mention it, I was having awful dreams."

"Disturbing dreams aren't unusual when the fortress is under attack. Come now, you'd better hurry. Your fellow travelers will be waiting."

"What's the hour?"

"Third before dawn."

Artka finished lacing his footgear, adding fur over-wraps, then followed Tren out the dorm mentally checking his gear, feeling like he'd forgotten something.

Harnet and Scang were already seated in the dining hall, wolfing down a robust meal of eggs, bacon, and bread. Captain Metid stood behind, gently rocking on his heels, his hands clasped behind. A steward ambled out the kitchen door with two platters, followed by another steward bearing four steaming mugs. A clatter of a dropped rucksack by the stairs announced Reddy's arrival, still somewhat groggy.

"Eat up men, while I give some instruction," Captain Metid said. "Go immediately to the stables when you're done eating. Give this note, written in my own hand, to the head groom. It says to make ready four swift steeds to cross the bridge. No, don't ask questions, Reddy, just eat. I'll do the talking. Now then, where was I? They'll give you sure-footed horses, trust them. Once you've reached the actual bridge, don't dismount for any reason. The bridge is barely twenty inches wide, allowing no room for dismounting. In nice weather you could leisurely stroll to the other side in a little over an hour, but you have neither nice weather nor an hour—nor do we."

All four riveted their eyes on the captain, slurping, munching, and swallowing as they received instructions.

"Your mounts are trained to run the bridge in fair and foul weather, so I say again, trust them, let them have their head, and for Splendora's sake, stay on them. If you dismount, you'll never see the other side. We have cloaks for your added protection—it's a raging blizzard out there—so cover up, even your heads. You have no need to see or try to guide your horses, they know the way and will take you to the eastern fortress. Give this message to Captain Gulundur, and him only, understand?" He handed Artka a sealed envelope.

The four nodded, mouths too full to speak.

"Good. Tell Gulundur we're besieged by crack Eroton troops, tophets—numbers unknown, all manner of cusps, and . . . " he paused, glancing at Tren.

Tren nodded.

Metid resumed, " . . . and three, maybe four chimeree."

Scang dropped his fork, his face turned as pale as his tunic.

"A chimeree?" Artka said.

"Neask is one of the chimeree, Artka. Dreads," Tren said.

Reddy and Harnet stopped eating, forks halfway to their mouths. "Three or four?" Harnet said.

"Maybe more," Tren said evenly. "Lurcan has sent the very gates of Inferna to attack. If you fail to deliver this message Lurcan may succeed in shutting down access to the bridge, preventing reinforcements and resupply missions into Carnalia. If that happens, it's a short matter of time until the long-awaited judgment."

"Come on lads," Captain Metid said, "eat up, it's bitter cold outside. Now, think, do you have everything? I know we're sending you off a mite early, but we must act quickly. The enemy, sneaking up under the cover of storm, thinks we're unaware of their approach, which is why we're making the most of this opportunity to send for help. At first light they'll try drifting some tophets on the river's currents that'll no doubt try to clamber up on the bridge, which is why you must be on the other side before dawn."

Artka suddenly remembered what he'd forgotten. He pushed his empty plate away, excusing himself. Captain Metid and Tren looked questioningly at him. "I, er forgot something."

"Usn's will wait fer yer at the stable, laddie. Be quick," Scang said, wiping his mouth with his sleeve.

Artka slipped down the hallway and quietly opened the door to the outside bailey. He was greeted by stinging crystals and an icy wind that whipped his breath away. He leaned forward, willing himself into the frigid blast. "I must remember to grab one of those cloaks," he said aloud to hear himself above the shriek of the wind.

Visibility was nil in the dark and swirling snow, yet Artka was sure of the well's position. There was a brief moment of doubt, but he forced it from his mind and waded through a half-foot of snow. He found the well and located a certain stone by feel. He brushed away the snow and gave a couple of sharp kicks loosening the frozen dirt around the stone. Pulling the stone out, he reached into the cavity and withdrew a leather pouch and tucked it in his belt. Then he replaced the stone and turned to retreat to the castle.

A sudden gust of wind took him off guard, sending him sprawling headlong. He immediately sprang to his feet, but confused by the dark and snow, had no idea where the postern door lay. He groped for the well to get his bearings but found only a void.

He ran left, then right, slipping and falling several times, finding neither well, nor wall, nor keep. Had he wandered onto the vast expanse of the parade ground? He slipped and fell again. In despair he sat shivering as snow cascaded deeper around him. It was useless to fight anymore. He should just lie down and die. Let the fortress fall, what did it matter?

A distorted noise caught his attention. A bluish glow filtered through the swirling snow. Hope surged. "Tren, Tren, I'm here." In another moment Reddy and Harnet grasped Artka's arms and dragged him inside.

"Artka, what possessed you to go out there?" Tren asked as Reddy and Harnet hustled Artka to the fireside. Scang was on his way down the spiral staircase carrying a thick blanket.

"It's not important," Artka said with a shiver, hoping to evade Tren's question. "How did you find me?"

"You were right outside the door. If you hadn't called out, we never would have found you."

"We waited for twenty minutes in the stables," Harnet said. "The horses are saddled. Our gear is packed. As soon as you're ready we can go."

"I . . . I don't think I'll ever be w-w-warm again. Maybe you three s-s-should go on ahead. I'll catch up later."

Tren said, "You're the reason anyone is going. You must go now, well, at least in a few minutes, else we'll have no chance of that message getting through before tophets bar the bridge. I don't think the four of you want to try getting past tophets, do you? Cusps are likely already positioned there to hinder messengers, so take heed."

Scang brushed Reddy out of the way and stood beside Artka. "Ere lad, drink this down. It'll git yer blood a flowin'. Then stand yerself up an' flap yer arms. Yer'll be warm agin in no time." Though Scang's voice was confident, his eyes were anxious.

Artka accepted the hot, dark brown liquid, gulping it down, taking little time to savor the sweet, deliciously different taste. "Mmm, this is good. What is it?"

"S'made in Eroton, but it be's awright. We calls it chocat. It'll gi' yer energy."

The beverage warmed Artka almost immediately. Following Scang's advice, Artka flexed his arms and legs. The chilling numbness was soon reduced to mere tingling. "I think I'm ready, as long as I'm protected from that vicious wind."

The entourage tramped from the dining hall through the kitchen where a steward handed each a fur-trimmed, hooded cape.

Scang said as he donned his cape, "Jest outside the door be's a rope. Grab aholt, and foller it ter the stable so yer don't git lost. Usn's be's right behind."

Tren was the last to step out into the raging snowstorm. Even with capes tied shut and hoods over their faces, cold wind drove snowflakes into their mouths, eyes, and noses, as if trying to suffocate them. The snow on the ground was already a foot deep.

"Are you sure horses can navigate this?" Artka shouted into the wind, but his words were swept away.

Artka suddenly found himself entering a lantern-lit stable where Captain Metid waited, tapping his foot and wringing his hands. Two stable hands stood alongside swinging doors, each gripping a pair of horses by the reins.

"Don't bother explaining," said Metid. "Tren can inform me later as to your delay. It's imperative that you go now. Remember—these are highly trained horses, trust them. Don't try to control them or you'll end up in the river. These are the most reliable ones we have. Let them have their head and you'll have no problems. You should be in the King's Gate East in less than half an hour. If not . . . "

"Which one of you is Artka?" asked a stable hand.

"I am."

"Take the lead horse." The man presented him the reins of a coal-black stallion. "He knows the bridge best. The others will follow. When you're ready, whisper 'Fort east' in his ear, and he'll do the rest."

Artka nodded and swung into the saddle. The others followed suit and indicated their readiness.

"I goes behind Artka," Scang said, challenging anyone to contradict him.

"The horse's name is Scarendous," said the stable hand to Artka. "He fits it well, so don't do anything to frighten him. He gets nervous around cusps. You don't have anything in your gear that would draw cusps, do you? If you attract them, Scarendous might lose his footing."

Artka asked, "What things would attract cusps?"

"Oh, it's hard to say. Maybe some Carnalian memento, or a Lurcanish coin, or jewelry with Lurcan's visage, or a dagg—"

"For mercy's sake, man!" Captain Metid said coming around the side of the horse. "What are you blathering on about? They must go, NOW."

"Take good care of my darlings," the stable master said, backing away. The doors opened and the blizzard screeched in. The horses jerked their heads up at the stormy blast, but soon calmed with the knowledge that they were about to cross the river to their favorite stable.

Artka leaned forward, his mouth inches from Scarendous' ear as he stroked the horse's neck, saying in a low voice, "Fort east."

The black horse leapt into the blinding snow and darkness as if it were broad daylight. The other mounts followed. Though uneasy at their animal's rapid pace, the four riders respected Captain Metid's warnings to not try to control the horses. The snow had gotten deeper, yet the horses neither slowed nor slipped.

Artka tightened his cloak against the tugging winds and choking snow. A few moments later Scarendous' solid hoof-beats changed to hollow *ka-thunks*. Artka's thoughts shifted to the twenty-inch-bridge he was now on and the raging river below. One misstep and the turbulent river would be their grave. Artka clung to the saddle horn, caring less about his cloak, eager for the hollow hoof beats beneath his horse's gallop to become solid again.

Temptation to see how his companions fared stole over Artka, but he thought better of it. Just shifting his weight to look backward could tip the horse off stride. Besides, in this blizzard and darkness, what could he possibly hope to see?

A few moments later the urge to look behind came stronger. But again, he reasoned, the risk was too great. He'd trust that his friends were safe.

Scarendous snorted and stutter-stepped.

Artka had always had a keen awareness of his surroundings about him, but in this extreme cold, swirling snow, darkness, and wailing wind Artka could neither see nor hear. Passage of time lost all meaning.

All that existed was now . . . a forever . . . changeless now . . . to be endured until . . . until . . . ?

Scarendous whinnied; his pace slackened.

A wave of despair like he'd never experienced washed over Artka.

"It's useless to fight the cold, wind, and waters below. It's senseless to flee, to try, to care." The wind ate his words as soon as he spoke them. An urge to pull back on the reins and stop Scarendous tantalized Artka.

Artka shook his head, but the dark thoughts immediately returned, eroding his resistance. What harm would it do to stop and think about the futility? Artka's hands crept forward and grasped the reins. Despair sucked at Artka's soul like a whirlpool.

~

Scarendous tossed his head and whinnied, trying to obey the original command in spite of the rider's confusing signals. Terrified and confused at the loathsome ghouls darting at him from all sides, Scarendous lowered his head and plodded toward the distant shore. The pressure on his bit increased though no verbal command accompanied the action, as was customary. He slowed, not sure what his rider wanted. Specters with bulbous eyes, displaying sharp claws and fangs swooped freely around his rider. Scarendous' terror intensified.

~

Scang, Reddy, and Harnet noted their mounts had slowed and were wondering why. They too had heard the hollow hoofbeats that signified they were on the bridge, and anxiously awaited the return to solid ground. But now, for some unexplained reason, their horses were coming to a standstill.

Was a tophet blocking the bridge? Or, had Artka met a kingsmen brigade already on its way across? Two groups heading in opposite directions on this extremely narrow bridge would, of necessity, come to a standstill. In such a case, one of the parties must reverse course, which, in this blinding snowstorm, would be disastrous.

The horses came to a complete halt.

Scang shouted at Artka, but the roaring winds sucked his voice away. He itched to dismount and investigate. Though the first hint of dawn filtered down from the leaden sky through myriad swirling flakes he could barely make out the shadowy form of a horse rearing, pawing the air.

~

Artka had a sensation of rising and falling as if in a dream. He faintly heard his name, but . . . it mattered not, nor did the growls and whinnies of a terrified horse, coming from . . . somewhere. Nothing mattered. Not the wet snowflakes melting inside his loosened cloak, nor the cold seeping into his body's core; and not the rising and falling sensation . . .

CHAPTER TWENTY-FOUR

"By the fire o' Logon's meteors," said Scang, recognizing the oppression assaulting him, "yer'll not take me wi'out a fight. In Logon's name, begone foul shadows." He swung his sword in wild arcs making the swirling snowflakes around him sparkle.

Reddy, third in line, caught glimpses of Scang's sword flashing in the dark; the sight of that light lifted his despair. He withdrew his own sword and remembering the drills Tren had drummed into them, traced a glowing rune with his forefinger as he shouted into the wind:

"I arose from the rock of the dead,
I have been rescued to rescue instead,
To defeat the hosts of Lurcan,
All to the glory of Logon!"

He repeated the rune over and over, retracing it with his finger each time.

Harnet, last in line, had been the first to anticipate trouble when he noticed his mount slowing its pace. Thinking a tophet might already be blocking the bridge, he withdrew his sword, making the cusps hesitant to assail him. Through the raging blizzard Harnet heard snatches of Reddy's runesong and fainter still, Scang's muffled voice. The first twinges of gray daylight revealed through the falling snow dim forms of his companions. "Logon, what should I do?"

He eased himself down over his horse's flank with one thought in mind—get to Artka. But the only path to Artka on such a narrow bridge was beneath the intervening horses.

"Madness," he said to himself as his feet dangled behind his mount's rump. He eased back another couple of inches, desperately groping for the bridge with his toes, hoping his horse wouldn't react. His feet found nothing but emptiness. But their lives depended on him taking this risk. Fresh out of options, Harnet released his grip on the saddle's cantle.

His horse, objecting to this ludicrous dismount, tossed its head and stamped a forefoot, but didn't rear.

Harnet landed softly on piled snow with his heels skidding underneath and between the horse's legs with a tail dangling in his face. Something—a hoof?—whistled past his right ear.

He rose to his feet behind the horse gently patting its flanks. "Steady boy. I'm not going to hurt you." It took another couple of minutes, but when the horse calmed, Harnet crouched to all fours and squeezed between its legs again crawling underneath. The horse gave a low whinny, but, to Harnet's relief, all four feet stayed put. He talked soothingly as he crept, stroking the horse's underbelly, pushing snow aside with his sword before him.

He emerged on hands and knees from under his horse and pondered his next step. Harnet started to rise and felt a tug! His heart skipped a beat—a tophet had him! He jabbed behind with his sword, and upon turning, saw the problem and laughed. He pulled his cloak free from the horse's forefoot, stood, and gently rubbed the horse's ears. His mount quieted, and Harnet turned his attention to the next horse in line.

Reddy, atop his horse, chanted one of the warrunes that Tren had taught them for battling cusps. Reddy was so intent on repeating the runesong that he didn't hear Harnet shouting.

In desperation, Harnet stretched out and tapped Reddy's shoulder with his sword.

Reddy yelped and swung his Child of the Stars behind so furiously that any foe of substance would have been devastated. Harnet's sword deflected the blow.

A lull in the windy blast encouraged him to shout, "Reddy?"

Reddy's voice came faintly, "Harnet? What are you doing? I might have killed you."

"No time to explain," Harnet shouted, "steady your horse, I'm crawling under." With that, he lightly tapped the inside of the horse's rear hocks with his sword. The mare parted them just enough for Harnet to squeeze through.

"Are you mad?" Reddy shouted back, but his voice was swept away as the gale force wind returned.

Harnet was already pushing through the horse's forelegs as Reddy concentrated on soothing his mare against the lunatic behavior of the man creeping beneath.

Once again on his feet, Harnet saw Scang's sword slicing the snowflake-filled air, accompanied by earnest, albeit indistinct, bellows.

Scang paused to catch his breath.

"Scang."

"Eh? Now whut?" The Eroton whipped his head around and looked over his shoulder. "Them nasties be's callin' me name aloud?"

Harnet raised his glowing sword. "It's me, Harnet."

Scang blinked. "Whar's Reddy?"

"No time to explain, just steady your horse, I'm crawling under."

"Yer doin' whut?"

"Crawling under—under your horse, I must get to Artka."

"Under me horse? Be's yer daft? Yer'll git trampled."

"Not if you hold him. Here I go."

Scang's over-sized horse, already jumpy, stomped its forefeet. Nevertheless, Harnet inched between the rear legs to the underbelly. The large horse neighed, lowered his head and shifted his forefeet together, blocking Harnet.

Scang tried to raise his horse's head by brute force, but to no avail.

Harnet tapped his sword's gleaming tip on the animal's nose, hoping to make him yield.

The horse remained staunch.

"Scang? Scang?"

"I hears yer Laddie."

"Your horse won't let me pass."

"I kens. I done everything short o' beheadin' the fool beastie, but he's stubborn as a rusty nail."

From beneath Scang's horse Harnet saw Artka astride the rearing mount. Why didn't Artka have his sword out? In frustration and without considering the consequences Harnet whacked Scang's horse squarely on the nose with the broadside of his sword. "Get your obstinate mule's head out of my way."

The horse raised its head so quickly that Scang was nearly flipped off backwards. Pulling himself upright he shouted, "Thet got his attention, laddie."

Harnet tapped the inside of the forelegs with his sword, and they parted.

He squeezed through, regained his feet, then approached Scarendous.

"Artka?"

No response. The horse reared again. When it came down, one of its forefeet nearly slipped off the snow-covered bridge. The steed tilted to one side, then slowly straightened.

Harnet was stymied. If he approached, the terrified horse could bolt off the bridge. Meanwhile, Artka wasn't responding to his shouts. Had he braved three tramplings only to be frustrated here?

Tren would have known what to do. But didn't he also have access to the same wisdom as Tren? Maybe not Tren's experience, but Tren's resource was just as available. He looked at his blade. "Logon, now what?"

One of Tren's lessons came to mind: "Whenever you're confused, when everything looks hopeless, as long as you cling to your sword, there's hope. If you lose sight of that hope, stop—even in the heat of battle—and toll your weapon. Your way will become clear."

Harnet slipped his hand beneath his cloak. "This is silly," he said. "Something must be done and soon, and the only thing I can think to do is sharpen my sword." He withdrew his hand and shouted again, "Artka," to no avail. Again, his hand stole inside his cloak and fingered the toller. "Oh, why not?" he said, withdrawing the implement. "It certainly can't hurt."

Awkwardly wedging his sword's haft against his foot, he stroked the blade. As soon as the file touched the blade a high-pitched hum resonated into the air.

Startled, Harnet paused. The hum died away. He stared in wonder at his sword and stroked the blade again. Once more a high-pitched but pleasing hum rose above the screech of the storm.

Scarendous stopped rearing and cocked an ear.

Harnet eagerly sawed away at his blade, quite pleased with himself. Whether it helped or not, he felt better just hearing the sweet strain of . . . could it be called music?"

Another hum joined his, different—lower in pitch, but harmonizing. Harnet glanced over his shoulder and saw Scang's sword no longer wildly flailing the air but laid across the Eroton's lap. Seconds later, another tone added a third harmony. Reddy too, was tolling his weapon.

The wind faded away, though snow still pelted down, at least, they could converse.

Scang and Reddy were laughing like children. Harnet too, giggled, as if he'd just been released from years of sadness into the dazzling sunlight of mirth.

"What are you laughing at?" Artka snapped.

"Artka," Harnet said, "are you all right?"

"Of course, I am. What'd you expect? Why are you laughing like loons, and why did we stop? Aren't you aware of our mission's urgency?"

"Well, I—I don't believe it. Do you mean to tell me you don't know what's been going on?" Harnet stopped filing, but the others continued.

"Harnet?" Artka asked in alarm. "Why are you—what happened to Scang and Reddy?"

"Listen, can't you hear them?" The joyful music faded, leaving only the hiss of falling snow accompanying the laughter.

"Well, if you're all finished with your merriment, may we resume our journey?" Artka said. "I'm chilled to the bone."

Harnet, cocked his head, but decided to sort things out later. "Right, Artka, just let me get back to my horse and I'll—"

"What? You're not on your horse? How did you manage that, let alone why?"

"I'll tell you later." Then it dawned on Harnet that getting back to and remounting his horse might not prove so easy.

Scang already had a solution. "Ere laddie, kin yer see me blade?"

A blue glow projected out in front of Scang's horse's. "I see it."

"The reins ter me horse be's right beside. Grab aholt wi' both hands, an' swing yerself out o'er the river so's yer flies up ter me. I'll take keer o' the rest. This here horse be's sturdy 'nuff ter bear usn's both."

"But Scang—"

"Yer gots nobbut choice. Too much time be's lost already."

"Uh, I think I'll walk."

"Not in this snowstorm. Yer'll slip an' fall afore any o' usn's kens. Now do like I says."

Harnet sighed, tucked his sword and toller away, stepped up to the horse and gripped its bridle.

The horse's ears flattened, and he bared his teeth. Before the horse could act on his intentions, Harnet flung himself out over the gray emptiness toward Scang. He reached the vertex of an arc and for a moment hung suspended, then gravity was reinstated, and he tumbled toward the icy waters below. The horse yanked sharply away on his reins. Harnet's benumbed fingers slipped, then lost their grip. He plummeted toward the turbulent river.

Suddenly he jerked to a stop dangling upside-down, knees painfully bumping the side of the bridge.

"I gots yer laddie, not ter worry," Scang said. The giant's massive arms hauled Harnet upward by the tail end of his cloak until Harnet was able to slip his leg over the horse's neck.

"I almost fell," Harnet said, his eyes flashing in anger.

"Now, now, lad, I kenned it'ud be awright, I asked fer Logon's help." Then to Artka he called, "He be's safe aboard. Let's go."

Harnet glared backward over his shoulder but Scang merely smiled and hummed a runesong, ignoring his passenger's pique.

Artka gently prodded Scarendous' sides, leaned forward and whispered, "Fort east."

Scarendous, exhausted, resumed breaking through knee-deep snow. Scang's horse followed without prompting, as did Reddy's. Harnet's rider-less mount brought up the rear.

Scang and Harnet kept their swords at the ready, out to either side. "It's a good thing they gave you a large horse," said Harnet. "But he shouldn't have been so stubborn."

"Stubborn gits the job done, though, don't it," Scang said. "A less stubborn horse might o' let yer pull him off'n the bridge when yer swung out. Whut was yer a thinkin'? Yer mighta been drownt."

"What was I—?" Harnet choked.

Scang chuckled.

"So, what was all that back there?" Reddy called to his companions.

"Cusp attack," Scang said. "But there's summat I doesn't ken."

"What's that," asked Harnet.

"Cusps only gits powerful like thet when somebody believes their lies—or else is disobedient ter Logon. None o' usn's has done any o' thet, so, how come we got attacked so strong? What thinks yer, Artka?"

"Huh? Oh, I don't know, Scang," said Artka. "Let's just enjoy the quiet, all right?"

Artka had difficulty remembering the ride from the time they left the stables. He felt useless and had begun to consider jumping into the churning river. At any rate, the singing swords dispelled the trance. He was chagrined that he hadn't been the first one to remember to toll his sword. After all, he knew Tren better than his friends.

~

The snowy darkness gave way to a gray, snowy dawn. Scarendous calmed seeing light beginning to filter through the overcast skies. Far below and on either side of the narrow bridge stretched the Flaming Sword River like a wide ribbon of inky blackness. Sensing his favorite stable ahead, he quickened the pace. He feared the cusps that specifically targeted his rider with their darting in and out and their hideous faces and horrid screeches. He could only be free from the cusps if he was free of his rider. Leaping off the bridge seemed the only recourse to be rid of the terrible shadows when a soothing sound reached him, reminding him of someone kind and strong, who gave shelter to frightened horses. When another tone joined the first, and then another, the cusps fled.

They now drew near the stable that was warm and dry, with molasses in the oats, and a good rubdown—oh, how he anticipated those rubdowns. He was greatly relieved to resume the journey; after all, it was his responsibility to break trail to the safe haven.

CHAPTER TWENTY-FIVE

ARTKA AND COMPANIONS, STILL CAKED in snow, stood atop a parapet overlooking the eastern gateway. On the drawbridge below a narrow file of Runers was just setting forth. Captain Gulundur had been waiting at the gate when the foursome arrived, for, as he explained, he'd sensed trouble brewing across the river. Artka delivered Captain Metid's message and the post became an anthill of activity. Within twenty minutes a company of mounted cavalry headed across followed by three companies of Sharpointer infantry.

"That's some bridge," Reddy said, studying the span stretching into snowy obscurity. "I'd always heard that large companies needed to break unison on long bridges lest the vibration cause collapse."

"Logon's bridge is indestructible," Captain Gulundur said, reviewing his troops standing among the four. "No one seeking the king's benefits must be prevented from reaching Ecclessa."

"If the fortress on the other side fell, could Lurcan send his armies across the bridge?" Artka looked to the tall, dark-haired, mustachioed captain. "Could he invade Ecclessa?"

"Oh no, lad, not even if he laid waste to the fortress on that side. I believe only humans pierced by a Child of the Stars may cross Logon's Bridge. Besides, the one thing Lurcan isn't likely to do is re-purpose anything of Logon's—like his swords, or this bridge. It's rare, but even when the powers of darkness take possession of kingdom things, the truth of Elyon's realm is so inherently entwined, that any who hunger for truth will perceive it and find their way to Logon. Lurcan, however, will try to make counterfeits. He dissuades his masses from crossing the bridge by ridicule—like exaggerating the danger of something so narrow and straight."

"But I've heard that tophets and cusps get into Ecclessa," Reddy said.

"Cusps float on air currents, much as fish swim in water, but tophets, ahh, that's somewhat of a mystery. They travel on legs, or whatever mode of locomotion they adopt, that much we know. But, it seems they also retain some of their ethereal nature as well, for they don't sink in water. It's theorized that they jump onto the turbulent waters way upstream and propel themselves toward Ecclessa hoping to not get swept away by the swift currents into Lake Maniways far below. Of those that attempt the crossing, some actually make it."

"But, the river is hundreds of miles long," Harnet said. "Surely a creature that doesn't sink mustn't have too hard a time getting across."

"It's over a thousand miles long, but there are so many eddies, back waters, rapids, and whirlpools in the river's expanse that anything afloat is totally at the current's mercy," Gulundur said. "Even so, the most determined do make it across, and those who do are dangerous."

The final company passed through the gate and the captain invited, "Come inside and take some nourishment."

They followed down the stairway, through the courtyard, and into a great dining hall where a roaring fire warmed the room. King's Gate Fortress East mirrored King's Gate Fortress West with one exception—the absence of walls, save along the riverbank.

Captain Gulundur led through the nearly vacant dining hall, peppering the four with questions: what were the battle conditions when they left; how did they come to be stationed at the bridge; what was their destination in Ecclessa; and of what brigade loyalties were they?

He paid particular attention to Artka's answers. "Ah, here we are, have a seat at my table, lads." He then clapped his hands and a steward appeared. "Flench, bring four tankards of spiced tea, and some cheese and biscuits for these men." Then turning to Artka he said, "Surely Logon indicated which brigade he wants you in?"

"He told me to seek out a sage in the mountains who would guide me."

Gulundur pressed his fingertips together and pursed his lips. "And the three of you are going with him?"

They exchanged cautious glances but nodded.

"Hmmm, there's something you're not telling me." He shifted his piercing gaze to Artka. "What's the name of this so-called sage?"

"Saygus."

Gulundur threw back his head and roared with laughter. "What? That fiddle-headed grouch in the Prophecy Mountains? Well, I suppose even his sort are of some use, but for the life of me, I can't figure out what."

"Is there something the matter with Saygus?"

"Matter? I don't think matter is the right word. Crackpot, eccentric, recluse, those terms are more apt. I doubt he'll receive you even if you do manage to find his lodge, which, will be no easy task, he's taken great pains to hide away in those mountains."

"All alone, like a hermit?" Reddy asked.

"Might as well be, it's just his family and himself, as I understand. There's a village nearby in the foothills, but I doubt he has more than casual contact with them. Now, there would be a proper destination for you single, young men," he concluded with a knowing wink. "Are you absolutely sure Logon sent you to seek out Saygus? He's not highly regarded by any brigades I know of."

"Logon told me Saygus would guide me to my assigned brigade," Artka said.

"Perhaps you misunderstood, lad. Look, why don't you and your companions rest here a few days? Brigades are always coming and going; maybe yours will be one of them. You'd save yourself a lot of trouble trying to locate that old coot. And with the weather so harsh. What say you?"

"A day or two restin' might do usn's good," Scang said, "leastways 'till the snowstorm passes, but then usn's gots ter move along. And, they's some things even captains oughtn't look too far into, if'n yer kens my meanin'."

Gulundur regarded Scang with a raised eyebrow, then Artka. "Very well," he said. "I'll not press you. But it's plain you're conspiring to keep me in the dark. Nevertheless, for my part, I'd be remiss if I didn't warn you about Saygus."

Captain Gulundur had their full attention.

"You'd best learn the mystery surrounding his past before you lean too heavily on his advice."

"What do you mean?" Harnet asked.

"Must be close to twenty years now," Gulundur said, "when Logon waged a campaign in the Forbidden Mountains. Saygus captained a Sharuner Brigade."

"Never heard of them," said Harnet, who considered himself knowledgeable about Ecclessite military matters.

"I suppose you could call them a blended brigade, a combination of Sharpointers and Runers. Anyway, Saygus' troops made good headway through the rugged mountain passes down south, intending to launch a surprise raid straight into the heart of Craniantium. Had they succeeded, Lunatum, Sophista, possibly even the stronghold of Decepta, would've fallen. A brilliant plan of approaching through the hidden passes of the Forbidden Mountains had been conceived, requiring a special man to lead. Saygus was appointed. He'd been one of the planners and was somewhat familiar with the territory. He was also chosen because his brigade, though few in number, demonstrated greater passion for rescuing Carnalians than other brigades. This was due in part, they claimed, to the extra shine they put on their swords. Every man in the brigade had at least half his sword shining.

"Saygus and company were but a few miles from Craniantium when Lurcan's irregular spies discovered them, leaving little time to summon sufficient defense of their cities."

"Irregular spies?" Harnet asked, his brows wrinkled.

Gulundur returned their intense stare. "You know, certain bats, carrion birds, scavenging animals."

The four nodded as if recollecting, although this was new information to Artka.

Gulundur resumed, "Tophets were sent, but Saygus' men unmade several of them and the remainder were driven back on their first assault. Cusps didn't even dare approach that valiant corps. Firedrakes and dreads were too far away on other missions, so, it was that Lurcan's personal attention, albeit remotely, was drawn to the threat closing in on Craniantium. Saygus had every advantage and was expected to deliver a crippling blow to the empire.

"Five weeks later, Saygus emerged from the southern mountains alone, defeated, a broken man."

"Why? What happened?" Harnet asked.

"No one knows for sure. Oh, there was a court of inquiry. But, before the tribunal rendered a judgment, Logon let it be known that he accepted Saygus' explanation in full. They had no option but to acquit Saygus. A motion was made to de-commission Saygus but Logon even prevented that. It turned out as if he'd been de-commissioned however, for no one would have aught to do with him after that. Eventually, he and his family disappeared. Rumors made the rounds that he and his family entered the wilderness of the Prophecy Mountains, a self-imposed exile, no doubt punishing himself. He's been the next thing to a hermit ever since."

"But he must have truthfully related what happened," Artka said, "otherwise Logon wouldn't have accepted his report, would he?"

"Ah lad, you'll learn that Logon often lets consequences overtake a man rather than mete out immediate discipline."

"But, are we to understand that the tribunal believed him guilty?" Harnet pressed. "Surely he must have offered a defense."

"He did. But only Logon knew the whole story. The judges on the tribunal were given just enough facts to satisfy the records but were never called upon to render a verdict."

"Well then, who's to say there was any malfeasance?" Reddy said. "I mean, maybe he told the truth."

"Exactly what Logon had written into the record. Only he knew for sure. It wasn't anyone else's business to pass judgment if Logon declined to do so."

"I'd like ter ken his side o' the story," Scang mused. The others nodded. "Does yer ken any o' whut he said?"

"It's been a long time, and I'm not sure I remember it exactly, but Saygus' story goes that the downfall occurred after setting up camp on a lookout over Cosmopolis Pike, the main road to Sophista. Saygus took two men and spied out the territory, selecting ambush spots. The plan was to block the road, isolating Craniantium."

Two stewards arrived, placing tankards and a platter of cinnamon rolls drizzled with honey on the table.

"Help yourselves lads," Gulundur said. "When Saygus returned to camp to brief his troops he found some twenty Craniantium Ecclessites, calling themselves Wisests, whom we now know to be deceivers, had joined themselves to his command. They had an alternative plan for the conquest of Sophista. The Sharuners were to yield their swords to the Wisests, who would then smuggle the weapons into the heart of Sophista under a load of hay. The leader of the Wisests argued that the Sophisticates had been warned and thus, were on the alert for strangers with glowing swords. But if Saygus' men carried no such swords, they could infiltrate the city disguised as merchants or migrant workers come to glean the fields. Once inside, they could reclaim their weapons from the hay-cart, deploy and take over strategic points of the city. When the Craniantiumites realized they'd been so easily invaded and occupied, Sophista, whose population eschewed violence for any reason, even refusing to defend themselves, would surrender, thus avoiding casualties."

"Clever," Harnet said.

"Ah, but Saygus insisted that kingsmen must never relinquish their weapons. Arguments ensued. The Wisests persuaded many Sharuners their plan was superior because it avoided open conflict. The camp became divided. The disagreement went on for two days, the longer debate continued, the more were swayed to the Wisests' opinion. Even Saygus' subordinate officers were eventually won over.

"Saygus argued two main points over and over: One, never let loose of their swords for any reason, and, two, the Sophisticate government might not collapse as easily as they hoped. Saygus' plan, admittedly, was dangerous, calling for cutting off the road, besieging and taking over the city, and battling any reinforcements from Carnalia."

"Ere now, a captain be's a captain," Scang said. "Whut right did any o' 'em have ter second-guess their captain?"

"Precisely the point one of the tribunes brought up during the trial: that a good commander would have just given orders, and that would've been that. But Saygus wanted men to follow him because they trusted his leadership, not because he had to pull rank. As far as I'm concerned, none of this is where the fault lay. I'm just relating the official record, since you asked."

"So, what was his mistake, as you see it?" Artka asked.

"No one, including Saygus, ever questioned the validity of the Wisests. After all, they were unknown in Ecclessa. Now we know them for what they are—counterfeit kingsmen in cahoots with Lurcan. For whatever reason, Saygus and his men received them at face value, ignoring the evidence before their eyes—that none of the Wisests bore swords. Considering they were hard-by Decepta, that should've been their first consideration. They were even too bashful to ask to see their chest scars, not wanting to be labeled as suspicious.

"On the third day, the last Sharuner holdouts abandoned Saygus, going over to the Wisests. Saygus sadly watched them hide their swords in an ox-cart and break up into groups of three and four. They intended to rendezvous two days hence at a selected landmark on the outskirts of the city.

"From a high vantage point, Saygus watched his disarmed, disbanded company stretched out along the very road he'd planned to blockade. To his horror, a dozen, black-caped Carnalian cavalry—the only empire forces in the vicinity—appeared from the desert bordering Craniantium and Pitland as if by sorcery. They mercilessly slaughtered the vulnerable kingsmen. Had the Sharuners kept their swords, that Carnalian cavalry would have had no chance. But as it turned out, the Ecclessites were massacred to the last man. At least, that's how Saygus described it, being the sole surviving witness."

"I believe his story," Artka said.

"Yes, of course you do," Gulundur replied, unperturbed. "But you weren't there for the questions he couldn't or wouldn't respond to."

"Like whut?" Scang asked.

"Why was the Advisor not consulted to evaluate the Wisests plan? And how did Saygus survive, a sought-after fugitive all alone, deep within enemy territory? According to his testimony, infantry reinforcements arriving later that day spied him and gave chase, so, how did he evade capture for more than a month while being hotly pursued in enemy territory? Do you understand why the tribunal, and others, believed there were too many moth holes in the fabric of his story?"

"Surely Logon had good reason to dismiss the charges," Harnet said, looking not at Gulundur, but Artka.

"And I'm sure I heard Logon right," Artka said.

"Just the same," said Gulundur, looking away, his attention drawn to a commotion in the outer hallway, "be very careful if you do find him. Now, if you'll excuse me, I have duties needing my attention."

His guests rose as the captain departed.

Reddy said, "What do you make of that?"

"I dunno. Seems like he be's wantin' ter put his nose inter our business, an' cain't seem ter say anythin' encouragin'," Scang said.

Artka sipped from his mug. "Nevertheless, I'm sticking to what Logon told me. After all, I've never been to Ecclessa like the rest of you. I thought everybody in Ecclessa would be like Tren. I never expected to have to sort out whom to trust."

"We were all like that at first," Harnet said. "We thought Ecclessa all was bliss and blessing. How could anything of Logon be otherwise? But we found out, as you're now discovering, such thinking is naive. Sure, there's no darkness in Logon, but his servants are only rescued Carnalians, and until they become more like Logon, can and occasionally do revert to their old nature. There's no real safety outside Splendora. On the contrary, Logon warned us to be prepared no matter which side of the river we're on. That's why he gave us such a wonderful weapon. That alone should clue us in that all isn't celebration and frolic, even in Ecclessa."

"He's right," Reddy said. "Many recruits aren't discouraged by cusp attacks in the least, but let a fellow kingsman speak harshly, and they call it quits."

"Thet's whut separates true followers o' Logon from them whut jest wants ter escape the destruction comin' on Carnalia."

"Well, to avoid causing envy," Artka said, "I think it best we not tell anyone of the new brigade." They joined hands in a pact then took their empty tankards to the kitchen.

An amiable steward washing dishes said, "So you're going to the interior? I hear there's been an increase in tophet sightings lately. But, I got this news a week ago from a Runer brigade heading to Carnalia."

Sobered by that information, the four spent much of the day lounging near the fireplace in the keep, talking quietly among themselves. Occasionally one or another would toll his sword, but their thoughts always returned to the battle raging just across the river. In addition, the rumor of tophet creatures on the loose in Ecclessa made prolonged concentration on tolling difficult.

In the middle of the afternoon a soldier strode through the great hall announcing that a messenger had arrived from the western fortress. Artka and his companions scurried outside to hear the briefing. They joined a small crowd of off-duty attendants in the snow-covered courtyard, eagerly listening as the messenger gave his report from atop his heavily-breathing horse.

" . . . almost crashed the gate. Captain Metid wants to know why you delayed in sending support. He also requests more troops, Sharpointers and Wholebladers if you can get them, if not, whatever's available. That's about it, sir, begging permission to return to duty."

"First go to the mess and get some refreshment," Captain Gulundur said, "and acquire a fresh mount from the stable. This one's all in a lather. When you get back, tell Captain Metid that we responded in record time, so I don't know what he's talking about. I'll send as many able-bodied warriors as I can muster on such short notice. Oh yes, the four you asked after, there they are." Gulundur pointed at Scang, Artka, Reddy, and Harnet on the fringe of the crowd.

The messenger nodded, dismounted, and after handing his horse's reins to an attendant, approached the four. "Artka?"

"That's me."

"Walk with me. I have a word for you." Without waiting for Artka's reply, he hastened toward the kitchen. The foursome followed, half jogging to keep up.

In the dining hall a steward bearing a mug of hot chocat and a plate of steaming beans mixed with ground mutton met them. The rider sat at the nearest table and gulped his food. Artka sat across from him with his friends, waiting patiently.

"I have a message, like I said, from Captain Tren," he managed between bites. "Hard to understand, some of it, but he assured me you'd grasp the meaning." In went another mouthful which was presently washed down by a swig of chocat. "He said: you must not delay. Be on your way by daybreak at the latest. Now this is the part I don't get, and I quote so as not to lose any of his meaning: 'the spitter crossed successfully.' Does that make sense? If it does, that's all that matters." He took another mouthful.

Artka paled. "Tell Tren his message is understood."

"Okay, but I doubt I'll see him again till after the battle. He led a counterattack into the center of the enemy's line, probably saved the fort. I never saw Erotons run so fast as when Tren's sword changed from bright blue to brilliant yellow, filling the air with wondrous sounds. It was truly . . . beautiful."

"But, he's too injured to fight. He shouldn't even have been in the battle, much less led an attack," Artka said.

"He had the brightest sword and was the only one who knew what to do. When this battle is over, I'm transferring to a Wholeblader brigade."

Artka glanced at the messenger's sword, it was sharp only for an inch or two from the point but interspersed along the blade were brightly glowing runes. He was a Runer.

Having completed his meal, the rider stood. "Well, back to the war." With that, he jogged toward the stable with the same urgency in which he'd arrived.

"What now, Artka?" asked Reddy.

Anxiety was in all their eyes except Scang's, who alone seemed unaffected by Tren's message, but then, his craggy face was always difficult to read.

Artka said, "I think we should go now, like Tren suggested, and not delay."

"Right," Scang said.

"But it's still snowing," Reddy complained, in no hurry to leave warmth, food, and the promise of a soft bed. "The snow must be three feet deep. From here we go on foot, you know. It'll take all day to go two leagues. Wouldn't it be safer to wait for the storm to stop? Maybe the battle will be over then and Captain Gulundur will spare us some horses."

"Now laddie, if'n Tren thot it'ud be best fer usn's ter wait, he'd a said so. Artka be's right. We leave now."

"I agree," Harnet said. "If that tophet is still upcountry, the older our trail, the harder for him to track us, the more distance between him and us, the better. Our swords haven't enough light to penetrate its cloaking mist, and if it came to a battle, I doubt we'd hit a vital spot before he rendered us defenseless with his spray."

"It's decided then?" Artka asked, looking to Reddy.

Reddy lowered his eyes, but slowly nodded. A hand touched his shoulder, and he looked up into the broad, bearded face of Scang. "Usn's all be's scairt, laddie. But, we mustn't let fear paralyze usn's. Logon never sends his servants on vain missions. He'll see we gets through."

"But don't you see that's precisely the problem. Artka is the only one Logon has actually sent. The rest of us are tag-a-longs."

"Does yer want ter stay here?"

"Yes . . . no . . . I don't know."

"You shouldn't come then, Reddy," Artka said, "unless you're absolutely sure Logon wants you in this new brigade."

"New brigade?"

None of them had noticed Captain Gulundur approaching. "So, that's what you're hiding. Logon is forming a new brigade. Well, well. And all that talk about Saygus was to throw me off, wasn't it?"

Artka declined a response, saying instead, "Captain, we thank you for your hospitality. It seems best for all concerned that we get on our way now."

"What? In this storm? Before you even know the outcome of the battle?"

In answer, the four travelers rose from their seats, silent, resolute.

"At least tell me what type of brigade is being formed. Sharpointer? Wholeblader? Onedger? Come on," he urged. "You know I'll find out sooner or later, for all brigades pass through these portals, eventually."

"Meaning no disrespect, sir, but at that time, you'll know," Harnet replied. "I believe if Logon wanted you to know, he'd have informed you."

Gulundur backed down. "Of course, I mean no harm. My duties as keeper of the eastern gate often frustrate me, especially when something big is afoot. It's my job to co-ordinate brigades to effective outcomes, and sometimes I overstep my bounds trying to garner personal information. Please, forgive me."

"We do forgive you, captain," Artka said. "But, be warned. Logon advised me to keep the new brigade secret. You found out by accident, and perhaps that was Logon's way of informing you. Now that you know, you also bear responsibility."

"Well said, lad. I accept the rebuke."

CHAPTER TWENTY-SIX

THE HEAVY SNOWFALL HAD STOPPED, but thick, gray clouds hung low and threatening. A trail of slowly-rising, steamy breaths lingered over the furrow left behind by the four who were well out of sight of the fortress. Scang led, breaking path through the thigh-deep snow.

"I hope tophets have as much trouble moving through snow as we do," Harnet grunted to no one in particular.

Pausing, Scang said, "Save yer breath, laddie. Yer'll need it oncet I gits a goin'." He drew a deep, frigid breath and defiantly lunged ahead, spraying snow to all sides. Several minutes later Scang stopped again, sucking in great draughts of air.

"Would you like me to break trail for a while, Scang?" Artka asked. "You must be exhausted."

The Eroton made no reply as, with limbs churning, he furiously re-assailed the snow-pack.

Artka, tramping snow down for Harnet and Reddy behind, smiled, remembering his first meeting with this self-sacrificing giant.

A violet-hued, snowy contour blanketed the land. They had gone only a couple of miles, but in their state of fatigue and cold, it felt like leagues. Reddy, last in line, complained of cramps.

Scang drew to a halt, lifted his shaggy, snow-encrusted head to get his bearings, then veered right, aiming for a stand of trees. "If'n usn's kin git another half mile ter them trees, usn's kin build a fire fer the night."

A howling wind swooped across the open steppes creating a blinding wall of snow. The four pulled their hoods over their faces. Scang turned his back to the blast, bending over, waiting for the blast to abate. But the gale intensified.

This wasn't a stray squall, but a revival of the storm they'd encountered on Logon's Bridge earlier that day.

"Grab aholt o' each other," Scang shouted. He seized Artka's cloak and pulled him close.

Following Scang's cue, they all gripped each other's cloaks. Scang, flailing arms and legs, re-assaulted the snow with maniacal fervor. Several minutes later he sank to his hands and knees. "Lost me bearings," he shouted to those behind.

Just then in a detonation of lightning and thunder, the full fury of the storm struck, sucking their breaths away. Scang turned about and huddled them like chicks under his outspread arms. The wind's icy fingers tugged at their coats and cloaks. Snow blinded their eyes and clogged their nostrils. Never had any of them encountered such ferocity in a storm.

A cape draped over Artka's head and he found himself face to face with Scang. "It be's no use, Artka. Usn's will never gain the shelter o' them trees now. I fears usn's will freeze right here. Mebbe we shouldda stayed the night in the fortress."

The sound of a toller scraping across a blade caught their attention. Adapting Scang's idea, Artka groped for Harnet's huddled form, draped his cape over him, and asked, "Why are you doing that?"

Harnet, visible in the pale light of his sword, said, "it worked on the bridge. The swords sang, and the storm settled down. I thought it might work again."

A cold blast of air and a lifting of their capes brought Scang's snowy visage into their impromptu shelter. Under an arm he dragged a shivering Reddy. "Best do summat soon afore usn's gits froze solid."

Packing down the snow around them and affixing their capes into the snow banks on either side as a roof over themselves, they carved out a small cave affording protection from the storm.

"Toll your Children of the Stars," Harnet said. "It worked before, it'll work again."

"Well, unless anyone else has a better idea." Artka said, extracting his sword and toller. Scang and Reddy followed suit. Reddy shivered so much that he couldn't keep his file on the same spot.

"I-i-i-t's n-n-not w-w-working," Reddy said after several moments. "I-i-it won't vibrate n-n-now."

"Keep trying," Harnet said. "It has to work."

They redoubled their efforts, to no avail. There was no musical pitch, no vibration, no bright light . . . nothing. And the gale shrieked on above them.

Reddy's arms sank wearily to his sides. He sat and stared blankly, confused, drowsy. Artka and Harnet began shivering. Even Scang's immense bulk wasn't impervious to the penetrating cold. His fingers were turning blue.

The storm, increasing in ferocity, whipped wildly about their cape-shelter, heaping inch after inch of snow over them.

Reddy slumped onto his side more asleep than awake, his sword slid to the snow-packed ground in front of him. Harnet began slurring words, mumbling on and on about someone named Pekkel. He also no longer tolled, but instead, stared fixedly at some spot in the snow burrow's wall and dropped his sword. It settled near Reddy's.

Artka's hands and feet slipped into numbness. His feet that had been so cold that they hurt, began to feel warm. He tried to focus his thoughts: what was it he should be doing? He forgot. He was so tired. If only he could sleep a little while, then he'd wake up and remember. But . . . he mustn't give in to sleep because . . . because . . . ?

Something large sprawled forward beside Artka, nearly bringing down the makeshift cape canopy. Artka was fading, but through his hazy thoughts he recognized three swords lying in close proximity to each other on the snowy floor of their little huddle. He must sleep, but, before he did, he must lay his sword overtop the others. This done, unconsciousness conquered him.

~

The sound of trickling water woke Artka first. He opened his eyes and saw in the combined light of the four swords that the cape-roof drooped here and there, but in its place a crusted snow-roof had formed over them. He propped himself up on an elbow and glanced at his sleeping companions. A wave of warmth wafted over his face. He searched for the fire but found nothing other than the prone bodies of his friends and their swords on the ground. He nudged Scang with his foot.

Scang rolled over, opened his eyes and asked, "Whut?"

"I don't know Scang. We ought to be frozen to death."

Scang sat up. "Heat! Whar's it from?"

"Can't say."

Artka lifted Sky Saber off of the other swords. Within seconds an icy chill crept back into the snow-cave. Harnet and Reddy sat up, rubbing their eyes, inspecting their surroundings with wonder.

"Hey! We're alive!" Reddy said.

Ignoring Reddy, Artka said, "Scang, why is it getting cold again?"

"Yer askin' me?"

Artka turned and demanded of Reddy and Harnet, "All right, what did you two just do? The heat stopped just as you sat up. What'd you do?"

"What heat?" asked Reddy.

Scang said, "The heat started fadin' afore they woke. It musta been summat yer or me done, Artka."

"All I did was put my sword in my belt."

"An' where was it afore that?"

"There," Artka pointed to the three swords lying close together. "Across them."

"Put it back, just like it was," said Harnet with a shiver. "Let's see what happens."

Artka shrugged, took the sword from his belt and placed it across the other three.

Instantly a wave of warmth rose from the contiguous swords.

"Logon said there were powers in these weapons that few ever discovered," Artka said in wonder.

"We should've noticed the ground beneath the swords was bare," Reddy said. "They're obviously the heat source."

The four grinned at each other, huddling around the swords, talking excitedly. Outside their shelter, the storm still raged.

"Do tophets freeze?" asked Reddy after they calmed down from their excited discovery.

"Not unless fire freezes," Scang said. "When snow hits fire, whazzit do?"

"Melts."

"Well, tophets be's nobbut fire whut's took on temporary shape, lad. When snow hits 'em, it turns ter steam. Fact is, thet spitter seekin' usn's, probly be's meltin' his way through this storm right now."

Reddy shuddered.

"But," Harnet said, "Will he find our trail?"

"Right now, we hain't gots a trail," Scang laughed.

"So, we're safe, covered over like this, don't you think, especially with no tracks betray our presence?" Artka said.

"Yep. I'd say so, unless . . ."

"Unless what, Scang?" Reddy asked.

"Well, now thet it's been brought up, summat's been botherin' me since the bridge."

"Speak what's on your mind, Scang," said Artka, not looking up.

"Awright. Since usn's been attacked on the bridge, I cain't help feelin' one o' usn's has gots summat o' Lurcan, or at least Carnalia, on his person. Thet's whut drew the nasty beasties to us'ns. If'n thet be's true, a tophet might locate usn's by his sensors. Don't make no difference whut the weather be's like, or how much distance it'll foller."

Silence reigned until Artka broke the silence, "Any idea who might have this object?"

Scang thoughtfully observed Artka for a long moment before saying, "Yer."

Harnet and Reddy stared wide-eyed at Scang. "How can you think such a thing?" Harnet said.

Scang ignored their resentment, keeping his eyes on Artka.

Artka finally raised his head. "I was told that Logon made them."

Reddy and Harnet shifted their gaze to Artka.

"Show usn's, laddie. Yer kens I'd die fer yer. I wouldn't be askin' if'n it weren't important."

Artka reluctantly withdrew the leather pouch he'd retrieved from the courtyard well. All eyes watched as he extracted the shiny dagger, placing it on the ground in full view. "There, if anything on me is attracting lurcanish agents, that's it. The man who gave it to me said Logon made them, that they're a complement to the sword."

"What did Tren say?" Harnet asked.

"He thought one of the dreads had something to do with making them. In fact, he dissuaded me from wanting one, but when I woke the next morning, this was on the foot of my bed. I figured it wouldn't do any harm if I kept it but didn't use it. Besides, it might be Logon's will for me to have it, since it just . . . sort of . . . appeared without my seeking it."

Reddy bent down and studied the engraved runes on the dagger, missing no detail of blade or handle. "It sure is beautiful, a miniature replica of the Children of the Stars."

"I wouldn't mind having one myself," Harnet mused, "unless of course, they do turn out to be Lurcanish."

"I dunno. I jest dunno," Scang said. "Looks awright. Fact is, it looks as much summat o' Logon as anythin' I ever seen."

"So, I can keep it? At least till we know for sure if it's of Lurcan?" said Artka.

"It'd be a shame to get rid of it if it's made by Logon. Look how it sparkles even in this dim light," Harnet said.

"Oh, awright. Keep it. Jest till we finds out more about it."

Artka's shoulders slumped. The thought of parting with it was hateful. If he had to, he had to, but, until he knew for certain, he'd keep it. He returned it to his pouch, which he now hung openly on his belt.

Secure in their snowy chamber, warmed by the combined swords and encouraged by each other's friendship, the four chatted until sleepiness stole over them. Before yielding to slumber, they agreed to keep guard in shifts. In the morning when the storm abated they'd break out of their snow-cave and continue their journey.

Scang wanted first watch, but the others convinced him that since the burden of breaking trail lay primarily on him, his greater value was in being well-rested. After sharing a meal that had been provided by the Fortress East kitchen crew, Artka and Reddy took first watch. Scang and Harnet promptly fell asleep.

There wasn't much left to talk about, and Reddy nodded off long before it was time to wake Harnet. Artka watched him drift, deciding to let him sleep. He could watch alone. He leaned back against his pack, thinking of Logon: remembering his kind voice, the gentleness of his eyes, the confident authority of his presence . . .

Artka's head snapped forward with a jerk. He'd been dozing. He shook his head, but his eyelids were so heavy and his need for sleep so pressing. He tried different ploys to stay awake: listening to the trickle of melted snow under the swords—no that made it worse; he then tried gauging the intensity of the wind or timing the snores of his friends. But his blinks lasted longer, his breathing became deeper, and he gradually succumbed.

A noise unrelated to the storm roused him. It wasn't nearby, but neither was it distant. Rather than the heavy dragging of a tophet, it seemed more like a horse-drawn sled—except there wasn't a horse alive that could pull a sled through this deep snow. Within minutes the noise faded, and though he listened, the sound didn't come again. It was nearly time to wake Harnet, but Artka wanted to listen a little longer in case the sound returned.

The next thing he knew, Scang's massive hand gently shook his arm. The snow roof of their shelter had turned bright yellow, ice crystals were melting into droplets.

"Storm's over," Harnet said. "I guess we were all too tired to watch till the storm's end. We just woke a minute ago."

"It must be mid-morning, judging by the sunlight on our roof," Reddy said.

"Time ter git a goin', laddies." Scang pulled his sword from underneath Sky Saber and thrust it through the crystalline roof. He stood to full height and squinted against the ultra-bright vista.

"How deep is the snow, Scang?" Artka asked gathering his sword and pack.

"Up ter me chest, which would be yer chins. I best git started." He lunged at a corner of their shelter, ripping into the snow which was no longer light and fluffy, but wet and heavy. Fifty yards into the task they realized the full impact of what they were up against. "Usn's ain't gonna make much headway today." After a quarter of an hour Scang sat and faced his companions, breathing heavily, his face flushed. "I cain't do much more o' this, lads. Yesterday the snow was light, givin' way. Not so today." He kicked a clump of snow from between his feet.

"I remember," Artka said, "Sergeant Love telling us stories about tying branches to his boots so he could walk on top of deep snow. We all laughed, thinking it was one of his tall tales."

"Of course!" Scang said, slapping his thigh. "Snowwalkers lets yer walk atop o' snow. All usn's needs is some o' the right kind o' tree branches." He stood on tiptoe to get his bearings to the copse of trees he'd spied the previous day. "Ah, there they be's. An' it looks ter be hemlocks among 'em."

His giant frame furiously lunged into the snow sending white spray in all directions. Artka struggled behind, followed by Harnet, then Reddy.

Scang's exuberance slowed after several minutes, however, and progress was again slow, exhausting work. Twenty minutes passed, then Scang abruptly halted. "Hullo! Whut be's this?"

The others clambered alongside the huffing Eroton. In open-mouthed wonder they beheld a path seven feet wide with only a few inches of slush on the ground, as if a road had been cleared through the deep snow just for them.

"It kinda wanders back 'n forth far as I kin see," said Scang, looking out over the top of the snow pack. "Whut couldda made it?"

"Uh, I think I might have heard something last night," Artka said, "like something gliding through the snow. But I was so sleepy, I wasn't sure if I really heard anything, what with the storm howling and all."

"What'd it sound like?" Harnet asked.

"It was swift, like a sleigh—only there were no hoof-beats. It faded after a bit, and didn't return, so I wasn't sure if I'd dreamt it. I didn't feel it was worth disturbing everyone's sleep."

"What do you think, Scang?" Reddy's voice wavered.

Scang considered, then said, "I dunno. Summat melted this here snow, but whut couldda done it, I be's afeered ter think. Lookit thet in yonder slush. Ain't thet a footprint?"

They gathered around the track that Scang indicated. Harnet knelt down for closer inspection. "It appears to be the claw mark of a giant crawdad, or scorpion."

Artka blanched, remembering the night he was sprayed with venom. "Oh, no!" "Giant scorpion?" said Scang. "Hain't thet the critter whut—?"

Artka nodded.

Reddy fingered his sword handle, looking nervously up and down the trench.

Harnet was already several paces down the path, investigating more tracks. "Hey, look at this gob of green slime."

"Tophet blood be's green I heered," Scang wrinkled his nose.

Artka prodded the congealed gob with his sword point and was startled as it sizzled away to a smoky wisp. He quickly retracted and examined his blade. None stuck to his sword and the gob cooled immediately, but the foul stench of tophet permeated the air.

"I guess there's little doubt now. The tophet that attacked Tren and me at the gate was wounded. It appears they don't heal too well, but fester," Artka said.

"It would also appear he's following you, Artka," Harnet added. "I've heard it said that tophets never give up a victim they wounded."

"Thanks, I needed to hear that."

"You want to know what you're up against, don't you?"

"But how did it come so close to finding us out here in the wilds?" Reddy asked.

They all turned to Artka.

"All right, all right, I know. The dagger." Regretfully, Artka opened the pouch to withdraw the offending item. "I'll just throw it away, I guess."

"Nay, Artka, nay," Scang interrupted. "I gots me an idee thet we oughtta use it ter undo our foe. I hain't 'zactly sure how jest yet, but it be's too dangerous ter let such a thing lyin' about now thet we kens what it does. Come spring thaw summat might find it an' draw the tophet after hisself like yer done."

"But isn't it dangerous for us to keep it?" Artka asked. "That gliding sound I heard must've been the scorpion searching for us—and nearly finding us, all due to this dagger. It's too dangerous to keep."

"When yer took the object, yer took the consequences whut comes with it, lad. But I be's athinkin' the Advisor gots a plan. Hang on ter it fer jest a bit yet, till usn's kin figger it out. Besides, thet tophet's not near here anymore, else the trail wouldn't be so cold. See, the slush is froze ter ice where the sun ain't shinin'? It be's a while since yer spittin' friend been hereabouts. He was close, but musta give up."

"Maybe the combined power of the touching swords made him shy away," Reddy suggested, "or at least confused him."

"Would it be safe to follow this path, then?" Harnet asked. "It sure would be easier than breaking trail."

Scang rubbed his whiskers, peering up and down the melted pathway. "Fer a wee bit, mebbe. Leastways till we gits ter them trees and kin make snowwalkers."

The four followed the melted trench, their heads bobbing just above the surface, with the exception of Scang who stuck chest and shoulders above.

He informed the others that the trail no longer meandered but headed straight for the same clump of trees he'd been aiming for. Then added, "Best git ready, thet tophet might be a waitin' ter ambush usn's jest inside the tree line."

"We're as ready as we can be, Scang," said Artka. "We have no choice but to get to those trees, tophet or no. We must have snowwalkers. Without them he'll surely catch us; with them there's a chance of escape. Who's to say for sure if he's lying in wait? If he isn't, we'll move along to our destination quicker, and if he is . . . "

"But, it's a spitter," Reddy said. "He'll disable us with his spray."

"Artka be's right. This be's the only way—straight ter it, like men, not runnin' away like dogs. If'n we dies, we dies like men."

Reddy gritted his teeth but said nothing. The knuckles on his sword hilt were white.

"Let's get it over with, then," Harnet said.

"Arter the beastie, lads."

The four turned a corner, swords at the ready as they marched a hundred yards down the pathway, straight toward a dark, brooding copse of trees.

CHAPTER TWENTY-SEVEN

FOLLOWING THE TOPHET-MADE TRENCH THE four entered under a fringe of fir trees. They paused in the shade, letting their eyes adjust from the brilliant, snowy fields to the shadows dominating the grove.

"Yers wait here," Scang said. "I wants ter sneak up on 'im. Mebbe I kin find where he be's a layin'. I doesn't think he kens usn's comin'." Without waiting for agreement, Scang hunched over and ventured alone along the shadow-mottled path. Before rounding a corner he called back in a hushed voice, "I be's right back. Don't go nowhars."

Artka, Reddy, and Harnet scarcely breathed. They kept watch long, anxious minutes after Scang disappeared, listening intently, sword in hand, ready to leap into action. Several more moments passed with nothing more than a breeze whispering through the conifers. A cloud crossed the sun, deepening the shade and lowering the temperature in the grove. There was still no sign of Scang. Ten minutes turned into fifteen. Concern turned to worry.

Twenty minutes passed. The sun burst with renewed glory upon the crystalline vista, dazzling their eyes afresh, causing them to squint. Artka was about to suggest someone go see what became of Scang when a yelp was borne on the wind, followed by sounds of heavy thrashing in the underbrush.

"There," Reddy said, pointing. "See it, way deep in the wood?"

Snow cascaded off a small tree.

"Let's go!" Artka said, charging down the trench, sword out before him. Harnet followed, with Reddy on their heels.

Scang's shouting grew louder as they got closer, but the words were indistinguishable. Perceiving the action was just around the corner they slowed their attack, not wanting to rush headlong into a trap. In the excitement of the moment Artka almost threw back his head to bellow his lion-roar battle cry, but the Advisor checked him.

Instead, as Artka turned the corner, he took up his new battle cry, "Lo—g—on!"

Reddy and Harnet, charging behind Artka, took up the same cry. They skidded around the corner, swords projecting before them. The trio slid to a sudden halt, staring open-mouthed, the war cry dying on their lips. Then they burst out laughing.

Scang, dangled upside-down, one foot caught in a snare, bellowing loudly in his native tongue. As soon as he saw his friends, the Eroton tirade ceased. "Well, qwitcher gawkin' an' git me down."

Harnet was the first to control his merriment. "Artka, I don't believe I've ever seen a hare this large snared before. Ah, this Ecclessa is a wondrous land."

"Don't believe I have either," Artka said. "What do you think we ought to do with it?"

"Why, take it along for food, of course. Especially the way Scang eats."

Scang glared from his inverted position. "I'm warnin' yers—" His tone and visage communicated that he'd better be let down immediately or else they weren't going to think his predicament humorous much longer.

"Only teasing, Scang, only teasing," Harnet located the ropes wrapped around a nearby kingwood tree.

They untied the ropes and using a sapling's trunk as a brake, lowered Scang. The small tree, removed from its supporting brace and suddenly taking the burden of Scang's full weight, dipped low. Scang plopped in the slush and mud face first. His torso and feet, however, were hung up on the brace, causing his face to remain entombed for several moments while they hurried to get the rest of him lowered to the ground.

Muffled Eroton oaths erupted from the slush on either side of his face. When Scang was finally on all fours and managed to raise his head, the sight of the Eroton's beard packed with snow, mud, and ice was too much for the young kingsmen causing them to collapse in a fresh round of laughter.

Scang's face grew redder and his eyebrows arched, but then, realizing what he must look like, he too cracked a smile, chuckled, and soon guffawed loudest of all. Gales of laughter resounded for several minutes as they rolled on the icy pack, holding their bellies.

When they finally regained composure and settled down, Scang reported his findings. "I follered this here path clear ter t'other side o' the woods an' seen it jest kept a goin'. 'S a funny thing—the trail be's headin' right where we be's agoin', as if'n the beastie kens our destination."

"Perhaps it'll ambush us when we come along," Artka said.

"How can it know where we're going?" Harnet asked.

"Probly be's guessin', but it be's a powerful good guess. One o' the names fer tophets means 'knowing ones'."

"Well if it knows let's not use its trail," Reddy said.

"Thet would be best. I don't think it figgered on us'ns makin' snow-walkers," Scang said. "But, if'n we takes too long gittin' ter the Prophecy

Mountains, the passes will git too deep an' we'll be froze out till spring. I sure doesn't fancy wanderin' around all winter wi' a tophet asniffin' after us'ns."

"Nor me," Artka said. "So, let's get busy with those snowwalkers."

"Awright, I'll show yers how it be's done." Scang, wiping the remaining slush and mud from his face led toward the shelter of some trees. "Some calls 'em 'branch shoes' 'stead o' 'snowwalkers'."

He broke path through the snow, which, in the grove was only knee deep. They soon found a hemlock with branches supple enough to be wrought, yet firm enough to not break under duress. Scang hewed off several branches he deemed usable, stripping bark, twigs and needles. He then wove them into a lattice until the resulting web was double the width and length of his foot. The others copied his every move as Scang explained each step, quickly learning the skills of securing ends and bolstering the edges against unraveling. Finishing, Scang demonstrated fastening withes around his ankles to keep the snow-walkers secure. Within two hours each man was outfitted with his own, handcrafted set of snowwalkers.

"I ain't perzactly real experienced in usin' these here things, but I remembers summat instructions I heered oncet," Scang said. He imparted what rudimentary instructions he recalled about keeping feet slightly apart and not shuffling. With an effort, he clambered atop the edge of the tophet-trench to give a brief demonstration and immediately disappeared from sight.

The others scurried to dig him out. It wasn't long however, until they were all cavorting like children atop the snow, playing tag, racing, and often as not, sinking out of sight in the deeper snow. When they'd gained enough skill to travel, they gathered their gear and set off on an oblique course away from the tophet-trench. Later, when reasonably sure of avoiding any chance of crossing the tophet-trench, they'd tack back toward their main objective.

"I be's glad we thot o' snowwalkers, Artka. Sure, saves me energy."

"I'm surprised you knew how to make them, seeing you've had no practical experience using them," Artka placed his foot in on of Scang's tracks.

"Me an' me brother used ter make anythin' whut come inter our minds. We was gifted thet way, makin' things outta wood or metal, even stone summat times."

"Your brother?"

Scang's voice lowered, "He be's dead."

"I—I'm sorry."

Harnet, changing the topic, posed, "I wonder who set that snare that caught you, Scang."

"Good question," Artka turned to look back at his friend. "Tophets don't set snares, do they? So, it must have been set by men. Whoever set it likely knows how to get around in deep snow, too. It's a riddle, alright."

"Here's another riddle," Reddy called from behind. "What were they hoping to catch? That rope was way too thick for small game like rabbits, or even deer, not to mention totally useless for tophets."

"I wondered about that, too," Harnet agreed. "You don't suppose it was set for humans?"

"But who would snare humans in Ecclessa?" Artka asked. "Aren't we all on the same side?"

"Then you explain it," Reddy said, "unless tophets do set snares."

"Nah!" Scang said. "Tophets mainly chase down their quarry."

"Well, you were the one caught in it, Scang. What do you think?" Artka asked.

"I doesn't like ter mention such things, but Logon allows fer critters ter roam about freely, big critters—an' dangerous."

"Like what?" Reddy scanned the horizon.

"Jest . . . beasties."

Reddy shuddered. "Oh, don't tell me. I don't want to know."

"Jest the same, we'd best be akeepin' a keen eye out. Thet tophet might not be the only danger usn's be's facin'. From now on, no more sleepin' on watch."

~

The lowering sun cast long shadows in front of them as they trekked mile after mile across the snowy expanse. Artka lifted his gaze and caught a shiny reflection in the distance. "Hey, looks like a castle."

True enough, a fortified wall glinted like a gold nugget between the white foreground and the murky, forested background.

"Take hours ter git there," Scang hunched over and plodded on.

"At least we won't have to spend another night in the cold and snow." Harnet shifted the sack to his other shoulder.

Without further comment the foursome veered toward the castle, each silently nourishing hopes of warmth, food, rest, and perhaps, news of Saygus.

The moon was rising as the party topped a knoll and saw the looming fortress as a dark shadow presiding over the snow-covered approaches. Yellow lights glittered from a few windows of the keep.

Artka and Scang halted, waiting for their companions to catch up, their frosty breaths floating in the chilly air around them.

Reddy huffed alongside. "Something's wrong here. I don't know what, exactly, but something is, well, odd."

"I can tell you," Harnet said, drawing alongside. "Look at it. It's crumbling. Even from this distance and in the dark, you can see that the watchtowers are eroded and the walls have gaps large enough to admit a tophet."

"Harnet, yer've hammered the nail square on the head. The place be's fallin' apart."

"Who would live in such a place?" Reddy asked.

"Let's find out." Artka started downhill. "Even if it's falling down, it's shelter, and hopefully good food and company."

Agreeing, they trudged onward, heading toward the portcullis and drawbridge.

"Uh, this might sound strange," said Harnet as they drew within a few hundred paces, "but before we get any closer, I think we ought to hide our snowwalkers. Whoever is in this rundown castle doesn't need to know we can travel on top of the snow."

Artka laid a hand on this friend's shoulder. "Are you serious?"

"Very. I have a gut feeling about this place, more than its dilapidated condition. We know nothing about the brigade quartered here, but I sense that something is amiss. The less they know about us and our quest to find Saygus, the better. Please, humor me, at least until we find out if my feelings are valid. In fact, we ought to retrace our steps a quarter mile or so, hide our snowwalkers, and have Scang break a fresh trail, making it look as though we've waded through deep snow."

Reddy and Scang groaned.

"Does yer ken whut yer be's askin' o' me? Jest mebbe yer bein' over-imaginative."

"No, it's not my imagination. This place is dangerous. Not as dangerous as a tophet, maybe, but there's danger here. I sense the Advisor's warning."

"Yer kens usn's gonna lose another hour, mebbe more, doin' this doncha?" Scang shook his head. "Time thet we could be enjoyin' a warm meal if'n yer be's mistaken."

No one answered but seeing the resolve on Harnet's face even in the moonlight, Scang shrugged. "Aww, awright. Let's git at it."

They retraced their trail a quarter mile, cached their snowwalkers in a snowbank by a tree trunk, and followed Scang as he wearily, grumpily broke trail.

More than an hour later they arrived at the moat, exhausted and irritable. The drawbridge was up.

Artka hallooed and banged on the wooden posts, but to no avail. There were no greetings, nor challenges, nothing. There wasn't even a watch. Looking around Harnet spotted a bell dangling from a post and went over to ring it, hoping someone would respond.

After examining it he turned and announced, "It's got no clapper."

"Uh-huh. Foller me, lads."

They tagged along after Scang across the frozen moat and pounded on the underside of the drawbridge with the pommel of his sword. The resounding *thunka-thunka-thunka* echoed through the inner courtyard.

No response.

A breeze brought faint sounds of laughter, fiddle music, and tabrets.

Scang hammered again. *Thunka-thunka-thunka.*

"All right, we've satisfied convention," Artka said. "Let's let ourselves in. I think we can scale yonder breach."

They waded along the frozen moat to a broken-down portion of wall. Artka climbed on Scang's shoulders, grabbed an overhanging rock, and pulled himself onto the parapet. Harnet threw their rucksacks up to him one at a time. Then Scang hoisted Reddy and Harnet up to join Artka. The three of them let down a rope and braced against the Eroton's weight as Scang scaled the wall.

The walls were windswept clear of snow, but the inner court-yard was still snowed in, with only essential pathways open. The four jumped down eight feet into the snow, then made their way to the keep along one of those narrow pathways.

Music and merriment from within were so loud that Artka doubted his knock on the door would be heard. The others agreed. They heaved the door open and entered.

A noisy atmosphere of people playing darts, dancing, chatting, eating, and drinking greeted the foursome. No one paid them any attention. They stood waiting to be recognized and invited in. Finally, a corporal backing away from his dance partner bumped into Harnet. He turned to make apologies and only then noted the strangers.

He smiled, bowing low, saying, "Ah, now, we've got some visitors, travelers, and in such bitter weather. Well, come right in and join the festivities. I'll notify his Excellency that you're here." He turned and left, looking back with a curious stare.

"Wait," Artka shouted after the corporal.

The corporal paused.

"What's the celebration? And why are there no watchmen on duty? What manner of brigade is this?"

The corporal approached them again. "Just come in from the cold and so full of questions. Ntch ntch. I should think the first thing you'd want would be refreshment, not answers. Your attitude could be misunderstood, you know."

"Well, I don't mean to be—"

"No, of course you don't." The corporal grinned a little too widely. "Come, I'll show you to a table. When his Excellency is free, he'll be glad to greet you and answer any questions." The corporal meandered through the room of whirling couples, guiding the foursome to a table near the hearth.

Scang whispered over his shoulder, "Yer be's right, Harnet."

At the unoccupied table the corporal said, "Here you are. I'll send a waiter directly."

With that he was off, weaving in and out across the dance floor. The four glanced at each other, then again at their surroundings. Scarcely any one paid them notice though they looked a sight, bundled up for snow and cold instead of finery in which the occupants of the hall were garbed.

"Let's try to be inconspicuous." Artka gave them a lopsided grin.

"Looks more like a Carnalian pub than an Ecclessite brigade," Reddy said. "Don't see many sharp swords."

Artka studied the occupants of the banquet hall, then gasped.

Scang followed Artka's eyes and discovered the same thing. "Daggermen!"

A dagger hung from each person's belt, both men and women. Many had no sword, yet every person sported a dagger. Harnet and Reddy stared open mouthed. Then Harnet tugged Artka's sleeve and pointed to the doorway as a dozen Carnalian warriors entered.

Scang impulsively leapt up, drew his sword, shouted, "Lives for the King!" and charged across the room.

Startled dancers scattered out of Scang's way amidst much consternation and shouts.

Artka, Reddy, and Harnet stood to their feet unsure what to do as Scang barreled across the room.

The first Carnalian in Scang's path backed hurriedly away as he fumbled beneath his cape and extracted a Child of the Stars barely in time to ward off a thrust aimed at his heart. "H-h-hold friend, I'm a kingsman, see?"

"Whut!" Scang slid to a halt.

The soldier parted his battle gear revealing a scar. "I'm an Ecclessite. I've been to Logon's Rock, just like you. Don't you know that there are no Carnalians in Ecclessa?"

Scang just stood blinking, speechless.

The revelers resumed their activities, many commenting, "Crazy Sharpointer," and "think everyone has to be just like them."

"I, I be's sorry." Scang's face turned bright red. "I thot . . . well, yer garments, an' battle gear . . . "

"Well, no harm done," said the man. "Don't be so quick to cleave someone's ribcage, okay? Say, who are you, and how did you get here? There's no open road through the snow, save from the village, which is where we're from, and I know you're not from there."

"Usn's, uh, jest come in from the west. Spent the night out in the blizzard. Only jest arrived moments ago ourselves."

"Dreads' gates! There are more of you?" He searched the room. "Oh, I see, over at the hearth."

Scang sheepishly nodded.

"My name's Braxmore, from Conformity, the village down the road, heard of it? No? Well, little matter. It's not even on the maps, being overshadowed by this brigade, as it is. Mind if I join you and your companions?"

Scang paused briefly. "I suppose not."

One of Braxmore's cronies smiled indulgently and said, "Be careful they don't recruit you."

Scang led Braxmore to the table where Artka, Reddy, and Harnet followed their progress across the dance floor with skepticism in their eyes. "Uh, this here be's Brakmer, er . . . ?"

"Braxmore," said the lanky Conformitarian extending his right hand.

Reddy took his hand but held it limply, not sure what to make of him. "I'm Reddy, and this is Artka, and he's Harnet, and you've already met our gladiator, Scang."

"Er, yes, yes I have, and quite an impressive gladiator he is," Braxmore forced a laugh.

"Why are you still dressed like a Carnalian?" Artka ignored the proffered hand and brazenly stared the man eye to eye.

"You're new here," Braxmore said.

"Just passing through, actually," Harnet said, taking the man's hand and pumping it once.

"Well, that explains it then, doesn't it?" Braxmore apparently wasn't going to be put off by Artka's rudeness, nor outdone by it.

"Such as?" Artka asked.

"Well, this outpost is leagues out of the way. No one comes here unless they're seeking a dagger. Or unless they're so unskilled at navigating that they've lost their bearings and ended up here by accident."

"Something like that," Artka said. "Do you mean Ecclessites actually come here seeking daggers?"

"Do they come? Allow me to inform you, this is the best, not the only, mind you, but the best place in Ecclessa to obtain one. Why? You might well ask. This is the only place where you can receive a dagger from His Excellency, the most renowned authority alive on dagger lore and use. In fact, I'd wager that once you hear His Excellency speak, you'll abandon whatever other plans you might have, and stay here."

"But, daggers attract tophets and cusps!" Reddy said, a flush spreading over his face.

"Oh, my pitiful sir, I had hoped that by now the rest of Ecclessa would have been enlightened."

Annoyed at Braxmore's condescension, Artka prodded, "Enlightened? What do you mean?"

"You all believe in such things? Come now, you're having me on. No, I can see you're not. You actually believe in tophets, cusps, dreads, and such, don't you? Don't you realize that unenlightened kingsmen invented such things to explain their own moral failures?"

"What?" Harnet cocked his head to the side and arched his brows.

"Oh, come now, how can intelligent, educated people accept excuses like 'cusps made me do it', and such." Braxmore studied the four. "No wonder Carnalians avoid Ecclessa, with people like you—no offense—running around, being an embarrassment with such foolish notions."

Harnet said, "Then why did Logon put warfare runes on the swords, if they don't exist?"

Braxmore sighed. "The runes, it's always the runes with you Sharpointers, isn't it? Yes, yes. I've seen the runes, and that's precisely where the problem lies. When you toll your swords, you light up only a portion of runes connected to a certain issue and you assume you've received 'a message from Logon'. Don't you understand you'll never ignite all the runes on your sword? And unless you do, you'll never grasp the complete message." He laid his dagger on the table. "Case in point," he said, pointing to a rune, "see how this corresponds to the same rune on your swords? It says:

Fallen flames will grace no more,
Purest land or purest shore,
Creatures vile have they become,
Taking form from swampland scum.

"Sort of sounds like your tophet creatures, doesn't it?"

"That's exactly what it sounds like," Artka said. "And it goes on to tell how to combat them."

"Ah, but—did you notice the smaller rune beside it?"

They all leaned over and inspected the dagger closely. Indeed, there was a very small marking that wasn't in evidence on their swords.

"Go ahead, check your blades. It's not likely any of you have uncovered this rune yet, but it's there, waiting for you to grow in enlightenment so deeper truth can be revealed to you."

Harnet laid his sword on the table. Tren, in the week before they set out, had taught them the raised rune, and since it was a basic rune, its primary meaning was gleaned even without making it glow.

"Only after years of sharpening will this lesser rune become evident," Braxmore continued. "It says:

Frail mind of men dreaded this grief,
So the King allowed superstitious belief."

"But, I've battled a tophet!" Artka said.

"And lived to tell about it? My, my, don't you understand that if there really were such things, no man could duel them and survive? Not even such stalwart Sharpointers as yourselves. Therefore, your experience belies your beliefs."

"Do you believe Lurcan exists?" Harnet sat back with his arms crossed.

"Does Lurcan exist?" Braxmore looked up at the ceiling and stroked his chin. "Well, to that, I'd have to say, yes. But, probably not in the same way you do."

"Dreads gates!" Harnet's fists pounded the tabletop. "Either he exists, or he doesn't!"

"Who among you have seen him?" Braxmore leaned back casually.

"My father works as one of his ministers," Artka said. "I've seen the evidence of what the emperor does to those near him."

The front legs of Braxmore's chair came down with a thud. "But have you yourself actually seen the emperor?"

Artka shifted his gaze to his companions. "No."

"And do you know why? Because he's an impersonal force."

"Ridiculous." Scang's brow furrowed. "I never heered such nonsense. If'n they hain't no sich thing as a tophet, I'd like ter ken whut melted its way through snow searchin' fer usn's."

"You . . . you actually believe there's a tophet . . . that melts its way through snow, and is searching for you? Incredible, oh, this is too rich." Braxmore's hand covered his lips but his features vibrated with mirth. "I'd, Ahem, I'd very much like to see this creature, or at least the trail you claim it melted."

"Fine! Yer come along wi' usn's, an I promises yer'll not only see its trail, but I'll feed yer to him!"

"Scang!" Artka said.

"You know," Braxmore said, "I'm intrigued. Why are the four of you roaming about the wilds in such inclement weather? Where did you come from? What are you searching for? I have a proposition—suppose you take me along."

"When water burns!" Artka said. "And, you never did tell us why you wear Carnalian battle gear instead of the tunic Logon issued."

"Ah, you're trying to distract me from the topic of coming with you. You know deep down that whatever trail you claim to have found has a perfectly natural explanation, don't you? My rational explanations would only expose your fanciful beliefs, threatening your confidence in what you choose to believe." Braxmore sat back, satisfied that he'd scored a vital point. "Very well, I've decided to tell you why my friends and I are dressed this way. I hope my example of being forthright will encourage you to reciprocate."

"Whut's all thet mean?"

"It means," Harnet said, "he's prying into our business. But, it won't work. Tell us what you like, Braxmore, but you'll get no more information out of us than what we're inclined to give."

"So be it," Braxmore said. "Two days ago, some of my friends and I set out from Conformity, for the King's Gate, on our way into Carnalia to rescue lives for the king."

"How do you expect anyone to recognize you as Ecclessites?" Artka said.

"We don't. Glowing swords and white tunics have long offended Carnalians. So, his Excellency has devised a brilliant plan whereby we can walk unknown amongst them, causing no offense, acting and talking like them, raising no alarm. Then, at just the right moment, we reveal our true loyalties. They'll be amazed that we're Ecclessites, and so, will realize that King Elyon and Logon aren't all that bad. They'll let us pierce their hearts and lead them to Logon's Rock. Beautiful plan isn't it?"

"It'll never work," Harnet said. "It's been tried. Not only does it dishonor Logon, but Ecclessites who try that ploy usually end up reverting to Carnalian behavior, their tunics get stained and their love for Logon dwindles."

"Come now, Ecclessites everywhere are like that, not just Conformitarians. You can't condemn the whole idea because of a few failures."

"Well, this much I know," Artka said, "the reason I kept struggling toward Logon's Rock was due to the goodness I saw in Tren, my rescuer. If Tren had acted like a Carnalian, I wouldn't be here now."

"Oh, you just think that. Anyway, back to my story. We were already a couple of miles out when a sudden snowstorm came upon us. We turned around and hurried back. We've been here ever since, occasionally making trips to the village for more supplies, like tonight. Since the snows came so early, looks like we'll be here till spring. So, will you."

"Not likely," said Artka. "It's our intention to leave at first light."

"Oh? And have you some magical way of traveling through chest high snow? Unless of course your mystical tophet will come and melt another path for you." He couldn't hide the taunting glee in his eyes.

"You'll never know." Artka ignored the jibe. "Anyway, we want to reach the Pro—uh, place we're headed before winter really sets in."

Braxmore sat back then said, "I'd sure like to meet whatever you think is a 'tophet.' My companions won't mind if our journey to Carnalia is delayed for an indeterminate time."

"It's best for all concerned that you not accompany us," Artka said. "We'd always be arguing."

"His Excellency teaches that debate is the beginning of reason. What are you afraid of? I really want to come along, and once I've made up my mind."

"Artka says, 'NO!'" Scang thumped his fist for emphasis.

Braxmore folded his arms and observed Scang, then the others. Finally, he stood and said, "Well, we'll see."

CHAPTER TWENTY-EIGHT

AFTER FINISHING THEIR BREW AND a warm meal, the four travelers were ushered to an upstairs room that contained six beds. As they prepared for sleep, a knock came on their door.

"Come in," Reddy said as he unpacked his rucksack.

A plump, but regal captain dressed luxuriously in a red cape clasped across the neck with a golden chain, entered. Two attendants followed, the first of them being the corporal who had first greeted them. "His Excellency, Captain Sofista," announced the corporal.

The four gawked at the captain's opulent attire.

"It's customary to bow," the corporal said.

"Tut, tut, Corporal, they're guests remember, newly arrived from Carnalia's shores, by the look of them. We can't expect them to be aware of our customs. You may return to your duties, both of you." Both attendants bowed and left.

The captain turned his attention to Artka. "Braxmore informs me you're the apparent leader of this, er, expedition. Is that true?"

"Nay! I be's the leader," Scang said. "So yer kens ter deal wi' me."

"Scang, we're guests," Artka said. Scang scowled and backed down, busying himself unpacking his gear. "We, uh, followed Scang through the snow. He was the only one strong enough to break trail, so I guess, in that sense, you could say he's our leader. I apologize for his outburst. We've had a long, tiring day."

"Marvelous! I've never seen anything like it, the way you handle him, I mean. I'd always heard Erotons made ludicrous servants, but he—"

"Scang is no servant, except of the king," Artka said curtly.

"Easy laddie, we be's guests," Scang muttered lowly looking up.

"Oh please, forgive me. I meant no harm," Captain Sofista said. "I'm truly sorry if I've offended, especially when I believe I can be of great service to you. I have here, gifts which will, I'm convinced, make up for my insensitivity and convince you of my earnest desire to benefit you."

The four glanced doubtfully at each other, but Sofista was undaunted. "I don't blame you. One must be cautious, and all that, especially since," he eyed their swords, "your current guidance seems to stem from that unwieldy, antiquated blade of tedious dictums and vague stories. If superstitions are your standard, you cannot help but eventually fall into fanaticism. Then every passing shadow becomes a cusp, every rustle in the bushes a tophet. Myths will begin to control your lives."

"But—" Reddy dropped his rucksack to the floor.

A glance from Harnet silenced him.

"I see, you're not comfortable enough to speak freely. Well, I understand. I remember being newly arrived in Ecclessa, myself." Sofista paced before the door. "Oh, I was so zealous that my Glint-Shine glow brighter than all other recruits' swords. It didn't take me long to realize that a glittering blade was going to take a lot of time and effort, as I see you've begun to discover. After a few months I realized that Logon didn't truly expect me to spend so much time trying to put a keen edge on the sword. Surely, he would've made it easier if it was all that important. So, I found another way." Sofista spun on his heel and faced the four, spreading his arms as if to embrace them. "Brigade officials rebuked me, telling me I was tampering with time-honored tradition. They meant well," Sofista said with a shrug, "but were too narrow-minded to see beyond their own swords. They jealously tried to force outdated rules on me that were established by ancient generals intended for another day and age. All because I had discovered this ..." The captain produced a sparkling dagger from within his robe.

The four sucked in their collective breath.

Sofista didn't seem to notice. "See, all the necessary runes are already revealed. One need not endure hours of tolling just to obtain a mere scrap of information. All the teachings of the Child-Stars were forged into the dagger and are easily discernible without such time-consuming labor and mind-muddling superstitions."

Sofista resumed pacing. "My superiors warned me of dire consequences, but I rapidly learned the dagger's lessons and showed them up for the shallow-minded, ignorant soldiers they were. They looked so foolish—unable to answer my arguments." Sofista turned. "Many veterans—not to mention countless recruits—took note of the wisdom I possessed over those still mired in outdated, conventional methods. Not a few resigned from their brigades to study under me. Thus, I formed this brigade based on the daggers—hence the birth of the Daggermen Brigade.

"It's so much easier to study and use a dagger and less wearing on body and mind. You don't have to worry about its sharpness disappearing, either. How much time have you spent re-tolling runes that have gone dull even though you never got a chance to use them? These daggers reveal all the runes in even a cursory glance, without all that labor. So now, may I assume you're willing to give these daggers a try?"

"I already tried one," Artka said, "and found it only brings danger, whether or not it seems to say the same things as our swords—"

"Tut, tut. You're too bright a lad to stay enslaved to silly superstitions. But, no matter, as you attend my lectures, I'm sure you'll come around. Uh, I must warn you . . . that fear of daggers is symptomatic of an unbalanced mental condition. Daggers bring comfort, not harm. Why, many Daggermen have been released from craven fear of King Elyon and his rigid rules of conduct found in the sword's first lessons which make Elyon appear harsh and cruel. Much labor has to go into the blade before runes appear revealing he's really all-tolerant." Sofista stepped closer. "Elyon's wrath is balanced against his tolerance, giving a fuller picture. In fact, don't be surprised to discover that he accepts all Carnalians into Splendora, whether they've been to Logon's Rock or not."

"Thet bundles it! I heered 'bout all o' this drivel I cares fer," Scang said. "Yer calls Logon's very words superstitions? Bah! We kens a tophet be's achasin' usn's, an' it hain't no superstition."

"You prove my point," Sofista said. "Your man Scang is convinced that such apparitions are real. Simple minds succumb so easily, you know. Scang could become dangerous to himself—and you. Thanks be to Logon you arrived here when you did. Who can say what tragedy has been averted by your blundering into our midst?"

Sofista's low, soothing voice had a calming effect in contrast to Scang's outburst.

Artka wondered if he wasn't being too imaginative? A quick glance at his companions reminded him that he, of all present, had the most reason to know tophets weren't superstition.

Harnet spoke up, drawing Sofista's attention. "I do have a question." He extracted his sword and toller and casually passed the file over a portion of his sword which was glowing. "You say that you formed this brigade?"

"Yes," Sofista replied, his eyes fixed upon Harnet's sword.

"But, I was under the impression only Logon could order new brigades," Harnet said.

"Well, obviously Logon has given us a great deal of latitude. After all, I have formed this brigade, haven't I?"

Harnet tolled with quicker strokes, "And are we to assume that Logon commissioned you as commandant?"

"What is Logon's commission except the will of his people? I'm the leader because I know the most dagger lore. Say, young man, do you have to do that now?" A bright red color had crept from Sofista's neck upward to his face despite his fatherly demeanor.

"You mean tolling? I'm sorry, does it disturb you? I'm sorry. I think I found what I wanted to know, anyway." He tucked his toller away.

Sofista's color returned. "There are sad stories, you know, about adventurers—such as yourselves—zealous for Logon's glory, who unfortunately, ignored sound advice, and clung to their own misinterpretations, instead. Sometimes their bodies were discovered, sometimes not. Tragic, tragic. I'm determined that that not happen to you. Beyond any shadow of a doubt, I know that Logon's intent was for you to come to this brigade."

"Bah!" Scang said.

Artka, however, was deep in thought. It was a "new brigade" after all. Maybe this was Logon's plan, not that he actually find the dubious

Saygus, but only search for him, and in the search, stumble upon this new brigade.

Reddy looked to Sofista with a smile and open, friendly eyes.

Harnet's attitude was indiscernible.

Captain Sofista seemed so wise, so comforting and sincere—Artka found himself wanting to believe him. Had it not been for the man's reaction to Harnet's tolling, this affable, paternalistic man who'd assured them he knew best might have enchanted him.

"We'd like to talk it over, "Harnet said, "alone. We'll let you know."

"Fine, fine, that's all I ask. I'm sure it's Logon's will you stay, so I'll just—oh, I almost forgot—" From beneath his robes Sofista produced a folded leather apron and laid it upon the nearest bed. He untied the strings, unrolling it to reveal four shiny daggers. "Gifts for you. Please examine them as you discuss my offer. If nothing else, consider them mementos of your visit should you decide to leave come spring, though I strongly doubt you will."

The four couldn't take their eyes off the dazzling daggers.

Sofista picked one up, saying, "Since you don't need all four, I'll retain one. Now each of you has his own. See you at breakfast? My lecture follows the morning meal, see you then." He left and closed the door behind him.

They scarcely noticed the captain's departure as the four gazed at the daggers, studying the intricate detail of not only the slivery blade with gold-flecked runes but also the handle with the wings delicately flowing upward to form the hilt guard. Even Scang and Harnet weren't immune.

"Might we be wrong?" Reddy asked in a faraway voice, reaching for one.

Harnet shook his head. "Don't touch it!"

Sofista's mellifluous spell broke. They all took a step back.

"Quick, cover them so we're no longer tempted," Harnet said. "If we even touch them we might become as susceptible to *kyllorn* like cusps and tophets as Artka is."

Scang draped a towel over them.

"What's happening to us?" Harnet asked. "I know what I've seen and heard, yet I was almost convinced."

"I found myself wishing he was telling the truth," Artka said. "It would be so much easier to stay here than face the unknown out there."

Reddy sighed. "I did believe him. At least while he was in the room."

"Usn's best leave tomorrow, afore his lecture. They's summat o' cusps hereabouts. In fact, it wouldn't surprise me if'n the captain hisself t'warn't but a cusp in a man's body."

"You go too far, Scang," Artka said.

"Does I? Dincher see how he glared when Harnet tolled his Child of the Stars? No man loyal ter Logon would act like thet."

"The man is under cusp influence, no doubt," Harnet said. "But that doesn't make him a cusp. I was most concerned about you, Artka. You were affected quicker than any of us."

"Probably because I already possess a dagger, just having it makes me want to keep it."

"Isn't there a rune that says, 'touch not the unclean thing'?" said Harnet. "Well, since yours, Artka, has already been touched, we'll not leave it here where it can be used to beguile someone else. We'll be sure to get rid of it in such a fashion that no one will ever again fall under its spell. Meanwhile, let's not even entertain the thought of handling these," he said, pointing at the lumps under the towel.

~

Morning stole softly into the room.

Artka blinked, lifted his head and looked around. Scang snored—a sound to which they 'd become more or less accustomed. Reddy's head was buried under the covers but Harnet also stirred.

"Harnet?"

Harnet rolled over.

"Let's toll. Things could get scratchy today, so we'd better be prepared." Artka swung his feet to the floor.

"Let's include Scang and Reddy," Harnet said lowly.

"Right."

Harnet playfully tugged Reddy's covers off while Artka gingerly tapped Scang's shoulder, standing well back, remembering that Scang often relived old battles in his dreams and if roused during one of those, might lash out. But Scang woke peacefully.

Reddy, on the other hand, pulled the blanket back over his face. When Scang's hand joined Harnet's on the other end of the blanket however, he abandoned all thought of resistance.

They sat on opposite beds, two facing two, tolling where each had left off. Thoughts of Logon filled their hearts and minds. Artka and Harnet's swords each had a couple of inches shining bright blue on one side. Scang had a little more, Reddy a bit less.

A rune in the middle of their swords—where none of them had tolled—started glowing of its own accord. At the same time Reddy gasped and pointed at a column of twinkling lights hovering under the lintel just inside the doorframe.

"Hello," Artka ventured, wondering how, or even if, he should communicate with the roamer. Before he could say more it faded from view.

"What was that all about?" Reddy's arched his eyebrows.

"A roamer," Artka said. "I encountered one near Logon's Rock. This was a messenger from Logon, I'd guess."

"But, it didn't say anything. What message did it bring?" Harnet asked.

"Look ter yer sword. All o' usn's has gots the same untolled rune aglowin'. I'd lay a wager if'n we toll by thet rune, we'll git the roamer's message."

All four immediately fell to tolling the edge by the glowing rune. "I . . . I can read it," Artka said.

> *"Only one weapon to pierce man's heart,*
> *Not to destroy, but new life impart,*
> *Only two edges forged in sky fire,*
> *Shall lead men to heart's true desire,*
> *Only three voices tolled runes know,*
> *King, Prince and Advisor, these only show,*
> *Xychirion's great power expressed on this blade,*
> *Pretenders will fail, false voices will fade."*

"I think," Harnet added, "I should read this other rune, too. Though it's not part of the same rune, it's also aglow.

> *"Let walkers four be wary of curse,*
> *Lest hopes be darkened and curse wax yet worse."*

"Hey, could that mean us?" Reddy said. "How can that be? These runes have been on the swords since Logon returned to his father?"

"I once heard a captain instruct about this rune," Harnet said, "or part of it, anyway. This is one of those runes that declare these Children of the Stars are Logon's only sanctioned weaponry, funny how we tend to forget such things if we don't review them often."

"Yes," Reddy said, "but what about the walkers four?"

"Well, that refers to Old Baraham," said Harnet, "his son Laffer, Laffer's son Supplan, and Supplan's son, Bounder. Remember how King

Elyon sent them into Ecclessa with a promise that their descendants would fill the land? Then all Ecclessa would be—"

"Nope, I don't remember much," Scang said. "I hain't heered o' them but mebbe oncet. Anyways, I believes thet rune be's meanin' usn's. Hain't jest chance thet a roamer lit up thet particular rune: we be's four walkers whut needs ter be wary o' the curse o' daggers."

"Scang has it," Artka nodded. "Although I wouldn't want to make every rune about four travelers apply to us, I think Logon is warning us that evil will befall us if we tarry. We ought to leave right after breakfast, like we planned."

"Why not right now?" Reddy asked. "It gives me creeps just being here."

Harnet shrugged and looked to Artka.

"Well," Artka said, "I think it'd be all right to have a warm meal in our bellies before we go out into the cold and snow."

"I'm so glad you said that," Harnet said with a laugh.

"Well, I still feel creepy," Reddy said, "but, I'll agree to a full stomach."

That decided, they tucked their swords and tollers away and went to the main hall. Gone were the festive decorations of the previous night, the dance floor was now all tables and benches as befitted a military mess hall. A few early risers were up and about, none had swords, but without exception, everyone sported a dagger. The four seated themselves and waited for a steward to take their breakfast orders.

"Good day gentlemen, I see you're early risers like I am," Captain Sofista said as he descended from a platform. "But, where are your daggers? Don't tell me you still have doubts. I heard a rumor that you weren't too pleased, but I thought surely once you carefully examined my gifts, you'd be convinced. It's an insult, you know, to turn down a gift from a friend."

"We just don't see it the way you do, I guess," Artka said.

"Hmmm. I also see you still think there's virtue in trying to light up your swords. I'm disappointed. Don't you know that those Child-Stars are too bulky for actual combat. New recruits feel guilty about not using them when they see diehards, such as yourselves clinging to outdated methods. I'm sure you see what a difficult position you've placed me in."

Realizing how this conversation would end Artka scanned the room for exits. There was only one—the main door, at the far end of the room.

"So, we've noticed," Harnet said, picking up the lagged conversation to distract Sofista from guessing Artka's intentions.

"Uh-oh." Sofista's tone brought Artka's attention back. The captain's pudgy finger traced the glowing rune on Reddy's sword. A dark scowl contradicted his condescending tone as he said, "How peculiar that all four of you happen to have the same rune aglow, but none of you had it glowing last night. Why, you're no better than Runers who sharpen only the parts of the blade that interest them. I'd thought better of you. But, I suppose, superstitious as you are, I can't expect integrity, even in sharpening your swords. But, why, I wonder, that particular rune?"

"It just sort of occurred," Artka said.

"I see. I don't suppose it would do any good to tell you that that particular rune is slightly distorted on your swords. It happened often during the primitive forging process. You can't expect to take fishermen, farmers, and herdsmen and turn them into weapon smelters overnight without some mistakes, can you?"

"Logon did," Harnet protested.

"Yes, well, if that's what you choose to believe. Nevertheless, let me read the corrected draft of that rune—and, might I add, that I am an established authority." He laid his dagger on the table for all to see, located the nearly identical rune, and read aloud:

"One of the weapons to pierce man's heart
Not to destroy, but new life impart,
Both of two blades forged in sky fire,
Shall show men their desire's true heart."

Artka compared it with his own sword:

"Only one weapon to pierce man's heart,
Not to destroy, but new life impart,
Only two edges forged in sky fire,
Shall lead men to heart's true desire,

"There you see," said Sofista, "a slight deviation of the wording and the meaning is substantially changed, isn't it? Authorities agree that the dagger rune is the more accurate. As for that other bit, about the four walkers, I hope you don't think—"

"Oh, that's about Baraham and his descendants," Artka said.

"Good, good. Well, I'll see you at my lecture following breakfast? I plan to give instruction on something the four of you should find rather engrossing."

"Oh, well, sorry, but we're leaving right after breakfast," Reddy blurted.

The others groaned.

Sofista's smile vanished. "I can't allow that! Why, it's bitterly cold, and all that snow. No, no. It's quite out of the question. I forbid it."

"We're under higher orders, sir," Artka said. "You see, this morning a roamer visited us and delivered a message from Logon that we are to hasten on our journey."

"A roamer?" Captain Sofista made a covert motion behind his back with his hands as he addressed his guests. "I see . . . a roamer. And he gave you . . . a message?"

"You believe us?" Reddy said.

From around the room Daggermen headed to aid their captain.

"Oh, I believe, all right. I believe that you will lie to a commanding officer when your wild imaginations tempt you hither and yon in search of what you think is devotion to Logon." He clapped his hands and shouted, "Now!"

A dozen daggers were whipped out and pointed at the four.

"I'm sorry to have to do this," Sofista said, "but, in time, you'll see it was for your own good. Now, I'm afraid I must insist that you surrender those swords."

CHAPTER TWENTY-NINE

ARTKA, SCANG, HARNET, AND REDDY pulled out their swords and stood back to back.

Stunned, the Daggermen retreated, but their perimeter surrounding the four wayfarers held.

"Gentlemen, gentlemen," Captain Sofista said, "it's useless to resist. I can call a hundred more men to subdue you, if necessary. Be reasonable, lower your weapons. Outdated swords won't save you from my power, nor, I fear, from injury. Unlike Logon's swords, these daggers aren't harmless. I'd rather you didn't force us to use them."

"Just what are your intentions?" Artka said.

"Nothing more than to have you join us." Sofista chuckled disarmingly. "And to teach you to use daggers more effectively than you'd ever be able to wield those clumsy slashers. When you've begun to reach enlightenment, a few months at the most, we'll release you, and you may do as you like. Certainly, you see the wisdom of avoiding unpleasantness?"

"So," Harnet eyed the Daggerman opposite him, "that's why there are no watchmen on the walls. You only keep people from leaving. Anyone entering is like a fly in a spider's web."

"Right yer be's, Harnet," said Scang, an angry glint in his eye as he took a step forward. "But, I gots me a slasher whut'll shred this spider's web."

Sizing up Scang, Sofista's men took another backward step. "N-n-n-now hold on there," Sofista said. "Artka, control your man. Your swords can't harm, remember?"

"Let's jest see 'bout that." Scang lunged.

Startled guards dodged out of harm's way abandoning their vulnerable leader. The broad side of Scang's sword hummed as it glanced off Sofista's cheek. His Excellency bellowed and sprawled backwards over a table. The smoky odor of burnt flesh permeated the air.

A low swipe from Artka's sword swept a Daggerman's feet out from under him. The other guards bounced off of each other getting out of the way. A path to the door was clear.

"Let's go," Artka cried.

A dagger flew at the four, but Reddy's sword intercepted it, shattering the knife. As its pieces skittered across the floor Artka noted that the dagger's exterior shine was plating only—inside it was the same black metal as Carnalian swords.

Knapsacks in one hand, swords in the other, Harnet, Reddy, Artka, and Scang rushed the doorway, snatching cloaks off hooks as they escaped. Sofista lay belly-up on the floor, his stupefied guards gawking down at him, too bewildered to take the initiative of pursuit.

Daggermen just coming into the courtyard halted and watched in astonishment as the four exploded through the door but then stood stock still just outside reconnoitering the bailey. None of the Daggermen dared challenge them.

A commotion drew Artka's attention behind him again to the fuss in the dining hall.

Captain Sofista's bodyguard paid effusive, if not timely, attention to their fallen leader; helping him to his feet, dusting him off and straightening his clothing. Sofista put a finger to his swollen cheek, whimpering as feeling returned. In the middle of his cheek was a blistered imprint of a rune that read

'Only one weapon to pierce man's heart . . .'

Sofista howled in a rage, "Bring them to meeeeeee!"

"Let's go." Artka took off down a snow-packed path leading the others around a corner of the keep and then toward an exterior wall.

Scang suddenly skidded to a halt. "I be's right back." He winked at Artka and ducked around a corner.

"Where—" Artka called after him, but he was gone.

"Hey! Artka, wait, take me along," cried one of the Conformitarians.

Over his shoulder Artka identified Braxmore as one of those who'd witnessed their escape from the dining hall. He churned across the yard through thigh-deep snow.

A growl-like grunt in his throat Artka turned around wishing Scang hadn't left him to solve this thorny problem alone.

Braxmore broke clear of the deep snow, and gained speed jogging down the path, waving his arms, yelling, "Wait."

Artka, wanting nothing more to do with Daggermen and their vile fortress, turned and brandished his sword at Braxmore.

Braxmore slowed to a walk, furrowed his brow, and studied Artka's fierce expression, not sure if he was bluffing.

A second-story window shutter swung open and a huge form flew through the portal and landed atop Braxmore. The falling body turned out to be Scang, hugging a bulky bundle to his chest. He rose, considered Braxmore who lay crumpled at his feet for a second, grunted, and was off again, his long legs quickly catching him up to his friends.

Artka fell in behind and the quartet raced full tilt to the breach in the wall.

Artka, Scang, Reddy, and Harnet scaled the wall and dropped to the frozen moat outside the castle's precincts, then clambered up the moat's outer bank. Scang re-broke their trail that had partially drifted shut during the night. Artka watched the drawbridge for any sign of pursuers. A black-clad figure climbed through the same breech from which they'd just jumped.

"Oh, Pitland! He's gaining," Artka said.

"Who?" Harnet asked, squinting against the rising sun's glare off the snow.

"That obnoxious Braxmore fellow, sounds like him, anyway. Scang, you should've landed heavier on him."

"How long till we reach our snowwalkers, Scang?" Reddy asked, huffing as he scooped handfuls of snow out of the trail.

Scang lifted his head, gulping in deep breaths. "Cain't say fer sure. Some places be's completely drifted shut."

"Uh-oh, here comes trouble," Artka said.

Clanking chains indicated the drawbridge was lowering even before any activity was seen on the up-raised planking. As the planking of the floorboards leveled out dozens of anxious footmen jostled on the descending floorboards eager to give chase.

Scang's arms flailed with renewed vigor like windmills, ripping a path as fast as he could, but it wasn't fast enough. The posse would be on them before they reached their cached snowwalkers. Artka and Harnet kicked snow back into the trail, which at best would merely be only a slight hindrance.

Reddy snapped his fingers. "Remember how we got warm in the snow cave?"

"Yes, the swords," Artka said, annoyed at the interruption.

"And that the snow under the blades was melted, right? Why not?"

Artka stared at Reddy for a second, then shrugged, "It's worth a try."

The four clustered together, touching sword points to the snowy pathway; the sword tips flared fiery red, sizzling the snow away.

"Hah!" Scang said. "Tophets hain't the only ones whut kin melt through deep snow. Wish we'd a' thot of this sooner."

They progressed at a trot as they jointly swung their swords back and forth, obliterating the snow in a hiss of steam. Progress wasn't swift, but it was quicker than Scang re-breaking trail—and Scang wasn't drained of his strength. But Braxmore still gained on them; and so, did the Daggermen who were off the drawbridge and only fifty yards away.

Braxmore, chasing after the mysterious travelers, abruptly stopped when he came upon the melted trail. "What? How? Artka, wait—" he called, "I want to come with you."

"Scang, I think you'd better discourage him, and then fill in some of the path behind to slow the rest of them down," Artka said. "Three swords ought to produce enough heat to cover the short distance left."

"It be's me pleasure." The giant turned and charged back up the pathway, howling like a banshee and waving his sword.

Braxmore skidded to a halt, rubbed the lumps from his last encounter with the Eroton, turned, and fled.

The pursuing Daggermen noted Braxmore's retreat. A shout went up, "They're attacking," and the foremost pursuers having no desire to get face-branded, turned and collided into the oncoming ranks, turning in angry confusion on each other, cursing, fists flying, and daggers slashing. Blood speckled the snow as they nicked each other in their rush to get away.

Scang smiled as he started filling in the trail.

Braxmore, spying the bedlam ahead, glanced over his shoulder to check on Scang's progress and noted that the giant was headed back the other way. He took up the chase again, hunching over to stay hidden.

Artka, sitting in the slushy path with his companions donning their snowwalkers, saw Braxmore bob above the snow wall to peek at them as he approached, presumably to see how close he was. Then a clamor on the trail behind distracted him. A cavalry unit led by Captain Sofista himself pounded across the drawbridge. Braxmore dodged into the snow to avoid being trampled by the soldiers and their captain as the entourage galloped past.

The four, fussing with laces and bindings, paid Braxmore little attention. Though the Conformitarian was an annoyance, Artka was relieved to see that he'd scooped out a niche and got safely out of Sofista's way.

The horses rushed past Braxmore's hideaway, after which the man emerged and stood observing, mouth agape.

The horses however, reached the end of the melted pathway at full speed and had been unable to stop. They rammed into the high snow banks and then into the rear of each other. Riders were ejected from their saddles and became partially buried in the snow.

Footmen rushing to the aid of their unhorsed comrades streamed past the stunned Braxmore, knocking the Conformitarian back into his niche.

One rider had been launched beyond the others, furiously kicking his plump, inverted legs in a futile effort to free himself; the more his legs pumped the more imprisoned he became. Artka chuckled. That rider was Captain Sofista.

Trotting along, Artka looked back and saw the commotion as mere specks on the white expanse behind them

"Whut be's yer chuckling at, Artka?" Scang huffed as they trudged down a slope.

"I saw Sofista's face, eyes wide as cups and saucers, flying off his mount. *Kerplop* he goes, head first with nothing but his boots sticking out."

"Serves him right," Reddy said. "He was trying to force us to take daggers. I hope they leave him there till spring."

"Now, now, Reddy," Harnet said, "in spite of his faults, he is an Ecclessite, someone who at one time in his life appealed to Logon for mercy. It's not our place to wish him evil."

"Be that as it may," Artka said, "Ecclessites had better be warned to stay away from him. How will others avoid such snares unless they're warned?"

"I suppose," Harnet said "that if we honestly related our experience, it would be okay, as long as we don't embellish."

"Usn's shouldda kenned right off summat be's amiss when we come up ter the walls an' seen nobbut on guard. Almost every principle our sword taught got violated at the Daggermen Castle."

"But we needed a good meal and a warm place to sleep," Reddy said.

"Wanted, not needed," said Harnet. "We were fine in our snow burrow kept warm by the glow of our swords, and as it turns out, we would have been safer had we remained afield."

They traveled a few more hours before taking a break, talking less frequently to conserve their breath on the upgrades. A rock outcropping that had been blown clear of snow offered shelter from the wind, so they gladly dropped their packs and rested. Upon examining the structure, they guessed the tallest spire to be some thirty feet in height. Reddy, an inveterate rock climber, decided to have a brief look around despite the numbing breeze. From his perch near the jagged top he surveyed the whitened countryside interspersed with several stands of trees.

"How far can you see?" Harnet called.

"A few miles, maybe a couple of leagues. Over there's a larger wooded tract leading up into some mountains. It'll take us a couple of hours to get there."

"An' how far be's them mountains?"

"At least two days journey on snowwalkers."

"Thems will be foothills o' the Prophecy Mountains," said Scang.

Reddy picked his way down the rock face and donned his snow-walkers again.

Just then a faint roar was borne on the wind across the snow-swept prairie. Harnet whipped his head around. "What in the name of . . . ?"

"Shhh, there it is again," Artka said. "I know the sound well, but never expected to hear it in Ecclessa."

"Well, what is it, man?" Reddy said, nervously searching the landscape.

"Well since Carnalians can't enter Ecclessa, I'd have to say that's a lion—maybe more than one, by the sound."

"Aye, a pride o' them, sounds like."

Reddy gasped.

Scang shielded his eyes against the glare and scanned the horizon. "Hain't jest ordinary lions. The only-est lions in Ecclessa nowadays be's black lions, like from Craniantium," Scang said. "Artka does a fair imitation. Once yer sees one, yer'll fergit fear o' most everythin' else."

"Even tophets?" Reddy said.

"Well, mebbe not tophets. But them lions be's twenty feet long an' more than ten feet high at the shoulder, wi' teeth big as daggers. An' though they might live in Ecclessa, they hain't loyal ter neither side. They'll savage Carnalians an' Ecclessites alike. They're jest beasties whut's always hungry. And they're smart, in some ways like men."

Another faint roar echoed up to them. They listened with heightened interest.

Artka said, "We'd best be on our way."

"How do you know which direction is safe?" Reddy asked, gripping his sword handle. "We don't want to accidentally stumble into lions."

"Those roars came from our left," Artka said. "Although the way the wind swirls, it's hard to be sure. I think we'll be all right if we make for those trees you spotted where we can spend the night."

"Does deep snow hinder lions?" Harnet asked.

"Cain't rightly say, laddie. But we best not be stayin' out in the open fer long, wind carryin' our scent around like it do. They'll be sniffin' usn's out. Might's well go yonder as anywhere. Leastways there we kin build a fire which will tend ter keep 'em at bay."

They shouldered their rucksacks and resumed their trek, Scang leading, then Artka, followed by Reddy and last, Harnet.

The trees were more distant than Reddy's estimate and their shadows were well stretched out ahead of them by the time they reached the shelter of the woods. They camped just inside a thick fringe of trees in order to keep a backward eye on their trail. They took several minutes to scoop out a wide, campsite hollow so that they'd be hidden beneath the surface under a wall of snow on the field side and concealed by thick spruce and hemlock trees on the other. Scang allowed they might treat themselves to the luxury of a fire, providing it was kept low. This brightened their mood considerably. A fire would warm and cheer them through the night.

Adding to their delight, Scang produced a parcel of butcher's wrap. He sheepishly explained, "I figgered it warn't nobbut use turnin' down a good meal whut was offered." He unwrapped the parcel revealing four thick, prime-cut tenderloins pilfered from the Daggermen's kitchen.

"So that's where you went," Artka said. "Harnet, you're best at fire-starting, go to it."

Harnet saluted, saying, "Aye, aye cap'n," and rummaged in his rucksack for his flint. "Reddy, see if you can round up some kindling."

Twilight passed into darkness as they lay close to the fire watching greasy droplets sweat from their steaks and flare on the hot coals below.

Artka stared sleepily into the flames. "We'd better take shifts, two at a time. We can't risk being surprised by Daggermen, tophets, or lions. You know, the deeper we go into Ecclessa, the more dangers we seem to attract. I feel that we won't be safe again till Saygus guides us to our new brigade."

"Me an' the red-haired lad will take first watch," Scang stood and stretched the kinks out of his legs. He grabbed a stick and lazily poked some coals.

"My name is Reddy, not 'red-haired-lad'."

"Well o' course it be's, laddie, course it be's. Well, c'mon little feller, let's usn's take a looksee around while our steaks sizzle." Scang effortlessly hoisted the reluctant youth to his feet. "Usn's won't be long."

Artka and Harnet passed the time tolling their swords while the steaks cooked and Scang and Reddy scouted around.

"I've been wondering, Harnet. You've been an Ecclessite longer than me so maybe you can help me understand something."

"I'll try."

"All the different Ecclessite brigades confuse me. How can we be so different, even at odds, yet claim to follow the runes of the same sword?"

"Oh, is that what's bothering you? Well, if it's any help, it confuses me too. I try not to think about it."

"How can you not think about it? Here we are, just barely escaped from an egomaniac who thinks his daggers are superior to Logon's Children of the Stars but meanwhile, Sharpointers are jealous of whole-blade warriors like Tren, because he does better in battle, yet disdain sharpening the whole sword, claiming that was only for the ancients." Artka lowered his voice, realizing he was getting worked up. "Then there are Runers who only sharpen by comforting runes. Onedgers accuse those not following the first edge of the blade of not being fully rescued, while Otheredgers think the second edge is all that matters, and anyone bothering with the first side has renounced Logon's amnesty and Tipsters are satisfied with so little but Sageruners want—"

"Enough, Artka, enough! Don't even try to understand it. I decided that the best thing for me was to find the brigade Logon wanted me in and serve there. I thought I knew where that was, until I met Tren . . . and you."

"But, what if this new brigade is just as critical of other brigades?"

"Hmm, good point."

"I wish I'd stayed with Tren."

"He sure knows how to use his sword. I wonder where he is, and what he's doing."

"So, do I. We're in a fix, aren't we? We can't do anything but follow what we guess are Logon's directives. Even so, I hope I never think the brigade I'm in is the only one capable of doing Logon's work."

"When you put it like that, it does sound absurd," Harnet said, thoughtfully tolling by a rune. "I think maybe, we're learning that now."

"I hope so," Artka replied. "Well, those steaks smell about ready. I'm going to eat. Then I'm going to get some sleep. I don't know where Scang and Reddy are, but, I'm hungry now."

"They'd better get back soon, or their steaks will be charcoal," Harnet said, lifting his from the spit. "I'm glad Scang liberated these, but wasn't it wrong to steal?"

"We'd have eaten this much and more had we stayed. I guess Scang figured Logon wouldn't mind us taking along some provision." Harnet peeked into Scang's bundle. "He not only got these, but other food-stuffs as well, which we'll be thankful for later on."

Silent as a ghost Scang suddenly appeared. He held a finger to his lips. "Summat's a stirrin' in yonder woods," the giant whispered.

Artka and Harnet tucked their tollers away but not their swords.

"Where's Reddy?" Artka asked.

"Keepin' watch. Snow ain't deep in the wood. C'mon, an bring thet meat, it oughta be done by now."

Harnet scattered the ashes, gathered the remaining steaks, and followed.

"Cover yer swords."

They followed Scang into the dense woods, sneaking through trees and climbing ridges to where Reddy kept watch.

"Pssssst," Scang hissed through pursed lips.

"Psst. Pssssssst," Reddy answered from the dusky woods.

Scang led over a fallen tree and down an embankment to a grouping of boulders. They sidled alongside Reddy who was on his belly peering into the shadowy forest. Artka slid behind a large, snow-topped boulder and studied the dark trees silhouetted against the moon-washed snow. Seeing nothing of note he was about to ask Scang what it was about when a thrashing—not unlike stags fighting when in rut—shattered the silence.

"Does yers hear thet?"

Artka nodded. "All this stealth for rutting bucks?"

"Mebbe," Scang whispered. More thrashing erupted from the forest. "Let's git closer." He belly-crawled forward.

Artka, Harnet, and Reddy slithered behind, dipping into a slight depression then up the other side. The thrashing got louder.

Scang paused on an overlook, motioning the others alongside. "Thar be's the source o' the noise." Scang pointed to an oak tree surrounded by younger trees and several saplings. There was a misshapen, stunted hemlock grotesquely entwined about the oak's bole.

The oak suddenly shuddered as if in a strong wind, but the air was still. Several saplings surrounding the oak rustled in the same non-existent wind. The misshapen hemlock swayed wildly, almost as if trying to wrench itself free of its roots.

Artka tugged Scang's sleeve. "It's an animal."

"Why so 'tis."

"It's choking," Reddy said. "Don't you hear it?"

"Now that you mention it, I do," Artka said. "Let's go down." They carefully picked their way down the hill.

"It be's a—" Scang said in awe.

"Craniantium lion," Artka finished, staring wide-eyed.

The beast hung suspended, fighting for breath, frustrated, fearful. The ground beneath the lion was torn up and bare of snow; this life and death struggle had been going on for hours.

Even in the moonlight the lion's rippling muscles were evident. His claws were as long as short-swords and his mouth large enough to engulf a man in one chomp. Only one hind foot dragging the ground supported the great cat, barely keeping him alive. The large oak had a thick rope secured to upper limbs that looped around the beast's neck, bearing the immense carnivore's weight.

Even as they approached, the great lion twisted in a violent but vain effort to free himself. Within seconds his limited air supply was spent, and he had to pause and refill his exhausted lungs through the tiny aperture of his strangled throat.

"Cor, would yer lookit thet." The mystery over, Scang gnawed off a bite of steak which he swallowed whole, then said, "I seen lions afore, even black lions, but I never seen one the likes o' him." He circled the suspended beast, keeping a respectful distance from the paws and thrashing tail that had splintered nearby saplings. "Say thet's the kind o' rope I got snared in t'other day."

"So, it is, Scang," Harnet traced the ropes to their tie-off.

"Well, what do we do?" Artka asked, taking a bite of steak.

"Do? Whut kin yer be meanin'? Jest let him ter his fate, thet's whut. If'n we cut him down, he'll attack usn's, an' likely eat us wi'out so much as a burp an' a thank-you. No, no, don't interfere."

"But we can't let him suffer," Harnet protested. "Let's at least put him out of his misery."

"An' how be's yer gonna do thet? The only place ter strike him dead wi' one, quick blow, be's twenty feet above yer head. Yer'll only add ter his sufferin if'n yer tries anything else. An' likely get kilt in the process. Lookit him. He won't last half the night out. He don't even ken usn's bein' here. Leave the critter ter his fate."

"Scang's right," Artka said. "The only thing to do is let him die in dignity, without an audience. What a shame for such a magnificent animal to die so . . . so . . . "

"Ignominiously," the Eroton said.

Artka, Reddy, and Harnet stared at Scang.

"Whut?"

"Scang," said Artka, "sometimes you amaze me."

The four headed back toward camp. Their anticipation of restarting the fire and sleeping cozily overcame caution as they neared the campsite.

"Oh drat, I've dropped the dagger pouch," Artka said. "Go on ahead, I'll be only a minute. I thought I felt something slip from my belt back at the boulders."

"Be quick about it," Scang whispered. "Me an' the red-haired lad wants ter git settled inter our watchin' spots."

"Right." Artka backtracked and found the dagger pouch at the boulders as expected. He paused to examine its contents, withdrawing the glittering steel blade, which, even in the wan moonlight, sparkled invitingly.

"I loathe the sight of you as much as I'm drawn to you," Artka muttered. "Tempt me not with your dazzle; I'll not be deceived again, not since I saw your seductive power over Sofista's mind." He stuffed it back into its pouch. "I'd leave you here, you accursed thing, but we agreed to either destroy you or put you out of anyone else's reach, so I unwillingly bear the burden of you for now."

Alarmed shouts echoed through the forest, shattering the silence.

Artka tore heedless through the woods, sword in one hand, dagger pouch in the other. The clashing sounds of steel on steel mingled with angry bellows, spurring him faster. Before he covered half the distance to camp all went suddenly quiet. He slowed to a walk, then stopped and listened. All was silent.

CHAPTER THIRTY

ARTKA TUCKED HIS SWORD BENEATH the folds of his cloak and slunk toward the encampment. Roaring flames sent sparks high into the night sky. A signal? Artka nestled under low-swept branches just outside the flickering glow of firelight.

Scang sat beside the fire, hands bound behind and knees tethered up tight to his chest. Behind him, likewise trussed, Reddy and Harnet, sat back to back. A dozen wilderness men garbed in hairy, black capes sprawled around the perimeter looting their captives' supplies, devouring whatever took their fancy, stuffing less savory items into their own rucksacks for later use.

Two men interrogated Scang. One brandished a club under Scang's nose.

"Five or six. So, where are the others?" the man demanded.

Scang said, "I tole yer, there hain't five or six o' usn's. Cain't yers count, one, two, three."

"Liar!" The man brushed the club across Scang's nose. "There are four packs here, so we know there are more than three of you. Now, you're gonna tell me where your companions are, or I'll bust your nose."

"S'been busted afore, an' probly will be agin, so go ahead."

"Stop it Da'rot," said the other. "Can't you see he's Eroton? They're used to beatings, you won't get anywhere that way. Besides, it's not that important. Sofista's men will soon be here, then we'll turn these three over to them. Come daylight, we'll pick up the trail of the others."

"Seems to me, Darfe'," said another as he rummaged through Artka's pack, "Sofista said there were four thieves, not six."

"Well, these four might have plans to meet up with the other two. I ain't taking no chances." Turning back to Scang he threatened, "Sofista has special ways of teaching people not to steal. You'll be sorry you ever crossed him, I can promise you that."

"Hey Darfe'," interrupted another of the wilderness men.

"What?" the leader snapped, irritated at the interruption.

"I was just thinking, didn't we set a snare hereabouts?"

"Yeah, so?"

"Maybe me and some of the lads should check on it."

Darfe' scratched his stubbly chin, warily scanning the surrounding wood. "Won't do no harm, I guess. Go ahead. Take Da'rot with you, before he does something stupid."

Da'rot grudgingly rose and followed, as did another man, passing into the darkened forest mere steps from Artka's hideaway.

Artka chewed his lip. Every rescue plan he conjured was flawed. These seasoned woodsmen were unlikely to be overcome by a one-man-surprise-attack, and surprise was the only thing in Artka's favor. He studied the nine gathered around the fire looking for any weakness to exploit. He was close enough to identify their black, hairy capes as lion skins. These men were lion poachers. Those rich, ebony pelts were status symbols among Carnalian officers. These renegades probably carried on an illegal trade with the enemy. Each of them had a Child of the Stars, but only the very tip gave off any light. A couple possessed daggers, but not all. They all wore tunics beneath their capes, but if they were Logon tunics, they were discolored with stains.

The snow right beside Artka crunched, startling him.

"Darfe'," Da'rot said returning from the forest, "we got us a big one. Biggest I ever seen."

"Really?"

"Yep. But, he ain't dead yet. He's so big one of his feet drags the ground. He's losing strength though and will soon die."

"Hmmm. I thought I heard one roaring earlier in the day. Hontr, you and your skinners go take care of him. The rest of us will wait here for the Daggermen."

Hontr jumped up from the fireside, rummaged through his sack, and pulled out his skinning knife, then pointed out the six men he wanted and with them disappeared single-file into the woods.

Darfe' kicked at a mound of snow, exposing a hidden snowwalker. He chuckled, admonishing Scang, "You foolish, foolish man. Did you think snowwalkers could escape skishers?"

Scang stared sullenly into the woods, knowing Artka must be watching. But though Scang looked directly at his hiding place, Artka didn't reveal his presence.

"Why Logon bothers rescuing you Erotons, I really don't understand," Darfe' said. "You'll never change your ways. You can't even speak right. You're all just a bunch of thieves and cutthroats."

"And you're prime examples of Ecclessites?" Harnet said.

"What do you mean by that?"

"Well, look at you. Your Child of the Stars is dull, your tunic is greasy and soiled, and you're holding fellow Ecclessites—three men on their way to an assignment—prisoner for bounty. You call that exemplary behavior?"

"Ain't no brigade within two hundred miles, except the Daggermen's, from which you nicked food and other valuables. There's nothing wrong with detaining liars and thieves."

"Then why is my tunic bright and clean?"

"Don't mean nothing," Darfe' grunted.

With Da'rot and seven skinners gone, the odds were four to one. Artka wasn't likely to get a better chance. A surprise attack might take out one, possibly even two quickly, but he'd have to fight the others. Well, that was a chance he'd have to take.

He gathered his feet underneath and was about to launch himself at the nearest poacher when one of the guards pointed across the snowy fields saying, "Torches heading this way. They see our fire. Looks like Daggermen breaking trail on foot."

Darfe' joined him peering across the snowy expanse. "I see them. Should be here in about half an hour, I guess. Good. I hope Sofista will be satisfied with these three, so we can get back to trapping and quit chasing escapees."

It was now or never. Artka broke from cover brandishing his sword.

The four poachers turned and stared.

A sudden explosion of snow off hemlock branches on the opposite side of the clearing revealed another man hurtled into the campsite, drawing the poachers' attention away from Artka.

"What ho, Darfe'," said the newest arrival. "I see you've traded lion hides for man's skin."

Darfe' strode toward the intruder with an axe in one hand and a skinning knife in the other, then stopped and said, "Braxmore? What are you doing here?"

"Braxmore?" said Artka, sliding to a halt.

Darfe' continued, "I suppose you two are the advance for that group slogging through the snow?"

"Sort of," Braxmore said, winking at Artka. "We've come for the prisoners."

"Okay, soon as I get paid, I'll be only too glad to release them." Darfe' held his hand out. "Caughter only three of them. There might be one or two more somewhere about."

"Uh, you don't quite understand, we've come for the prisoners." With that Braxmore withdrew his sword, which, like the lion poacher swords, was dull except for the very point. Braxmore touched his sword tip to the ropes binding Scang.

The ropes parted and in half a blink the giant rolled to the side and seized Darfe's legs, knocked them out from under him sending the leader crashing to the ground.

Artka squared off against two lion poachers while Braxmore swung his sword wildly at the third.

The two attacked Artka, one flailing his sword, the other waving a dagger. Sky Saber moved of its own accord in Artka's hand to meet the sword. The dull weapon tumbled from the man's hand as he yelped and clasped his wrist. The other man with the dagger ducked low and swiped at Artka's stomach but missed.

Artka conked him on the head with his sword's pommel; the man crumpled.

Braxmore wasn't faring as well, only when the poacher saw Artka's second opponent hit the ground did he flee into the woods screaming for help, following the man with the sprained wrist.

Scang sat astraddle the squirming Darfe'. "Ouch, yer bug! Cut it out or I'll bean yer." Grinning up at Artka, he said, "Sure was easier when we kilt our enemies."

"We don't have much time," Braxmore said, loosing Reddy and Harnet.

"Just what are you doing here?" Artka said.

"Like I told you back at the castle, I want to join you."

"How did you—?"

"Later. First we've got to find and destroy their skishers so they can't chase us. Then you've got to teach me how to walk on snow."

"Skishers?" said Reddy and Harnet in unison.

Braxmore probed under snowy piles and behind tree trunks. "Long, slender slats of wood, they make a *skish* noise as they glide over snow."

"Like these?" Artka said, holding aloft wooden slats three-inches-wide and as long as a man is tall.

"Exactly," Braxmore said, striding across the campsite.

"There's a stash of them here," Artka said, leaning behind a rock and brushing away the concealing snow.

"Break them quick and put them on the fire."

"No, no! Don't destroy them," Darfe' begged. "They're our transportation in deep snow. That's how we escape the lions. Destroy them and we're doomed."

Artka hesitated.

Braxmore pressed his point. "You must destroy them, or they'll be on our trail and overtake us in minutes."

"No, I promise. We'll just pretend to chase you."

"Look, Artka," Braxmore said, "he'll say anything to save his skin. Once Sofista realizes the lion poachers can't travel atop the snow he'll take them to Daggerman Castle in your place. Sofista has had an uneasy alliance with these poachers only because he hasn't been able to catch them. It would serve them right, after all, they were planning to deliver you to the same fate."

"Don't listen to the liar," Darfe' said, still pinned under Scang's weight. "We'll die by lion attack if we don't have our skishers."

Artka leaned several sets of skishers against a rock, asking, "You're not afraid of Sofista then, only lions?"

"Yes, yes, only lions. It would be murder to leave us without skishers."

Artka's foot stomped through the first set of skishers, breaking them in half. "Learn to face your lions with Logon's swords, the way Logon intended, instead of fleeing on skishers."

"Artka, Yes!" Braxmore triumphed, happily trouncing more skishers and dumping the shattered pieces on the fire. Darfe' went limp, mumbling about hiding before Sofista's patrol arrived. Whatever else he said was muffled by Scang's hand.

"Shouldn't we keep some skishers for ourselves?" Harnet asked.

"Have you ever used them?"

Braxmore looked at him. "No, but it shouldn't be much more complicated than snowwalkers."

"They're trickier than they look. Sofista's men would catch you before you learned to get along without falling. Stick to your snowwalkers—speaking of which, I don't have any."

"Hain't enuf time ter make yer some. Sorry," Scang said, checking on the Daggermen's progress. "Looks like yer be's on yer own, Braxmore." He got off Darfe' and started gathering his belongings back into his knapsack.

Braxmore said, "How can you harbor ill feelings after I freed you?"

"Scang, he's right," Artka said. "You'll have to carry him."

"Whut you say?"

"Quickly, they're closing in," Reddy said, recovering the rest of their snowwalkers. "Those other lion poachers will be back any moment, along with the Daggermen, and you'll still be arguing."

Heeding Reddy's advice, they bent to the task of donning snowwalkers.

"I mean it Scang," Artka said. "You carry him until we're out of danger."

Scang muttered something in Erotonese and darted angry glances at Braxmore. No further protest was made however, and the decision stood.

Harnet gathered the last of the odds and ends of their scattered goods as a shout sounded from the forest followed by lion poachers charging out of the trees.

"Time to go," Artka said, climbing atop the snow pack. Reddy hefted Scang's rucksack along with his own, followed by Scang piggy-packing a tight-lipped Braxmore hugging Scang's neck. Last of all, came Harnet, side stepping, sword high to fend off any poacher arrows.

No arrows came. The lion poachers, seeing flames greedily devouring their broken skishers, realized their own jeopardy and hustled Darfe' and the others into the cover of the forest just as the torch-bearing Daggermen broke through the other side of the campsite. Thirty men gave chase to the retreating lion poachers, ignoring the five fleeing atop the snow.

CHAPTER THIRTY-ONE

DAYBREAK OVERTOOK THE FIVE WEARY travelers climbing into the foothills of the Prophecy Mountains. The actual mountains were still a good day's journey off. They had a prolonged stop only once—to make a set of snowwalkers for Braxmore. After that Scang resumed leading, his longer stride setting a demanding pace. No one complained except Braxmore who was left to figure out by trial and error how to walk on snow for himself.

At first, Braxmore had difficulty. His leg and back muscles had never been so challenged. His companions were travel-hardened and somewhat skilled at snowwalking, he wasn't. He lagged half a mile behind, huffing and puffing, but accepting his lot, thankful that they hadn't abandoned him—and that the Eroton no longer carried him. Most of all he was grateful that Logon had brought some Ecclessites into his life who were different. Longings were awakened that hadn't stirred since first meeting Logon. Jaded years sloughed off his soul as he plodded in the four kingsmen's wake. The night he was nearly skewered by Scang jolted him out of his sense of complacency; and though he concealed it, he recalled times when he'd actually heard the Advisor's voice.

Pausing on an up-slope to catch his breath, Braxmore shielded his eyes and searched ahead for his companions. He tried not to complain about cold, hunger, steep ascents, or the fact that they occasionally disappeared over ridges without so much as a backward glance. "Just because I'm not as conditioned as they . . . "

Up ahead, Scang, Artka, Reddy, and Harnet weren't as travel-hardened as Braxmore thought. "Scang," Reddy said, "I'm so tired, if I tripped, I'd be asleep before I hit the snow."

Scang, surveying the panorama, answered with a grunt which was taken as agreement. "Be's the pest still a-comin'?"

Harnet turned to look. "Yup. One thing you can give him credit for—he's tenacious."

"So be's a hair in a biscuit." With a growl he gestured toward the base of a small hillock where a small, dark cave-opening was visible in the craggy rock-face. "Yonder's a crevice. Usn's kin rest there a bit."

"Right," Artka said. "I'll wait here for Braxmore, so he knows where we've gone."

"Cain't he foller our tracks?" Scang obviously had little use for the Conformitarian dogging their trail.

Artka bit the inside of his lower lip to keep from smiling at Scang's attitude but made no reply.

Scang shrugged and headed for the cave. Reddy and Harnet followed. Artka waited atop the knoll, surveying Braxmore's progress.

Braxmore, seeing the others drop from sight, tried to hustle faster.

Nothing else in the white expanse moved except a flock of birds flying low in the distance. Braxmore would be another fifteen minutes or longer, so to pass the time Artka withdrew Sky Saber and gave it a few strokes with his toller. Minutes later he checked on Braxmore's progress and scanned the horizon again. Braxmore was within hailing distance. The flock of birds—ravens by the look of them—seemed to follow their trail.

Artka cupped his hands to his mouth and shouted, "Hurry, Braxmore, there's a cave, we'll rest."

Braxmore waved and renewed his efforts.

Artka's toller was hovered above his blade as he watched the birds overfly Braxmore. The lead bird was unusually large, even for a raven. Without taking his eyes off them Artka tucked his toller away and defensively raised his sword. The birds hoarsely called to each other. They now obviously were following the kingsmen footprints. As they came closer Artka noticed that the lead bird was a buzzard.

Braxmore half-stumbled up to Artka, wheezing billows of vaporized breath.

The flock circled the craggy cliff twice and then flew back over Artka. The buzzard split off from the main body and swooped directly down at Artka, pulling up just out of reach of Artka's sword, screeching, "Yeearrk."

Artka's neck hairs bristled. The scavenger flapped up to a safer altitude, rejoined its companions and headed back the way they'd come.

"What was all that about?" Braxmore said, gulping in a draught of air.

"Spies, I think."

"Spies? In Ecclessa? For whom?"

"Whoever it is, they'll soon be on our trail."

Braxmore searched the snowy landscape and said, "Where did Scang and the others go?"

"There's a little cave," Artka pointed. "We'll rest there."

"I'm all for that." Braxmore headed down the slope.

Braxmore, weary beyond anything he'd endured prior, stumbled and nearly fell on his face. Scang waited just inside the entrance. Harnet and Reddy were sprawled on the cave floor fast asleep, heads resting on their knapsacks. Reddy hadn't even unfastened his snowwalkers. Braxmore plopped down beside them. Three swords, their glowing points conjoined, were on the floor emanating a cozy warmth into the stony enclosure.

"Did you see that buzzard leading the ravens?" Artka asked Scang. "I think I've seen it before. They were spies."

Scang nodded. "I'll watch then, yer git summat sleep."

"I don't think that's necessary. Even on skishers, it'll be hours before anyone catches up. We need to sleep. I think we're safe for the time being." With that, he added his sword to the pile, unfastened his snow walkers, laid his head on his knapsack, wrapped his cloak about him, and promptly fell asleep.

"Well, I'll jest keep watch anyhow," Scang said, nestling into a niche that afforded a clear view of the approach. Within a minute, however, his chin also rested on his chest.

A rivulet of snowmelt trickled into the cave's adit beneath Scang's upraised knees, past the sleeping men, under the congruent swords, and down, down into the dark, mysterious underworld of the Prophecy Mountains.

~

Scang dreamt he was fending off a large wolf with his bare hands. The beast wasn't dangerous. Its objective seemed to be pinning Scang to the ground. If Scang could just free his arms—and if the beast would only quit slurping. Scang's foot kicked at the animal's underbelly, but instead its ice-cold mouth grabbed his foot.

He struggled to get free—and rolled into the rivulet beneath his legs.

"Gaaaahh!" He said disgustedly, rising from the stream. His outcry roused the others. Moving slow, blinking weary eyes, they gathered their possessions.

"Sun's going down," Harnet said and yawned, leaning against the wall by the entry to scan the snowy scenery.

Artka joined him. Long, bluish shadows stretched over the white expanse, and mists hovered ghost-like above the snow in the bottom-land. A gusty breeze kicked up and swept upward, rising over distant hilltops; snowflakes skittered across the crusty snow like white, swirling feathers.

"I'm hungry," Reddy said rummaging in his knapsack but finding nothing edible.

"Hain't no use lookin', little feller," Scang said. "Them lion poachers done cleaned usn's out."

"Look, my name isn't litt—"

"Shhh!" Artka slipped back inside and retrieved his sword from the floor.

"Two men coming," Harnet ducked low and whispered, "following our tracks."

The others took up their swords and crowded just inside the doorway.

"We kin take 'em," Scang said.

"And do what with them?" Braxmore stepped in front of the giant. "You can't tie them up because no one would find them in this barren land. They'd starve, especially this time of year."

Scang growled under his breath.

"Braxmore's right," Artka said. "Besides, they might be the bait in an ambush meant to catch us."

"Well, whoever they are, they're coming right for us," Reddy said.

Artka turned to inspect their hideout. "We could explore those deeper recesses for another way out, or we can defend this cave."

"Wait," Harnet said, "they're not Daggermen or lion poachers. I know them." He bolted out the entry, waving his arms, calling, "Halloo!"

"Harnet! Come back!" Artka said. "You don't know—" But it was too late.

The new arrivals on snowwalkers waved back and quickened their gait. Harnet waded through the drifts and embraced the newcomers. The other four watched helplessly from inside the cave, unable to assist should it prove to be a trap.

Reddy straightened up. "Well, as sure as the sun shines in the day, it's Brendle, and Corporal Clepy!"

"So 'tis." Scang twisted his beard between his fingers.

Harnet, having dashed out without snowwalkers, huffed and puffed as he churned through the snow leading the newcomers to the cave.

Artka welcomed Brendle who was the young kingsman who had been offended at Tren's tale of the unarmed kings. Corporal Clepy had introduced him around in King's Gate Fortress West. Greetings were exchanged then questions flew. The newcomers expressed surprise at the warmth in the cave and Reddy delightedly demonstrated the swords' ability to generate heat. Brendle revealed that he carried food supplies and all other matters were momentarily dropped.

While satisfying their hunger Clepy said, "We have news."

They gnawed salty, dried meat, waiting to hear tidings from people and places far away yet near to their hearts.

"The day ye left, the day of the blizzard," Clepy said, "we were attacked, and the fortress would ha' been breached, had it not been for Captain Tren, thanks be to Logon. As it was, we barely held our own. The enemy launched a massive attack with frightful creatures and men whose hearts weren't easily pierced. We only rescued a few in the first wave, many casualties occurred on both sides. We were outnumbered ten to one, and with the storm, it was impossible to determine where their next assault was coming so as to bolster our defenses. It was snowing so hard we could barely see our opponents. Our Children of the Stars had to guide themselves. If it hadn't been for Tren's influence . . . "

"Yes, yes, we know," Harnet said. "But, tell us of the outcome."

"Aye, the outcome," Clepy said. "Captain Metid kept watching the bridge, waiting for reinforcements, but all that came was more wind and snow. He doubted ye'd made it across and tried to lift our spirits by saying, 'Looks like we'll soon be in King Elyon's palace.' We resolved to die honorably and therein found peace.

"Shortly afterward a thunder of hooves echoed from the bridge and reinforcements burst into the courtyard. We took courage and our enemy was dismayed. I guess they'd counted on us not receiving any help.

"Then Tren galloped out on a white horse, his sword flashing brilliant colors and giving off high-pitched musical sounds. He called for all whose swords resonated with his to join the counterattack. Mine was aglow and vibrating, so I scrambled down off the ramparts and joined the throng surging out the sally port. Some say they saw a cloaked figure with arms extended standing upon one of the parapets," Clepy said with a tilt of his head.

"I saw him," Brendle interrupted. "It was Logon."

Clepy said, "Well, most of us never saw—"

"It was Logon."

Clepy shrugged. "Anyway, we went out and won many to Logon. It turned into a rout. As the snow hindered our defense at the first, it likewise hindered their retreat, resulting in many Carnalians being rescued.

"I followed Tren's wake the rest of the day. Twilight found us on the edge of the Swamp Tophet. That's where many wavered, remembering the abhorrence of that foul place and the evil it breeds. Tren made camp. The faint-hearted were told they could return to the fortress in the morning if they so desired. There'd be no dishonor to those who returned. They'd fought bravely facing death all day but those who felt the urgency of pressing the attack should carry the fight into the swamp on the morrow with Tren. They, and they alone, were called by Logon to do so."

Clepy fell silent.

Brendle stared at the floor.

None disturbed the moment, though their ears burned to hear more.

Finally, Clepy swallowed the lump in his throat. "Tren told us that there were at least three chimeree—dreads of the gates—that lurked in the swamp, along with a multitude of tophets, many still in the process of shape-taking, but nonetheless sinister and dangerous.

"Many of the valiant quailed at the thought of facing dreads and tophets. Nevertheless, about fifty of us longed to press the battle. After a restless night of watching and listening, Tren divided the task force into two groups—those who were to return to the fortress and train the new recruits, and those who were to push deeper into the swamp. I took my place among the fifty going into the swamp, but Tren took me aside and wanted me to lead the expedition back to the fortress, saying there were dangers along that road as well, and he wanted someone in charge who still had spirit enough to fight. I was given a field commission, journey lieutenant. Of course, when we got back to the fort, I was just a corporal again. Oh yes, Tren also gave me a message for ye, Artka."

"For me?"

"It's a wee bit curious, and some of it I dinnae understand."

"Git on wi' it man," Scang said.

"All right, dinnae rush me. Tren said: 'Hurry, seek no shelter until the sage be found.' Then he said something about a spitter looking for ye. Do ye ken what that means?"

"The venom-spraying tophet that melted a trail through the snow," Harnet said. "Then it is the same tophet."

Brendle paled. "Tophet trail in the snow? You—you don't mean a trench through the snow, do you?"

"The same," Harnet said. "It seems tophets are able to melt their way through deep snow, clearing a trench down to bare ground."

"Oh my," Braxmore said. "A wide trench? That's a tophet trail? That's what I followed from the Daggermen's castle to your camp in the hemlocks. I didn't quite get to the end of the trail, for when I saw the bright campfire I broke out, waded through the deep snow and hid in the brush till I knew what kind of reception I'd get."

"And is that how you and Brendle located us, Clepy?" Artka asked. "So, it's been following us all along. Why hasn't it attacked? How did it know we came this way after we entered the Daggermen Castle?" He went to the cave's mouth and looked out. "The buzzard!" He turned around. "How far away does the trench end?"

"We climbed out of the trench just below that hill," Clepy said, "before those trees. I didnae like the look of the trees, thinking it a likely place for an ambush. Then Brendle discovered your snowwalker tracks. We donned our snowwalkers and . . . well, here we are."

Scang said, "So, it found usn's agin?"

"And not just any tophet, but the spitter," Artka said.

"Hadn't we better get going then?" Reddy said.

"Where?" said Braxmore. "If such things exist, and I now believe they do, wouldn't it be easier to defend this cave than be caught in the open?"

"Come here and tell me if you see anything unusual," Artka said. "Up there, on our path toward the mountains."

They peered out the entrance. Braxmore said, "I don't see much of anything except mists rising off the melting snow, is that what you mean?"

"That's all anyone sees," Harnet said, "unless his sword is bright enough to pierce their enshrouding mists."

"Look closely, Braxmore," Artka said. "See most of the mists are drifting over the ridge then dissipate in the breeze."

"Yes."

"Now, look to the left. What's that mist doing?"

"Just lingering." Braxmore's eyes widened. "Do you mean to say that that's a—? Maybe there's no breeze there."

"Other mists are swirling past, but it remains impervious. That my friend, is a tophet. It must have arrived just before Clepy and Brendle and watched as you met us."

"Aye, thet be's a tophet awright. But why sets it yonder?" Scang scraped his toller across his blade.

"Waiting for reinforcements?" Harnet posed. "Don't forget, if he's the one that was driven away at the gate, he's hesitant to feel the bite of our swords again."

"We're trapped." Braxmore stepped backward into the enclosure. "And if it shoots its spray into this cave . . . "

"Thot yer said this 'ud be a good place ter defend?"

"That's not called for, Scang," Artka said. "Braxmore is right, we do seem to be trapped. There are seven of us now. How many did it take to drive him off that night?"

"Dozens as I recalls, mebbe even a couple o' score. He warn't too impressed, we only jest made him retreat. Seemed ter be extra strong."

"Then direct attack is out," Artka said.

"Thanks be to Logon," Reddy muttered.

"There's a time to fight, and a time to slip away." Clepy tapped a faint rune on his sword. "We'd best investigate the depths of this cave. Maybe there's another exit."

"I'll bar the entry while yers looks around," Scang said.

"Nay," Clepy said. "Artka, I think we should stick together, don't ye?"

"I agree, Clepy. But if it makes you feel better Scang, you can bring up the rear of the column."

"Aye, I'll bring up the aft then."

Clepy laid his hand on Artka's shoulder and whispered, "There was a little more to Tren's message, Artka, but I think it can wait." Then aloud, "We'd best not delay; that beastie's reinforcements might arrive any moment."

Artka nodded, took one last look at the fading daylight and followed Clepy, Brendle, and the others into the eerie darkness of Lurcan's Womb.

CHAPTER THIRTY-TWO

AN HOUR SEEMED LIKE A day for the seven descending into caverns of blackness where the silence could almost be felt. The combined light of their weapons seemed meager in the vast void, revealing only a few yards of their path before being swallowed by the ubiquitous night. Clepy led into the yawning oblivion, since his sword was brightest, followed by Artka, Brendle, Harnet, Braxmore, Reddy, and finally Scang who stepped off a dozen paces then suddenly whirled around with his sword at the ready as if to say, "I ken yers be's there."

The walls of the tunnel spread wider and the ceiling rose, fostering an eerie sense that the world had disappeared except the stone pathway beneath their feet. Stalactites constant dripping water loomed somewhere high overhead. As they descended the temperature rose; the novice spelunkers loosened their cloaks and walked silently into the uncharted abyss surrounding them, as if fearful to interrupt the somber quiet with idle chatter.

Their path consistently went down, almost leveling out at times, and other times more steeply down, but ever down, ever dark, ever silent.

At times Artka fancied he heard scurrying sounds behind or off to one side or the other but said nothing. If no one else heard, it must have been his imagination, or if others had heard, they wisely kept mum. It wouldn't do to awaken superstitions and fears of the unknown in this foul hall. The overbearing darkness made him long for sunshine, blue sky, chirping birds, a fresh breeze—anything but dark, stuffy, silent caves.

Uneventful hours passed as they shuffled steadily down. Their knees, unused to a continual downward slant, ached for relief. Their calves began to quiver—presaging muscle cramps. And still they pressed silently onward, downward.

"I hope we soon turn back uphill," Reddy said in a hushed voice, finally daring to break the silence.

The smallness of his voice disquieted them, impressing on them just how immense and alien an environment they trespassed. Would this trek never end?

Clepy held up his hand as the company rounded a turn. "Listen." Even his whisper was distorted, unnatural.

"To what?" Artka strained to hear anything other than his own breath.

"Sounds like a breeze. Can ye nay hear it?"

"I hears it," Scang said, "but it don't sound like no breeze. Nor be's the air any fresher."

A faint roar increased, then as suddenly, decreased. Moments later it reoccurred and disappeared again.

Harnet chuckled. "It's not the wind," he grinned. "It's water, or, more accurately, a tide. Listen. Breakers rushing onshore . . . now . . . running back out. Hear them?"

"But," Braxmore said, "there's no body of water large enough for a tide in the Prophecy Mountains."

"Maybe not on the surface." Harnet patted his nearly empty water skin. "It must be an underground lake, hopefully the water is drinkable."

"Let's find out," Clepy said.

They resumed their journey at a slightly faster clip, nearly jogging down straightaways, rounding corners, but ever downward. The amplified sounds of tidal swells suggested a body of water much larger than a lake—perhaps an underground sea? The crashing surf intensified as they approached.

Artka edged around Clepy and was the first to detect a greenish glow reflecting off the cave walls. "What's that?" he asked.

No one answered; no one could venture a viable guess.

The seven navigated a final corner and beheld a vast, luminescent sea stretching beyond sight. Breakers onshore were brighter than waves farther out, yet a green haze hovered above the waters seemingly to infinity. Way offshore, rogue waves running contrary to the tide resulted in marvelous, shimmering displays of green light. The kingsmen gaped spellbound.

"Hullo," said Scang dipping his hand in a swell, "it hain't the water whut's green, but summat kind o' scum afloatin' in it."

Clepy scooped up a handful and brought his sword close. "It's an algae of some kind, like as grows in ponds. I suppose this would be as good a place to rest as any."

"It looks deeper over there where there's less algae," Reddy said. "Let's see if it's drinkable."

"I'll come wi' yer little feller. Let's try by them rocks, so's usn's don't stir up no sand 'n grit."

Brendle, Braxmore, and Harnet flopped down on a sandy beach, situating their rucksacks as backrests.

"Ow, I've never ached so much in my entire life," Brendle said.

No one had any sympathy to spare. Clepy and Artka stayed afoot, transfixed by the beauty of the subterranean sea.

"I'd like to hear the rest of Tren's message, Clepy," Artka said.

Clepy studied the pitch-blackness behind them. "I guess it's safe. Not even a tophet could guess the paths we've taken. Now, where did I leave off?"

"Umm, the last thing you said was about the Spitter. That it was seeking me."

"Right. Then Tren said something about Lurcan's agents drawn to ye by some object ye possessed? That part I dinnae ken. Do ye take his meaning?"

Though the shame went deep, Artka confessed to owning a dagger.

Clepy stroked his beard, saying nothing.

"I still have it."

Still no response.

"We felt it was too dangerous to just discard," said Artka, prodded by Clepy's silence. "If Tren knew I had it on me, why did he let me jeopardize the mission?"

Clepy said, "Once ye've been told something, but failed to listen, the next lesson often comes from hard experience. Have ye larnt your lesson?"

"Oh, have I! But, what can I do about it now?"

"Normally I'd say be rid of the foul thing, but not now, not down here. I think ye should keep it a wee bit longer, until we find a proper way to dispose of it. But, I hope ye really have larnt your lesson, for if ye haven't . . . "

"Believe me, I have."

"Ere, take a look-see at this," Scang barged up and interrupting them, thrusting a long, thin fish between Artka and Clepy. "It gots nobbut eyes. The shore be's lousy wi' 'em, an' they don't ken ter swim away. The water be's good fer drinkin', though a mite warm. The little red-haired lad thot he'd take a swim afore comin' back."

"Ugh, Scang! Whatever would ye do with that thing?" Clepy asked, studying the pale, squirmy creature.

"Why, eat it, 'specially since our provisions been et and there hain't nobbut else down in this dark hole ter feed on."

"But Scang, we can't cook," Artka said. "Even if we found fuel to burn, the smell and smoke would alert whatever creatures lurk in these quarters to our presence, including those tophets that might be snuffling around for our spoor."

"Who said summat 'bout cookin'?"

"Ugh," Artka and Clepy groaned in unison.

Brendle detached himself from Braxmore and Harnet, joining Artka's huddle. "Excuse me, but don't you think it's time we left these caves? We don't know if it's day or night now, and it won't take much more meandering to get thoroughly lost."

Artka and Clepy glanced at each other. "Brendle, we thought ye knew," Clepy said, "we have no idee where we are."

"But, you do know the way back, right?" Brendle's voice rose.

Clepy's shaggy locks shook as he said, "I'm afraid if Logon doesn't guide us, we're lost. I thought ye kenned the risk we took avoiding the tophets."

"Well yes, I did, but thought we'd have found our way back by now."

"As we all hoped," Artka absent-mindedly tolled his blade. A faint vibration filled their ears and a rune on Artka's Child of the Stars glowed softly.

Clepy's sword also hummed though he wasn't tolling, and the same rune as on Artka's was aglow. The two swords resonated with a harmonious, intertwining melody. The others gathered close, including Reddy, dripping wet from his swim, his clothes clinging to him. Artka and Clepy spontaneously erupted into song:

"Where can I go the Advisor is not?
Where is the place unknown to the king?
What name has the land where no mention
of Xychirion is made?
When I sleep in pits deep, my king is nigh,
Or pursuing the sun upon the high sea,
Xychirion's hand will light the path,
His covering will always shelter me.
Pursuing horrors can't overwhelm,
For the watchful eyes of the Great King,
Behold all, for all is in sight,
To the great Creator of light."

The music ceased, and the singers fell silent, but the glow from the two swords intensified. Rays of light shimmered from both swords and joined to form a silvery beam that sliced through the gloom, shining on and revealing an aperture in the rock walls of a cliff some twenty feet above the breakwaters.

"Behold," Clepy said, "our pathway."

The beam from the two swords began to fade.

Scang said, "Usn's best be a-hurryin' afore the light goes out. Usn's will never find thet cave in the dark."

"But how can we scale that," Reddy said. "It's too high, and in those tricky breakers, there's a strong undertow, you know. I had to fight it when I was bathing to keep from being swept away."

"What are you saying?" Harnet asked.

"And there are deep holes all along the shore. One misstep and one or all of us could be swept out to sea. In this darkness we'd never find our way back to land"

"He has a point," said Braxmore.

"The beam is fading," Clepy urged. "We'd better hurry." He picked up his gear.

"But . . . " Reddy's voice faded.

"No buts, Reddy," said Artka. "The Children of the Stars wouldn't show us an impossible way. It may be difficult, even dangerous, but we must trust the runesong and the light."

"Well said." Clepy directed his sword toward the cave. "Let's be on our way. No sense waiting for the beam to vanish entirely."

They hoisted their gear and waded toward the cliff. Artka and Clepy discovered they needn't keep pointing at the portal, for no matter where they stepped, the beam stayed fixed on the cave.

"Whut amazin' weapons," said Scang.

"How much more amazing is the one who forged them?" Harnet replied.

As they waded across the glittering, green surf, numerous fish swarmed to them and nibbled at their leggings.

Scang turned to them. "Stuff yer sacks." He gleefully followed his own advice by jamming a fistful of the wriggly creatures into the side pockets of his pack.

"Scang's probably right," Clepy said. "There's no telling how long we'll wander these dark, barren passages. Much as I hate to admit it, we might have to depend on these fish for food. Oh, and if ye haven't already done so, fill your water skins, too."

The others copied Scang, somewhat less enthusiastically.

"So much for the superiority of the Eroton palate," Harnet said under his breath.

"Ahh, raw fish be's a delicacy, lads. Yers'll see," Scang said with a chuckle.

~

Blist, lurking in the benighted distance behind a stalagmite, quite able to see in these familiar haunts, watched the largest of the men hoist the red-haired youth to his shoulders. With a mighty upward thrust the lad was propelled to an outcropping ledge where he secured a handhold, hoisted himself up to the tunnel entry, and then dangled a rope to his companions. One by one the men climbed out of the rollers. Blist inadvertently hissed in frustration.

The giant, the last man in the surf, turned and peered at the darkness—as if the fool could see in the dark! The man returned attention to the rope under his armpits and ascended the cliff aided by the concerted effort of his friends.

"A curse upon those needles," Blist muttered. "And a curse upon their maker . . . " He immediately winced, recalling that that had already been tried by one more powerful than he. But how he hated those shiny weapons that were able to penetrate his cloaking mist. He'd been just about to devour those two warriors at the castle gate, too. They were rightfully his. It would have been quite a feat to have taken the injured one with the fully glowing sword; what fame he'd have had in Pitland, Cosmopolis, and Inferna. But, he'd retreated; he, Blist, fleeing impudent mortals, all because of those shiny-tipped swords.

But, he wouldn't be denied. He hadn't trailed the deserter across Ecclessa to be cheated now. As for the other warrior that stayed at King's Gate, the one with the fully glowing sword—now that he was recovered from his injuries—was too much for Blist to handle alone or even with his cronies.

But, ahh! The young man coiling the rope—the deserter—still carried the false blade. The fools hadn't figured out that Brida's agents could zone in on its presence. The clever little men could go nowhere without being tracked, especially down here.

Blist was mildly surprised that they'd come to this chamber of all chambers. This was where Brida had openly denounced King Elyon aloud for the first time—and nothing happened to him! This was a happy place, one of the few under Ecclessa, although recently, that too was changing. This dank, lightless chamber referred to by his own kind as the *Beneath* and *Lurcan's Womb* was the opposite of Splendora. The deep darkness became midwife to corrupt schemes that, when carried out in the upper world, distorted Psychanon into Carnalia. Lurcan and his minions enjoyed the darkness because it was so unlike Elyon's realm. It was here to this chamber that Brida brought other *kyllorn* of his order and enticed them to mutiny. Here they dragged lowly creatures from above which they perverted into mutant, loathsome, deformed shapes which they would later assume in the festering environs of the Swamp Tophet.

When Lurcan, then called Brida, felt confident enough to launch a rebellion, it was in these dismal halls he received the allegiance of his supporters; any reluctant sympathizers were harangued and bullied until they yielded to full insurrection. They'd assembled *kyllorn* ranging from high order to low, to become dreads and firedrakes, tophets, cusps, scavengers, irks, and even more loathsome creatures—all that had succumbed to Brida's boastful words and subtle accusations against the king.

"A curse upon Zindrad, too," Blist muttered, then quickly scanned his surroundings. Ambitious snitches would be only too glad to bear tidings of that hasty oath. Zindrad, one of the dreads, would certainly wreak vengeance upon him if the source of that curse were discovered.

Assured that he was alone, Blist turned full attention to the man coiling the rope.

So, they knew about the tunnel Lurcan named after Carpul, lord of the firedrakes, did they? Well, Blist knew where it led as well; past the chimney vent and the path to the outside adit—and he knew a short cut. He'd gather his squad of disgraced roamers and mercilessly pounce upon the kingsmen just when they were filled with hope at returning to their own world.

Blist dragged his hulk up the twisting passages reminiscing about the early days of the resistance when they expected Elyon's throne to topple. Brida, who'd devised the swift-acting powers of violence and hatred, would ascend as the new Master of the Realms.

But, Blist sighed, that was long ago. Things had turned out quite differently. The battle was hard pressed on many fronts now, and they were barely able to hold their own against mere mortals at times.

Thus, nursing bittersweet memories, the tophet, still oozing slime from the nicks received at the King's Gate West portal, made his way along familiar trails back to the outer world where he would brief his subordinates on his plan. Though wounded, he was the only venomous tophet in the warparty, and therefore, the highest ranking. Ah, how clever he'd been to spin a venom-spitting form about his scorpion shape. While others took beatings from those annoying needles, he only needed to enshroud the battle zone with a venomous spray; then satiate his flesh-lust on paralyzed kingsmen. Just for fun, he'd sting that giant with his tail, make him writhe in agony while he slowly devoured him. During the rescue at the gate that Eroton had delivered the most telling cuts. Revenge would be blood-sweet. Thus, with fantasies of debilitating the seven travelers he wended his way back up and out of Lurcan's Womb.

~

Scang crept away from the cave's opening. "'Twar a tophet awright. I heered him draggin' hisself along, makin' no attempt ter be quiet."

"Then we got up here just in time," Braxmore said. "Do you think he knows where we went?"

"I think nay, but even if he does, it's unlikely he'll be able to climb up here and follow," Clepy said. "I just wish I knew where this tunnel heads, and how long it'll take. I dinnae like surprises, especially when tophets are afoot."

The seven resumed the journey, Clepy and Artka going first and second; the others in order with Scang bringing up the rear. The trail rose steadily; before long other leg muscles ached from the constant uphill push.

Several hours into the climb Reddy breathlessly complained, "I'm tired. Can't we stop and sleep? It's been a long time you know . . . "

"I dinnae think it wise," Clepy said. "There surely must be an exit soon, perhaps just around the next corner. We'll all sleep better when we get out of this oppressive atmosphere."

Reddy and Brendle groaned. Scang, more exhausted by the uphill push than the others, appeared ready to physically argue the point.

"Ach," Clepy said, "I guess it will nay hurt to be rested a wee bit. But we'd best set a two-man watch."

Harnet and Brendle agreed to take first watch, using the opportunity to toll their blades. The others fell out, stretching aching muscles as they laid down and soon fell asleep. Artka followed suit, albeit fitfully, troubled in dreams by strange voices and distorted faces.

Artka woke; a hand shook his shoulder. For a brief instant he thought he was in the Valley of Shadows, waiting for Tren to lead him away from the cusps. Realizing where he was, he sighed. Brendle then roused Braxmore.

"All's quiet, not even a drip," whispered Harnet. "I've never heard absolute silence before, except, of course, for Scang's snores and Reddy muttering." He lay down and covered himself with his cloak. Within minutes he and Brendle slept peacefully, undisturbed by voices and dark visions.

Artka gave Braxmore some pointers on tolling as they kept watch. Braxmore hadn't made much progress sharpening on his own, having fallen under Sofista's spell early in his Ecclessite career. As their watch passed they chatted as they tolled, sharing their experiences at Logon's Rock.

When their time was almost up, and they were about to awaken Scang and Clepy, they heard a faint scuffling sound from the tunnel above. The sounds stopped, then came again, stopped, and then came again. Something was progressively, cautiously moving down the passageway toward them. Clepy, held his sword ready and roused the others. Artka broke into a cold sweat; both hands gripped Sky Saber's haft.

A brilliant blue light suddenly shone up the passageway off the walls revealing a turn just ahead. The light intensified until a fully lighted sword came into view. Even at that distance merry runes were identified along the blade's length. A man followed the sword around the corner, his hand shielding his eyes. Upon spying seven dimmer swords before him, he halted.

Artka joyfully leapt to his feet and raced toward the newcomer. The only person he longed to see more than Logon was this man. He nearly tripped as he ran in his excitement, crying out, "Tren! How ever did you find us?"

CHAPTER THIRTY-THREE

"HOLD YOUR GROUND!" COMMANDED A stranger's stern voice.

Artka froze. Upon taking a closer look, it wasn't Tren.

"Who are you? And what are you doing in these wretched halls?" the stranger asked.

"I'm Artka, and these," he pointed, "are my friends. I—we've—been sent to the Prophecy Mountains by Logon, to—"

"Keerful Artka," said Scang.

" . . . to find a man named Saygus."

"Saygus? That scoundrel? What could you possibly want with him?"

Harnet joined beside Artka. "Do you know where we can find him?"

"I'll ask the questions. What do you want with Saygus?"

"We . . . er . . . are seeking his advice on a matter," Artka said.

"And you thought to find him down in these defiled halls?"

"We came into these caverns to evade a tophet," Artka said.

"What? With all your swords, you fled from a tophet?"

"He be's a spitter, if'n yer kens whut they be's." Scang drew alongside his friends. "An' jest who might yer be, ter be askin' all manner o' questions?"

"Well, well. An Eroton has been to Logon's Rock. Can the Final Reckoning be far off? Enough of this banter. You tell me, and tell me true, what business have you in Lurcan's Womb?"

"Lurcan's Womb?" Artka frowned. "As to its name and history we plead ignorance. Like I said, we seek Saygus, a sage. We were told he resides somewhere in the mountains above. That's all we can reveal. Will you help us, or not?"

"What makes you think Saygus will receive you? He has a reputation for throwing uninvited visitors over cliffs, you know."

"Logon sent me—us—"

"Oh? First, it's me, then it's us? I think you are Daggermen sneaking into the Prophecy Mountains through secret ways that Lurcan's agents have shown you. Or might you be friends of the lion poachers who plunder these game-rich mountains?"

"Sire, ye misjudge us," Clepy said. "We truly are on a mission from Logon, not Lurcan. Why else would our Children of the Stars glow?"

The stranger observed them. "True enough. But, before I consent to aid you in your quest, I must know your business with Saygus. He regards his privacy highly and wouldn't take it kindly if I let just anyone have audience with him."

"May we take private council?" Artka asked.

"Alright. A few hundred paces behind me there's a junction of three caves. When you reach a decision, meet me there. But, don't tarry long, there's danger afoot." The stranger lowered his sword but eyed the group for a full minute before turning back.

"Hmmph! Seems mighty full o' hisself, don't he?" Scang huffed.

"But, his sword," said Reddy, "I've never seen a sword that bright. Not even Tren's."

"Ah, but can he be trusted like Tren?" Brendle asked.

"Anyone with that much shine on his sword knows Logon well," Artka said. "And anyone who knows Logon that well ought to be trusted, at least until they prove otherwise."

"But remember Captain Sofista," Braxmore said, "he knew the runes, and everything."

"Sofista didn't have a glow on his sword or obey the runes," Harnet said. "He merely learned some runes in order to argue against them. Knowing runes doesn't make the blade glow, only sincere obedience puts the light of Logon on both man and sword."

"I agree," Artka said. "So, I think it's safe to reveal our mission."

They searched each other's eyes.

Clepy finally said, "Face it lads, we need to trust somebody, and this fellow is clearly on Logon's side."

"Yes, and he has more reason to be suspicious of us than we of him," Harnet said.

"Aye," Clepy nodded in agreement.

The seven gathered their sacks and water bags and went to meet the stranger, Artka and Clepy leading.

They found him at the junction of three caves as he'd said, seated, resting against the wall. His brilliant sword lit the cavern walls and ceiling. "Well?"

"Sir," Artka began, "when I was healed of my chest wound, Logon sent me into the Prophecy Mountains to find Saygus the Sage, who, he told me, would direct me to a new brigade being formed. That's about all there is to tell."

"All seven of you?"

"We belonged to other brigades, sir," Reddy said. "All but Artka. We received permission from our commandant to join Artka in seeking his new brigade."

"All of you?" The stranger stared at Carnalian-garbed Braxmore. "No Daggermen or Conformitarians among you?"

"Uh, well, actually, I sort of joined up along the way," Braxmore said.

"S'more like he attached hisself, like a tick," said Scang.

"But, he's proven very useful," Harnet interrupted in Braxmore's defense.

"Extend your Children of the Stars toward me," the stranger said.

The seven complied, glancing wonderingly at each other. To each in turn, the stranger laid his sword overtop theirs, carefully matching up only the portions they had aglow with his own. As he did so he peered into each one's eyes. None dared look away from the man's penetrating gaze.

When finished, the stranger said, "Well, at least you're all sincere, even if you are a mismatched crew, not to mention in a foul place."

"Then you'll guide us to Saygus?" Artka asked.

"And if I told you he's not receiving anyone?"

"Surely your recommendation—" Artka persisted.

A wave of the stranger's hand silenced him. "I said you were sincere. I didn't say your mission was valid."

"What do you mean?" Harnet said, replacing his sword in his belt.

"I mean there's no brigade in the Prophecy Mountains, old or new."

"But there must be. Logon said so. You can't possibly know what's going on in all of these mountains."

"Very little escapes my notice in these mountains. I have many informants."

"Yes, but we were sent to find Saygus, not you. He'll know the brigade we seek."

The stranger sighed. "I'm afraid Saygus can't help you any more than I can."

"Why is that?"

"Because I'm Saygus."

"You?"

"Preposterous!"

"Yer be's lyin'."

"Nay, nay, friends. Be not angry because I withheld my identity. Of late, there's much evil abroad, even in Ecclessa. Besides, you would have kept your quest from me had you not needed my help."

"Now see here, me good man," Clepy said, color rising to his cheeks, "we journeyed a long and dangerous road to find this Saygus, and ye dinnae look much like a sage to me."

"Oh? And just how does a sage look? Should my beard be white instead of dark? And longer, say to here?" He tapped his sternum. "And should my features be wizened and wrinkly, and oh—a staff to assist my wobbly legs would be a nice touch, don't you think?"

Clepy accepted the rebuke with smile. "Well, we hardly expected a, a—"

"Warrior," Artka said. "I confess, I too, expected more of what you described than what you are. You're so . . . young."

"Young I'm not. At times I feel ancient. But walking in the light of Logon's runes slows the aging process."

"Well then, since you must be Saygus—for no one with such a glow on his sword would easily deceive—you must know something of the new brigade," Artka said.

"I told you, there is no brigade. In fact, until a couple of days ago, the entire range was devoid of human life except for my family. Even villages in the valleys and foothills shut themselves in early due to the heavy snow down-country. Then word came to me of five snowwalkers closely followed by two others, who were in turn, followed by seven tophets. Since then the weather turned warm, melting some of the snow, so I came out to investigate."

"What? With seven tophets on the loose you came out alone?" Reddy said.

"Seventy tophets are no reason to not come out if they invade my mountains."

"But, there are spitters," Reddy added.

"Only one, and he's somewhat incapacitated by several small wounds."

"You must've been quite close to discern that," Brendle said.

"Close enough, but I knew their natures when they were but fuzzy mists way below my lookout."

"How?"

"Ah, that's an ability the Advisor has given me. Logon gives special functions to certain ones to accomplish his work. But, enough of that for now. We must decide what to do, for I barely escaped detection by slipping down a hole, which, as it turns out, happened to be this cavern."

"Escaped?" Harnet asked.

"From tophets."

"I thot yer weren't afeered o' seventy tophets," Scang challenged.

Saygus regarded Scang for a moment, then replied, "For myself, I fear them not. Those who have accomplished their sword's second shine know how to resist Lurcan's strongest tophets. My children however, like all of you, haven't completed their first shine. If those tophets knew I was absent from my home, they'd likely quit following you and attack them. They despise me and would do anything to hurt me or mine. I thought it prudent to hide, so I slipped down this cave, one I'd never investigated before, indeed, was unaware it existed. I was searching for an exit when I happened upon you."

"Seems like tophets are suddenly everywhere." Reddy shuddered.

"Everywhere? What do you mean?" Saygus asked.

"Scang saw—or rather, heard—one as we climbed out of the breakers into this tunnel."

"Breakers? You were at an underground sea?"

"As far as we could tell it was a sea. It's dark down there, you know," Harnet said.

"Then . . . this is the passage I've sought for years."

"You wanted to find this cavern?" Harnet asked dubiously. "Whatever for?"

"Until you're familiar with the mystery runes revealing the end of days and the Final Reckoning, you won't understand. But tell me, how far to the sea?"

"Several hours," Braxmore said. "Perhaps a day's trek."

"Mmm. A fair journey then. Too far for today, especially with a tophet down there, too."

"Too?" several voices chimed at once.

"Didn't I make it clear? I slipped down this cave to avoid a cluster of tophets that were heading straight for me. They set an ambush about the entry. At first, I thought they'd seen me, so I prepared to sally forth and do battle. Then I heard them hissing and snorting about, waiting for their victims to exit. They must have meant you."

"How could tophets up there know anything about us down here?" asked Harnet.

" I see you know very little about the depths you've been *holidaying* through. Well, I'll fill you in, but I must be brief. Lurcan's agents know these halls well. You do know that Brida was jealous of Psychanan? Good. Before the War of Splendora, Brida, now known as Lurcan, used to roam these mountain tunnels from time to time until his jealous moods passed. He didn't ask King Elyon to rid him of the foul moods, preferring to keep them. Everything else that he had was gifted to him by King Elyon: his beauty, musical ability, power of oratory, privilege and dominance, position as prime minister, all given to him, but the foul moods were his own and he perversely treasured them. He owed thanks to no one for them—especially not the king.

"To Lurcan's way of thinking, the very darkness of this *Beneath* diminished all the good Elyon had created. Here he nursed spiteful feelings into cruelty, violence, and greedy ambition. Brida fantasized over these concepts, loving them as his own offspring. Some legends say those fantasies came to life, becoming *kyllorn* such as cusps, tophets and dreads. I don't believe that. Instead, I think that Brida lured some of the king's servants into this dark domain where his clever arguments in combination with the oppressive darkness, eventually seduced them to evil. Thus, Brida gained a following. Almost instantly they degenerated from Elyon's glorious servants into vile, hateful beings.

"Brida bode his time, waiting the right opportunity. When that time came, he summoned his fellow mutineers to these halls and with stirring words provoked them onto the irreversible path of rebellion."

"This darkness caused all that?" Brendle looked around, eyes wide in fear.

"It's more like this darkness amplified the night they harbored within."

"And we've been immersed in this gloom for hours and hours," Harnet's face mirrored Brendle's.

"Fear not, your Children of the Stars were ever in your eyes as you walked here, were they not? Though your swords vary in keenness, they constantly reminded you of Logon, therefore your hearts didn't brood upon darkness. Evil, selfish thoughts can't overcome Logon's life in you unless you let it. Had you not each had your own sword, I dare say disloyal thoughts to Logon might have arisen, if not outright madness. But, I discerned your hearts when I touched my blade to yours and found true devotion to Logon."

The seven breathed a collective sigh of relief.

"Well, now what?" Artka asked.

"Before that's decided, you must answer my question, Artka."

"Very well."

"How long do you intend to keep your dagger?"

They all gasped. Artka felt a sudden flush on his face. "How did you know?"

"How I know isn't important. But, your answer is."

"I loathe it."

"I know, but, that isn't what I asked. Can you bring yourself to be rid of it?"

"Here now, thet be's no way ter be talkin' ter the lad," Scang said.

Saygus' glance rebuked Scang more than words. "Artka can speak for himself."

"You make it sound as if I want to keep it."

"That's still not an answer."

Artka took note of his friends' consternation toward Saygus. A sudden, awful knowledge of the power he possessed dawned on Artka. He could persuade his friends to ostracize Saygus, protecting his private feelings. But, if he pursued that course, would he not be acting like Sofista? He finally answered, "I . . . I don't know."

Artka's friends turned from eyeing Saygus to eyeing him.

"I wish I'd never touched that cursed dagger."

"If it were a clear choice of keeping the dagger, or following Logon, could you be rid of it?"

"Oh, yes."

"Good. There's hope for you. The toxic effect on your mind by merely possessing one of those foul things is far worse than any venom from a spitting tophet, especially down here in what's called The Beneath. The dagger's power is magnified in Lurcan's Womb. Indeed, if I'm not mistaken, you're already wrestling with its increased strength."

"Not to interrupt, sir," Clepy said, "but Artka and I, and the others as well, feel that there's a reason for his having kept the dagger this long."

"Um hmm, but only if Artka has the will to follow through, if he fails, or even hesitates, great harm will come to us all."

Harnet asked, "Do you know how to destroy the dagger or don't you?"

"Now, now, don't get your temper kindled. I have a plan to defeat the tophets and get rid of that deceptive masterpiece at the same time. But only if Artka has the grit to face the tophets alone and if he can summon the will to be free of it." He searched Artka's eyes. "How say you?"

CHAPTER THIRTY-FOUR

ARTKA SAT ALL ALONE IN the hallway of the cave, two weapons lying on his lap. He mentally rehearsed the consequences of his choices. Logon's sword took hours of sharpening to learn of Ecclessite ways, whereas the dagger in his lap was already fully revealed. The dagger even reflected Sky Saber's glow but distorted the sky-blue color into a prismatic rainbow. He sighed and put the sword behind him, dousing its light from the cavern. With the light gone, the dagger seemed alive, crying out for his affection.

Saygus had warned: "Neither resist, nor yield to the darkness. Either way, your will cannot but lose that struggle. You must use only your will to commune with Logon."

"Logon," Artka said softly, "you're my liege." He had to force the words out, as if something surrounding him in the darkness was preventing utterance of those words, yet, with the effort, the oppression lifted a little. "Logon, I choose to serve you." His words must not be mindless repetition; recitation by rote was not from the heart, nor did it commune with Logon, and therefore, was of no effect. "Advisor, please guide me."

Artka stood, stretched his achy legs, stiff from the long, uphill climb, then headed for the exit.

~

Blist roused from his reverie; he sensed the dagger's approach. He'd been re-living the glorious, early days of Lurcan's rebellion and hoping such victories would return—as seemed quite possible now that the war had begun again in earnest. But now the deceptive blade was coming toward them; the victims drew near; his squad was about to be rewarded. But his senses identified only one mortal coming. A moment of doubt flitted across his mind. Where were the seven that climbed into Carpul's Tunnel?

But wait . . . why did the manling stop just inside the entrance instead of coming out in the open? Had something alerted him to the ambush? That untraceable third portion of Splendora's Royal Personage was always interfering . . . Had he gotten involved to disrupt this hunt?

A subordinate hissed, "Where are the others? One won't feed all of us."

"Silence fool!" Blist put aside his misgivings.

"But where are they?"

"How do I know? Maybe the darkness drove them mad and they killed each other off. Maybe they blindly wandered into the chimney and fell to their deaths. This may be the only survivor, or the others may be straggling behind. Now, shut up before you give us away." Blist flexed his tail stinger.

Heeding the warning, the other tophets backed away. Since only one manling had shown up, they rightly expected that, as leader of the expedition, Blist would lay claim, leaving them leftovers . . . or nothing. They wouldn't object too much however, for they all had a healthy respect for that stinger. Ah, the wisdom of assuming such a formidable shape.

He must wait . . . maneuverability in the cramped entry would be severely limited for a large tophet, especially if the manling proved an experienced swordsman. But why did the manling linger? What was he doing? Didn't he know he had arrived at the exit? Was he going to sleep before exiting?

One of Blist's eyes turned toward dawn creeping into the eastern sky. Day was approaching, and the Bright Sword of the Mountains might come snooping about. Saygus, well-known among tophets, was fierce and fearless; some rumored he was cut from the same pattern as the Ecclessite generals of old who could dispatch a hundred tophets with a wave of their sword. Blist's small patrol was vulnerable in the extreme if Saygus happened upon them. Every day spent this deep in his domain was dangerous; the sooner they accomplished their objective and left these mountains, the better. He didn't want to duel with men such as that again!

Birds greeted the approaching day with a cheery rhapsody.

Blist shuddered at the disgusting sound. Still the human lollygagged. Blist hated uncalculated risks, but matters must be forced before full daylight. The great scorpion aroused himself, flexing pincers and stinger simultaneously to impress his subordinates. Looking over the squad he selected and pointed at Frang, a large beetle with powerful jaws and claws, saying, "Time to prove your worth. Lead the attack into the cave."

"Me? Why should I go? You've got the venom."

Blist's tail bobbed; Frang's objection ended. Whatever waited in the cave couldn't be as bad as the venom in that tail sac. Frang resentfully obliged.

~

Artka cocked his head. Was something stirring outside the entrance? To the uninitiated, such noises would appear natural: a breeze whispering through the trees, a scurrying rodent, or a bird probing beneath leaves for a tasty morsel. But Artka was learning to not dismiss such portents.

Saygus had assured him that the tophets, having come this far into Ecclessa, were determined not to leave without tasting blood.

A hulking mist obliterated dawn's light filtering through the doorway. Artka's heart thumped. Saygus had been reasonably sure a lesser tophet—not the spitter—would be sent in first. "Reasonably sure" wasn't much comfort. Every tingling nerve urged him to "flee," but he must wait for the spitter.

Clawed feet scrabbled on the stone floor of the entry; Artka involuntarily sucked in his breath. Reek filled the cave. Artka slowly reached his free hand behind and gripped Sky Saber.

Then a second form—massive compared to the first—blotted the entry. Its stench overpowered the reek of the first tophet.

Artka's eyes watered and he fought a gag impulse, whispering, "This is it. Logon, help me."

Saygus' last minute instructions echoed in his mind: "Under no circumstances use the dagger except as discussed."

Artka wanted to put the dagger in its pouch but Saygus had been adamant: " . . . the dagger must be kept at the ready, in hand at all times."

Sky Saber twitched slightly in Artka's hand. His throat suddenly found voice, "Logon!"

He whipped the sword to the fore. Illuminating the cave's interior, the sword's glow pierced the fore part of the mist. Artka caught a glimmer of multi-faceted eyes and drooling mandibles of a horrendous, black beetle.

The beetle hesitated as if to calculate his attack. As if he'd never assailed a warrior with a partially-glowing sword primed for combat before. A pinch from behind and a shrill hiss however, spurred him forward. With jaws agape, the beetle lunged.

Loose stones clattered under the tophet's clawed feet. It rushed forward, intending to pin him against the wall.

Artka's hand was guided in an upswing as he ducked low. The sword point bit into something crunchy. A pincer spun across the floor, crashing against the wall where it came to rest, but still spasmodically opening and closing.

The beetle screeched and lifted a spurting stump for inspection. Smoky green effluent squirted into its own eyes.

Avoiding the hot, frothy slime, Artka slashed again at the head.

Half of one of the beetle's mandibles hung down, useless; more slimy, green blood spouted, greasing the floor. The creature roared again, blindly groping with its remaining pincer.

~

Blist was furious that the Ecclessite was too incompetent to dispatch even a weak tophet? Had he known the kingsman was so inept, he'd have taken the offense himself. The beetle was now a hindrance instead of a clever opening gambit. "Get out of my way, worthless fool!" Blist sent threats via the mind-link tophets shared. He poked the beetle's carapace with a pincer.

"Where would you have me go?" the beetle retorted. "I fill the cavern almost as much as you, besides, I can't see. I don't know where the manling is."

Blist was in no mood for excuses. He wanted to have at the manling now! His tail stinger scraped across the low ceiling on its way to pierce the beetle's thorax. "Get out of my way. This is no warrior, but a recruit. Get out of my way!" The tail-stinger flicked again.

Liquid fire jetted into the beetle's interior. Forgetting how over-matched he was, he instinctively tried to turn and pinch Blist.

Stone chips from the tophets knocking each other about showered down on Artka as he backed away and crouched in a cleft of the wall.

Outraged, Blist thrust his body overtop the beetle. Frang tried to rise, jamming himself and Blist between floor and ceiling. The beetle's remaining pincer slowly reached up, fumbling about until it clamped onto Blist's leg.

~

Deep down the tunnel Saygus and companions heard the ear-shredding scream as they finished last minute preparations. They paused, their thoughts going to Logon on Artka's behalf.

"Thet be's tophets fightin'," Scang said.

"Why would tophets fight, that's not part of the plan, is it?" Reddy asked.

Harnet said, "No, it's not. That shouldn't happen unless . . . "

"Unless what?" Reddy tied off the end of a rope and tugged it to make certain it was secure.

"Unless," Saygus said what no one else wanted to admit, "it's over a body." He cinched the rope, checked its tension, and added, "But, we must hope for the best, and prepare as if our plan will still work. The Advisor wouldn't give us a plan unless it would accomplish Logon's goal—providing everyone does their part."

"Yeah, but mebbe his goal is ter bring usn's straightaway ter Splendora."

No one replied.

~

Frang was wedged sideways, blocking the tunnel, unable to face Blist squarely, and equally unable to locate and fight the manling. The lava of Blist's venom pumped throughout Frang's mass, driving out all thought except awareness of intense pain and desire for relief. He convulsively clamped down again on Blist's leg, clinging tenaciously.

Blist's fury and appetite was whetted by the cringing manling's paralyzing scent of fear borne to him on air currents. He must have this manling! Blist considered spritzing his sleeping venom to prevent the manling's escape but realized the beetle's bulk would only block the spray from permeating the chamber. Besides, he wanted the manling fully aware as he was rendered piece by piece.

~

Artka, though daunted, was not paralyzed by fear as Blist supposed. He, too, was frustrated, for his jabs hadn't unmade the first tophet. The plan had been for him to eliminate the first, weaker tophet, briefly confront the leader, then flee, inducing pursuit. Instead, he helplessly watched the two struggling mists, neither one gaining an advantage. He kept waiting for the stronger tophet to disembody the lesser, so he could carry out the rest of the plan. But the beetle had a seemingly unlimited ability to endure pain without being unmade. It just wouldn't explode and vanish.

The realization gradually came to Artka that tophets, like roamers, weren't granted the ability to unmake each other. Torment, yes;

dominate, yes; unmake, no. Artka must join the thrashing combat and unmake the lesser tophet.

What chance did a mere mortal have of surviving that fight between two behemoths? A flailing limb could crush him. Even where he crouched Artka had to duck chunks of rock nicked out of the granite wall by the combative tophets. Nevertheless, Artka's duty was in throwing himself into that fray. His mouth went dry and his stomach tensed; but there was no other way. Only when the beetle no longer encumbered the way could the spitter be drawn into pursuit.

Artka pushed away from the safety of the cleft, leveled Sky Saber in front and rushed at the titanic scuffle, crying, "In the name of Xychirion, the Mighty."

The glowing sword point met only brief resistance as it penetrated the beetle's outer carapace. The beast's interior felt mushy. A foul odor belched from the wound. Artka's eyes watered and his nostrils tingled. As the glowing sword point disappeared into the beetle, light all but vanished from the cave. The monster jerked violently, trying to turn on him. Artka clung to his sword with all the strength every muscle and sinew in his arm had. The dagger in his other hand threatened to shake loose.

Artka squeezed his fingers tighter.

Artka was yanked this way and that, then off his feet, but managed to keep a grip on his sword. Saygus had said to expect a flash of flame, not a violent thrashing.

Artka's feet touched ground and he withdrew his sword. The cavern lit up with a soft, bluish glow. Green blood and mealy matter splattered the walls and floor. Artka thrust again. His foot slipped, but his sword found its target. Artka jumped back to avoid another thrashing, but instead, a deafening roar filled the cavern.

~

His thrust had entirely missed the beetle; instead slitting the other tophet's tail as it bobbed for yet another strike at the hapless beetle.

Blist's-venom sac ruptured, spraying the chamber ceiling. Some venom seeped into the edges of his own wound and Blist tasted a sample of the agony he had so gleefully inflicted on others. This pain and embarrassment only renewed his efforts to get past the impotent, catatonic beetle. He wanted this impudent manling to agonize as he had never made any human suffer. Blist slammed against the beetle's hulk. With full attention focused on the manling, the huge scorpion, dribbling fluid from its violated venom sac, again attempted to squeeze overtop the beetle, unaware of a rising pincer.

Frang's claw latched onto Blist's sliced tail, mangling the flesh yet more, emptying the contents of the sac.

The scorpion jerked violently upward, hitting the ceiling so hard that a crackle resounded throughout the mountain, growing into a low, grinding moan reverberating deep into the bowels of the earth.

The tophets outside the entrance backed away fearing the mountain was about to fall on them.

~

Stone chips showered down around Artka's friends as they waited anxiously down the tunnel.

Artka, with a strangely renewed burst of energy, sprang at the pinned beetle, thrusting his sword past the mangled mandibles and into the oral cavity. The leathery head covering yielded with small popping sounds. Sulfurous flames erupted around Artka, knocking him backward. The yellow ball of flame screeched out the doorway and vanished into the early morning sky.

Artka didn't comprehend the words, hearing only growls, but he was well aware of the menace bearing down on him. Still dazed by the explosion, his head throbbing and vision distorted, Artka regained his feet, paused a moment to get his bearings, and steadied himself against the wall. A sudden jolt pierced his shoulder—his dagger arm. Artka sank down and cried out.

Blist's stinger was withdrawn. Artka picked himself up and sagged against the wall, rubbing his shoulder where a small blotch of blood appeared. Was the monster waiting for him to go mad with seizures and pain? Would he make him beg for death? Would he devour him slowly, preventing loss of consciousness? From what Artka had heard at any moment now the writhing, sweating, skin rash, gnawing the tongue, grinding teeth and tearing out hair might take effect.

Blist inched forward to seize his prey.

Artka jumped aside, avoiding the pincers.

"Ha, your sting of death is drained. Where now is your victory?" Artka taunted.

Then he spied the dagger on the floor—underneath the scorpion's head. It had been shaken loose when he was stung. The dagger was key to Saygus' plan.

Shadows crowded into the entry behind the scorpion. The other tophets were jostling for position to get leftovers.

Artka's left arm started turning numb though his fingers still moved, but for how long? He must somehow retrieve the dagger while he could.

Raising his sword, Artka leapt forward at the mist filling the cavern.

~

Blist was amused. The fool was actually bringing the battle to him? Did he love the dagger that much? Oh, Blist had respect for the sword coming at him, but wasn't impressed with the kingsman wielding it. His pincers alone could easily repel the attack.

Suddenly the sword burst forth with a piercing, yellow light and a cacophony of harmonies, overwhelming Blist's senses. That, in itself, might have made some impact on this war-hardened tophet, but he'd battled powerful kingsmen before, and even roamers with similar powers. But in the center of that bright, yellow glare was something that no other being in the cave saw—a sight known to make mighty dreads quail, indeed, even Lurcan must back away and flee from that apparition. Blist saw another hand joining Artka's on the sword's haft— a hand belonging to Xychirion, the Invincible! A flame burned in his eyes and he was girt for war.

Blist, covered his eyes out of sheer terror and couldn't skitter backward fast enough. He hadn't expected to face this horror until the Tremendum.

~

Artka saw light burst from his sword and heard the powerful rune-song, but nothing else. He watched the tophet withdraw and was only too glad to leap forward and pluck the dagger off the floor. He wrapped it safely in his benumbed fingers and pressed the attack—just enough to goad the tophet into giving chase.

The tophet's retreat was blocked as he collided into the jumble of lesser tophets entering the doorway. Artka took a wild swipe; a pincer dangled by shreds.

~

Blist howled again; pain jolted him back to reality. Logon was nowhere to be seen. The sword's bright light had receded. The foolish, young warrior stood alone before him, preparing to strike again with his pathetically dim sword.

The manling leapt, striking him again, then backed off, visually checking his hand to make sure the dagger was secure. Blist's forefoot below a knee-joint fell away. Blist teetered off balance, vainly slashing his usable pincer at the manling who amazingly still retained enough control to dodge the blow.

The enraged tophet, oozing slime from many nicks, hobbled on seven legs after him.

~

Artka had been warned to keep the tophet in hot pursuit. Though wounded and stumping along on only seven legs, the tophet maintained a rapid pace. With Sky Saber's light guiding, Artka pushed the bounds of safety, scampering along the tunnel's pitted floor; he must not be careless and stumble or get caught from behind.

A burning sensation progressively crept down his left arm. Artka's breathing became rapid, his pulse thready. Even so, he forced his fingers tighter around the dagger. He dared not transfer the dagger to his good hand, for to do so would require tucking his sword away, and he'd have no light to avoid rocks and chuckholes covering the tunnel floor.

~

Blist hustled after his prey, no longer afraid of encountering Logon. Nor did the mystery of the missing manlings distract him. Only one thought burned in the scorpion's vengeful mind: get the insolent

Ecclessite. He pushed his wounded body to its utmost; everything but revenge could wait.

Blist was worried that when his victim reached the junction of three caves, he'd dodge into the short, vented passage and foolishly dart over the precipice into the "chimney" and plummet to his death. He must catch the manling before that happened.

A host of sensory readings suddenly overwhelmed Blist: Frang's blood, his own ruptured venom sac, manling blood, sweat, and fear—and the dagger; all mingled together. He'd be less distracted if he ignored all sensory data except the dagger.

The dagger suddenly veered sharply to the right—into the chimney's tunnel. No, no, no, not when revenge was so close . . .

~

Near exhaustion, Artka staggered to the end of the tunnel and halted on the very edge of the drop-off, his head spinning, the searing pain in his arm and hand had now spread to his neck and upper chest. There was precious little time to execute what must be done. The nothingness under his toes told him this was the brink of the shaft. He put his sword away and with his good hand groped for the object Saygus promised would be ready. He couldn't find it. Had he misunderstood? Was there another tunnel he should've dodged down?

"I'm here but wounded." Artka broke silence, contrary to Saygus' warning. He had to know if they were here.

Clepy's hushed voice asked, "How badly are ye hurt?"

"Can't use my left arm."

"Then dinnae try climbing the rope," Clepy said. "Use the alternate plan. Have ye got the dagger?"

"I couldn't forget that." He groped again with his good hand, leaning his body dangerously over the emptiness of the shaft until he finally found the object.

Scuffling steps approached at the end of the tunnel.

Artka had mere seconds to bait the trap. If the Spitter saw through their plan, one burst of sleeping venom would saturate the tunnel, the shaft and everything within fifty feet, putting them under its sleep-inducing power, sending them all into the yawning depths.

Artka grimaced as he pried the benumbed, cramped fingers of his left hand open. The dagger was sticky with his own blood. Struggling against unconsciousness he inserted the dagger. Dizziness forced him to stand still. One false step would send him over the edge into the chasm.

~

The scorpion stalked down the entry, unwilling to spook his quarry into the abyss if he hadn't gone over already.

In ages past Lurcan had named this passage, "the chimney," for it was virtually a flue drafting air upward from the innards of the earth to vent into the sky several hundred feet overhead. Blist perceived a human form—and the dagger—lingering at the rim of the drop-off. The Ecclessite hadn't tumbled into the abyss after all. He was trapped. Now, if only the fool didn't wisely jump to his doom . . .

The scorpion made a calculated rush down the tunnel.

CHAPTER THIRTY-FIVE

ARTKA TENTATIVELY FELT HIS WAY out along a slim ledge rimming the sheer wall of the pit. The ledge was so narrow that his toes hung over nothingness. He stopped a few feet out and groped for a handhold on the rock wall.

~

Blist, waiting in the entry, estimated the distance; he must not let momentum send him over the precipice. As nearly indestructible as he was, the fall would certainly undo him. But the manling still lingered on the edge. The dagger, focus of all Blist's attention, was just ahead, along with the unmistakable, tantalizing aromas of fear and blood. He gauged his pounce, hoping that fear—or wisdom—wouldn't make the kingsman leap. The snatch would require a delicate, precise maneuver, but Blist had done this sort of thing before. When he secured his catch, he'd begin flaying this impertinent Ecclessite, dangling him over the nothingness, making him suffer without hope.

The manling hovered on the edge. Did the fool think he wasn't seen?

Then another aroma—one he should recognize, caught Blist's attention. But, this was no time to categorize smells; he must secure the manling first. Scent identification could come later.

He lunged with surprising agility for a wounded beast his size, covering the distance in two swift bounds, sliding to a halt just short of the chasm. A pincer shot out and successfully seized the manling about the waist. He squeezed but there was no resistance, no writhing, no agonized scream. And the torso was oddly disjointed, separating between the scorpion's claws as he clamped tighter. Blist wasn't willing to release his prey until the puzzle was solved.

A large rock tumbled from somewhere overhead, plummeting harmlessly down into the void. There were vibrations of something trailing after. A rope? Now why would a rope—?

The line snapped taut, and as it did it whipped around Blist's pincer, tugging him forward onto his wounded stump. It happened so fast that he hadn't thought to release his victim—which he now recognized as Carnalian clothing stuffed with eyeless fish—the familiar scent he hadn't taken an extra moment to analyze. Clever!

The weight of the rock impelled him toward the edge, but his bulk and strength were greater than the weight of any boulder a lone man could roll off a ledge. A doubt flashed through his thoughts: a small group of men—like the mysteriously missing six—could heave a substantially larger rock over the edge.

Blist tried to extricate his snagged pincer from the rope wrapped around the mannequin, but the rope had already knotted. He was caught and being inexorably dragged toward the precipice. A fish-stuffed dummy and dagger had suckered him to recklessly take the bait. Blist straightened his legs, clawing at the tunnel walls. His slide halted just as he reached the very edge; in another moment he'd snap the rope with his mandible, setting him free.

The other tophets, unaware of Blist's predicament and not wanting to miss out on any scraps, charged down the short tunnel ramming into Blist's ruptured tail, providing the necessary nudge to shove Blist, rope, rock, fish-filled dummy and dagger into the abyss. Blist's eyes rotated wildly as his clawed feet scraped naught but air. The manling he'd pursued all the way from Carnalia was a few feet off to the side on the slimmest of ledges, pressed against the wall. He, Blist, monster of battles, terror of underlings, and bane of enemies outsmarted by a raw recruit with little more than inches aglow beyond his sword tip. It would take months to acquire a new form, and a year or more to form a shape as useful as the scorpion. But he would come for this manling, yes, he would come. In his outrage Blist sprayed sleeping venom as a parting shot at his nemesis.

Blist's sudden disappearance over the ledge baffled the remaining five tophets. They sniffed and snorted, and finally decided to retreat and regroup. Stinig, a wasp-shaped tophet with shriveled wings, took leadership by virtue of his stinger. He started to lead the squad back toward the junction of three caves.

Without warning, a brilliant, blue light pierced his clustered eyes. Stinig whirled around, colliding into his cronies, crying, "It's a trap. It's a trap. The Bright Sword! Flee."

~

Artka teetered, bringing his sword from beneath his cloak. He watched the spray from the monster get sucked into its own downdraft.

Artka's left arm now felt afire. Saygus had warned them all that the monster's unmaking when it landed would create a shock wave that flew up the shaft. Artka swayed, struggling to stay conscious, waiting for the tophet's explosion.

Saygus jumped from the outer tunnel into the midst of the tophets, slicing right and left, hewing heads and limbs as quickly as his sword arm could move. Four disembodied phantoms vanished up the chimney passage one right after the other in bright yellow flames.

The remaining tophet fled down the tunnel and hurled himself over the ledge.

Clepy's voice came from overhead, "Artka lad, are ye alright?"

Those on the landing above had their swords out, peering over the edge.

Artka's sword glimmered from an impossibly narrow ledge rimming the chimney.

Saygus appeared at the pit's edge, illuminating the entire section of the shaft. Spotting Artka out on the ledge, he ordered, "Stay put until both fireballs pass. I don't think either has landed yet."

Braxmore, who had contributed his Carnalian clothing to be the dummy stuffed with the eyeless fish, said, "Our plan worked, didn't it?" He wore only his tunic, breeches and outer cloak. "It's a good thing you knew about this cave, Saygus, and the rock hanging over the upper ledge."

"As I said, I discovered it only a short while before I found you. I'm glad I resisted a childish impulse to tip that boulder into the pit. The Advisor warned me not to, and I obeyed, though I didn't know why at the time. Otherwise we wouldn't have had the deadweight to drag the spitter over. His sleeping venom would have posed real problems. Look out, here he comes."

A faint boom preceded a fireball from the depths. For a brief moment, they glimpsed the silhouette of a large ant outlined against the ascending flames of the unmade scorpion.

Saygus backed away from the shaft to avoid the rising tophet. The ball of flame took the most direct path to the exterior world, soaring straight up the shaft, passing the wonder-struck men, veering out of sight a hundred yards overhead.

"Is it gone?" Reddy asked, "or will it come back looking for us?"

"No, it won't be back," Saygus said. "Once disembodied, they fly back to the swamp where they took form. But, don't celebrate yet, the other one still has to pass. Stay put."

Artka teetered. "I . . . don't think . . . I can hold on much longer. I'm dizzy, and sick."

"You must hang on," Saygus said, stepping out onto the ledge. "I'm coming."

Face to the wall, Saygus inched toward Artka. When he was within an arm's length of Artka, the second tophet hit bottom, exploded into flame and became a rising fireball.

"Grab my hand, Artka."

Artka's knees sagged.

The second fireball sped upward then passed them, not as hot nor as concussive, following the same path as the first. Artka's body tilted away from the wall, sucked toward the updraft.

Saygus lunged, catching Artka's sleeve.

Artka, whimpering, barely conscious, dangled limply held by Saygus' hand.

Saygus also leaned precariously, dragged off balance by Artka. As Saygus lost his balance he jabbed his sword into the rock wall. Stone chips sparked away; a crevice opened as the sword penetrated the rock face providing enough of a chink hold to keep from toppling into the abyss. Artka hung over nothingness, suspended only by Saygus's determination and the sword sunk in granite.

A gritty voice rang out, "Hang on . . . "

A dark form hurtled off the ledge above. Scang, clinging one-handed to a rope, was swooping down to their rescue.

A husky arm encircled Saygus' waist. Scang's momentum dislodged Saygus' sword from its niche and all three swung out over the void. Saygus' grip remained firm. He shut his eyes, concentrating on not letting Artka slip. Then, like a pendulum, the airborne trio swung back toward the lower ledge.

Harnet and Brendle, having slid down to the tunnel's entry on another rope, caught Saygus' cloak. Grunting and tugging they hauled all three back to the landing.

Saygus gently laid Artka on the rocky surface, then, sparks in his eyes, stood to full height, glared at the Eroton and scolded, "Scang, you should have consulted me before slinging us out over that pit!"

Scang sputtered and blinked several times.

Saygus bent back to examine Artka's injuries. "We must get him to my lodge before the poison spreads. I'm surprised he isn't in much worse condition considering he was stung by a scorpion tophet. Most never survive the initial strike; indeed, only a mighty few can even fight once stung. That must've been some battle."

"Is it safe to go up yet?" Reddy asked. "I counted. Only six tophets were unmade, two went down the shaft, four sent directly up the shaft by your blade. If there were seven, as you said, one still lays in ambush."

"The other was probably unmade by Artka. Safe or not, Artka needs attention as soon as possible."

Scang and Brendle formed a makeshift litter out of their backpack braces and bore Artka up the tunnel.

It took half an hour to retrace Artka's route back to the battle scene. They were heartened as they advanced by the morning light reflecting off the walls of the cavern. At the last turn they stared open-mouthed at the site of the conflict. A shaft of sunlight blazed through the doorway, fully illuminating the scene.

A severed mandible and a still-twitching pincer were off to one side, pieces of a lower leg on the other. Reeking smoke rose from pools of stinger venom, which Saygus warned against touching. Green, slimy tophet blood was splattered everywhere as if by some demented painter.

They didn't pause but headed out into the welcoming daylight. They emerged blinking and smiling at the fresh air, glad to be on the surface of the world again.

As Clepy and Scang re-examined Artka, Saygus went a little way uphill and piled one stone on another just above the cave's entry. Then he made another pile several yards downhill. These he aligned with some object in the distance known only to him. He then covered the portal with rocks and dry brush, making it look as if it was just part of the hillside.

"What are you doing?" Braxmore asked.

"Setting markers so I can find this entry to the Beneath again, and the brush is so no one else does."

"Well, I can see that, but why?"

"When you've lit more runes, and gained some battle experience, Logon may reveal things about the Beneath that he's shown me. Until that day, you'd best stick to the runes he reveals to you."

"And ye, dear Braxmore," Clepy said, "have more to learn than anyone else here when it comes to sharpening the runes."

"Well, I just wanted to know."

"It's the king's pleasure to hide secrets, and a warrior's glory to discover them," Clepy said.

"Well said, corporal." Saygus climbed back up to the others. "But, enough of that, how is Artka? Is he conscious?"

"About the same as we figgered down in the hole," Scang said. "At times he wakes, or at least opens his eyes."

"Then let's be on our way."

Harnet suggested making a better litter, to which Saygus consented. It took several minutes, but a more durable, comfortable stretcher was constructed, and the party set off.

Clepy and Harnet took the front handles of the litter while Scang would hear of no one else bearing the back. Reddy followed, then Braxmore, and last of all Brendle keeping a lookout to the rear.

Saygus led up, high above the tree line, toward craggy peaks and thinner air.

All the men were keenly aware of what they owed Artka. Artka's arrival had re-kindled a yearning to walk with Logon.

~

Onward and upward Saygus led the small band into the Prophecy Mountains, lugging their beloved companion. Saygus' expression was somber, not only out of concern for Artka; with medicine and proper care, Artka would recover. But, he wondered why these valiant men claimed Logon had sent them? There was no brigade in the mountains. Furthermore, winter snows had come early, complicating matters. Artka's recovery would likely take several days, days that would deplete his family's limited resources. In addition, even a few days waiting while Artka healed would waste precious time Artka and his friends needed to get back to the lowlands before deeper snows fell.

Saygus studied the travel-worn squad tagging along behind him. They hadn't even a day's provision among them. What was Logon up to?

It had to be a gross misunderstanding . . . unless—No! Logon couldn't possibly expect that . . .

Saygus focused on the trail ahead. As they passed familiar markers, he said, "We're about three hours from my lodge, perhaps a little longer. But we'll take a brief rest here."

As the group fell out, Saygus mounted a large rock to scan the horizon. His sharp eyes were drawn to distant, snow-covered slopes. He withdrew his sword, Dread Bane, and aimed it at the field in question. The bright bluish haze surrounding his sword magnified the image. Herringboned 'V' patterns marred the otherwise unblemished snow. Skishers! From that distance it was difficult to tell how many men had made the crisscrossed tracks, but he had a good idea who made them. "Poachers," he muttered. "Now what would they be doing up here this time of year?"

"Uh, we didn't have time to explain everything," Reddy said. "What with getting the rope around the rock just so, and the fish to stay in the clothing, and you going down the other way to block off escape routes, we didn't get to tell you about our escape from the Daggermen, or the encounter with the lion hunters, or—"

"So, tell me now."

With Harnet and Scang occasionally adding comments, Reddy related how they'd nearly been imprisoned by Sofista and then were caught off guard in the wooded tract by the poachers.

Saygus said, "I see. And now you think they're hunting you, is that it?"

"Seems likely."

"I agree. Though I've had a few run-ins with the lion poachers myself, which has left them desiring not a little revenge. Well, small chance they'll find us once we reach my lodge."

The eight resumed the trek in relative silence. Saygus occasionally left the path, scrambling upon an outcropping rock for a look around. Thus, they traversed the rugged, terrain another hour. Eventually they descended into an obscure valley filled with conifers. The trail, with its scrubby, gnarled trees lining either side, dropped steeply. They gradually passed through forest glens that flowed with brooks of clean, clear water—a verdant paradise compared to the barren, snow-covered, rocky plateau they'd just traversed. Snow had disappeared in this valley; and as they went lower they found more trees still clinging to the last leaves of autumn.

Saygus pointed at a wisp of smoke against the blue sky. "That'll be my eldest son, Sajon, smelting ingots. I hope he hasn't sent a marker into the sky for your poacher friends to see."

The trail leveled off and widened out; bearing Artka was less arduous. None of the carriers had let anyone spell them, though their arms and shoulders ached with fatigue.

The setting sun cast long, purple shadows from the peaks across the broad valley as the squad drew up at Saygus' lodge, weary, but encouraged at the prospect of a home-cooked meal and their best night's sleep since leaving King's Gate Fortress.

CHAPTER THIRTY-SIX

ARTKA WOKE AS A MOIST cloth was placed on his forehead. The large, blue eyes of a beautiful maiden with auburn braids peered down.

Her eyes widened as she realized Artka was waking. "How do you feel?" she asked. Her voice was light and musical. Her clear, unpretentious eyes held his as she waited a reply.

"Fine. No, sore, uh . . . I really don't know."

She tilted her head and laughed.

"Who are you?" Artka asked, regaining his wits. He probed his shoulder, feigning only mild interest in her answer. The puncture had closed, and the discomfort was bearable.

"Sejisca, eldest daughter of Saygus, and that," she pointed to a slender, raven-haired girl toting an armload of firewood, "is my younger sister, Cocee."

Both girls were girted with leather belts supporting a latticed scabbard. Visible through the latticework were the glowing edges of their Children of the Stars.

"Do you remember the battle with the tophets?" Sejisca asked.

Artka quit examining his shoulder and lay back on the pillow. "Tophets. That's about all I do remember." He raised up on his elbow again, asking, "Is everyone else—"

"Be at peace, Artka. You're the only casualty. The plan worked gloriously."

Artka lay back down. "I ache."

"I don't wonder, if half of what my father said is true. None of us, including my father, understand how you were so lightly affected by the scorpion's stinger."

"Oh that." Artka chuckled. "I'm afraid it was due to a misplaced thrust. I intended to kill the beetle but missed. Instead, I slit the scorpion's venom sac, draining its fluid."

"If thrust with a true intent, the Children of the Stars never miss," Sejisca said. "You were just aiming at the wrong target." She lifted a bowl of water off the floor. "Rest now, it's late. There'll be time for questions later."

Artka watched as she walked away. And he watched Cocee finish stacking her armload of wood beside the hearth, then tend a pot that was suspended in the walk-in fireplace. Both Saygus' daughters were beauties.

Artka reluctantly turned his attention to his surroundings and was impressed with its friendly ambiance. The dwelling itself was constructed of lodgepole pine logs, carefully crafted and squared off so that little or no chinking was necessary. The main room was fifty feet by thirty, with doorways leading into other rooms. Spare but sturdy wood furnishings built for function and comfort, not elegance, were situated around the room. The floor was tongue and groove planking, laboriously fitted and then fastened with pins. A cooking fire glowed cozily from the fieldstone hearth. Though the lodge was rustic, it had none of the squalor often associated with wilderness living. Instead, nature's glory embellished the lodge.

Over the mantel hung a somewhat frayed, discolored banner that resembled the gallant battle flags of old that Artka had seen on the interior walls of King's Gate Fortress. A blue fringe bordered a silken field that had once been white but now bore the yellowing of age and downdraft smoke. Adorning the field was an emblematic blue-edged sword with crimson runes along the blade's fuller, holding a crown on its point.

"It's the Sharuner Brigade banner," Sejisca said coming kneeling before Artka. "My father was captain. In their day, I'd be willing to venture, that they rescued more lives to Logon than any five brigades put together. Here, I've brought you some broth. As long as you're awake you might as well have some nourishment."

Artka received the steaming bowl gratefully, only then realizing how hungry he was. "Thanks."

"Cocee, bring some bread to sop up his broth, will you?"

The younger, dark-haired girl put her broom in a corner and went to a trestle table laden with foodstuffs. She threw back a covering towel and sliced off a slab of brown bread which she lathered with butter then bashfully brought to Artka. He took a bite, unable to take his eyes off the attractive sisters. Cocee giggled and hurried back to her chores.

"I think she likes you," Sejisca whispered with a twinkle in her eye. "From the moment they brought you in she's been hovering over you."

Artka blushed. Could Sejisca read his thoughts as easily as she did her sister's? He dunked the granular bread into the broth and took another bite.

A doorway opened, and a chill breeze blew in accompanied by tramping feet disrupting the quiet of the lodge. Scang, stooping under the lintel, entered, followed closely by several others, two of whom Artka didn't recognize. They all shed outer garments and hung them on hooks near the door. Sejisca went to the taller of the two strangers, stood on tiptoe and kissed him lightly on the cheek. Artka's heart sank.

The man Sejisca kissed spoke to the other unknown man and they both went to Artka's side.

"Artka," began the one Sejisca had kissed, "Sejisca tells me you're doing better. I'm glad. You had us concerned. By the way, I'm Sajon, and this is my brother Hudge." The other man smiled.

Saygus interrupted, "Now, now, don't bother Artka. Get ready for dinner."

Sajon and Hudge nodded warmly at Artka and went to wash up. "They mean well, Artka. I hope my sons didn't disturb your rest."

Artka propped up on his elbows. "Your sons? Not sons-in-law?"

Sejisca and Cocee looked at each other, turned bright red, and suddenly remembered chores at the far end of the room. They glanced shyly and giggled as they scurried past Artka.

Artka's face warmed.

"Ah, yer gots a nice, healthy color back inter yer face, lad," Scang teased. The room erupted in laughter. Artka's face grew warmer.

"All right, enough of that," Saygus said. "I'll not have you tormenting a wounded soldier. After all, he's been through an ordeal. The state he's in, I suppose any young lady could capture his admiration."

"Father!" Cocee chided from across the room.

A fresh round of chuckles followed. Her father's jibe had found its mark. The raven-haired beauty haughtily tossed her head and busied herself with meal preparation.

Saygus knelt beside Artka's cot, lowered his voice, and said, "I must speak frankly, Artka. There truly are no brigades within a dozen leagues of us here. Your valiant journey has been in vain."

"Father, we're ready," Sajon called from his seat at the table.

"I'll be right there." Then turning back to Artka he added, "My supplies are limited. If I keep all of you here, we'll all starve toward the end of winter. I can't let that happen, not if I can prevent it. It grieves me to say this, but, you and your friends must return to the lowlands as soon as you're fit for travel and the weather allows." He shook his head, as if wanting to say more, but turned and went to the table where the others respectfully waited for him.

Artka laid his head back on a pillow and stared at the ceiling. "Why did you send me here, Logon? And why did my friends tag along?" He rolled over, closed his eyes and listened to the dinner conversation. Eventually their voices faded to a dull, background drone and he dozed.

~

A hand gripped Artka's foot, waking him. Saygus leaned over him, flanked by Clepy and Scang. "Are you well enough to come outside?"

Artka blinked and looked around; it was pre-dawn.

He'd dozed the night away. He swung his legs over the cot and shivered as his feet touched the cold floor. "I feel much better for having slept."

Scang draped a cloak around Artka's shoulders.

"Where are we going?" Artka hoped they weren't being sent away already.

"I'd like your opinion on something. Don't worry, it's not far. We'll be back by breakfast."

"How be's yer, Artka?" Scang asked, catching hold of Artka as he leaned to one side.

"Dizzy, with a slight headache, but, otherwise, I'm fine. My shoulder hurts some."

Saygus handed fur-lined boots to Artka. "As I thought," he said, "you've slept off most of the venomous effects. Come quickly, or there'll be too much light."

Artka looked curiously from one to the other as he laced the boots but said nothing. No one offered any explanation.

The sting of cold air dissipated Artka's grogginess as they crunched across a yard laden with heavy frost.

Saygus led up a trail to a spot that overlooked the vast panorama toward Carnalia. He pointed to the northwestern sky. "What do you make of that?" Several glowing red spots were visible between mountain peaks. "I can see thirty leagues from this lookout, and in clear weather the sky over another ten. Those glowing spots are some fifty miles distant. What do you make of them?"

Artka looked from one reddish glow to another. "I have no idea. Fires, I would guess?"

"Mm," Saygus grunted, looking along the flat of his sword's blade. "I don't think so. I've seen whole villages afire that had less glow and more murk, if you know what I mean. No, I don't think they're fires, but I'd guess Lurcan's handiwork is somehow connected with it."

"Look," Clepy said, "over there. Another one just lit up, off to the left, see it?"

Saygus examined the new spot through the intensifying haze of his sword. "That one's closer."

"Might it be dreads?" Scang asked. "I means, I don't ken, never havin' seen dreads afore, but I heered plenty."

"No, Scang, dreads don't glow, except maybe their eyes. Besides, there are only ten dreads, and there are at least two score glowing spots.

This is beyond my experience. I asked you up here, Artka, hoping that maybe something your friend Tren might have said would explain this."

"Is it . . . " Artka choked, " . . . the end of Carnalia?" His thoughts went to Jeda, his parents, Bilrood, Poppitt.

"No, Artka, I think not. That day will be more spectacular, I'm sure. Although, whatever is happening may herald the beginning of those events."

The four stared as more spots appeared. Saygus pointed out a dense cluster, saying, "That's the direction of Logon's Bridge."

The rising sun was just below the horizon brightening the sky, outshining the glowing spots, making them disappear. A clanging bell interrupted their vigil. "We've been up here long enough, my friends," Saygus said. "No doubt Sejisca will be perturbed that I've stolen her patient without permission."

Artka blushed, but no one noticed. It was good to be up and about again. His headache was gone, and he felt rested, though sore, and quite hungry.

Several minutes later they filed into the lodge. "Really, father! And in such chilly weather," Sejisca chided.

"Now girl, the man is nearly whole again, lacking only exercise to recover his health. If you women had your way, we'd all be in bed at the slightest cough—"

"Hush dear, before you start an argument you can't win." A tall, dark-haired woman stood in the doorway. She bore the same ageless quality as Saygus, with the same air of wisdom and experience.

"Evebryl, you're back," Saygus said. "Gentlemen, my wife. She's been in the village below, tending ill people, as I mentioned." He turned to his wife and said, "You must have traveled all night to get here. What happened to make you hazard such a journey?"

"Several wives received word that Logon is about to finally answer their requests concerning the activities of their husbands. I'll fill you in later."

Saygus introduced his guests, giving her a sly wink when he came to Artka.

"Tell me, how do you feel, young man?" she asked.

"I'm fine."

"Well, I hope you're good and hungry, for my daughters have evidently prepared a feast. Saygus, dear, I need to discuss that matter about the poacher's wives. Sajon, please give thanksgiving in your father's stead lest breakfast be delayed."

Saygus shrugged, feigning helplessness as his wife took his hand and led him to another room. "I may rule the wild and savage mountains, but my wife rules here in my den."

"Oh, stop it, you old mountain lion." Evebryl playfully cuffed him.

Sajon extended his arms toward the rafters. "To King Elyon, our provider, and Logon Xychirion, our liege, we give our thanks."

"So be it," everyone chorused. For the next several moments the only sounds were utensils scraping dishes as hungry men filled and re-filled their plates with bread, eggs, and thinly-sliced, fried venison dipped in a tangy sauce.

Sejisca glanced at Artka and flushed with embarrassment to find him staring at her. Both immediately dropped their gaze, busying themselves with their plate.

"'Tis akin ter eatin' wi' Erotons," Scang said, paying the cooks a compliment.

Cocee's fork clattered to her plate. "You're Eroton?" A look of revulsion overspread her face.

Scang's face turned red.

"Cocee," Sajon said sharply, "do you think your heart needed less piercing than anyone else? Maybe you need to review the third course of Atel's runes again. And you owe our guest an apology."

Cocee lifted her eyes, repeating out of obedience rather than sincerity, "I'm sorry sir. It's just that . . . " tears coursed down her cheeks, "Erotons are so evil! When father took me to Logon's Rock we were attacked by Erotons. My father drove them off, but they said such vile things." She jumped up and fled the table, pausing briefly to don a cloak and grab an empty water bucket before running out the door.

Everyone sat in stunned silence.

Finally, Sejisca said, "Please excuse my sister. She was thoroughly frightened by the experience. She was very young. I'd better go see if she's alright." Sejisca rose, giving Artka a quick glance, then followed out the door in her sister's steps.

Hudge said, "No one blames you, Scang. In fact, your being here is forcing her to face what she's been avoiding."

"It grieves me ter pain the little lass. Me heart goes out ter her."

"Well, it little matters, anyway," Artka said. "We'll soon be leaving."

"What?" chimed several voices.

"I'm afraid our being here is an imposition on our host's resources. Saygus told me their supplies won't see the winter through if we stay. I, for one, don't want to be more of a burden than I already am."

"But what about the new brigade?" Braxmore asked.

Artka swallowed a morsel of venison and sighed. "I confess, I don't understand why Logon sent me, or why you, my dearest friends, were inclined to seek out a new brigade with me. Saygus assures me there is no such brigade. It's hard not to think it was all a cruel joke."

"Banish that thought from your mind," Saygus said, emerging from the private conference with his wife and taking his seat at the head of the table. "Never, never mistrust Logon. That's the work of cusps and will come to no good. Doubt your own understanding, doubt my word, or doubt your friends if you must doubt something. Even doubt your own sanity, but never, ever doubt Logon or his runes."

"But there's no other logical explanation why—"

"Father!" The door flung open and Sejisca stood silhouetted against the morning light, her tone full of alarm. "Cocee is nowhere to be found, and," she gasped for breath, "and there are men's footprints in the frost."

The men all rose as one, withdrawing their swords and grabbing cloaks off the doorway hooks on the way outside.

"Lion poachers," Scang said. "They'll pay dearly if'n they harms a hair o' the lass's head." His long legs rapidly carried him up the path following Sejisca.

Sejisca paused at a turn in the pathway, pointing down at the ground. The others gathered around as Saygus stooped to examine the frosty imprints. "There were seven, maybe more. And this one," he singled out a particular footprint, "is bearing a burden that I would guess to be Cocee."

"You can tell all that?" Reddy questioned.

"See the depth of his left heel print? She's slung over his left shoulder, and by the look of it, put up quite a struggle. His companions' footprints go in a straight line but his waver back and forth. He's probably getting kicked, scratched, and bitten. He'll pay for bearing her, if I know my daughter."

"What could they want with her?" Harnet asked.

"I'm not sure I want to know. Let's get her back before they accomplish their intention." He headed up the trail with the others close behind—with the lone exception of Braxmore who stopped and tolled his sword.

"Wait," he called.

They turned.

"I don't know much about such things but could this be some sort of trap."

"Aw," Scang said with a growl, "time be's awastin'."

"Hold on Scang, I think Braxmore may have something," Saygus said. "At any rate, it wouldn't do for one with a reputation for sagacity to foolishly run into a trap. What rune is that?"

"Rune? Oh, I didn't even realize . . . "

"What rune?"

"Drog-heeda?" Braxmore struggled with the unfamiliar pronunciation.

"Drogheeda, of course! Braxmore, my lad, the Advisor lit up your sword to warn us of a clever ruse. Now I know what they want with Cocee," a smile played on his lips, "and why I sensed Cocee, herself, is in no real peril."

"Well?" Braxmore said.

"Cocee is bait to draw us away from my lodge. You said there were twelve of them? There's only seven that were here. No doubt the rest of their thugs are in hiding, observing us this very minute from some vantage point, waiting for us to rush up the trail in hot pursuit so they can swoop down and claim my lodge—which has been their goal for years even though they could never locate it."

"We can't just let them run away with your daughter," Harnet said.

"They'll most likely turn her loose somewhere up on the plateau. She'll be all right. Their objective is to get us out of the way, so they can occupy my lodge."

"Let's get back there, then," Reddy said, turning downhill.

"Nay, let's not be twice hasty. I'm called a sage by some, so I'd better act the part. Sejisca, go keep your mother company. The rest of you, circle around as if I was pointing at a mark in the trail while I detail the plan."

CHAPTER THIRTY-SEVEN

ARTKA'S KNEES SUDDENLY BUCKLED. BRAXMORE caught him just before he hit the ground. After a brief discussion Braxmore supported him down to Saygus' Lodge. The others watched until they were inside, then Saygus led the rest up the trail and around a turn. With one arm around Braxmore's neck, Artka shoved the door closed.

Evebryl and Sejisca looked up from clearing the table. "Is she found? Is she safe?" Evebryl asked.

"Artka," Sejisca asked, "what's wrong with you?"

Stepping free of Braxmore's support, Artka said, "Nothing, I was acting as if I'd had a recurrence of weakness so the lion poachers watching us will think the lodge is under-defended."

Braxmore went over to a window, lifted its curtain and peered out.

"Lion poachers? But what of Cocee?" Evebryl said.

"We haven't much time." As Braxmore moved window to window, surveilling the open area around the lodge, Artka informed Evebryl and Sejisca of Saygus' scheme. Evebryl nodded and immediately removed all decorative weaponry off the walls, stashing shields, halberds, axes, dirks, and spears in a rear antechamber. Then she and Sejisca concealed their Children of the Stars beneath their aprons.

Artka returned to his cot, pulled his blanket tight around his neck, clutching Sky Saber beneath the cover. Braxmore paced window to window, sword drawn.

An uneventful quarter of an hour passed.

"Here they come," Braxmore said. "Two, five . . . oh, there's more over there, five more on that side, uh, six, seven. That's it. Twelve in all."

"Is Cocee with them?" Evebryl asked.

"No." Braxmore tucked his sword in his belt, making no effort to conceal it. "Well, here goes." He threw the door open and called out in greeting, "Welcome Darfe', I thought I recognized your merry band's handiwork."

"Braxmore? We might have known you'd be here," returned a gruff voice.

"Think not ill of me, I beg you. I was deceived, but now realize my error. Have I not proven my good intentions by persuading the able-bodied men to pursue your false trail? And now I open the door to you, asking only to join your band."

"Darfe'," said Da'rot, the second in command, "this Conformitarian has proven slippery more than once. He's only offering what we already have. I say we reward him with his life but turn him out."

"What say you to that, Daggerman?" Darfe' studied Braxmore.

"What can I say? How can one resist the will of twelve? But before you make a final decision, let me advise you that within is the wife of the Bright Sword of the Mountains, and his eldest daughter, also Artka—whom you've already encountered. He's been confused by too many captains and wounded in a deadly conflict with a tophet, though now he's nearly recovered. No doubt you observed him appearing weak and leaning on me for support just a bit ago. That was all in pretense, intended to fool you."

"Braxmore," scolded Evebryl from behind the door, "you're betraying us. What are you doing?"

Darfe' asked, "And, what of the others?"

"They've seen through your plan. Saygus is a pretty shrewd character. His plan is to deceive you into thinking your plan is working. They'll come flying over the hillock and down the trail any moment now, which is my cue to slam the door, shutting you outside in the yard, leaving you exposed to their attack."

"Braxmore!" Evebryl lowered her voice.

Braxmore shoved her back inside, urging, "Darfe', be quick and enter, for lo, here come your adversaries with vengeance in their eyes." He avoided Evebryl's angry glare.

"We outnumber them twelve to eight," Da'rot said. "Why suffer siege when we can fight and get it over once and for all?"

Saygus and Scang shouted angrily as they charged over the hill.

"Da'rot forgets what a fierce warrior Saygus can be," Braxmore said. "And I'm sure that Eroton is equally dangerous. Quick, get in here before it's too late."

The charging warriors formed a battle line as they drew closer. Saygus shouted, "Shut the door, Braxmore. What's the matter with you? Shut the door."

Sejisca and Evebryl tried to force the door, but Braxmore wedged his foot in the opening.

Darfe' decided. "All right, we go in. We can always come out and fight at our leisure." He pushed against the door, forcing Evebryl and Sejisca back into the room.

"One more thing," Braxmore said as the black-pelted lion poachers filed into the lodge, "both women have swords hidden in the folds of their aprons, and the lad on the bed has his beneath the coverlet."

Artka sat bolt upright. "Braxmore! Scang was right. We should've left you behind."

"I'm sorry, Artka, but, trust me, it's for your own good." Braxmore slammed the door shut and dropped the latch bar.

"Why are you doing this, Braxmore?" Sejisca pleaded as one of the lion poachers roughly disarmed her.

Braxmore said, "Daggers are the weaponry for our day. The day of the original generals is long past, and so is their weapon. Modern campaigns can't be fought with glowing swords or too many warriors would be disqualified. Besides, daggers don't require long, boring hours of tolling."

"I trusted you Braxmore, believing you really wanted to live by the runes," Artka said. "I thought the battle with the tophets removed your doubts."

Braxmore shook his head. "I'm sorry, my friend. That changed nothing."

"Don't call me friend. You betrayed us. You're as foul as Claygall." Artka turned his face away.

Evebryl and Sejisca huddled together, comforting each other.

Lion poachers stationed themselves at each window. Artka was forced to join the women, keeping all the hostages in one place.

Saygus' voice hailed from outside, "Are you cowards that you hide behind women? Come out and fight."

"He the lion calls coward calls himself wise when he holds the lion's den," Darfe' quoted a Carnalian proverb through a shuttered window.

Ignoring Darfe', Saygus turned his comments to Braxmore. "Braxmore, what have I done to deserve this treatment from your hand?"

Braxmore sheepishly looked to the poachers for support but found only suspicion. He dropped his gaze to the floor.

Saygus persisted, "Answer me, Braxmore. How have I mistreated you to warrant this behavior?"

Braxmore said nothing.

Da'rot crossed the room and suggested, "Darfe', they're within bow-shot."

"No. I want no one harmed unless it can't be helped. They'll leave for the lowlands once they've had a taste of the bitter night air."

"What if they don't?" Da'rot asked. "What if they lay siege, or burn us out?"

"They won't. Not with the man's wife and daughter here. We've already won—without a fight. As long as we have hostages, we're safe. After the men have gone down to the lowlands and snow blocks the passes so they can't return, we'll escort the women to the valley and turn them loose with enough supplies to keep them until they find their way to the village where some of us have wives."

"And what about Braxmore and the whelp over there?" Da'rot pointed at Artka.

"What say we give them their choice?"

"You know my decision," Braxmore said. "Besides, if I go out there, they'll tear me to pieces."

Da'rot grunted, "And rightly so."

"Well, I'll stay and protect the ladies from the likes of you," Artka said.

"Suit yourself, lad, but, believe me, the women are under no threat from any of us. After all, we're Ecclessites, too. We came here by way of Logon's Rock, just as you did. We've no ill thoughts toward the ladies."

"I'll stay just the same."

Saygus' voice intruded again, "All right, Darfe', it seems deceit and betrayal have carried the day. State your terms."

"Terms?" Darfe' called back. "There are no terms. We've won, you've lost. Be happy with your lives and a couple of good days to travel before the snow flies. And, you'd best hurry, for the night and morning skies were both red, a sure sign of hard weather."

Artka looked around the lodge rubbing his shoulder which was roughed up as he'd been rudely disarmed.

"Your arm still hurt?" Sejisca made a show of tending to his bandages, then whispered, "What do we do now?"

Evebryl said loud enough for all to hear, "Your father will think of something." Though her words were hopeful, her face wasn't.

From out in the yard Saygus said, "At least send out my wife, daughter, and injured guest. You have the lodge and supplies. That was your goal."

"Now, you know better than that since you're supposed to be such a smart man, Saygus. I'm sure you understand why we can't just let your womenfolk go yet. As for your guest, he's chosen to remain with your wife and daughter." Darfe' stepped back from the window, pointed outside and ordered his men, "Keep an eye on them. Let me know if they try anything."

"They're just standing in the middle of the clearing, talking," said one of the skinners.

"Well, keep a watch, though I think we need not fear. They're smart enough to know when they've run out of options." Darfe' and Da'rot went to stand beside Artka. "You don't appear too terribly wounded."

Artka looked away, declining to comment.

"I think come spring we'll turn you over to Sofista. He's been in an ill humor since you and your comrades escaped. I can probably get on his good side again if I make a present of you."

Artka glowered.

"And what about me?" Braxmore said.

"Ah yes, you're a different problem. I don't trust you enough to let you join my band, nor to send you away, either. I think I'll keep you here with us over the winter, but in the spring, you'd better find your own way to the lowlands. Sofista would likely want to apply his reformation methods on you, since he heard you helped them escape. Oh yes, you'd better give me your sword as well. I don't trust anyone who makes the attempt to shine his sword, even the paltry bit you've done."

Braxmore unhesitatingly yielded his sword haft first. As the lion poacher chief turned away, his pelt parted slightly and Artka caught sight of a dull Child of the Stars tucked in his belt. Only the very tip shone, the part Logon illuminated.

"You all have swords?"

Darfe' was taken aback. "Well, they're from Logon, aren't they? Aren't all Ecclessites supposed to have one? Dumb question. That's one of the things we part ways with Sofista over. Though he tolerates swords, he's trying to eliminate them from his brigade saying they're too rigid and confining. I think since Logon gave them, we ought to show some respect and keep them."

"But you've let them stay dull. The light hasn't increased on them. Why haven't you sharpened them? Don't you understand Logon's will and purposes are revealed in those runes and that his strength is manifested in the shine?"

"Haven't needed to. Long ago we decided not to go to Carnalia or be warriors anymore. Now we live off the bounty of the land, which are mostly lion pelts. Since we don't rescue lives, what need have we for keen swords?"

"Men and women throughout the empire risk their lives daily to rescue people to Logon, but all you want to do is slink around the mountains and live off the land? I may only be a recruit and not very knowledgeable in such things, but this much I do know: sharpening your sword does more than prepare you for battle, it puts Logon's light in your mind, and helps you be sensitive to the Advisor's voice."

"Well, I try to stay out of things too high for me. That's where you went wrong, lad, believing all that poppycock. Look at the mess you're in now. In years to come you'll thank me. Fanatics like Saygus are best avoided."

At that moment the door shuddered, then lurched inward, cracking the latch bar. Another resounding crash followed, then another. The latch bar snapped in half, the door ripped loose from its hinges and fell flat. Scang jumped in and stood on it glaring around the room, ready to manhandle any and every one of them.

After a brief moment of shock, all but three lion poachers accepted his challenge; they charged brandishing hunting knives, daggers, and axes. Scang was shoved backward through the doorway where Saygus and company waited to meet the counterattack. Thrusts, parries, chops, and slashes continued for several minutes, neither side gaining mastery, though superficial wounds occurred on both sides.

One of the lion poachers remained inside holding a knife on the defenseless hostages. Another two watched the melee from just inside the doorway but couldn't get through to add their weapons to the fray. Da'rot broke away from Harnet's grasp and pushed his way back inside where he retrieved his bow. He stepped to an open window, notched an arrow, took quick aim, and shot.

Angry Erotonese words filled the air.

Saygus called an immediate retreat. All sounds of fighting ceased; the poachers cheered; yet none dared press the attack away from the safety of the lodge. Brandishing their weapons out the doorway, the lion poachers backed inside the lodge.

"Well done, lads. Now, be quick about setting the door to rights. And reinforce it so we're not caught off guard again," Darfe' ordered.

"I doubt that overgrown Eroton will be up to any more door smashing for a while," Da'rot said with a chuckle.

"Did you kill him?" Artka attempted to rise off the cot, but his guard shoved him back down.

"Nah. I just discouraged him a little," Da'rot turned and said. "I don't suppose there's any strong brew about?"

Evebryl regarded him narrowly.

"No? Well, I didn't think so."

Darfe' posted watchmen at the portals while the door was under repair. Nothing stirred in the clearing. All seemed peaceful: the sun warmed the ground causing the frost to dissipate, some golden and red leaves fluttered across the yard in the breeze, birds flitted about as small rodents scurried into the woods with seeds or nuts stuffed in their cheeks.

Two hours passed without further incident. A couple of the raiders complained of hunger, and to everyone's surprise Evebryl arose, went to her cupboards and prepared something for them to eat. Sejisca sighed and followed her mother's cue. Sejisca took a slab of dark, brown bread and a slice of cold, roast venison to each man while Evebryl supplemented it with a cup of hot broth.

Darfe' gave her a wondering look.

"It's what Logon would have us do," she said, her face neither warm and friendly, nor resentful.

With bread crumbs tumbling from his mouth, Darfe' said, "Gronch, you and Wertie go out and see what the Bright Blade is up to."

"But, but they'll kill us," Gronch whined. "Or hold us hostage."

Darfe's open palm slapped the top of Gronch's head. "I'm not accustomed to being second guessed by a twaddle-headed goose. Now get out there and prowl around. Find out what they're up to."

Gronch rubbed his scalp but said nothing as he and Wertie, a blemish-faced adolescent, exited the re-fortified door.

Another uneventful two hours passed; the atmosphere in the lodge relaxed a little.

Darfe' paced, anxiously waiting for Gronch and Wertie to return. "Where are they?" he muttered. "They should be back by now."

Artka's anger smoldered.

Sejisca leaned over and whispered, "My father taught us to look for something of Logon in each other when we squabbled as children. It might help."

"In them?" Artka only wanted to think evil of the intruders. Then he remembered that they, too, had once met with Logon and had been assigned to a brigade in Ecclessa. Though he didn't want to, little by little, he saw glimpses of the crown prince in them, though not much, to be sure.

Outside the late afternoon shadows lengthened across the clearing. Darfe' was increasingly concerned that there'd been no sign of his scouts.

In the distance a nightingale called softly, once, twice, and then fell uncharacteristically silent.

Braxmore rose, stretched, and then approached Artka where he leaned one-handed against a supporting column.

Sejisca, finished with offering food to the poachers, started back across the room; Artka shifted his position inviting her to sit beside him—and so he didn't have to face Braxmore.

Braxmore leaned over and said, "Please, Artka, I meant no harm, you must understand my motives. I did this for your own good."

Artka looked up, nostrils flaring, eyes wide as he fairly shouted, "For my good? You lied, betrayed, and used us in return for the mercy shown you. I should've listened to Scang and left you for the wolves."

The lion poachers, recognizing the preliminaries of a fight, migrated toward the two hoping to stop them before they tangled.

Braxmore stood away from the post and lowered his voice, "The things you believe are outmoded and dangerous. Nobody can live by those standards anymore. If you'd just give me a—"

Outside, the nightingale sounded once more.

Artka leapt up and grabbed Braxmore by the throat. The two grappled and crashed to the floor, wrestling and grunting.

Sejisca let out a piercing scream and ran across the room to a window.

Several poachers rushed to separate Artka and Braxmore.

In the ensuing chaos that drew everyone's attention, Sejisca slipped into the pantry and with one swift motion tossed back a bearskin rug, revealing a root-cellar-trap-door. She tugged on the bolts until they gave way.

The trapdoor flew open and within seconds the room was filled with earnest warriors and shining swords. Each loyal kingsman found a vulnerable poacher to press his sword against.

"It's over, Darfe'," said Saygus, increasing pressure on the poacher's jugular. "Tell your men to drop their weapons and lie face down on the floor, or your head will be the first to roll."

"Logon's swords can't hurt us." His words were defiant, but his eyes reflected uncertainty.

"Shall we find out?" Saygus pressed harder.

There was a moment of indecision, then Darfe' said, "Do as he says." The lion poachers stood stock still, their weapons half drawn.

Saygus pressed harder.

"Do it!"

His men slowly complied. The poachers who'd become entangled in the fight between Braxmore and Artka gradually disengaged. Too late they discovered that Artka and Braxmore had quit wrestling each other and instead, clung to as many poachers as they could grab, keeping them from the fray as Saygus invaded through the pantry.

Braxmore got up from the bottom of the pile, brushed himself off, grinned, patted Artka on the back and said, "Well done Artka. I truly believed you were angry at me."

"I had to make it convincing, didn't I?" Artka laughed.

"Blast me for a double fool!" Darfe' said. "Knavery! If I ever get my hands on you Braxmore."

"What makes you think I can let you go free, now that you know the location of my lodge?" Saygus stepped between them. "I'll either have to build a jail and incarcerate you, or turn you out on these mountains in the dead of winter to try to fend for yourselves . . . "

"That's not Logon's way, and you know it."

"Now be's a fine time ter be rememberin' Logon's ways," Scang said, filling the doorway. He lugged a barely conscious Da'rot under his arm. Scang dumped his burden in the middle of the floor among the other captives.

"Where'd he come from?" Saygus asked.

"He come aflyin' outta the front door as soon as yers went up the root cellar door. He run his ugly face plumb inter me fist. Carryin' a bow, he were, too. Imagine thet." Scang massaged his bandaged thigh.

"Scang," Evebryl said, "you really were wounded. Let me wash your injury, how serious is it?"

"S'jest a flesh wound. I let on worse than it be's, so our retreat would appear more real-like. Even so," he glowered at Da'rot, who was slowly regaining awareness, "it couldda been worse."

Da'rot's swollen eyes blinked.

Evebryl tore off Scang's hastily applied dressing to get a better look, much to the latter's protests.

Sajon and Hudge bound the captives hand and foot with ropes from the poacher's own gear.

"Leave 'em trussed up an' hangin' from a tree in lion territory," Scang said, wincing as Evebryl poured a reddish-brown solution into his wound.

"It's a tempting idea, I'll admit," Saygus said, "but, I'm afraid it's out of the question."

"What if," Brendle suggested, "when we leave we take them, blindfolded and bound, down to the lowlands and set them loose before winter fully sets in to survive by their own devices?"

Before anyone else responded, Cocee entered the doorway with Gronch and Wertie in tow, their hands bound tightly behind.

"Child!" Evebryl jumped up, leaving Scang to finish bandaging his own wound. "Are you all right?" She enfolded her daughter in her arms.

"I'm fine, but I can't say the same for my charges."

Indeed, Wertie looked disconsolate; but Gronch . . . Gronch's cheeks were blackened, swollen, and puffy, as were his eyebrows and forehead. A trickle of dried blood showed beneath his nose, there were bare patches in his beard and the left side of his head was plucked nearly bare.

"Daughter, what happened?" Saygus examined the men. "I thought we left them securely tied? Did they try to escape that such a bashing was required?"

Cocee lowered her eyes and meekly said, "The fault wasn't theirs. They accepted their fate, even after you and the others left they just sat quietly. Scang stayed with me until you gave the first nightingale signal, then he went to the top of the knoll to catch any that might try to escape. I didn't want them to think they could pull any tricks on me because I was a girl, so I got right in their faces and warned them. It was then that I recognized this roughneck as the one who grabbed me and slung me over his shoulder. I was outraged and lost control, and . . . well, you can see for yourself. I never realized such violence was in my own heart." Tears coursed down her face as she approached Scang. "Dear sir, I judged you for your past, even while un-Logon-like feelings lingered in my own heart. Please forgive me."

Scang searched the girl's eyes, loving her honesty, penitence, and courage. "I fergives yer lass, wi' all me heart."

Saygus put a hand on his daughter's shoulder and said, "Today daughter, you begin to understand why Logon died even for you."

"I never saw it that clearly before. I knew the runes declared everyone unworthy, but I never saw how much I personally needed his sacrifice." She turned to Wertie and Gronch, "I'm so, so sorry please forgive me for treating you like that. You didn't deserve that." She sobbed.

Gronch looked at Wertie, tears rimmed his eyes as he looked back to Cocee and said, "I, I'm sorry too for manhandling you like that. I didn't mean nothin', but I didn't have to be so rough."

"I hate to interrupt, Saygus," Clepy said, "but we need to decide what to do with the prisoners. Daylight is fading. Harboring this many prisoners, even for a single night, will drain your reserves even more. I suggest we leave right away and turn this lot loose in the Beneath where they'll be forced to toll their swords and live by that light or go mad. Then we'll make our way to the village ye spoke of and try to find someone who will sell us supplies for our return."

Saygus considered and said, "I have no idea what Logon would have us do. The village you mentioned is out of the question, however, it's too far south, and the path is full of false trails. Without a guide, you'd never make it before the snows come again. I wish there were some way you could stay as our guests, but that's impossible. My supplies are over-taxed as it is. You do understand, don't you, Artka?"

"I'm disappointed, but I understand your predicament. As Clepy has suggested the most feasible solution, I suppose we could find our way back down those tunnels to the underground ocean, then trust our swords to lead us out, as they did before. If that's the plan, we should leave now."

"I'll come along and guide you as far as the entry to Lurcan's Womb," Saygus said. "Recheck the bonds on those prisoners while Sajon and I gather provisions to keep you for a few days."

Scang took it upon himself to double-check the knots that secured the lion poachers, finally grunting an affirmative.

"Darfe', you meant us ill," Saygus said, draping a food sack over one shoulder, "but I reckon you'll face whatever consequences your actions deserve in Lurcan's Womb. If you don't go insane, and if you emerge, you'll be changed men who will no longer be a threat to anyone in Ecclessa. In those gloomy halls you'll be forced to light up your swords or perish. Hopefully, you'll take advantage of the opportunity and reacquaint yourselves to the Children of the Stars."

"You could do us worse, I suppose," Darfe' said, resigned to his fate. "I hope you bear no ill feelings, Captain Saygus."

"Don't call me captain. I'm just the watchman of the mountains, hoping to live out my waning stewardship where the breath of Lurcan seldom fouls the air. Evebryl, I'll be back by sunrise."

Saygus opened the door and found a tall, hooded stranger standing on the stoop, poised to knock.

"Is this the lodge of Captain Saygus?"

All eyes fixed on the stranger, as if he were familiar.

"I'm Saygus, my good man, but no captain am I. There's no brigade hereabouts to command, hence, I'm no captain. There seems to be a lot of mistaken notions lately concerning a mountain brigade," he glanced aside at Artka, then back to the stranger, "but, even as I assured my friends, there is no such unit. Now, how is it you've come looking for my lodge?"

The stranger ignored Saygus' question and said, "I see valiant men and women before me, each armed with a potentially mighty weapon. How say you there is no brigade in the Prophecy Mountains?"

Every rune on every sword suddenly sprang to light.

"Your eyes deceive you, sir. What appears to be a group of Ecclessite warriors is in reality a divided band. These in bonds, are just within the hour, captured, guilty of villainy, and treachery."

The stranger's hand went up. Saygus fell silent. "Be loosed," the man said.

The ropes, knots still tied, fell off Darfe' and his men.

"See here now," said Braxmore, stepping forward, "these are dangerous men."

"I dare say," the stranger said with a chuckle. "You are all dangerous. But, you must cease being dangerous to each other. There," he pointed in the general direction of Carnalia, "is your enemy, still deceiving and abusing his citizens." The man threw back his cowl.

"Logon!" several said at once.

He entered the room. "To think you've used my swords to argue, fight, and threaten. Mighty powers meant to pull down and expose the enemy are invested in those weapons, but you've allowed yourselves—like many of my brigades—to be tricked into disputes about runes and blade edges and lifestyles. And you've drawn each other's blood. Woe to those who bicker with each other rather than rescue men and women doomed to perish." Logon turned to face Saygus. "And some have drawn aside from the war, thinking their own grievances too great to bear."

Saygus sank to his knees, tears streaming over his cheeks. He took Logon's hand in his and said, "My Liege."

Logon withdrew his hand, looked kindly down at Saygus, took a step backward to look at everyone in the room and said, "Say no more 'there is no brigade in the Prophecy Mountains,' for I commission you, Saygus, as general at large, and as captain over this, the Singing Sword Brigade. Train these men: in sword warfare, rescuing lives, enduring hardness, and recognizing lurcanish agents. I know well the rejection and bitterness your heart has tasted, but your loyalty and courage in the Forbidding Mountains is highly regarded in my father's court. My name is slandered among the rebellious so is it too much to ask of you to endure the same dishonor?"

"No, my Lord."

"I charge you, Saygus, prepare these men, all of them—lead them even within the very walls of the enemy's fortress, should I so order. Strive to fulfill this charge, and your reward shall be made steadfast before my father.

"Have no care for provision, I will provide good weather for more crop-harvesting as well as for hunting and also for building. Thus, your family, and the families of these men, will be sustained as you train them over the deep of winter."

Logon turned to the others. "Clepy, Darfe', I charge you: put away your differences, obey Saygus as he forges one unit out of the two. I commission you both as sergeants. Darfe', you and your men have done harm in Ecclessa, yet, you are forgiven, for I see that you still fear me. Let that respect keep you in line or you will answer to me."

"M'lord, how can we repay you?"

"You can't even begin, Darfe', but it's good that you desire it. Nevertheless, the consequences of the harm you've done will eventually overtake you. At that time, if you seek my face, you'll receive strength to endure."

Logon turned to Artka. "You've done well, recruit."

Artka felt a rush of shame, knowing that the affair of the dagger was known; yet now that it had been destroyed, it was as if Logon entirely forgot the matter.

"Study hard, Artka, apply yourself to Saygus' example.

"Tren has been captured through no fault of his own. He's in my keeping, however, and will be useful again. I have no brigade ready to venture to his side, indeed, few would be willing. You're ready of heart but are unskilled. Apply yourself to learn my methods with all diligence. Are you willing to face even the Chimeree, should I so order?"

"M'lord, I'll go wherever, whenever you say."

"And I," Scang said.

"And I," chorused Braxmore, Harnet, Brendle, Reddy, and Clepy.

"Then obey me now and forgive these your brothers. Be ready when I call. A great evil has been loosed and many fortresses are under siege, and the King's Gate Fortress East knows heavy battle each day. I've bolstered their forces with roamers—you've noted the glow of their defenses in the early morning sky—yet the war is hard pressed. Soon the Final Reckoning comes, so prepare. There's much that is yet to be done."

The doorframe was suddenly empty.

Artka blinked away his tears. "Here am I, send me," he whispered.

EPILOGUE

As Logon promised, the weather held fair long enough for the men to build a small barracks and some cabins for the married ex-lion poachers. The snows had begun in the lowlands but not the highlands; non-hibernating animals were driven up into the mountains, providing bounteous hunting.

When the structures were finished, firewood laid in, and game and other foodstuffs smoked, dried, or preserved, Saygus led a small contingent by secret paths to the village to fetch the poachers' families. Many of the poachers' wives had spoken regularly to Logon about their spouses returning to Ecclessite ways. Thus, the inclusion of them into the Singing Sword Brigade was seen as nothing less than Logon's answer.

As Saygus led the caravan of poacher and their wives and children into the mountains the winds blew from the north and the unusual highland warm spell ended. The first flakes of the year's winter blizzards hissed around the caravan as they entered their new lodgings.

All through the deep of winter Saygus trained his nineteen soldiers in physical endurance, runelore, and sword drills. The penitent former poachers devoted themselves to re-learning Logon's ways, eager to put their lawless past behind.

Artka and friends sharpened their swords with added diligence. Many were the nights they stayed up discussing insights from the runes and discovering hints of the powers Logon had hidden in their swords.

418

Artka's admiration of Sejisca also grew, as did hers for him.

So, it was, that in obedience to the solemn charge laid upon them by Logon Xychirion, the Singing Sword Brigade was birthed. They grew strong in Logon's ways, dedicated themselves to love and service, and applied themselves to the secret of making their Children of the Stars glow brightly, reveal hidden runes, and even . . . sing.

WATCH FOR THESE UPCOMING BOOKS IN THE *SAGA OF THE SINGING SWORD BRIGADE* SERIES

For more information about
J.M. MacLeod
&
Inception of a Brigade

please visit:

www.facebook.com/john.macleod.188

For more information about
AMBASSADOR INTERNATIONAL
please visit:

www.ambassador-international.com
@AmbassadorIntl
www.facebook.com/AmbassadorIntl

If you enjoyed this book, please consider leaving us a review on
Amazon, Goodreads, or our website.